A TIME OF NEED

A DARK EAGLE NOVEL

BRENT A. HARRIS

A TIME OF NEED. Copyright © 2017 Brent A. Harris. All Rights Reserved. Printed in the United States of America. No part of this book may be used or reproduced in any manner whatsoever without written permission except brief quotations. For information, contact Insomnia Publishing, 11 Avery Rd, Londonderry, NH 03053

Cover image designed by E. Prybylski

www.insomnia-publishing.com

ISBN-10: 0-9988047-1-1

ISBN-13: 978-0-9988047-1-2

This book is dedicated to my children Aurora and Alexander; all your choices matter.

ACKNOWLEDGEMENTS

Thanks goes out to good friend and huge supporter Stephen Hunt whose helping hands have steadied this project from the first bits of prose on the page. I've also been helped along by good friends Ricardo Victoria and Rob Edwards. Thanks goes to my mom and dad for helping me realize my passions. I'm sorry you never got to see this book, mom. Further thanks goes to the National Parks service and librarians everywhere.

The most important thanks belongs to my wife Stephanie who is not only my best friend but my unwitting beta reader and sounding board for every idea that crosses my mind. She does not deserve such punishment. I also want to thank the fine folks at Insomnia Publishing for helping me make my dreams a reality. While there are many people who helped with this book, any mistakes are my own.

POINT OF DEPARTURE

Braddock's Road, Monongahela River, British America
July 9th, 1755.

IN retrospect, General Edward Braddock realized he should not have survived. Maybe the French ambush had gone awry. Maybe someone had been out of place. Maybe he had just gotten lucky. For an instant, he experienced a feeling that things should be different. Now, engaged in the chaos of battle and on the brink of defeat, he had no option but retreat.

Personally, the French and the savages could have the damned Ohio Valley and the damnable heat that went with it. His red woolen coat stank, and his white uniform blouse had long since turned yellow. His red silk sash wrapped loosely around his chest. The summer humidity made his buff breeches sticky, wedging uncomfortably under him.

Despite this, his allegiance lay with his uniform, and he would not betray it. Braddock held his hunting sword high as he wove between cypress semi-evergreens and massive white oaks. On some of those trees, scalps of his men hung like trophies. He passed them, and his stomach tightened. The mount he rode was his fifth since the ambush started; the others had been shot out from under him. His men had lost the will to fight. Many lay dead. Of those who lived, most had fled. Still, Braddock rode on among his remaining soldiers.

As far as he was concerned, everything around him— the undrinkable water of the Monongahela River, mosquitoes, venomous vipers and savages—was trying to kill him. Those things weren't found back home in Scotland, and his nice thick uniform would have served him quite well in the highlands. But, like everything in the British Colonies, what served well at home was often a hindrance here.

He spied his *aide-de-camp*, a young Yank—sweaty and flustered—not meters away, returning from the head of the column to the rear. Braddock rode to him, then recoiled and reared his head back in disgust. "You smell like the wrong end of a horse." George Washington cut an imposing figure on horseback. But not today. Up close, he looked pale and wet. Several folded blankets padded his saddle, most of which were soaked in a slick, brownish mess.

"We are overrun, sir. We cannot hold," Washington said. Sweat poured over his face, but his mouth and eyes remained dry. "The Ottowan and Potawatomis Natives are breaking our ranks. The French are keeping us penned in."

The Scotsman gave it one last thought, then said, "If we cannae hold them here, then we must fall ba—"

His horse bucked as if stung by something sharp. Braddock grabbed ahold of the reins too late. He couldn't get a tight enough grip on them. He felt light, then the sensation of flying. His sword flew out of his hand, and his sash came undone. He heard the snap in his leg as he hit the ground. His right leg, below the knee, twisted sideways against the momentum of his fall. Then his horse fell dead on top of him and crushed Braddock's broken leg. He let out a bellow of pain which rivaled the cannon firing and matched the haunting war whoops of the savages encircling his men. The next thing Braddock knew, two of his men held him propped up by the shoulders.

"Do I have your orders to call for retreat?" Washington sat above him, still on his horse.

Everything felt distant. He managed to nod. "Aye."

"Very well. I shall carry the orders myself to the men and drag them away if necessary. If we cannot have victory, we shall at least share no shame in our withdrawal." Though the spirit of death hovered around Washington, Braddock thought, he didn't act the part. Washington actually shot *him* a look of concern, then spoke to the two men. "Get the general to safety." With that, Washington turned away.

The two men attempted to haul the wounded general back up the road, keeping the weight off his leg, but had no luck.

Braddock gasped. "No lads, let me rest a bit." He turned a finger behind him. "There. Get me up on the rise, steady as you can." He grunted with each step.

A moment later, he looked down just in time for him to see his *aide-de-camp* fly down the hill. Braddock heard two distinct shots fire, both muzzle flashes aimed at Washington. If either of them hit, Braddock couldn't tell, but Washington rode on. *Bloody 'ell that luck.*

Braddock was a general in the best equipped, best trained army in the world. One British soldier was worth ten savages. Or, so he thought. The wilderness challenged that assumption. Washington pushed him to accept that things were different here. Braddock had at first sneered. As if a Yank knew anything about proper British soldiering. What Washington did not know or understand was Braddock *had* changed. He *had* adapted his method of soldiering to face the peculiarities of the New World. Apparently, Braddock thought as he saw the destruction of his army all around him, he had not changed them enough. Perhaps, in the future, he should take his aide's advice closer to heart. Maybe Braddock had underestimated him.

Later, when the British made good on their withdrawal, it did not surprise him to learn they owed much of their orderly departure to the work of Washington. The sickly, flux-riddled Yank had performed more admirably then even some of Braddock's best generals. They would all live to fight another day as they made their slow and arduous way to Ft. Duquesne to liberate the Ohio Valley from French invasion.

Braddock would not have believed it had he not borne witness to it. Maybe the Yank had enough British blood in him yet to make a proper soldier. Braddock raised an eyebrow as he tried to envision the youth in a bright red British uniform instead of the Colonial rags he wore. In his head, the result was smashing. "Hmm," he said to no one. "Who would-ev' thought?"

PART ONE

"A man without enemies is a man without character."
—unknown

ONE

Honduras, West Indies
October 7ᵗʰ, 1764.

BENEDICT Arnold knew he was a great man. In pursuit of convincing the world of that truth, he found himself in a tavern at the busy seaport in Honduras after a difficult and full day of unloading his ship, *Fortune*. He wanted nothing more than a bite, some ale, and a bit of sleep before he and his crew sailed out at first light to the Caribbean. If he stumbled across a girl or two before then, he might find a way to accommodate them. However, his priority was to finish the wretched dock notes. *Thank God for the British. They've civilized this country with paperwork.*

Everything about the tavern had the same dull quality as the washed-out, grey wooden planks holding the structure intact. Inside, it was just as plain, except for the few exotic girls in bright dresses and a blue and gold macaw perched near the bar. A few local Mestizos and Negroes sat around empty tables, but tradesmen took the rest of it. Arnold's plate of rice and fish sat cold, and he had a pile of papers pushed off to the side. Instead of eating dinner and finishing his work, he found himself confronted by a displeased gentleman. Apparently, Arnold had found time, despite his busy day, to offend someone. It would certainly explain the flintlock pistol aimed at his nose.

Arnold was particularly attached to his aquiline appendage, easily his most recognizable feature next to his chiseled chin and charming smile. Honestly, he preferred to keep everything right where it belonged, so it wasn't altogether the worst way for someone to get his attention. The man with the pistol wore a knee-length blue waistcoat, which struck Arnold as impractical for the jungle. His badly sunburned skin marked the man as obviously English. Arnold didn't recognize the face, but he didn't have to. He realized who the man was: Captain Lawrence Croskie.

"When you arrived this morning," Croskie said, "did you not receive my invitation?" The man took his time with his words, and his breath reeked of rum.

"I did," Arnold said, sighing inwardly. The drunkenness, the aggression. The situation had an air of familiarity from the time before his father died.

"Then why did you fail to join us for drinks onboard my ship?" Croskie turned to wave his hand around the dimly lit tavern. Others joined Croskie now. "Yours was the only new ship in port that failed to honor tradition, to show respect worthy of a gentleman of the Crown. Are you not a gentleman?"

The British and their rules of civility. Well, Arnold could show him where to stuff those. "I was otherwise disposed. Our cargo needed offloading and, as you can see here," Arnold pointed to the pile of forms he had shoved to the side a moment earlier, "I remain engaged with my duties." Arnold smiled. "I meant no offense. I was to pay my respects in the morning, just before departure." Arnold was telling the truth... this time.

"You have slighted me, and I do not take to being insulted." Croskie gestured again at the tavern around them and said, "I see you would prefer to slop with savages." He then pointed to a lovely exotic girl with a bright dress and continued, "Have you enjoyed the finer delights too? Have you spread your filth?"

Arnold frowned. Maybe his smile wasn't so charming after all. No, he had not had a side of laced mutton this evening, at least, not yet. And Arnold did not have the French pox. "Do you have a point, *El Capitan*? Please, sit. Lower your pistol. Your arm must be tired. Let me buy you a drink."

Croskie lowered his pistol for a moment, as if giving his arm a rest. He raised it right back up. "Do you think I would stoop so low as to indulge in your offer of company when you so blatantly ignored mine? Your time amongst the savages has turned you into one, I think."

The large blue and gold bird ruffled its feathers, puffed out its chest, and spread its wings. It gave a loud squawk. Arnold furrowed his thick brown eyebrows and asked, "To which savages do you refer?" He gestured around the tavern. "Not these fine Spanish Colonists here?" Then, he shot a wounded look toward Croskie. "Or do you refer to your own kinfolk of the American Colonies, which are sometimes mistaken for its natives? I understand your confusion. I suppose we savages all look alike to you." Arnold wondered how many Mestizos knew the pompous British oaf had just insulted them.

"I offer you civility, I offer you friendship, I offer you my good name, and you sit there mocking me?" Captain Croksie sobered, his eyes turning sharp. His long, thin frame seemed to broaden, and his voice deepened. "You sir, are a damned Yankee," he went on, pointing his pistol wildly over the dirty table. He snorted with derision before continuing, "You are destitute of good manners or those of a gentleman. I should shoot you where you sit."

Benedict Arnold's brown eyes narrowed and focused. His face tightened, and sweat beaded on his brow. He had been called a "Yank" before, but it still rubbed him raw. Arnold sighed in relief—he had made the right call in ignoring the invitation. Captain Croskie had proven himself an unbearable drinking companion.

Conversation in the tavern cooled as the exchange heated. Arnold saw patrons sliding to the edge of their chairs, hands disappearing behind waistcoats. Some of those men were his crew. Most were not. Several burly men had entered the tavern and joined the thin British sea captain. Others fell back, guarding the door. Croskie had brought friends. How nice. It seemed to Arnold, the more still the air became, the more of his own sweat and other foul smells filled his nostrils. He had never been free of perspiration on any of his port visits here, but the sweat he felt now did not come from the heat of the Honduran sun.

Arnold struggled to remain composed. The captain had not come here just in response to some perceived slight but rather to make sure Arnold knew his place as a Colonist. *Well, tradesman, today you'll receive more than you've bargained for.*

"You feel slighted because I didn't show for drinks. And I feel slighted because you have publicly insulted me and interrupted my meal," Arnold said, seizing upon a course of action. "I can give you a chance to do just that; I'll give you that shot." Arnold took his glove from the table and offered it to Croskie. "I challenge you, but with one condition. We must resolve this matter not on the morrow but right now, here, outside."

Arnold convinced himself the captain would decline to duel. Not tonight anyway. Arnold hoped the embarrassment of having to refuse it would at least make the halfwit hurry away. Croskie had no reason to accept. His inebriation gave Arnold the advantage. There were several reasons duels typically occurred in the morning. There were the practical matters to attend to: both had to find seconds and surgeons, and both would want to spend the evening as if it might be their last. The whole ordeal was designed to unnerve, until one person inevitably apologized and the matter could be put to rest. Arnold bet Croskie would do just that.

"Challenge accepted."

Or, I could be wrong. Arnold's brow wrinkled, and for a brief moment, he almost let his outward composure slip. He knew himself to be an intelligent person, but clearly, he must have been more exhausted than he thought. The hogsheads of salted meat were as heavy as they were numerous. Perhaps he had taken ill.

In any case, now he had to think of something else, fast. Arnolds had fought duels before, but he still did not wish to leave anything to chance. He looked squarely at the captain. "You say I misplaced my honor, but it seems I misplaced my own flintlock." He felt the weight of his pistol tucked into his waistcoat against him.

"Perhaps you left them both with a *señorita* back in her room?"

Arnold soured. He had a sudden urge to upend the table and disarm the man, but he took in another deep breath and let the moment pass. Now, he was quite certain he wanted to duel.

"Take this one. It should suffice." Captain Croskie flipped his weapon and handed it, stock first, to Arnold.

Arnold couldn't explain why the captain had disarmed himself or why he now held the weapon, which he examined. Even in the low light, Arnold could see the pistol was a thing of beauty. It had the usual wooden stock, but everything from the firing mechanism down was decorated brass. Certainly more extravagant than his plain, wooden, pirate-style flintlock. But, his had gotten the job done many times over. This weapon looked like it had never been fired at all.

"Very well," Arnold sighed as he stood, taking the firearm and placing it on the table. "I will meet you outside. But, if this is to be my end, I would like to have something in my stomach first."

Croskie nodded then turned away. Others followed along with a few of Arnold's men. He watched Croskie head out of the tavern. Then Arnold took the pistol and tucked it into his waistcoat next to his own. It didn't fit well and hung heavily but felt secure enough. Arnold took out his flintlock, the pistol he trusted, and held it close by to obscure the fact that it was a different weapon. The fading light outside should also help conceal it, he hoped. Leaving his plate untouched, Arnold left the tavern.

The warm air did nothing to lessen the perspiration building on Arnold's skin. He felt paler than his tanned skin belied, as if he were a shadow walking through the motions while watching them from afar. *What, by God's bones, was I thinking? Why do I have to take everything so personally?* More specifically, why did he feel it necessary to shoot any man he didn't like?

Captain Croskie stood outside with his arms folded across his chest and a smirk on his face. Something about the captain just set him off. Arnold's gait intensified, his free hand clenched, and crimson burned into his furrowed brow.

Croskie and a second man took their positions, and the other man gave Croskie a pistol. Arnold gave him a once-over. He was large and young but had the telling composure of experience. Arnold presumed the man was Croskie's first mate. The young man tapped his foot impatiently. He probably didn't want to be here either, Arnold realized, discovering he had a liking for the irritated young man. Arnold couldn't wait to help him get promoted. He felt for the comfort of his own pistol. *Congratulations, your captain was just reassigned with higher orders.* Arnold's face broke into a smirk of his own.

The captain must have noticed, for he shrank back. Croskie staggered a bit as he took to his mark, and his shoulders dropped when he noticed the growing crowd of onlookers. *Too late, prig.* Arnold had never dueled this late in the day before. Too close to tea time. His stomach rumbled.

"At your mark!" the first mate announced. He stood off to the side, quite a bit away from the duelists but somewhere in the middle between them. Arnold decided not to shoot with a second.

It was, of course, highly improper. But then again, so was this whole bloody affair.

He knew the drill. The two of them would stand approximately thirty yards apart. Then they would take turns shooting at each other like civilized men. Arnold understood the irony, but he resolved to show the captain what true honor meant in the highest tradition of retaining one's good name. Honor no longer existed in some old custom of ships at port. It came from being true to oneself.

Arnold saw the distance had already been roughly marked out, and Croskie had taken his mark. Arnold stepped to his and made a show of bowing to the captain in front of the audience. *Here is where things get interesting.* As the challenger, Arnold must stand still as Croskie took the first shot. This method ensured duels were kept to a minimum; if you challenged someone, they shot at you first.

It was the worst feeling in the world to stand there, waiting for another man to end your life or wound you while you could do nothing about it. Unless, of course, you ran away. Despite his outward bravado, Arnold's legs felt weak, and he struggled to keep himself upright. He wanted to run—he really did—but he would not. He stood there, as still as he could. He realized then that his sobriety didn't help. He should have at least finished his drink.

In the harbor of Honduras, in front of the sloop *Fortune*, the sun fell behind thick jungle. The evening sky erupted into a violent clash of red and blue. Purple outlined the horizon. Arnold watched as Croskie took aim. Despite his inexact execution, Arnold knew even sloppiness could kill.

Thunder cracked, and everything else went dead silent. Arnold let out a breath without realizing he had held it in. He was still alive. At least he hoped he was. Smoke filled the air and smelled of fire and brimstone, which concerned him for a moment. He looked down to check the most important bits first, then examined his legs. Satisfied, he used his hands and ran them over his torso and then both arms. Everything seemed in order. He had not taken a round.

Arnold's hands found a small new rip in his waistcoat, just below his elbow. The shot had only ripped his clothing, but it had been close. Even after seeing the hole, Arnold had a hard time believing it. Croskie had fired at him and ruined his coat. Arnold's breathing quickened, and his skin flushed. Croskie seemed unconcerned, even though the next shot was Arnold's. *Odd.*

Arnold wasted no time. He balanced his weight on the balls of his feet, against the movement of his body, squared his shoulders and moved the pistol forward with his right hand. He kept it close to his chest as he steadied his aim with other his other hand. His practiced stance placed his flintlock at the center of his body which should place the ball directly into the center of his opponent, give or take the horrible inaccuracy of the damned things. Arnold fired.

His movements were precise, so now it was up to where the ball wanted to go. Thunder roared again, and Captain Lawrence Croskie stumbled backward before collapsing. When smoke cleared, Arnold saw Croskie lying propped upright by his left elbow. A dark red stain sprang from near his right shoulder. The captain gaped at him, his expression surprised despite the torment on Croskie's pale face as he tried to say something and failed. Then, Croskie took a gasp and spat, "You bloody Yank!" Another grimaced gasp. "You damned, bloody Yankee... You shot me! How could you?"

Arnold's shoulders sunk. He wasn't too pleased with the outcome and summed it up thusly: First, he had clearly missed, evidenced by the whining coming from what should have been a corpse. Second, the captain hadn't stopped with the insults.

Fortunately, Arnold had a solution to the second problem tucked into his waistcoat. He approached the fallen man. "Why do you persist in calling me a Yank as though it is an insult? I happen to embrace that moniker, yet you attempt to make such a profanity of it." Arnold pulled out the second pistol and brandished it. "I do hope we can resolve this problem."

Croskie's expression of defiance shifted to one of panic, and he gulped air. "Don't shoot. I apologize, I did not—" He struggled for air, then said, "By my honor, I did not mean to offend you."

"That's unfortunate." Arnold slowly approached the prostrate figure. "Because I do not accept your apology. It's worthless. You didn't change your vitriol until after I brought this out. I think that means you aren't really sorry." Arnold grinned. "I won't miss a second time. Not from here, and not with the pistol you were so very anxious to hand me." He revealed Croskie's pistol. Croskie's brows shot up. "I should kill you where you lie. Your death will serve as a warning to those who would tread on my good name."

"But," he said, "you lied about being unarmed."

"I know. I suppose that is what damned Yankees do."

From a distance of a few feet, Arnold raised the pistol at Croskie and, with a knowing grin, put his finger on the trigger...

Croskie's eyes widened, and his mouth fell open, spilling the truth. "No, please no. In the name of the Almighty, you do not want to fire that, I rigged—"

...and fired.

The sea captain remained upright. Only now, Croskie sagged, and his face flushed, this time, in shame.

"You must have had such a low opinion of me to have threatened me with nothing more than a blank pistol. A low opinion, indeed," Arnold said. Croskie trembled, not looking at him. "I hope your judgment has now been altered."

Ever quick to anger, Arnold set to vengeance. He flipped the pistol around, and the hot brass burned his flesh. He took two quick steps toward Croskie and swung the weapon downwards at his skull. The wooden stock made contact with a satisfying crack, and the captain fell unconscious. With the proper care, Croskie might live. Might.

Arnold's men stood their ground, hands on their weapons, looking for signs of trouble. Croskie's burley men looked on expectantly. The first mate stared for a moment but then heaved a sigh. He called out for men to carry Croskie to the surgeon back aboard their ship. The men obeyed, and the first mate turned away and headed back inside. Arnold chuckled. He'd buy that man a drink, maybe find a spot for him on his crew if he could. The Mestizos returned inside, ready to wash away the night's outside entertainment with further drink, leaving Arnold alone in the street.

The evening air brought a soothing ocean breeze, and Arnold breathed it all in. He looked out at the *Fortune* and over to the horizon, and his mind drifted off to sea. Benedict Arnold had been born into wealth. He came from a long line of Arnolds who already possessed greatness respected by all.

His father had ruined it. His consumption of rum cost his family their fortune. But, more importantly, it cost Arnold the respect his name once held. Being the son of the town drunk was a title he couldn't escape. It was even worse when he moved from the front pews of the local parish, where his family had sat for generations, to the back rows, then to be asked not to come at all. Now, the Arnold name held no meaning. At least until he could restore it.

As Arnold pondered the horizon, he heard the noise of the jungle return and saw the North Star appear low in the evening sky. As a sailor, he often used the star for guidance, and he looked to it now. True to its name, it beckoned him ever northward.

Somewhere in the Colonies of the Americas lay his true calling. Arnold knew he would meet many more men like Croskie in his attempt to claim his fame, and Arnold now knew he could overcome those challenges. Otherwise, his name would drift away with the sands of time as countless as the grains of sand on which he now stood. With those thoughts, he too went back inside. Even with the excitement and glory from victory, Arnold hadn't lost his appetite. In fact, he was hungrier than ever.

TWO

London, England
January 23rd, 1774.

THE crack of black powder brought George Washington's attention back from deep reflection. He grasped at the red sash around his chest, given to him nearly twenty years ago. The sky hung low with fog. Appropriately enough, it began to drizzle in typical London style. Musket fire erupted once more, and Major Washington of the King's Footguards lowered his head in silence.

The casket containing the remains of General Edward Braddock rolled by on horse-drawn carriage, past St. Abbey's Cathedral, and stopping at the lot where soldiers and family had gathered to pay their final respects. After the service, the casket would continue its journey to Braddock's final resting place in Scotland. Mere coincidence had Major Washington in attendance; he had come to the city for different reasons: attempting to purchase rank he could not afford. But, he was glad for the last chance to say goodbye. It salvaged a journey otherwise undertaken in vain.

Washington had traveled the world over since donning the British uniform, each time kissing Martha on the cheek, telling her that he would be home as soon as he could, and leaving the estate of Mt. Vernon in her and his cousin's care. He considered settling in London, but the idea of leaving the estate bothered him—he felt a strong attachment he could not explain. Washington could understand Braddock's wishes to be interred not among the fallen heroes of Britain housed within the cathedral, but in his home in the highlands.

Later, after most of the mourners had moved on, Washington remained with several soldiers who also knew Braddock well, even if they did not owe as much to the general as he did. Among them was General Thomas Gage. A time ago, Gage had been among those wounded in the Monongahela River expedition. One of his wounds must have been his pride, for Gage and Washington had never gotten along since.

The drizzle turned into an icy sleet, and Washington wrapped his coat tighter and braced himself. The two squared off a short distance in front of the carriage where their leader now lay.

"It is pleasant to see you again, old friend," Gage said.

"Speak truth, Your Excellency." He heard no trace of venom in Gage's voice, but Washington knew better. "We are not friends."

"True," Gage said. He stepped closer. Washington followed Gage with his eyes as he circled. There, Gage stood in his red and buff uniform, regimental bronze buttons shone to a mirrored surface, boots blackened. Except for puffed jowls and a receding hairline, Gage would be handsome. Instead, his features paired with his orgulous condescension and baritone voice. "Only because you continue to be but a sheep in wolf's clothing."

Washington winced. "I was there, too, you recall. I saw you carried away with your injuries just as the fighting began. I was in the thick of it. My valor should not be questioned."

"I do not question your valor. I question your circumstance. If God wanted you wearing that uniform, he would have put the proper blood in you. And may I remind you that during the battle, I wore the king's uniform while you wore rags."

"Now, I wear the same uniform as you do, Your Excellency. We fought together. You and I marched into Fort Duquesne—"

"It was British soldiering and tactics that won the war, not your coon-skin cap. You marched into Fort Duquesne because I had liberated it."

Washington tugged at his sash again. "General Braddock believed in me."

"Braddock is dead." The two stood in silence. The sleet eased a little, though the chill in the air didn't dissipate. "Braddock, rest in peace, may have pushed for your commission.

Lord Fairfax may have paid for it, but it was politics that handed it to you. You are nothing but a puppet to be called out to quell the rebellious actions of a wild few." Gage gazed at the casket behind Washington. "And even that has failed."

Washington knew his commissioning was in response to Colonial unrest. The British had involved themselves in Colonial affairs after years of self-reliance. Until the war in the wilderness, the Colonies had largely been ignored. When the British raised taxes and demanded of the Colonies to pay their fair share, the Colonials looked to Washington—until he put on a red coat. Protest died down for a time after that, but civil unrest had flared again, particularly in Boston. General Gage had been keeping the peace there during a protest when a civilian injured a soldier, prompting a deadly response. This had happened years ago. Gage seemed to hint at something much more recent. "What do you mean?"

"Your Colonial friends are at it again." Gage retrieved a wrinkled, yellow newspaper from his pocket.

Washington read it over, shielding it as best as he could against the elements. The Essex Gazette, a newspaper from Massachusetts, wrote of an eyewitness account. Tea had been thrown overboard at Griffin's Wharf in Boston Harbor. A lot of tea. Washington's shoulders fell.

"This isn't the only account," Gage said. "From what we can tell, a lawless band calling themselves the 'Sons of Liberty' disguised themselves as savages. They tossed all the tea from the *Dartmouth*, *Eleanor*, and *Beaver*. That is over four hundred crates of tea, perhaps ten thousand sterling worth."

Washington mulled it over, his eyebrows furrowed. That was indeed quite a bit of tea. But there was more to it. He could see what the British could not. "They dressed as what? Mohawk natives?" Washington tried to remember what tribes inhabited the area. "Not to disguise themselves, but to disassociate themselves from us, I think. Perhaps the dumping of the tea was more a sign of independence and less an act of defiance. The Colonists seem to believe they can manage their affairs without us."

"No," Gage said. "I know what it means. I am the one in charge there, and they are nothing but a mob. Maybe even the same mob that caused the incident at King's Street. That whole damned port must be shut down. Those radicals must be stopped—"

"As I have stated before, and it seems appropriate to say yet again, we are putting too much pressure on the Colonies. If we simply exercise some restraint, we can maintain our sovereignty over them."

Gage raised an eyebrow and pointed a finger at Washington. "Some think to question your allegiance with talk like that. We are talking of just one city, not revolution. The Lords are furious. They want action... No, they demand *results*," Gage corrected. "I am returning to take command of the situation. I will put an end to this infernal war drum that your people continue to beat."

Washington's face fell and went flush. He tried to recover, but not before Gage noticed. Washington hoped to take command of the British force in the Colonies. They were once, or were still, his people—that point confused him. Still, he knew the land and the politics. It should have been obvious that he was perfect for the position. However, Washington had been unable to secure enough money to obtain the rank of Lt. Colonel, and therefore ineligible to take such a command. "And what would you do to quiet the city?"

Gage snorted. "Follow the path of divine providence. The Colonies are our responsibility. They are a part of the king's domain. No matter their waywardness, God minds his flock. That is their fate." He took a moment to tighten his cloak against the cold. "That is your problem, George. You want control, to shape your destiny. Just like at Monongahela, you took command of the retreat when you had absolutely no authority to do so." Gage pointed at Washington. "You are wild and hasty, and all of this excitement brewing is the result of similar savages acting just like you."

"I tried to save you! I tried to save everyone. We could have all perished that day. Sometimes, a little wildness is in order." Washington turned to look at the casket, his jaw tight. "What would have happened if Braddock had died that day?" Washington's voice betrayed him and shook with fury he couldn't hide.

"I do not think Braddock would have been killed, but who am I to know? Fate is a matter for God, not mortals." The sleet became thick, fat flakes of snow tinged with soot from the many chimneys around them. Washington discovered he no longer felt the cold and clenched his fists. Gage said, "I am not as harsh as you may believe me to be. My purpose here is to inform you that new regiments are opening in anticipation of any action we must take against the city. We have already sent out contracts to the Hessians for men, but we will need British officers to lead them. I have put in your name to do so. It's an opening billet, so you will not have to purchase it. Save Martha's money, or pick her out a few fashions while you're here." Gage pulled his cloak around his shoulders. "I, for one, am getting out of this cold."

In all the years he had known Gage, the general still surprised him. Washington's agitation cooled and he regained his composure. He thought about what Gage had said. Using Hessians would not change the climate in New England. Boston, apparently, was near a state of open rebellion, and the arrival of paid mercenaries instead of fellow countrymen would add further insult. But perhaps, if Washington were there as well, his expertise could help mend the rift. He wanted to keep the British Empire intact. To accomplish this, they either had to back off entirely or, conversely, hit Boston without warning and with an overwhelming force, targeting only those inciting talk of treason. "Why would you recommend me?"

Gage had already turned to leave, but he stopped, and over his shoulder, he said, "Think of it as fighting fire with fire." With that, Gage departed without a backward glance.

Washington continued to mourn for Braddock in solitude and in silence. He stayed there until the carriage-driver whistled, and the horses drew it away.

He found himself in Virginia once again in the fields around the Fairfax estate, hunting with Lord Fairfax and horseback riding with Sally. He recalled the poetry and letters he had written to her. The arrogance he had displayed during the seven years he spent fighting in the wilderness. The pride he felt putting on the British uniform for the first time. The life he and Martha had carved out for themselves at Mt. Vernon, on the bank of the Potomac.

He returned to the present and gazed down at another river a world away. Thick, white snowflakes disappeared into the water. Washington had left the courtyard and walked past Parliament, not sure how, and arrived at the edge of the River Thames. In it, he could not see his reflection, nor anything but the churning, brown water mixing with falling snow.

He visualized himself, at first in a white shirt and blue jacket, riding a horse. Then, he saw himself in his red British coat and grey cloak. It was to this uniform he had a duty, a responsibility to serve His Majesty to the best of his abilities, even if his peers would never view him as an equal. Gage's words gnawed at him, forcing him to pick around the question that truly plagued him: *Could I fight my own countrymen?* Experience told him he would find his equal in America, and when he did, he had better know the answer.

THREE

Albany, New York
July 11th, 1775.

B ENEDICT Arnold marched toward the *Red Herring*, his mind a pendulum of thoughts. There was his brisk dismissal at Fort Ticonderoga which caused his fists to ball. Then, there was his upcoming meeting with General Schuyler, the gentleman from New York who had Arnold's appointment or, rather, the job Arnold wanted. Either way, past or present, his thoughts troubled him.

Part of Arnold thought about retiring, but his country was in a time of need, and war provided a man seeking to redeem his name the best opportunity to do so. Unfortunately, no one else seemed to appreciate this. Thus, the initiative he had taken in capturing the British fort went unappreciated as Arnold found himself passed over for promotion. Again.

These thoughts distracted Arnold from a small band of ruffians blocking his entrance to the pub. *Lovely*. He stopped to study them and frowned. A few blokes going on about their own tasks was one thing, but their attention all fell on him.

Arnold wanted to get inside and conclude his affairs with Schuyler. Afterward, he could return home to his sister, wife, and children in New Haven, Connecticut. Once home, he would pay his debts and arrange affordable cargo with easily reachable destinations for his ships, *Fortune, Peggy,* and *Sally,* past British blockades. Later, he could decide how best to use the brewing war to his benefit. It certainly wasn't helping his shipping business, but this was all predicated on Arnold's ability to avoid the trouble standing in front of the pub.

Arnold took several slow steps up the dirt road, and a knot of leathery, uncivilized men stepped out to intercept him, some holding weaponry—pistols or knives. Arnold survived two duels in Honduras and escaped several skirmishes with the British at Ticonderoga and Crown Point on Lake Champlain. He would survive this, too, but it was a bloody inconvenience. The July sun slipped behind a thick cloud, casting an air of gloom across the pub and street. A lone man, more scarred and cragged than the rest, took a further step out from among the rabble blocking the entrance. He pointed to Arnold. "Isn't there a bounty out for wandering redcoats?"

Arnold thought the men might be part of a militia, maybe on their way from Albany to Boston. He didn't know for sure. What he *did* know was this lot of would-be soldiers had mistaken him for being British. It didn't help that Arnold still wore his red uniform jacket, modeled after the British, complete with gold trimming and brass buttons. He may have been discharged from his duties at the fort, but he was still on official business with Schuyler. The uniform was a vestige from his militia days in Connecticut as well as his involvement with the Sons of Liberty. Besides, he looked smashing in red. Arnold knew he would have made a fine British officer if he hadn't decided to capitalize on the business opportunities here.

"I am Benedict Arnold, Commander of Fort Ticonderoga and Master of Lake Champlain," he said, placing his hands on either side of his opened red coat. He knew his gesture and tone were arrogant, but in truth, it put his right hand closer to his pistol. "My business is a matter of importance and urgency, so you would all do well to let me enter."

"Ticonderoga?" Another voice said. "I'n't a redcoat fort?"

"Not anymore," Arnold said, his voice low and threatening. "There is war brewing. For some of us, it has already started. While you lot have been sleeping, I've been fighting to protect your liberties. So let's say you let me pass, eh?" Arnold moved forward, ignoring the crowd. However, instead of parting to let him by, they locked together.

"You'll not find anybody sleeping here," the scarred man said and stepped in front of Arnold. "Wait just a tug. Where do you think you're going?" He jabbed a finger at Arnold's chest. "We're not done sussing you out."

"I order you to stand down and let me pass."

The crowd chuckled.

Arnold rolled his eyes. "While I applaud your commitment to safeguarding this drinking establishment," Arnold said, "I must protest your foolishness." Arnold sighed, wishing there were someone among the growing crowd who recognized him. Were that the case, he could sort this whole thing out. *Where is Schuyler?* Nobody ever accepted his authority. It was just like Ticonderoga all over again. "If you do not let me pass, the day will become a most unpleasant one." Arnold felt for his pistol.

"Boys, I believe we have a spy here." The scarred man caught Arnold's motion. Everyone else did, too.

"A spy? Do you think me daft?"

"Daft enough if you pull out that pistol."

"Then so be it—"

Arnold jerked his hand down inside his coat for his pistol. Everyone around him tensed, and some drew their weapons. At that moment, an unhealthy looking gentleman emerged from the entrance of the pub. Arnold relaxed. The sun broke through the clouds, casting long shadows.

"Easy, gentlemen. This man is with me," said General Phillip Schuyler, looking Arnold over. "Although I cannot attest to his choice of attire." Schuyler's eyes remained commanding despite his wasted physique. He gave Arnold a look of incredulity, then glanced over the crowd. They still seemed hesitant, turning their heads between General Schuyler and Arnold. Schuyler coaxed them further by saying, "I will purchase drinks for all who step inside." That did it.

Schuyler waved Arnold in, dismissing the group of militia, who collectively decided a free mug of ale or a gill of rum was worth whatever strangeness the man in the red coat brought to their watering hole. But not before the scarred man said, "You look like a man of means. Why so quick to the pistol when you could've simply bought us a drink?"

A look of confusion crossed Arnold's face. The thought had not occurred to him.

"Bah," the scarred man said. He shook his head at Arnold, brushed by him, and headed inside.

"You certainly have a way with people, don't you?" said Schuyler. The pair passed through the crowd, who paid Arnold no attention. "I suppose it's true what they say about you. You love conflict."

"I hope you do not believe everything you hear." They passed the bar. Arnold noticed a frumpy, redheaded woman behind it. Arnold took in her dark, red hair. Even plain, she was the first woman of note he had seen from his long spring and summer of military action. Nevertheless, he turned away when she eyed him back, chastising himself for getting caught looking when he had just been thinking about Peggy a few minutes earlier. The tavern keeper glowered at Arnold, but changed her expression when Schuyler produced a pouch of coins with the instruction to pour drinks for everyone.

"I tend not to judge one on hearsay alone. In your case, I am extra mindful."

Inwardly, Arnold groaned.

It wasn't unusual for a woman, usually a widow, to run a pub, nor was it unusual for a tavern to mix people from different levels of society. Aristocrats, generals, and farmers alike all shared an interest in warm beer and the latest news and gossip. Pubs like the Red Herring also functioned as jails, post offices, and assembly halls.

While Schuyler threw down coin at the bar for the round of drinks, Arnold looked for Schuyler's table so he could begin his business. In doing so, he looked around the stone built tavern for anything out of place. He thought it best to be cautious, seeing as people here appeared a bit jumpy. Nothing stood out. The room set aside as a cell was empty. Conversely, the postal slots stuffed with letters and packages. He hoped one of those letters was from Peggy, but knew it was wasted. She never wrote back.

Arnold found where the general had been holed up off to the rear of the tavern and near a side exit. He pulled out a worn wooden chair for Schuyler and one for himself and sat them at the makeshift table—no more than a hogshead to which three uneven planks had been nailed.

"Colonel Arnold," Schuyler said after taking his seat, "I have heard much about you, but I know little of what to believe."

Arnold responded with a puzzled look. "What do you know about me, and who spoke ill? I deserve an account of those who've spoken against me."

Schuyler continued without addressing the question. "I've heard you have a certain way of dealing with both your superiors and immediate subordinates, but we will get to that in a moment. First, I want to hear your account of Ticonderoga."

Arnold considered pursuing the issue, but refrained. It could wait. Over the next few hours, he gave Schuyler the account of the events of Ticonderoga and the subsequent events of Lake Champlain. They were both many drinks in when Arnold finished, and the sun sat low in the sky.

"Basically," Schuyler said, his words careful and slow, "you, hailing from Connecticut, took control of a militia from Massachusetts and then invaded the neighboring Colony of New York?"

"Well... yes. In defense of the whole of New England, not just a single Colony. We must get away from that mindset. Furthermore, it was perfectly within my charter—"

"Enough of that," Schuyler interrupted. "I'm not attacking you. I just wanted the gist of it. To tell you the truth, the thought amuses me." His face brightened, and he chuckled. "We are in agreement. New England must be safeguarded against military incursion from the north. Taking the forts Ticonderoga and Crown Point and securing Lake Champlain, went a long way toward guaranteeing just that." Schuyler swigged his rum. Then, he changed focus. "Not to mention, all the cannons you plucked from British hands for our own devices. I hear tell that they may be of some use to us in Boston." Schuyler leaned back deep within his chair, like a thin, bowing plank leaning against a wall. "Jolly effort, Colonel. Well done, indeed."

Arnold's eyes widened. He wasn't used to receiving proper credit for his effort nor thanks for it. For the first time in months, his shoulders stretched back and chest puffed out in pride for his hard-won victories. Earlier, Schuyler had one of his aides, a thick short man with a snug uniform, summon a cheese plate, which now arrived, bearing thick white cheese cuts, dark bread, and purple grapes. Arnold grabbed a grape and popped it into his mouth. "Thank you, but as you know, the state of the north is in terrible condition since I have had to resign my duties."

"You should not have resigned," said Schuyler, leaning closer with commanding eyes. His unhealthy features disappeared behind them. "You should have stayed on, in whatever capacity you were needed." Arnold's eyes widened as Schuyler continued. "What did you expect? You caused quite the consternation for New Yorkers by dragging them into the conflict. Did you seriously think when New York pulled their Congress together they would leave you up there in command? Bloody hell, Arnold. If they had left you there, I'm certain you would have been halfway to Quebec by now."

This is true. The British in the Quebec Province were few and stretched. The time to secure the border was—

"Politics," Schuyler exclaimed and settled back in his chair. "My home colony didn't want to be dragged into the same predicament with England Massachusetts is in. But you? You started something. Now, all of New England is in this together," Schuyler said, pointing a finger at Arnold. "I know a few things about politics. They are a dangerous business. It can kill a military man's career as quickly as a musket ball. And you are on the short list for execution. Your tenacity is not what General Hancock and Congress is seeking. It pains me to say, but reconciliation with the British is our current objective. My charter, under the new Continental Army, is only for the defense of the Colonies. You, good sir, could march right into General John Hancock's office and demand a pre-emptive invasion of Quebec—though it would never happen. You are too ambitious for them."

Arnold unbuttoned his red coat. The tavern's thick stone walls made it quite cool inside, even on the hottest days, but as the sun set, the stones retained some of the sun's warmth and left the air stuffy. As Schuyler finished off the cheese plate, it occurred to Arnold that their business had long since concluded. Schuyler wanted something else. Arnold broke the silence. "And what would you have me do?"

"I want you on my staff," said Schuyler. "My health can sometimes get the best of me. Your versatility at Ticonderoga—planning, coordinating and then leading both a ground and naval assault—were impressive." Schuyler's expression soured, and his voice dropped as he said, "Don't mistake me—I have heard stories about you. I know about your duels in Honduras. I know you threatened to duel one of your own subordinates at the fort, and when he declined, you gave him the boot. Quite literally, I may add. You have a propensity for making enemies, even within your own ranks, wouldn't you say?"

"I'll challenge any man who affronts me."

"I daresay you would. I've seen it first hand," Schuyler said, his eyes flicking to the front door where the earlier incident took place. "But you don't have the type of political backing to survive such an onslaught of enemies. Your conduct would come back to haunt you, but I have a need for such a character as you, and I can offer you some political protection. In exchange for your services, I will make you my adjutant general."

Arnold's shoulders shrank as the words rolled over him. He had to suppress a frown and the urge to pound his fist on the table, but felt sure that he had kept himself composed in front of the general. *He wants me to sit behind a table doing paperwork?* Arnold would be the one planning the battles. General Schuyler would take the credit for the victories. True, Arnold knew himself to be a master strategist, but he also thought himself more of a field commander, and a capable one at that. If anyone was to lead, it would be him riding out in front. Onward to victory—and glory. He couldn't improve upon his name from behind the lines with a pile of paperwork in front of him.

Instead of jumping out of his chair and throttling the pompous general, Arnold stood, the chair scooting backward on the hard surface, screeching as it did so. "I would serve this cause in any fashion I am able, with or without this uniform," he said, now with the idea of returning home to Peggy at the forefront of his mind. His back was stiff, and his rear was sore. He must have been sitting in that hard chair for too long, he thought. Further proof that it wasn't the life for him.

Schuyler, for his part, looked jolly. "I hoped that would be your answer. I will finalize the appointment with General Hancock, who will, of course, need to acquire approval from our new Congress. But I don't see any of this becoming an issue." Schuyler stood up and beckoned his aide to refill their tankards with a new drink—bourbon, topped off with tart cherries and sugar. He grabbed both and handed one to Arnold. Then, Schuyler said, "To your health, *General.*"

Arnold smiled. "I do like how that sounds." He looked at the ailing Schuyler. *To your health as well, General.* Perhaps it would not be all bad. How long could Schuyler survive, after all?

He was just about to finish the toast when a panting youth rushed in with a wrinkled brown envelope. Dirt covered his face, and his curly, black hair lay matted against his scalp. His brown, linen shirt clung to his chest. After a solid deep breath, he called out, "Mister Benedict Arnold?"

The room fell silent, and everyone turned toward Arnold. The scarred man from earlier let out a disapproving grunt, and

Arnold glared at the youth. The messenger rushed to the table while Arnold and Schuyler stood with tankards in the air.

"Mister Arnold, sir." The disheveled youth panted. "I have a message for you."

The mounting frustrations of the day caught up to him, and Arnold exploded in anger. He slammed the tankard down, spilling its sticky contents, "How dare you interrupt me while I am about my business." Arnold's large frame bore down on the boy. "You uncivilized cur. Do you not recall your manners?" His arm lifted in a threatening manner. While Arnold couldn't take his anger out on the general, he could take it out on the interloper.

Schuyler sat back down, arms crossed as he watched with a look of astonishment as Arnold berated the boy. "General Arnold, I think that is enough. I think this young man needs a breather and a drink, don't you?" Schuyler reached in and pulled a king's crown from a pouch. An aide brought a chair and retrieved a tankard of cheap, watered-down red wine. The boy sat and drank, catching his breath.

Arnold remained standing, leaning in, both hands balled and used as supports against the table. They ignored each other as Schuyler prompted the boy, "Go ahead, son. What do you need?"

"Beg your forgiveness, sirs," the boy said. "I have been attempting to reach Mister Arnold over the past few days since Fort Ticonderoga. I'd 'ave missed you here, too, but I overheard people talking about a man claiming the name of Benedict Arnold, who threatened a crowd of armed men this afternoon."

Arnold's face stretched into a forbidding frown. He was about to speak when Schuyler interrupted him. "What do you have for us?"

"I've a letter about a Margaret Mansfield." The boy produced the crumpled correspondence and handed it to Arnold.

Arnold stopped and stared. "Peggy?" Arnold asked, taking the letter. "But she never writes."

Arnold was dimly aware of Schuyler's eye on him as he began to read. As he did so, Arnold felt the blood drain from his face. He fell backward, collapsing heavily in his chair. It felt like his chest had caved in.

Schuyler frowned. "Is everything all right?" When Arnold didn't answer, Schuyler took two schillings from his pouch and gave them to the boy and then said something to him, but Arnold couldn't make it out. With that, the young messenger nodded and headed with an aide to the redheaded tavern keeper, leaving Arnold alone with Schuyler.

Arnold stared at the table, the sounds of the tavern fading into each other, becoming a background murmur against the thunder in his heart.

"General," Schuyler said, his tone loud as though he'd addressed him several times. "Arnold, return home and take care of whatever matters have arisen."

Arnold looked up, his mouth dry. When he first tried to answer, the words wouldn't come. When he found them, his voice sounded faint. Empty. "No, I mustn't. There's much to be done here. It's already too late anyway..." He trailed off. "...nothing to be done..."

"What's too late?" Schuyler sounded alarmed.

"My wife is... dead."

From the way Schuyler responded to the news, Arnold guessed he expected to hear something like that. Even in war, life at home went on, including the tragedies. He dropped his shoulders and frowned. "I am very sorry to hear that." Silence fell between them. The tavern had filled with its evening customers. Raucous crowds made their way in, and tankards of rum slammed down on the makeshift tables. But the stillness from Arnold's table pushed away all other noise.

"Colonel." Schuyler broke Arnold's dour reflection. "Your children should have their father. You must return home. Take tonight to rest. Tomorrow, we will breakfast together, and I'll supply you with provisions and a fresh horse. We'll get you home. We can talk about your role in my command should you desire to return at some point in the future. I assure you a place in my ranks." But from the way Schuyler said it, Arnold could tell that the role of adjutant general had just been taken off the table. *Perhaps I can make some good out of Margaret's passing after all. Very well.*

Inwardly, Arnold was relieved. He tried to mask that transformation, though he wasn't sure how successful he was in hiding it. "I suppose I cannot take the position you so kindly offered."

"We will discuss the issue more once the matter resolves. I will arrange a room for you."

"No, that won't be necessary." Arnold retrieved the letter from the floor, stood back up, and said, "I must be on my way immediately."

"Certainly. You can wait until you are refreshed. The letter has been following you around for weeks—"

Arnold pounded his fist onto the wooden table, and the room quieted. A thick trail of blood sprang from his knuckles. "No. I must leave now." Arnold sprang to his feet.

Schuyler stood, barely making it upright with a dry cough, but managed to intercept him. "Not tonight, Colonel. It is getting late, and you've had one bloody bit of bad news."

"All the more reason to leave. I am already late. My sister needs me, as do my children. I must go at once."

"Tomorrow morning, I insist."

"Now!"

Arnold towered over Schuyler, steaming, and Schuyler backed down. "If it would aid your bereavement to leave now... Well, it would appear I have little choice. At least allow me to provide you with some necessities and a horse. You will have need of them." Arnold nodded, so Schuyler called over his aide and gave him clipped orders.

While Schuyler made arrangements, Arnold slipped into thought. Though he wanted to get as far away from the general as he could, he wished the best for Schuyler. Despite his ailing health, Schuyler seemed like a damned good leader, and the war was going to need people like him. It wasn't Schuyler's fault he had been chosen over Arnold. So, for now, Arnold would focus on his home and his business now that his wife had passed. He would have to rely even more on his sister, Hannah. The war, and the Colonies, would have to succeed without him, at least until Arnold could find a way around the insult of being offered an assistant's job to a command that should have been his. That could come later. Eventually, the Colonies would realize they needed him more than he needed them. He almost let out a wry smile, but remembered he was supposed to be mourning Margaret. He knew he would when the time was right, or at least he believed that eventually, the tears and emotion would flow.

Once the provisions were loaded, Schuyler walked Arnold out. The air was still warm, and the sky was much darker under the new moon. Schuyler placed a hand on Arnold's shoulder and whispered, "Good luck."

Arnold nodded an empty reply, climbing on the brown horse and spurring it into action.

A few moments later, Arnold disappeared into the tree line surrounding Albany, leaving General Phillip Schuyler, head of the Northern Department of the new Continental Army, alone to carry the burden of command. Arnold once again escaped the life fate tried to hand him, and he would, once again, find his own path.

FOUR

New Haven, Connecticut
July 14th, 1775.

BARREL staves and hoops?" Benedict Arnold demanded answers. When he arrived home on his way to Albany upon learning of Margaret's death, he had no idea what to expect. All he wanted was to climb up the polished ash-wood staircase of his home on Water Street in New Haven and bury himself among the blankets of his own bed.

Instead, he found himself at the waterfront, arguing with his sister, Hannah, and a bureaucratic paper-pusher hell-bent on keeping Arnold broke. This, most certainly, was not the comfort of his own bed. He hadn't even yet made a visit to his wife's grave.

In the hot July sun, Arnold kept his red, wool uniform jacket closed tightly. Everything was so cold. He used his sleeve to wipe the sweat off his face. Despite the chill, he perspired like a pig. "Please, explain to me why my ships are loaded with such—"

"It is a sensible shipment," Hannah said. "Besides, it is least likely to be confiscated by the British. You need an honest stream of income now. You have financial concerns." Hannah wore a black mourning dress with her brown hair wrapped in a tight bun. She seemed older than her years, well past the point of ever becoming wed. She managed the apothecary, cared for Arnold's four children, took care of the estate—Arnold had driven his sister into spinsterhood. He regretted that now.

"Mum, would you excuse us so that Mister Arnold and I might discuss—"

"Finish that thought and it will be you stuffed into the ship's cargo hold," Hannah said.

"I meant no offense," said the dockmaster, an Irishman, with dark, close-cropped hair, light skin apparently stuck in a perpetual state of sunburn, and an accent which made it sound like his words rolled out. "But, I must ask Mister Arnold to sign the manifests. They are his manifests, no matter who arranged the cargo."

"And that is why I brought him here."

Arnold hadn't changed out of his uniform. He'd barely set foot into the house before Hannah dragged him off to the docks. He hadn't visited with his children, who'd been carted off to boarding school during Arnold's absence. "I didn't even know if you were alive, never thought I'd see you again, and there was business to attend to. Choices had to be made," Hannah had said. She was right, and Arnold was in no position to argue.

Dizziness washed over him as he dabbed the pen in the inkwell, leafed through the paperwork, and signed his name in the appropriate places. The job was done. Now, he could return home and climb into bed, so long as he suffered no further interruptions—

"And how is the fighting going on over there?"

Arnold sighed. "You don't want to know."

The dockmaster pressed. "Is it true what I've read in the papers?"

"The papers?" Hannah chortled. "Don't believe what you read in there. The papers have been unkind to Benedict since he left, publishing all sorts of lies about who did what—"

"Once again, I find myself apologizing, Mum," the Irishman said. Hannah took a step back, and nodded for him to continue. "I meant about the north, how they might possibly wish to ally themselves with us in the fight against England," he finished.

"It doesn't matter either way," Arnold said, shrugging it off at first, then pausing to think. "The north is not particularly well defended at the moment. The further we push north, the better our safety and security becomes here. If the people there wish to fight with us, it strengthens our cause." Arnold felt more clear headed now, the best he'd felt in several days.

"Stop now before you become embroiled in conversation, the both of you," Hannah said. "I need to get back and open shop."

"It's a pity we cannot simply sail up the Hudson and lend Quebec City our support," the dockmaster continued.

"No, the Hudson wouldn't get you near close enough to the city. There may only be a small garrison of redcoats there, but to reach the city quickly and quietly is another task."

"Well, the north is full of lakes and rivers... Perhaps there is another way."

"Perhaps." Arnold realized they had ignored Hannah, much to their peril. She said nothing and frowned at them. "We must be going."

Arnold closed with the dockmaster, ensuring his paperwork was in order and his ships would depart soon with what meager cargo they held. Then, he and his sister made their way up the half-mile distance from the docks as a mild sea breeze took some of the heat away from the sunny summer day.

Hannah wrapped her hands around Arnold's left arm. "Do you want to stop by Margaret's grave?"

Arnold stopped. "What?" The ocean breeze tore through him.

"It's on the way. At the churchyard. The tombstone should be finished and placed by now. I will give you some time to spend with her while I open."

Arnold had sidestepped General Schuyler's generous offer of employment by using his wife's death. But now that he was home and his wife's grave so freshly dug, the reality began to sink in. The chill and dizziness returned. He needed rest, but what he wanted to do was look at some of his maps. "I think I shall go later today when you can accompany me. Right now, I need washing and a change of attire."

"Indeed." Hannah shot Arnold a look of curiosity, but left it at that. "I will leave you to your own devices then, brother."

Arnold kissed her hand before she left him alone.

Arnold hurried home, climbed the stairs, and tore off his red uniform jacket before entering his study. He pulled a dusty stack of papers off a shelf and leafed through them, drawing out several crude maps of Quebec province. They were all wildly inaccurate, so it was only through comparing the maps to each other that Benedict could get a sense of the area. It wasn't too far off from Lake Champlain and the wilderness he had just spent the last several months in.

Yes, there is something here.

With some excitement, Arnold pulled out a chair and freshened up his writing supplies. He placed the maps down and sat. He was about to grab a quill when his head fell forward, crashing into his arm that rested on the table. Darkness followed.

Arnold awoke to the sound of silver chiming on china. He lifted his head, opened eyes, and wiped away a trail of drool. He gingerly took the offered teacup from his sister's hand. *Chamomile with a squeeze of lemon.* Just because they were at war with the British didn't mean he and his sister should sacrifice some of the finer things.

He hadn't realized how dehydrated he'd become and drank it down. It wasn't until his sister refilled his cup that his senses returned. For one, it was now dark outside, and several candles mounted on wall sconces and a lantern on the table illuminated the room. For another, he could see his sister's displeasure through the dim light. Arnold shivered.

"I see you've started with some scheme already." Hannah sat back down at a chair and small table beside the desk.

Arnold stirred his tea without answering.

"Benedict, why did you come back? I am not a hospital. If you are sick, you should seek treatment elsewhere."

Stirring did nothing to stifle his unease. Arnold tried to change the subject instead. "How are you doing? Is Margaret's death— How are you getting by?"

"Margaret's death is your concern. We are absolutely fine here without you. The boys are acquainted with matters of life and death. They understand. And I am busy managing your estate. Other than needing your signature on a piece of paper every now and then, I am getting along fine." She took a slow sip of tea. "You ought to be more concerned with yourself. You go off to war, you were supposed to improve our... your name, and I come to read things in the papers about your... exploits." She dropped the spoon on the saucer. It rattled loudly on the table. "Dreadful things."

It was getting warm. Uncomfortably warm. He changed the subject once more. "Where are my children? Earlier, you mentioned boarding school."

"Benedict the father. Suddenly, you want to see your children? Why, when you have no ability to comfort them."

Arnold shrank back, as if wounded. "I would like to visit with them."

"You won't strengthen your name staying in the house with children at your feet," Hannah leaned forward. She brought her attention to the maps on the table. "Your place is out in the field. It is the only place you can be a man, where you can redeem yourself—through victory or death."

"Why does it matter?" Arnold sat up in the chair. "Here we are, a year into the war, and I have failed. I was asked to leave Ticonderoga. I was asked to be a staff officer instead of being asked to lead." Arnold's voice rose. "And I face court martial for my boldness and willingness to act long before Congress even realized we were at war. It is preposterous. And here I am, near broke, bereft of my wife, full of grief and barely able to lift my head. What would you have me do?"

"Full of grief?" She folded her arms. The candles flickered. "I think not."

Arnold blew out a long breath of air and answered with silence. She almost convinced him she was right. *But, she couldn't be, could she?* Surely, he grieved.

Hannah ruffled through the maps on the table, her eyes squinting in the low light of the lamp. Then, she folded her arms. "Take some time. For yourself. You've always been at your best when you've stopped to think. I find it amusing that to others, it looks as if you've lost your mind, running off into the unknown, but I know you better than anyone else. It couldn't be further from the truth. There is so much thought behind your actions."

"From insult to compliment. Looks like I'm moving in the right direction. I'll claim victory wherever I can get it." Arnold wiped sweat from his brow and feigned a smile.

"Benedict, your mind is like a teapot. It's not working unless it's brewing something." She shook her head and continued, "It looks like you've picked up an ailment, so rest and get over it. Sort out your financial dealings, and for God's sake, grant me some sort of legal authority, so I don't have to deliver you or your letters to the docks anymore." Hannah went on, inching closer to Arnold, "Then, do what you've always done."

"Yes?"

"Act." She stiffened, and her eyes darted as if searching for a memory. "Do you know what Father said to me one time? He told me what the name 'Arnold' meant. He said it meant 'rule with eagles.' He said this at a time when he was a respected man of this city, and it's the best memory I have of him. Arnolds were meant to soar."

"How can I fly when my wings are clipped and my feathers tarred?" Arnold churned over the list of grievances against him. It seemed to grow with each iteration. Then there was Hannah, who could be counted on to bring him back down from the heavens, or, in this case, pull him back up from the depths of Hell.

"Your pride keeps you caged! You can be such a pompous ass. Do you even realize you have no choice? If you stay, you'll be a father, but not much of one. You'll dwindle and wane until you've become no better than ours. If you go, there is a chance you can become somebody fantastic or meet death in a righteous cause. In either case, your name is restored, and your sons can carry it on. Then you can be a father."

Arnold pondered her words. A thought formed on his tongue, but Hannah had not finished. "Smuggling is no longer an option. So, like it or not, even from the business side of this, you are involved. You won't make any money from shipping until this matter resolves, so you might as well place yourself well in this new system. Start thinking of allies in Congress and make sure you have the love of the men beneath you. War is the sole option you have to redeem the Arnold name. The Lord has given you this opportunity. Use it."

Arnold sat back, in stunned silence. His head throbbed. He was cold. And his muscles ached. Hannah was right again, but that did not mean he had to acknowledge it. Wax melted off the candles on the wall, dripping, cooling, and forming long, dagger-like shapes that hid in the darkness on the underside of the sconce. There was light... and then there was dark.

"This room is now blue." It was the first thing he could think of to break the silence.

"Do you like it?"

"Yes. I think it makes the room very regal. I do."

"Liar," Hannah said.

She proved correct for a third time tonight. He pressed his luck. "Am I really an ass?"

"Absolutely." She didn't smile. Her sarcasm was deadpan. If she were joking, there was no way of knowing.

"Thank you," Arnold said, "for everything."

She stood and departed without another word, shutting

the door behind her. The candles on the wall flickered in protest. Arnold felt hollow. He wondered how he had maintained the self-control not to plunge into a pile of pillows. Then he smiled to himself at the answer—he found his strength through Hannah.

Several weeks later

Adjutant General Horatio Gates, with glasses over his sloped and aging eyes, met Benedict Arnold with a hint of disproval. The adjutant seemed to shout, *"Who are you, and why are you bothering my boss?"*

Arnold had waited patiently for nearly half the day to see General John Hancock, the Commander-in-Chief of the Continental Army. He had found a way to traverse the harsh wilderness to Quebec by taking the Kennebec River and its land bridges up through the frozen north.

If it worked, and if they did it quickly, Arnold was confident he could take the city. Even if it failed, it would rock the redcoat army that a band of Colonials could strike so far into enemy lands. This would prove to the people of Quebec that Britain was not invincible. And sometimes, showing that the other side could be hurt was all it took for a once-strong empire to fall.

It had taken time and patience to meet with Hancock, both of which Arnold had in short supply, but now, Gates had finally summoned him. It was time for Arnold to blaze his own trail and prove he had the strength and temerity to restore his name and honor.

Gates opened the latch on the plain wooden door leading to Hancock's office, and showed Arnold in. With a deep breath and a bit of fake bravado, Arnold stepped through the threshold.

FIVE

Delaware River, Outside Trenton, N.J.
December 25th, 1776.

TO say it was bitter cold and dark would be a disservice to the truth, Lt. Colonel George Washington thought. There was no moon, and a blanket of black storm clouds covered the stars. Snow drifted over the forest floor in treacherous, impassible mounds. Chunks of ice choked the Delaware, funneling icy torrents downriver. The wind tugged at Washington, sitting astride his white, Virginia-bred Quarter Horse. From out of the foggy darkness, he heard snow crunching under hooves. Washington waited, suppressing agitation while the rider came into view.

Washington risked a whispered, "Colonel Donop?" The chestnut horse Colonel Donop rode, stopped, its nostrils flaring. Icy vapor formed around its nose. The Hessian commander looked a little out of place on horseback. Hessians, in general, were broad-shouldered, tinged with a darker complexion, and styled their hair by pulling it straight back, wrapping it in a point. Lt. Colonel Carl Emil Ulrich von Donop was no exception, but for keeping his hair in the English fashion.

"*Ja*," he said in a deep, guttural accent. It was becoming less strange to Washington, but he still didn't speak the Prussian tongue. The Hessian spoke little English, making communication... *interesting*.

"Report."

"Your Excellency," Donop spoke in his best English. "I speak most poor news. My regiment cannot cross downriver as we before believed."

Even the Hessian's best English took Washington a moment to piece together. When he did, he raised an eyebrow. "Why? Be quick."

"Ice... the river. Excuse me, I mean to say the ice has closed across the river."

"Surely your men can break it up? We must proceed with the crossing at once." The Hessians seemed to be under the impression that tonight's mission was optional. Even the normally determined Donop demurred.

"My English, it is not great. I think that I do not understand."

At that, another rider approached from the other direction. His horse trudged through embankments that reached the rider's feet in places. Instead of riding close, the second rider stopped too far away to whisper, then called out, "Herr Commander!"

Washington winced at the noise.

"*Halt die klappe*," Donop said, hushing the Hessian.

After a moment of trouble working his horse through the drift, the second rider joined them. He spoke, "*Entschuldigung, Herr* Washington. *Herr* Colonel." This rider didn't gesture to either man as he apologized, Washington noted, probably because the second rider couldn't make out either of the other two in the thickening fog. The second rider continued in German with Donop translating, "We cannot conclude the exercise upriver of our position tonight on account of the extremes of the weather."

Washington expected the response, although he saw the words encouraged Colonel Donop, who puffed out his chest. "He is right. We cannot make the crossing. Perhaps another night?" Donop suggested. "Come, let us seek warmth."

"No. As you can see for yourselves, gentlemen, the ice has not overtaken the entirety of the river at this crossing point." Washington didn't believe for a moment that the river was impassable at the two other spots, either, but he was practical enough to know when to pick his battles. "We will cross here, now, as planned."

"*Ausgeschlossen*," the second rider said. Impossible. Out of the question.

It was a word Washington had heard before. His imposing frame glared down, not that it mattered in the dark fog. "You are relieved of command. I expect your second to arrange to care for casualties and captives. Expect us late tomorrow morning.

If these orders are not fulfilled, both you and your second will receive lashings." Donop translated, stopping several times as if in confusion. Washington pictured shock on the commander's face.

"*Herr* Commander, *das ist eisig und kalte,*" Donop shook his head, "I mean to say, it is freezing. While I approve of the discipline, your Excellency, it is Christmas. We could do this another time, perhaps, when we have more support?"

Washington felt his face burning. He turned his temper toward Donop. "March your detachment to this juncture. You will cross the river with the utmost of haste." He took a breath and let it out in a cloud of icy vapor. "It is precisely because of the foul weather and holiday that we must cross at once." He paused again, giving them a moment to translate. "Are we of perfect understanding?"

The two Hessians nodded. Washington dismissed them, and they trudged back to their respective camps. He then made his way toward the trees along the Delaware. To the north and upriver lay a low ridge. East of that lay Princeton. Immediately downriver was his main camp at Trenton, where Donop was heading.

In all, Washington held a tenuous command of two regiments, and coordinated with Donop's regiment. Right now, they were broken into three detachments for each potential river crossing. His hope was they all would make the crossing that night. But, it appeared he was already down to a third of his strength. His surprise raid against a Continental outpost on the other side of the Delaware hadn't even begun, and it was already failing. But, if Washington had a regiment or two to use, even if it were a detachment of mercenaries, he refused to waste the opportunity.

Across the Delaware lay Pennsylvania. Washington's spy network placed a large number of continentals on the other side of the river, protecting the most likely British route into Philadelphia. No doubt this area was well fortified with *abatis*, breastworks, and artillery. That would not be Washington's approach.

The continentals knew how to shoot from behind a fortification, as Washington and the British had learned to their dismay at Breed's Hill a year and a half ago. It was meant to be the first and last engagement of the war. They were wrong. Breed's Hill, and nearby Bunker Hill, had turned a simple landing of

British regulars into a slaughterhouse. The British had ultimately won, but at a price so high they could scarcely call it a victory.

The two sides had been at a near stalemate since, with British progress slow and costly. Their master plan seemed tragically flawed to Washington—engaging the main body of the rebel force and defeating them, but not engaging them where defeat seemed likely. It tied their hands and kept the British to the cities while the rebels disappeared into the forest wilderness. However, there were other ways to strike which the British had not fully considered.

To that end, Washington approached the detachment of Hessians awaiting orders in the woods. The men huddled together beneath blue coats with red facings. Some had blankets. Most did not. Several earthen kitchens—mounds of earth, with spaces for a dozen small, hidden fires—provided little heat. What scraps of smoke it let out dissipated into the fog, but they would soon lose even that warmth. He urged them on.

Snow fell like cold, wet ash on the nine hundred Hessians as they made their way to the riverbank, hauling heavy, flat-bottom Durham boats. Others carried oars covered with animal skins to help silence their approach once in the river. Still others carried large poles for dislodging ice and steering. Among the Hessians were Loyalists, wrapped in furs, who knew their way around the river.

Sweat built under Washington's uniform despite the chilling storm. The current rushing down the river made crossing directly from bank to bank impossible. If carried too far downriver, they risked being spotted by Colonial sentries on the other side. Or the boats and the men on them might be swept down for miles before making it to land, or they could capsize and freeze to death within the river's icy thrall.

For the men who might make it to the other side, the situation remained precarious. It would take hours for all the men to cross. All the while, Hessians on both sides of the river would be subject to exposure and fatigue. If discovered, there was no escape for them. Rumblings of insubordination came from all around Washington as the Hessians crept toward the river, none too eager to be the first to cross.

Washington moved his horse to the embankment. At last, several Hessians boarded the first flatboat after heaving it into the river. A navigator had not joined them, which caused Washington some alarm.

As soon as they pushed out, the current caught the boat and slammed it down the river. Before the Hessians could react, ice crashed into the small craft, sending a spray over them. Ice stuck to the sides, making it impossible for them to steer. They attempted to use their oars to change course. His face flushed, and his knuckles whitened. *Boys, knock the ice off!*

The boat, weighed down by the thickening ice, lost control and crashed downstream. The boat flipped over, and the men slipped beneath the blackness.

The witnesses let out a collective gasp on the shore, followed by curses. Some Hessians dropped their burdens, splitting the Durham boats by wooden seams on the solid snow. Soldiers abandoned their oars and fled back toward the tree line. Only a few men, led by Washington and several officers, attempted any rescue efforts, but it was futile. The men were lost.

Soft snow turned to icy sleet and fell sharp as daggers.

"Soldiers, keep by your officers. For God's sake, keep by your officers!" Washington spun around on horseback, urging each soldier back, despite the language barrier. Officers who shared some words in common started to do the same to no avail. The evening broke into chaos.

Washington urged his steed down to the closest boat, now sitting empty in the water. He dragged the men closest to him and directed them toward it. This was his last chance to regain control. He was about to dismount when his horse found a piece of ice and slipped. The horse lost its footing, unable to recover. Washington felt the ground give way underneath him and himself rushing toward it.

Private Frederick Bakker wanted nothing more than to be back at home to a time from before he and his father had been thrown in jail. Before he had taken the offer to soldier for food and freedom. *And before I got on that* verdammt *boat to America.*

Maybe he'd like it as a farmer or a carpenter instead. He certainly hadn't liked working with his father as nothing more than a borderline criminal. Now, he found he liked standing in the snow with churning black water staring him in the face even less. *Snow... no, sleet. Wonderful.* He was so cold he could barely tell the difference, except that this stung more.

The first boat on the river capsized, and Bakker watched as four men disappeared. His heart beat faster. For a moment, he forgot the cold. Not a single one of them reappeared. They either drowned or froze underneath a sheet of ice. Thankfully, it hadn't been him or anyone he knew—as if he knew anyone other than Maximillian or a handful of the soldiers in his unit. But there was no way he was getting into a boat now. This idea? *Nicht sehr gut.*

The fate of the men on the capsized boat horrified him, and Bakker, like most of the others, abandoned his burden and started for the woods. He had no problem letting other people pick up the pieces. His part was over.

His mistake, however, had been to look, as he always did, to his sergeant for guidance. Maximillian, in turn, watched Colonel Washington. Bakker now did the same. Washington was a powerful, imposing figure, particularly astride his equally large white horse. In truth, Bakker found him intimidating, just as he found the harsh Colonel Donop, but Bakker liked Washington better. He appreciated his enthusiasm and novel approach to battle. Washington was, at least, willing to strike the enemy a blow, unconventional as it was. He respected that. Even if he wished he wasn't part of it.

But now, even Washington looked as if he were about to fail. His horse tumbled, threatening to send him sprawling along the ice or splashing into the river. Horror stretched along Bakker's spine, and his eyes widened. Washington would suffer greatly. The night was over. Bakker was torn between relief and—

But Washington did not fall.

Instead, Washington gripped the massive beast by the mane. It seemed to Bakker as if he had picked up the horse from on top of it—an impossible feat. And yet, Washington commanded the animal gracefully and calmly back on all fours as if they acted as one mind, as if nothing had happened. Just like that, the commanding officer recovered, and the beast looked as steady as ever. Bakker stood there in disbelief. His sergeant's jaw fell.

Washington ordered something in English. Bakker wished he knew enough of the language to have understood it. At least Maximillian did. A moment later, Washington dismounted in a single move which also looked impossible for a man his size. Then, he made his way into the first empty boat and climbed aboard. He just stood there, standing with one leg raised on the side of the boat, as if daring people onward. The boat did not so much as rock.

People around Bakker stopped their exodus into the woods. Officers pulled their men forward. Maximillian was only a sergeant, but he did the same. Bakker felt a tug on his sleeve as Maximillian pulled him down the embankment. He looked up at Maximillian, who stared back. Bakker wanted to pull away, but if he did, he would lose face in front of his sergeant and in front of his unit. He couldn't.

Slowly, reluctantly, Bakker allowed himself to be led down to the river. Fewer people crowded the front than a short while ago when they had all formed. Empty boats and oars lay near the shore, filling with sleet. Officers were less concerned with organization and more concerned with launching the first few boats.

Maximillian headed toward Washington's boat. Bakker warmed to that idea for a moment, but the boat had already filled when they reached it. Instead, a little later, Bakker found himself holding a deerskin-covered oar from inside a Durham flatboat. Now, in addition to being cold, Bakker was soaked in icy water from the seat and the floor of the boat. Bakker shuddered as he realized, with horror, that the night had just begun.

Shortly after, the boat launched from the bank, and Private Frederick Bakker from Kassel, found himself crossing the Delaware on a cold, dark Christmas night.

SIX

Delaware River, Pennsylvania
December 26th, 1776.

COLONEL Washington marched into the snow, burdened by worry. The crossing was taking all night and stealing into the morning hours. Reclaiming order from the earlier chaos had taken most of his time and patience. The slow crossing threatened once again to stop their attack before it even started. Washington breathed deeply to relieve tension. It did not work.

The few experienced navigators made repeated crossings, taking empty boats back and filling them with soldiers. Washington and the Hessian officers prepared the men and equipped them with dry ammunition, but the only thing the soldiers could do on this side of the river was wait until everyone else had crossed. And they had to do it in silence out in the cold. The men bit on their collars to keep their teeth from chattering.

The last boat completed the crossing just as sleet turned to heavy snow. It blended into the thick fog, making the path ahead impossible to see. Washington tightened his cloak. The weather would help mask their arrival, but the extreme elements tonight would take their toll on the men—some would die on the march. Washington trudged onward, pushing it to the back of his mind, but the worry that he had made a terrible mistake troubled him with every weary step.

It was this moment Washington would later look back on and realize he made his biggest miscalculation. In the darkness, he split his force into two groups. It had seemed a way to expedite things. Washington took direct control of the first column and sent the second column to flank the rebel position from the far side. This group marched away and disappeared into the fog and snow.

Nearly twenty-seven hundred men, mostly from the Pennsylvania and Massachusetts militias, composed the rebel outpost. The encampment, from what he could discern from his network, sat on a high, flat ridge overlooking a forested hill which sloped down into the river, pushing the water around it. It featured improvised but sturdy fortifications and was situated about a mile and a half inland. Snow covered that forested hill and the distance appeared much more than just over a mile.

In the daylight, they would've been ruined. Six-pound cannon and small mortar fire coming down on his men would've destroyed any attack they made on the position. Only this night, a night of celebration and foul weather, afforded the opportunity to strike the camp, so long as everything went to plan.

Washington moved his men on. Each of them now held a long Potsdam musket with bayonet. Some of the officers carried pistols that also allowed for a strange-looking bayonet to attach. He did not understand the point to it, but left the matter to the mercenaries. What was important was that they also all had dry powder, a miracle, considering the weather and river crossing, and a pouch full of musket balls. *Providence favors us this day.* Washington drew himself up, his spine stiff and straight as they reached the camp.

Time remained the critical factor. Daylight would ruin everything, and the sun would soon rise. Washington went over the plan in his head again. His first mission was simple: capture the rebel cannon before it could be used against them, then set a perimeter around this half of the outpost. Keeping the men quiet while the second column swept behind the breastworks now became his chief concern.

Thick fog still clung low to the ground, and snow continued to fall in thick flakes. Despite the early-morning sun rising from beyond the horizon, Washington could still see very little in front of him. That meant the rebels in the camp, even if they were awake, could not see them. The weather, or something far more powerful, seemed destined to allow this attack to continue. Morning had come, but no light shone on his endeavor. They remained hidden. Washington suppressed a smile.

He nodded, and a smaller unit moved ahead, tasked with searching for additional sentries or continentals out at the wrong place and time. They returned, reporting they had found no one awake near the camp. Everyone, they said, had passed out—apparently, having celebrated a little too much. No one expected the attack. Not even the sentries stirred this Christmas night. *Remarkable. Everything is proceeding as planned, despite our delay.*

Washington whispered, "Take the artillery." While Washington's men waited on the second column, they would capture the cannon and strengthen their position. The second column was under orders to do the same on their end. He couldn't see much through the fog, but he had been told of several six-pound cannons, unmanned, and a few service tents nearby with what he assumed were sleeping soldiers inside.

He frowned over the fate of those soldiers. They had to be killed, murdered in their sleep. Capturing them alive would be too risky. He motioned several of his men forward and whispered, "Quickly now, to duty and glory." But there was no glory in this. Washington removed his hat and lowered his head in silence. All he wanted was to keep his country united. This felt like a strange way of going about it, but necessary.

Several Hessians, armed with bayonets and knives, crept to the tents, widened the flaps, and forced their way inside. Washington imagined the horror, the wide-eyed shock as steel pierced skin and men awoke to their deaths. He tried to shut it out, but when he closed his eyes, the carnage intensified.

Moments later, the Hessians silently crept out. He could not see them clearly, but he pictured their hands and uniforms stained with blood. All of a sudden, Washington wished he were not so hot. He wiped perspiration from his forehead and neck with his sleeve. The first enemy casualties weighed heavily on his mind, but he forced himself to maintain his resolve. They could not turn back now.

He had to move. He again restated his intentions, which were quickly translated—correctly, he hoped. "Capture those cannon men, for those are the very keys to victory. Once we hold them, take positions surrounding the outpost. We will demand their surrender." If everything continued smoothly, there would be little left to accomplish and no further casualties for the day.

Washington ran through every detail of the plan in his

head once again while his men obeyed his orders. This was only a small rebel outpost, designed to give an early warning to General Hancock's main force. Hancock, he understood, was out on a Christmas tour, visiting commands in the area and reading to them from Thomas Paine's *Common Sense*. He would not be here. General Gates was with the main rebel body and General Charles Lee, the former British general and now rebel turncoat, had recently been captured and was paying hell for his defection. Therefore, if Washington and his men were quick enough, they should manage the capture of the entire rebel garrison. He needed to slow his rapidly pumping heart and carry out the—

Black powder exploded nearby. The still, unbroken air fractured within a heartbeat.

Bloody hell. Surprise was lost. There would be no call for surrender. The sudden urge to fight pumped through his heart, tearing through the terror which, before then, had threatened to engulf him. The fight was on. "Attack!" he ordered, raising his hunting sword high and his voice along with it. And the men did so, without need of a translator.

Washington recoiled as the initial shock wore off. In the heat of the moment, he realized that he might have given the wrong command. He was about to engage the enemy, where moments ago he was ready to abort the whole bloody affair. But it was too late now. Rebels tore out of their tents into the frigid air. Washington watched his men fly into the camp to meet them. A fog of war blanketed the camp. All he could do for the present was to look on in horror.

Private Bakker felt frozen solid. His feet were numb, and he couldn't feel his toes since the wet river crossing some time ago. He envisioned that his toes were gone, that instead he was walking on raw stumps. He wanted to stop. His eyelids hung low and heavy. He wanted to rest by a warm fire. But, every time he slowed, Maximillian prodded him along and sped his sluggish step. If hell were to ever freeze, Bakker was certain that this would be it. And all the while, the blizzard blew onward.

Something terribly loud burst through the long night of silence. It was some sort of explosion, which soon carried an echo through the camp. He thought it must have been loud enough to wake every living creature on earth. Bakker shuddered. His heart raced and his skin crawled. He wanted to run, but couldn't.

Back home in Kassel, he'd wanted to be placed into the artillery. The artillery units were prestigious, however, and Bakker lacked such polish. Maybe that was why he had remained still in the face of the mortar, for though it took a moment, he recognized it as such. Others around him called out in panic. Some ran. He couldn't. Maximillian grabbed him from behind and brought them both down to their knees into the icy snow.

They waited in silence. The mortar must have landed far away because no other explosion triggered. The next thing he knew, Maximillian picked Bakker up again. He was left alone for a blessed moment as the sergeant checked on every man in the unit. Bakker frowned as he returned. Maximillian seemed deliberately attached to him. *Just because I tried to flee that one time.*

A few moments later, he heard the snap of commands and was once again prodded forward. They went into the camp at a speed altogether too fast for it carried him away. They soon came upon the first row of tents, where the unit split off. In the middle of the path stood an earthen kitchen, where a cooking fire should be. Bakker found himself unconsciously holding his frostbitten fingers over it. He frowned. It was long since cool, frozen over along with everything else in this miserable wilderness.

Then, things got worse.

The tent in front of him opened. Before he and Maximillian could respond, at least six soldiers stepped out into the frigid air. Bakker's eyes opened, and he took a step back in surprise, wondering who was more afraid of whom. In between wafts of fog, the soldiers looked as if awoken too soon from a long hibernation. Their louse-ridden hair was oily and their faces overgrown with stubble. They rubbed at their arms, becoming even more dazed as the coldness hit them. Their eyes were as wide as his.

Bakker had no idea what to do. This was unlike any battle he'd fought in since being forced to join with the mercenary army just a short time ago. Until now, it had been mostly drills and a few small skirmishes, so Bakker just stood there. He looked toward his sergeant. Even Maximillian appeared frozen. They quickly lost the element of surprise, and they were already outnumbered. This did not look good.

"Halt. Halt!" Maximillian called out. Bakker realized that Maximillian had not been frozen, he had been thinking. He raised his musket at the men, and Bakker did the same. Now, it was the continentals' turn to freeze, but the soldiers still outnumbered the two. Maximillian leaned over and whispered, "Do not fire your weapon."

It took a moment, but Bakker nodded in understanding. If he fired, it would might slow the rebels down, but then he would have only his bayonet to defend with. Had things gone differently this morning, the bayonet was probably all he would've needed. The weapon itself was a great persuader. But now... well, things had kind of gone to hell.

"Kneel. Get on your knees, kneel!" Maximillian was at it again, though this time, the soldiers stopped listening.

"Surrender," Bakker said in Prussian. He tried to help, but it was no use. He realized that the soldiers did not understand them, although he thought their meaning should have been clear. Instead, the soldiers remained standing, several appeared poised to pounce. Bakker flustered and nervously waved the musket. Bakker continued to shift his weight while calling out to the soldiers. They were more bold, he less so. They were running out of time.

Then, out of the corner of his eye, the fog parted. He heard hoof beats. Bakker took a chance to look behind, taking a moment to recognize his company commander. He breathed in a sigh of relief. Certainly, he would know what to do. *No offense, Maximillian.*

"Rebels are everywhere!" The commander nearly trampled Bakker as he slowed from a gallop. Bakker stood, stricken with fear. He watched his commander fire a pistol. The shot tore into one of the soldiers across from Bakker. The man dropped with a cry into the snow, blood overtaking the white ground and staining it red. "No time for prisoners, no room, no comfort. We must be away. Back to the boats!" As quickly as he had come, the commander vanished, leaving Bakker and Maximilian to deal with the crisis.

Fear drained out of Bakker, replaced by confusion. The soldiers in front of him scattered. He reacted on instinct, no longer in control of his actions. He found himself raising his weapon at an approaching soldier. He couldn't tell if the soldier was about to attack or if he was going past him. There was no time to consider it, so he fired. His musket kicked hard back against his shoulder, nearly knocking him down. He lost focus on the soldier, then found him crumpled on the ground. Bakker couldn't tell if he had died. The body twitched, and Bakker jerked away.

He found himself facing Maximillian, who shot him a disapproving look. With an edge of frustration, Maximillian closed the distance between him and a soldier. The soldier appeared to reach for the stock of a musket buried bayonet first into the ground just out of reach. He never made it. Maximillian slid his bayonet into the man, letting his momentum do the rest. With a squeal of a stuck pig, the bayonet plunged into his chest, the triangular blade widening the wound with ease. The man died wide-eyed with blood trailing down them like tears. His mouth lay twisted open as if asking Bakker, *"What did you do?"*

Even through the fog, Bakker saw every drop of blood pouring from his mouth, every teardrop rolling down the man's face. It seared in his head. This is what they were paid to do. He had killed before—no, he had fired his musket before along with the rest of his unit—it was impersonal that way. These two men were dead at their hands. No question about it.

One soldier escaped, but the last two dropped to their knees, hands in the air. Maximillian stood above them and kept his musket aimed at them. Blood trickled down the bayonet. They all remained still.

"I just shot him. You—you just... what did we just do, what do we do now?" Bakker asked.

Maximillian appeared cool and relaxed. "We survive, and I suppose we return to the boats."

"With them?" Bakker gestured at the two soldiers. *How does Maximillian not care?*

"I believe that was the plan all along. So... yes."

Bakker wanted to move, to carry on with his duty. Instead, he found himself frozen once again. Maximillian was already moving. Bakker didn't understand how he shut it out. Those soldiers were dead. He had killed somebody.

"Come on," Maximillian called out, startling him. "Be glad it wasn't you."

The sky brightened as they made their way through the camp with the two captives. A cold pallor of smoke and fog still blanketed the area. Bakker and Maximillian led their prisoners through similar scenes of carnage. Soldiers from both sides lay in twisted ways. Bakker could not tell the dead from the living. They all spoke to him.

His breath shortened. His head felt uneasy and light. He was cold all over. Like death. Then something incredible happened. Laughing came through the fog. It began as a mild echo. He did not recognize it for what it was at first. His heart beat faster. He began to sweat, even in the still grey cold. It grew louder, as if the corpses laughed at him, and the sounds of whooping and mirth burst through the fog. It did not belong. How could it? *What was going on?* His heart stopped. Maximillian halted, the prisoners did, too, and Bakker found himself once again frozen in fear.

A light breeze pushed a bit of fog away. Bakker could see better now. His breathing resumed, and his head felt normal again. Before him stood other men in his squad, some sprayed with blood. They held at least three prisoners among them, dirty, bruised, still half-asleep. But the men around the prisoners were as happy as they could be.

He saw a man he recognized go into one tent and come out with a blanket and his hand around... something. Another man patted down one of the corpses and came away with a shoe. What surprised him the most, however, was the opened hogshead of rum in the center of the men. The dreamlike nature of the scene crept back over him. The rest of his unit was drinking and looting. They were merry. It felt so strange.

Musketfire erupted not too far off. It shattered the illusion, replacing it with cruel reality. "Sergeant, let's be rid of this place?" Bakker almost said please.

"All right, just as soon as we've had a moment to collect payment." Maximillian looked his men over. "Is the area clear?" He meant, of course, if they had finished looting.

"Just about."

One of the men turned to him. "Prisoners?"

"Ordered to take them with us," Maximillian said. "So we will."

Another man spoke. "What about this barrel of rum we liberated?"

"If you can carry it, spoils of war."

The statement met with nods of agreement.

"It is time to be going. Sticking around here any longer means more work."

Ja, the men agreed again, and a nearby shot of musketfire emphasized the point. The sulfur. It burned the inside of his nose.

They finished gathering their prizes and combined their prisoners. Then they trudged toward the river. Soldiers came from behind, their boots crunching in the snow. Every unit was out for themselves, and they were running out of time. Bakker hung his head low.

There was no place for him here.

Colonel Washington's aides and messengers had grown frustrated—they never found him in the same place twice. His translator could barely keep up and abreast, but Washington didn't spare him a thought. After unleashing bedlam, he'd regained his composure and was now on a mission of redemption and to pull some cohesiveness out of this mess. His face burned.

Nearby, he'd witnessed a company commander shoot an unarmed rebel. Then he'd run off, abandoning his men. Washington would get to him in due time and promised to hold back his anger—there would be time for proper punishment later. But at this moment, there was a battle to win. He sent off a company of dragoons to coordinate with the far column. When he finished, he turned back around to chase after the errant commander, catching up to the fleeing officer a short moment later. The common soldier was unkempt and untrained, but they could follow orders. *The officers are a useless lot.*

Washington brought his sword down on the unsuspecting subordinate hard enough to sting, but with enough restraint not to do lasting damage. "No!" he yelled, his temper bursting through. He swallowed hard and held it back.

Stunned, the officer spun his horse around and eyed his attacker. Washington returned the look with a glare that silenced the man before he could protest. "You will not abandon your men; you will not harm any prisoner. You will ride back, compose your boys, and make an orderly return for the boats." Washington felt the translation lost some of his intensity, but the Hessian nodded. "Get to your unit." The Hessian galloped off on his horse, back toward the outpost.

He never should have ordered the attack, but it was too late now. Washington supposed that was why he had been lenient on his officers. It was his tactical error, not theirs. He just hoped they could salvage some sort of victory from it. Washington sat in contemplation over his course of action for a moment. It was the longest he had remained still since the attack began.

The sound of concentrated musketfire filled the air. Washington's stomach tightened. The rebels were already regrouping. He spurred his horse toward the place where his aides expected him to be, near the cannon. Along the way, he redoubled his efforts at regaining control and pulling his men back. Like many battles throughout history, this one would be decided by speed in organization. Washington frowned. They had to regroup and return to the boats.

When he reached the command center, Washington was immediately bombarded with questions. He ignored them all. "Begin the withdrawal," he said. Washington looked around and saw relief flooding his aide's faces.

But one voice instead asked, "What do we do with the cannon, Your Excellency?" Washington jerked in surprise. He had forgotten all about them. They could no longer be used to persuade the camp commander to surrender. Washington could not use them either to fire on the camp, as a cannon did not distinguish from friend or foe. To capture it under these conditions would slow their withdrawal, but he didn't want to leave them for the rebels. He frowned. "Destroy them all."

"Even the light brass ones?" the voice asked again.

"Yes."

A few miners and sappers, the miracle builders, as Washington referred to them, started on the wooden carriages with axes. They placed bits of bayonet into the firing holes of the heavy iron cannon and then broke off the tips. Washington admired their work, as always.

Washington nearly smiled at their efficiency, but the fog dissipated, and time had run out. He could now see the camp before him, though it remained dense enough that he could not see the far side of it where his second column should be. He took a long look around. Washington frowned instead.

What he did see lay in ruins. Corpses littered the ground. Tents were flattened. Cartridge papers blew in the wind. This should have been a quiet morning. But, there was no trace of fresh, new-fallen snow anywhere to be found. No light gleamed from a morning's blanket of hilly, undisturbed snow. No laughter from children as they played with sleds or snowmen. It was times like these that Washington missed home and Martha's children playing in the snow at Mount Vernon. Fresh snow was supposed to be serene. However, the scene before Washington was surreal.

As the main bulk of his column made its way back toward the river, Washington stayed behind to await the second column. Washington wrung his hands in frustration. He should not have split his force in two. He chastised himself, for this mistake and all the others he had made. Perhaps the British were right. Maybe he was not a leader; he was just somehow lucky.

By the sounds of it, the second column was in trouble. Mustketfire shattered the air with increasing frequency. Washington tried to look out through his spyglass, but it could not pierce the fog. His men on the far side of the camp were in danger of being cut off. He took a deep breath. He could do nothing for them, except hold out hope that they could make it through. He directed some of the remaining units to fire into the rear of the rebels, but he knew they could not stay any longer. They were vastly outnumbered.

Washington tried to help, but all his firing did was bring attention to his position. Several rebel units broke off and turned to face him. He ignored them. Instead, he kept his attention on the area where his second column was to emerge from—if they were able to outflank the rebels. His field of vision filled with soldiers as musketfire splintered tree bark and scattered bursts of snow off the ground. His eyes watered from the smoke of black powder, and his ears begged for mercy.

Out of the corner of his eye, Washington spotted a lone soldier nearby. Hope soared that it was the first of his men. His heart sank. Instead of seeing blue and red, he saw the familiar trappings of leather and wool. He'd worn that a long time ago. The rebel raised a musket toward Washington. The musket seemed to be aimed right at his heart.

He tried to tell himself that the musket was horribly inaccurate and he forced himself to remain still. Washington's heart skipped, but he remained composed. What would happen, would happen. There was no changing history.

A rustle came from nearby the rebel. If it were more rebel soldiers, Washington and his men were lost.

Upon the first bit of blue that Washington spied, he immediately called out, "Hold fire." The last remaining men around Washington lowered their weapons. The second column had made it through. The lone rebel eyed Washington one last time but did not fire. Instead, he slipped away into the woods. Only then did Washington breathe a sigh of relief.

The second column of Hessians made their way to Washington's position. He relaxed a little and took in another breath of cold air. The weary Hessians made their way through the ranks along with a surprising number of captives. Washington's mood lightened for the first time since yesterday, but he would concern himself with the details of that later. It was time to get out of here.

The foul weather that had earlier helped mask their arrival now faded. The fog rolled along with their exit toward the river. They clung to it, no longer worrying about noise, no longer taking their time in stealth. They ran, keeping to fog and away from the rebels, slipping away toward the river bank.

Colonel Von Donop burst through the fog. Washington smiled for the second time that morning. It was becoming habitual. He was even more relieved to see that Colonel Donop and some of his regiment had done much of what they had been commanded. He sighed with relief as he eyed the reinforcements. The relatively fresh troops, along with Donops' artillery and a few hastily dug trenches with a line of *abatis*, could hold off the rebels long enough so they could make the crossing.

"Your Excellency," Donop said, his face beaming. Donop had regained his usual boisterous mood. "I am so glad you returned."

"Me, too." For the first time in two days, fatigue caught up to him, but there was little time for rest. "I brought company."

"Do not worry about it. I will welcome them. You cross the river." Donop turned away and prepared his artillery men. Washington stuck close. All they had to do now was to make the crossing before the rest of the Continental outpost showed up to stop them. Washington refused boat after boat as they came and went. He stayed in place as both columns of his Hessian regiment made it safely across. Then, he lingered as Donop's regiment made the crossing. Those that stayed behind covered their exit with a steady stream of musktfire joined by cannon and mortar.

The fog had vanished. The sun was out, and the rushing river waters reclaimed their dominion over the ice. The rebels offered heavier fire now, and it was unclear to Washington why they didn't reach out with one hand and overtake them. He was the last man into the last Durham boat, and now there was no one to offer cover fire except for the opening of a fraction of artillery from across the river.

As the flat-bottomed boat shoved off, a company of rebel militia rushed the icy bank. Washington saw the first man slip. A hand reached out and caught the faltering soldier by his waistcoat. It wasn't much, but it slowed the rebels enough so Washington and the men in the boat with him put some distance between themselves and the rebels.

Once the unit regained its composure, they raised their muskets and fired. Musket balls poured into them, peppering the Hessians and splintering the wooden boards of the craft. One Hessian took a round to the gut. Washington frowned. The boy didn't know it yet, but the wound was mortal.

Washington ignored the wounded soldier and grabbed a fallen paddle. They hadn't much time before the next volley. It came sooner than he expected, and the boat's navigator fell into the icy river. Washington couldn't tell if he had just slipped or had been hit. In either case, the river meant death. Washington took his oar and plunged it onto the water next to the navigator as the militia company on the bank reloaded. The navigator grabbed on to the oar. With all his strength, his arms and his back burning, Washington heaved the soaked man back into the boat.

He'd saved the man at the cost of losing control of the craft. It raced down the river, hitting ice and rock and spinning wildly. The craft splintered, holes from musket fire filled with water. The craft threatened to sink or capsize and throw all of them out. In either case, the river would finish what the rebels on the bank had started.

He rammed his oar into a nearby chunk of ice to regain control of his craft. Others on the boat went to assist him, shoving oars and poles into water, or wadding skins into the breaking craft to slow the leaks. The boat began to recover, but it was too late. Even if they salvaged it, the militia on the bank was ready to fire. They found themselves at a near standstill on the frozen river, the very epitome of sitting ducks.

Artillery sounded from Washington's side of the Delaware. Case shot tore into the rebels on the far bank. It gave no mercy to weak flesh and bone. Washington had to turn away as the shots hit. He could tell from their screams what the case shot had done. It stopped their attack cold.

Washington and the remaining men limped to the other shore. Relief filled their faces. They carried the wounded Hessian from the boat to the shore and up the bank. Their faces displayed exhaustion, but they marched on with what strength remained, following Washington toward the secondary camp downriver.

When they arrived at the camp, Colonel Donop once again rode to meet Washington. In the background, Washington could hear men shouting, sounding surprisingly festive.

"Colonel," said Donop. He gave Washington a hard slap on the shoulder. Washington cocked his head. It wasn't a greeting he was familiar with. "There is something I am excited to show you. You have done great work. You should see."

Curious.

All he wanted was to write his reports while the attack was still fresh in his mind and then get some rest. Instead, Donop led him toward a rabble of war weary Hessians. They encircled a hastily constructed wooden fence, taunting whatever was caged within.

Inside gathered a large number of Continental provincials—rebel soldiers. Washington's jaw dropped. He guessed several hundred men were in there. He didn't think they had been that successful. It wasn't the entire camp he had envisioned capturing, but it was a long way from the complete failure they had escaped.

"This is remarkable," Washington said. "Is this what you wanted to show me?"

"Nein, nein, this is just a taste!"

General Donop led Washington further into the camp. The celebration of the Hessians died down upon his approach. Hogsheads of rum and other golden liquids spilled into mugs and canteens, sloshing around and spilling on each other in toasts. Their pleasure stemmed from something in the center of the crowd.

He pushed his way through, then he saw. On the ground just a few feet away lay a corpse. It looked recent, as if the man had died a short while ago. Washington might have thought he were sleeping if not for a bloody mess oozing from the man's abdomen and the stink of feces as death let loose the bowels.

Washington would have turned away and let the men continue their celebration if he had not recognized the rebel at the last second. He didn't know how the man came to be here or how he had died, but Washington recoiled in horror. His face turned white, his fingers numb, and his heart felt like it stopped. What had meant to be a Christmas raid and capture of a rebel camp had turned into a massacre. And there, as evidence for it, was the last person Washington ever expected to see: John Hancock, Commander of the Boston Militia and overall General of the Continental Army.

The rebel commander was dead.

PART TWO

"These are the times that try men's souls: The summer soldier and the sunshine patriot will, in this crisis, shrink from the service of their country; but he that stands it now, deserves the love and thanks of man and woman." --Thomas Paine, *The American Crisis*

SEVEN

Near Annapolis, Maryland
April 19th, 1777.

THE sunny day made the tree-covered walk enjoyable even in the chilly April air. The deciduous trees budded along the winding path, and blue jays fluttered off branches as they called to each other in their mating dances. Martin Stevens decided to take a scenic route, avoiding fresh mud, and keeping to animal paths. As such, it took him quite a bit longer to reach his normal Sunday destination after the church service let out. But, soon enough, he arrived at the familiar, timber house.

The home sat on a small plot of land, its customary crop of tobacco still fallow from the winter. Nearby lay what remained of a patchwork of cold-season garden vegetables. Tools of various sorts leaned against the grey wood planks of the house. Roughhewn rope tangled and weaved over posts and fences to make a place for laundry to dry or tobacco to cure, although it was empty now. In fact, the whole place looked worn and empty—a cobweb left alone in a shuttered room.

The house once belonged to a veteran of the French and Indian War who had presumably rented it out and moved elsewhere. The farm hadn't seen much use of late and didn't look like it would come mid-spring, either. The new inhabitants were not farmers, but then again, he had already known that. Stevens had acted as best man at the wedding this past harvest to the couple now renting the place.

He approached the front door and knocked on the frame instead of the door. They had left the door slightly ajar. Knocking on it would have swung it wide open into the one-room home. The couple were still newlyweds, particularly in the cold winter months. He respected their privacy. Stevens wanted no part in walking in on anything like that.

A moment later, after some ruffling of sorts, a tall, thin man with bony fingers and dark hair answered. The door opened partway, revealing a darkened interior, a small bed and a slender auburn-haired woman who sat upright, with a sly smile, smoothing her dress. The tall man messed around with his breeches and said, with a noticeable moment of hesitation, "Ah, good Martin, you're late."

They had at least found something to do while they waited, he concluded, but nodded uncomfortably and returned a greeting. This was past his normal stretch of arriving, so they could be excused. *To be in love*, he mused, trying to force a grin back onto his face. The young woman stood. She wore a simple, flax dress, homemade, of course, but looked lovely in it. Her hair fell past her shoulders and to her waist, framing a rosy face and indulgent brown eyes.

As she approached, he greeted her. "It's good to see you again, Emma... Er, Missus Collins."

"Always a pleasure." Her words floated into the air.

Stevens watched her as she took his threadbare overcoat from him but diverted his gaze when she looked directly at him. "Thank you kindly," he said, turning his focus to Mr. Collins, or Henry as he knew him, to see if his awkwardness had been noticed.

If it had, Henry Collins gave no indication. Instead, he shut the door, made his greeting, and then stoked the fire, adding another log to it.

With the door closed, nothing but the fire illuminated the room. It took a moment for Stevens' eyes to adjust. While the home had frames for windows, it did not have glass. Animal skins covered them to keep the heat of the fire in, but it also kept the light from the sunny afternoon out. The tiny house, however, boasted wooden flooring which creaked with each step, and a hearth for the fireplace with bricks hastily piled atop each other. Stevens had been curious about how they afforded such luxuries but had never asked.

The couple offered Stevens his normal spot on the bench at the small, uneven table in the center of the room. He sat while an oil lamp was lit and placed at its center. The light spread poorly over the wooden table, but it was enough to reveal several items, one of which was a small pamphlet. Stevens didn't read well, so he couldn't make out the title, but knowing his friend, he was sure it had something to do with the war. On the other side of the table rested the things he had come over for: a small wooden board with tall, faded triangles; lead dice; small, round leather draughts; and a leather cup.

As Collins sat down at the other side of the table, three frothy containers of dark ale met them. Emma handed one to each, including herself, and smiled. "I've got work to do, so if you want more, you're on your own."

"Why don't you join us?" Emma's husband asked. He always did.

"I have work to do. Quite a bit more work, in fact, if you ask me, since the last list of British boycotts came out. You'd think we buy air from 'em. Besides, you know your dice games aren't my cup of tea... or coffee now, isn't it?" With that, she went to a chair by the fire, picking up a needle and thread as she sat. She occupied a corner behind her husband but in view of Stevens. There was a reason he sat where he did. As Collins set the board, Stevens thought about taking in the view, but he seldom did, and he chastised himself each time. He took a glance—

"What did you think of this morning's service?" Collins asked.

Stevens turned away and looked at the board. The hair on his arms stood on end. He stole a breath, buying time to respond. He didn't understand why he did this to himself. Collins was his friend. But a long time ago, Emma had been, too. Between that and Collins' refusal to talk about anything else other than the war, pretty soon he would have to stop coming here altogether.

He frowned on the inside and picked up a lead six-sided die and stared at it. The die had been formed by flattening the sides of a musket ball with the pips hammered- in. As far as he was concerned, it was a better use of a musket ball than what Collins had in mind. It weighed heavy in his hand. He rolled it without the cup and got a three. "The pastor seemed fairly passionate about something."

"Something?" Collins rolled a four. He would go first. "Now that's an understatement if I've heard one." His face contorted into mock shock. "That 'something' is the fate of our country." As he talked, he moved his draughts the requisite number of spaces.

Emma interrupted, scolding her husband. "You aren't already into politics, are you? Remember, our guest isn't as involved in it as you."

Quite right. He should've seen it coming. Even growing up, Collins was always into the parish politics while Stevens went out hunting with his father, trapping and sailing the Chesapeake or inland rivers. Sundays were the days when all three of their childhood lives crossed paths. From there, their friendship grew. But no friendships were without their difficult moments.

It was Steven's turn, and he rolled both dice with the cup. Four and a four, doublets. He continued his move.

"But he should be," Collins said to his wife, continuing the conversation. Then he turned back. "You know, I normally rib you about your disinterest in what goes on, but this is serious."

"It doesn't much matter to me who my taxes go to. King there, or king here. Haven't much thought about it." Stevens took a swig of ale, and drops of it spilled out and clung to the hairs of his close-shaved stubble. His heart just wasn't in to discussing this today. He'd need more to drink.

"Careful who hears you talk like that. Used to be in my father's time, talk of liberty would get you a painful ride on the wooden donkey. Now, praising the king will get you tarred and feathered."

"I'm all for it. People sound ridiculous when they talk politics. Should look ridiculous, too." Stevens received blank stares from the others. He ignored them and continued, "I'm not promoting one side or another. It's why I don't care much for taverns, pubs, and church. It's too political. I'd much rather be in the company of a good friend, passing the time drinking beer."

He also didn't used to have to watch what he said here, and he liked that. Other than his Sunday afternoons here with Emma and Collins, he didn't socialize much. Church was the other exception, for he found skipping too many sermons also sent people his way. They wanted to save his soul. He wanted them to leave him alone.

"Did you hear *anything* the minister said?"

"Something about having a crisis of common sense. I couldn't agree with that more. Lost me after that."

"No, no, not Paine's *Common Sense*," Collins said, picking up the pamphlet from the other end of the table across from the backgammon board. "This is *The American Crisis*. It's by the same author, so I understand your confusion. This is what the minister read aloud at church today. I was dying to reread it, so he let me borrow the copy, but I have to return it to him for tonight's service. You going?"

"One sermon a week is enough for me," Stevens confirmed. "Is that what ministers read now instead of the Bible?"

"My friend, we're in a whole new age. We don't just look for answers in the Bible. Instead, we ask questions we don't know the answers to."

"How very unsatisfying."

"But we *will* know. That's the point. There's a whole continent out there awaiting discovery. There's so much to know. It's an exciting time to be alive, but we must be at liberty to do these things on our own and not yoked to the Old World," Collins continued, the backgammon game forgotten now. "Church is so much more than lectures about eternal damnation and brimstone. You should come with us tonight. The minister's going to talk about the Christmas Day Massacre and what we, as patriots, should do about it. We're lucky we didn't lose the whole war that night. But if we don't build our forces back up, we will."

"You already sound like him. Maybe you should give the sermon." Stevens tried to change the subject and lifted his empty mug. "Emma, could I trouble you for another go?"

She shot him a disapproving look and held up the bit of cloth in her hands. "Try finishing this shirt for me, and I'll fetch the cask for you. Otherwise, you're on your own."

He was glad that she didn't get the refill. She seemed so soft. Perhaps it was the fire, but she appeared to glow even more so today. "What is it you're working on?"

"It's a uniform shirt for the soldiers."

"Well, I knew that. But the shirt looks finished."

"Oh, that. Yes. I'm embroidering it with my name, actually. All the women are. It's a touch we added, me and the ladies at the minister's house. We thought it might make it a bit more personal. What do you think?"

Generally, sentiment didn't mix well with war, though all he said was, "I think you're doing a lovely job." Stevens thought the matter was finished and the topic of discussion was over. He was wrong.

"Actually, I'm curious. This is your area of familiarity." Collins ignored his wife to steer the conversation back on topic. "How *exactly* did that redcoat, Washington, get those men over the Delaware?"

Stevens could get by all right by himself. He could feed and clothe himself off the land. But sometimes, one needed to escape. Such a time came two years ago when his friend started courting Emma. Sticking around would've caused him needless heartbreak. So, he retreated inward to the Potomac, working as a ferryman and living off the river. He had some experience with the question, but that didn't mean he wanted to answer it.

Before he left, Stevens encouraged his friend to end the relationship. Emma's father was a proud man with means. Neither he nor Collins met the criteria to be Emma's future husband, but the conversation ended badly, and Stevens left. He was quite surprised, then, to find the two engaged upon his return. *Lucky.* How his friend had done it remained a mystery. Like a card player, Collins held his cards close to his chest.

Collins and Emma had been married for months already, so it had nothing to do with an illegitimate child. As he glanced around the cheap house full of expensive luxuries, he knew it had something to do with money. It was a sad truth that Collins was not suited well for this world. *What trouble have you gotten yourself into?*

"Your thoughts?"

Stevens placed his hands flat on the table and took a breath. "I'm reminded of how Jesus walked on water."

"Yes?" Collins looked intrigued. His brow rose and he leaned in. Even Emma stopped working to listen.

"It's not difficult to walk across a river if one knows where the stones are."

Emma gave him a wink and smiled. Collins, on the other hand, scowled. "It's not a laughing matter." Collins' face went red, and he forced himself to keep his seat. "General John Hancock died that day, as did many patriots. Even more were captured and are now rotting in British prison boats. You've heard what goes on in those, haven't you? Our entire cause hangs by a thread because of one awful act. I mean, who attacks an outpost at Christmas?"

"It was an awful act, all right," said Stevens, "but war is nothing more than a continuous string of awful acts that ends only when there's no more thread. So what would you have us do?"

"We've spent time on the Maryland Old Line, Martin. We have militia training. Let's put words to action and pick up our muskets and fight. Otherwise, what Washington did to us will be the end of us. We will lose this war. Let us fight!"

Every Marylander spent two years mandatory in the militia. They left the Old Line long before the war started, and it was there where their friendship had really matured, to the point Stevens still considered Collins a mate even after Emma—a fact Collins appeared to have forgotten.

"Why? So you can march way up north? So you can protest awful acts by committing some of your own?"

"This isn't about you or me. This is about freedom. Independence. For all of us."

Stevens gaped, then recovered and kept his voice calm. "There is no such thing." Collins' mood changed from shy and meek to stubborn and proud. Stevens sighed. There had to be something else going on. He tried a different way. "That's about the stupidest thing I've heard you say, and I've known you a long time." He looked over at Emma, who had a sour look on her face. "You have a wife."

He continued looking at her. She looked like she was about to vomit.

Strange.

"It's more complicated than that," Collins stated. As if on cue, Emma stood, swallowed hard, then joined them at the table.

Why do I feel like I've just walked into a bear trap? Betrayed by his best friend. Again. Stevens sighed. He waited for the inevitable.

It was Emma who broke the silence. She clasped her hands together and smiled. "We're expecting!" Laughter danced in her eyes. "I'm so excited."

Like that, everything came together. It all made sense. Stevens sulked inwardly as he figured it out, but he forced a smile. "Well, congratulations are in order, Missus Collins."

The glow diminished for a brief moment. "I'm also a little bit nervous and scared, truthfully." Emma lowered her head. "There's so much to consider, to prepare. A child changes everything."

"Yes, it does," Collins said. "Which is why I've decided to join the—"

"We're already supporting the war, my love."

"No, that's you. You've supported the patriots since the beginning. You've done so much. Now it's my turn to give what

I can, however little it may be. We will both bring a better future for our child."

Stevens looked on in silence. He was glad that, thus far, they had ignored him.

"Please, Martin, don't let my husband go off to war. His place is here."

Never mind. "Well—"

"Don't you see?" Collins pleaded. "I'm going to have a child. That has made me realize, more than church, pamphlets, or...or...the Christmas Day Massacre, that I need to do more for him."

"Or her," Emma chimed in. "I don't mind a son, but you better prepare yourself if we have a daughter."

Collins continued, ignoring her. "I have to make this world a better one for my child to grow up in, and the only way to do it is to create a free and independent country."

"I said before," Stevens said, fighting his frustration, "there's no such thing as independence. We all rely on each other. How is an American king going to make a difference? The British have been doing all right for the past few centuries or so. How exactly does being free of them make us any better off?"

"They invaded our lands," Collins said, his face reddening.

"To reclaim what is rightfully theirs," Stevens held out open hands.

"By which right? How should one people have dominion over another?"

"I don't know. Why not ask a Negro next time you see one?" Stevens asked sharply, without thinking. He had no concern over the plight of those people, he didn't care, but it was a useful point for the argument. Anything to dissuade his friend.

Stevens stared down Collins. Collins had fire in his eyes, as if his mind were made. Collins was an idiot. A daft and useless idiot. It was no use. Stevens pointed an angry finger and said, "Look at you! You're thinner than your musket. Don't you remember how miserable you were back in the militia? You'd never make it as a proper soldier, not with a war going on. Why do you want to do this? Why—"

"I don't know!" Collins' face steamed. Stevens and Emma jerked backward. He, for one, had never seen his friend so heated.

Stevens stood, took the time to refill his ale himself, and sat back down at the table to a table trapped in silence. It took a long while for the silence to end, and it did not end how Stevens would have guessed. It was Collins who spoke, but what he said was quite unexpected. "Emma and I eloped."

Emma smiled and put a reassuring hand on her husband's shoulder.

"What?"

"I need to be honest with you here," Collins said. "We did not have permission from her father. We married anyway." He looked hollow. His soul poured out. The stubbornness vanished, replaced by desperation.

"I made a bloody mess of things," he confessed. "That year you were gone? My father made more off his tobacco crop. More money than any harvest before it. Almost thirty, forty sterling, in promissory notes. The land isn't that good for tobacco, not like down south. So, I didn't know how he did it at the time—certainly not with my help. But I set aside some of the extra funds."

Stevens wondered if he meant to say he'd stolen the notes. At least it was more honest than blackmail, which until now had been his theory. Collins continued, "The following harvest, my father made even more in promissory notes, but the crop had not increased one leaf. I didn't ask, and I didn't care. With the notes, we were able to marry, against her father's wishes. We were able to rent this place and start our life together... but, of course, our money ran out.

"I figured last harvest would bring more of the same, but it didn't. In fact, it was worse than either year and even lower than it had ever been before the war. I confronted my father, and that was when he told me he was involved in smuggling. He made extra money hiding goods smuggled in from the bay. With the ports closed in Boston and New York, it's the only way to bring goods in past the blockades. But the British aren't just blockading up north anymore. They're everywhere, including the Chesapeake. So, my father couldn't raise any extra income. There won't be any trade at all until the British are gone."

This is far worse than I thought.

Collins lowered his voice along with his head, as if in confession. "I was unwise with the money. I didn't know how fleeting it was. For this small plot of land to produce anything, it needs extra hands. The Lord knows my farming skills are almost useless. Instead of using the money to buy hands and the food, clothes, and means to house them, we got a creaky wooden floor and some bricks by the fire." Collins concluded, "Now we are without."

Stevens' first instinct was to rap Collins in his daft face, but Collins' honesty struck him. Collins had been sincere in his desire to treat Emma right, even if they had no right to marry in the first place. He couldn't begrudge him for that. Stevens would have probably done the same.

Today changed everything. He'd be going off to war soon, something he'd never considered. *What are friends for? To hang together until you hang separately*. He'd heard that one from somewhere a while back. It was still worth a chuckle.

Collins raised his voice and kept talking. "I've considered joining back up with the Maryland militia. The enlistment bonus will help keep Emma in our home, and I can send my pay to her, since they will feed and clothe us. A pound of meat a day. We will just be gone till year's end. Back before the baby arrives." He tried to put some happiness into it. "We've got to avenge what Washington did to us. We can't lose this war or England will strip all our liberties. I don't want that for my child. Besides, what else have you got to do?"

"Not get my ass shot off." Stevens smiled.

"I think his mind is already made," said Emma coolly. "We talked about this before, but not as heatedly as today. I don't think I can stop him." She looked directly at Stevens. "Tell me you will keep him safe."

He was afraid she would ask that. He did not have a response for her, and he would not lie. War was dangerous and unpredictable. So, instead he tried a new tactic. He turned to Collins. "You want to gamble? Then let's gamble. You've always been fond of dice games." He picked up the two lead dice and dropped them into the leather cup, then passed it over.

"You're willing to leave your future to the whim of dice?" Now, it was Collins' turn to sound incredulous.

"It'll be fate."

"I thought you didn't believe in fate?"

"Just having a bit of fun. We can risk it with the dice. They don't shoot back." He pointed to the leather cup that was now in Stevens' hands. "If you roll higher than me, then off we go to a place where we can die from dysentery, smallpox, or freeze to death overnight. We may even get lucky and be torn apart by a cannonball."

"I want no part in this," Emma pleaded. "Enough with that."

Stevens ignored her. This was his last attempt to get Collins to stay. Otherwise, it was off to war.

"All right, I'm game," Collins said. He took the cup, shook it, then placed it upside down on the table. Emma looked away. Stevens and Collins leaned closer. He lifted the cup. Two dice, each with one pip face-up. The lone dots stared back at him.

"Ha!" Stevens smiled and slammed his palm down on the table. Ale sloshed out of a long forgotten drink. "Luck like that could get you killed. No point in me rolling now, is there? Looks like we're staying."

"Best two out of three?" Collins asked.

"What? No!" Both Emma and Collins yelled in unison, throwing up their hands in a disapproval.

"You can't change your fate, mate."

Collins protested. "Make me honest, Emma. I mean it this time. No matter the outcome. You can hold me to it, I swear." Emma shook her head.

Collins turned his head back. "Come on, you roll first this time. After all my beer you've drank, you owe me at least one roll."

This wasn't going to work, either, Stevens realized. He picked up the dice and placed them back in the cup. Collins was determined. He might as well get this over with. "I do it to humor you, but when you lose again, you better hold true to your word. You placed it on your wife, remember? Best two out of three. I won the first. This would be the second go." With that, he rolled the heavy lead dice, looked down, and saw a three and a four. "Beat a seven."

Collins took the cup, jostled it around a few times, and then slammed the cup upside down. There was a nine when he lifted the cup.

"We are even. This last one decides it." Stevens took the cup and turned it over. The dice spilled out and stopped at an eleven. He could feel a wave of relief building up to wash over him. There was little chance to beat that. In all the years they had spent together, Collins was terrible at dice games. Maybe they would not be leaving after all. Stevens threw the dice back in.

Collins reached for the cup, but Emma took it from Stevens' hands instead, her warm skin touching his rough fingers. The moment was tender and gentle as he handed her the cup. But his smile faded as she said, "This is stupid." A tear ran down her cheek. She surprised them both by rolling the dice herself.

Out came another seven. It did not beat the eleven but it did not matter. Emma looked as if she wished to continue to cry, but wiped away the tear and stood silently. This was the known outcome all along. From the moment he had sat down in their home, he knew where this would end. The wave that should have brought relief to him moments before dashed upon the rocks instead.

They were going to war.

EIGHT

Freeman's Farm, Saratoga, New York
September 19th, 1777.

FALL had arrived on swift winds, bringing a deeper chill than usual for the end of September. The leaves on the maple trees had prematurely turned deep red, and the air felt heavier. For the third morning in a row, thick fog filled the command tent. Clumps of black moss spotted one side of it, and inside, the blankets were damp, which made it hard to sleep. The moisture ruined the paper, which made it harder to write and plan the upcoming battle, and the weather caused Major General Benedict Arnold's wounds to stiffen. He awoke in dampness from a rough night's sleep, surrounded by a mist of fog, wracked with endless pain.

In the two intervening years since his wife had passed away, Arnold had accomplished two important things. First, he had used his wife's death to avoid the paper-pushing job Congress and Schuyler had offered. Second, he started on a variety of successful military ventures of his own design that had made it impossible for Congress to ignore him—hard as they might try.

General Arnold felt so much older now. In those two years, both his body and mind had been through much. He sat up, the hurt in each of his wounds reminding him of how he had acquired each of them.

After his wife's death, he'd fallen ill from bad air on his journey home from Albany in the festering heat. Following his recovery, he'd nearly wasted away in the frozen wilderness on his way to capture the city of Quebec. It amazed him he'd convinced then-General Hancock of the plan; that he'd almost captured the city with just a handful of men was monumental. He'd just put that weight back on, plus a stone or two for good measure. Starvation was not something he'd wanted to repeat.

Arnold's left leg pained him the most, however. He had been shot during the Quebec City invasion. Despite the injury, Arnold escaped capture and saved his leg. Losing it would have meant the end of his military career. Instead of being admired as a hero, he would have been looked down on as a cripple. He could not allow that to happen. So, the surgeon did not hack off his leg. The leg still functioned, and that was good enough for him, though he paid the price in pain.

He sat at the edge of the cot and pushed damp blankets away, rubbing his face with his hands, then looking down at them. His hands. They had healed, but the ropes had left scars on them. Going back and forth between each cannon onboard the flagship *Congress*, assisted by the *Enterprise*, Arnold had almost single-handedly held off the British Navy on Lake Champlain, thereby delaying their invasion. But the ropes cut deep into his flesh, and the scalding black cannon burned him. He now made it a point to wear gloves from morning to night.

After a fit of coughing, Arnold rose, his bones cracking in protest. His leg shot out in pain and his toe flared with gout. He pushed the pain aside and started with his morning routine. In addition to the physical tribulations, Arnold suffered great personal loss. Of course, there was his wife, but there was also his business. It was failing on account of the personal money he had spent to finance the war and the lack of income from his trading business.

Also, Arnold's friend Dr. Joseph Warren, who had perished during the battle of Breed's Hill. Arnold needed every friend he had. He had been passed over for promotion, accused of theft and court-martialed—twice. Losing Dr. Warren, an influential man, was a terrible blow. Arnold would have to fight his battles without him.

Like Job, God had chosen Arnold to be tested. This was his crucible, his forge in the fire to be hammered into something remarkable—someone great. The new country of America needed him, but before he could lead them, he had to be baptized through water and fire. He understood. Each sacrifice put him closer to his calling.

However, those sacrifices would end today. His army was in Saratoga, just a day's ride north of Albany, New York. He knew this land well, but the British did not. They were under a guide, a Mr. Freeman. Somehow, Mr. Freeman had led his British overseers directly to his own farm—and right to where Arnold wanted them.

Not much of a guide. True, the terrain dictated the British advance to a certain degree, but it was ludicrous to fight Arnold here. That was all right with Arnold. He camped south of the farm, on Bemis Heights. To the immediate east ran the Hudson River, and to the west grew a thick forest. If Burgoyne hoped to break though Arnold's lines, he would have to outflank him there. And thick forests were a Colonial haven. Soon, the British forces in the north, under General Burgoyne, would fall. Arnold was ready.

Arnold finished dressing in his blue and buff Continental uniform jacket. He had just finished donning a thin pair of black riding gloves when the flap of his tent flew open.

Arnold did not flinch, as his aide, a bright young man from Connecticut, Lt. Colonel Eleazer Oswald, stepped in. Oswald, a hardy fellow, followed Arnold up the Kennebec to Quebec as a volunteer, only to be captured by the British during the assault on the city. He had served Arnold with distinction, so upon his release, Arnold pulled some strings and attached him to the Second Continental Artillery Regiment. However, Oswald often found himself wearing multiple hats—the second of which was as General Schuyler's aide.

When the new Continental commander saw Schuyler as a threat and had him cashiered, Oswald found himself once again in Arnold's service. Arnold made him his aide as well. Besides, Arnold liked him better than his own aide, a lawyer named Livingston from New York who carried a judgmental and self-righteous attitude. Arnold cracked an inward smile when Oswald came in. *Right on time, like a ship's noon-time bell.*

Oswald looked around the tent, in seeming shock at the clutter. Fortunately, the fog hid most of it. Oswald let it go. "What do you think of being in charge?" he asked. "With Schuyler gone, you're essentially running the Northern Department."

"Schuyler let me have a free hand anyway," he answered. Oswald often started Arnold's morning off with polite conversation. "I think he realized I was better off alone, especially after what I... *we*, almost accomplished at Quebec. No, it's the new commander I'm concerned about."

"General 'Granny' Gates, you mean?"

Arnold almost chuckled. "The same. No one's ever seen him except from behind a book with naught but a pair of old granny reading glasses sticking out. No one's ever seen him on the front lines, either. But, now we've all seen his true face. He toppled Schuyler and stepped right over General Lee to get himself promoted as General Hancock's replacement."

"To be fair, Lee was a guest of the British at the time," Oswald said. "He and I were paroled at about the same time. Bit of bloody bad timing that was, for both of us."

"Of course," Arnold said. Gates had put those old glasses down and struck. His congressional appointment to the post was ceremony. In truth, Gates grabbed the reins the same night they learned of Hancock's death, and he hadn't let go since. Schuyler could attest to that. *That man was a mystery. I could learn a few tricks from him, eh?* That said, Arnold didn't know if he would rather serve under Gates or Lee. All he knew of Lee was that he was quite foul-mouthed and eccentric. But he had heard rumors that Lee was a different man since being released as a prisoner of war by the British.

Gates, however, was unknown to him. Arnold had only met him once two years ago when Gates was an adjutant to Hancock. Now, Gates was in charge, and Arnold didn't like the new commander, because anyone who hid in the shadows, waiting to strike, was a snake. Arnold was an eagle.

Ah. Arnold found the answer to his question. *I would rather them serve me.* It was a matter of time. Sooner or later, Arnold realized, he and Gates would have their showdown. He licked his lips, relishing the opportunity.

General Gates' ascension occurred months ago, of course. But Gates' meddling with the Northern Department had come recently. If Gates hadn't interfered, Arnold was confident he would have already beaten the British forces. Now, he would have to wait for the days' end to finish the job.

"The preparations are all in order," Oswald said, switching topics. "The fortifications are finished, the trees are felled, and the *abatis* is in place. Majors Morgan and Dearborn are in position. We're just waiting for you to give the word to send the militia unit out. We'll draw those bloodyback bastards right to us, sir."

Arnold grumbled. Militia units were less than reliable, but his plan hinged on them. "They've been briefed, thoroughly?"

"Yes, sir. Find the British, take one shot, and run back to our position."

Arnold nodded. "And all you need from me is the go ahead?"

"Yes."

I'm too far behind the lines. Arnold sat for a moment. Sure, this was his plan, but now all he did was tell other people to put it into action. Then, hopefully, they did. "Tell them I've given the order." Arnold rubbed his eyes. "I'll be in the command tent shortly."

"Yes, sir."

"And Colonel?"

"Yes, sir?"

"Have Livingston fetch me a cup of coffee. Let's put the lawyer to honest work."

"Absolutely." Oswald broke military bearing and smiled.

Arnold stood, stretched, and felt the pain of his leg reminding him he had once been on the front lines, leading the charge. Maybe, just maybe, today's battle would shake up the monotony.

They should have been back on the Old Line in the Maryland militia—maybe the First or Fourth Regiment. But the allure of getting his hands back on a rifle, a weapon with far greater accuracy than the Brown Bess, was too great for Corporal Martin Stevens to resist. Because these weapons were so rare, harder to maintain, and much more expensive, they were reserved for the best. Without any false modesty, Stevens could say he was one of them. And Collins... Well, the hardest part had been teaching Collins how to shoot. *I've fended off a bear who was less stubborn.*

Stevens had slept well enough on the damp ground. Collins had not. Stevens shook his friend's shoulder, and a groan of protest answered him. The poor man hadn't even unrolled his blanket. Instead, he'd used it as a pillow. He shivered in the cool autumn morning. *He'll learn.*

While Collins stirred, Stevens retrieved breakfast from the earthen kitchen with the rest of his unit. He grabbed an extra hoecake for Collins—not that either one of them would even be able to eat the stale cornbread. Not from a lack of trying, but rather their stomach wouldn't let them—it twisted and turned. The thought of the upcoming fight made him anxious. Stevens managed to wash some crumbs down with a gill of rum. If Stevens' stomach twisted, he couldn't imagine how Collins felt.

When Stevens returned, he found Collins awake... mostly. He handed the hoecake over and met with the usual disproval. After they broke their fast, they broke camp. It seemed strange, such a normal routine, when they all knew what was coming.

Later, they both found themselves standing in loose order, strung along the treeline, awaiting the British. Stevens looked around. Most of the men in Morgan's five hundred riflemen were Marylanders alongside a scattering from Connecticut, from Pennsylvania, and New York. It was unusual to see men from so many places in one unit. Collins hadn't seemed to mind. He said once that they were all continentals. But to Stevens, everyone outside of Maryland, or even outside Anne Arundel, was foreign.

They all stood together behind the edge of the forest, between thin trunks of red-leaved maple trees. Red filled the air—in the leaves of the trees and in the leaves on the ground. Red was not the color he wanted in his mind right now, but it couldn't be helped. All Stevens could see in the foggy still morning was red.

Somewhere in the confusing rank and structure of their unit, stood their commander, Major Daniel Morgan, mounted on horseback. Dressed in all white, Morgan was a bear. He made his way through them, separating Stevens and Collins for a brief moment while he passed through to step out front.

"Boys," he began. The bear stopped in front of Stevens, and his voice resounded with the growl of a grizzly. "In just a few moments' time, our boys—our militia boys—will storm through our lines. They have the devil on their backs. Be restrained. Do not fire until ordered to do so. When the devil comes chasing after, we will give him his due. But not a moment before." Morgan continued down the line. Though he was farther away, his words reverberated in Stevens' chest. "We are the soldiers of the Five Hundred. We can shoot; we can stand firm. We can fire our lead into the beast's belly; we will run them off. And we will win the day for General Arnold, for country."

Stevens' heart pounded with pride, but he maintained his silent stance. Powerful men throughout history had a way of sending one to their death without making it seem so bad. He looked down each direction along the line of soldiers. Others whooped and cheered. Some raised their woolen liberty caps off their heads. Collins was among them, caught up in the euphoria. Stevens let him have his moment of bliss before the bloodshed began.

They quieted down and waited in silence for the militia to arrive. The general had moved back into position. Stevens stood still, careful to not lock his knees. He sent reminders down the line, though it wasn't his duty to do so. Collins pitched his weight back and forth, the nervousness returning.

Time crept on, but nothing happened. By now, men murmured about what could have happened to the militia unit. No one knew for certain. It was obvious by now something had gone wrong. Stevens cleared his throat, about to say something—

Footsteps. The red, wet maple leaves dampened the sound. It was faint, but soon enough, they recognized the British. Stevens raised an eyebrow.

"Bloody bloodybacks," someone whispered further down the line.

Stevens cocked his head. *Unusual expression.* He, Collins, and the rest of the Marylanders called them redcoats. He sighed inwardly. It didn't matter. Whatever they were called, they were marching toward them. The militia was not.

Collins looked around in confusion, squinting through the fog. "Are they coming?" He asked. "I don't see any of our boys. Where are they?"

"They aren't there," Stevens answered with a low voice, careful not to spread panic down the line.

Collins swallowed hard, but he kept silent and shifted from side to side once more.

All Stevens could see in the fog was the outline of red coats. More red. This was not how the general said it would be. They came closer. Stevens gripped his rifle and twisted his hands nervously around it. Drums and fifes played in the closing distance. Twigs snapped and footfalls crept closer. Voices in the distance drew nearer. Voices issued orders, but they weren't *their* officers' voices. The redcoats were preparing to attack.

Why haven't we been ordered to fire? They stood silently. Still, no word. It would have to be now, otherwise—

Major Morgan roared through the chill mist somewhere to Stevens' left. "Ready."

Relief swept across Stevens, but he turned and saw it had done nothing for Collins. His face held worry, pale and grey, like a worn tombstone.

Five hundred riflemen knelt among the trees, rifles in firing position, each one aimed at a different target for maximum effect. Stevens did likewise, picking out a man holding a hunting sword from atop a horse behind a cluster of redcoats.

From his periphery, he saw Collins' weapon teeter a bit, so he reached out to steady him. "You're going to be fine."

"Of course I am," Collins said. He still shook. "Providence will win us the day."

Stevens dropped his shoulders. "You'll have to do your part first." The Lord wasn't the one who had spent the last several months teaching his friend how to shoot straight, relatively straight, or how to survive the first few weeks as a soldier. But Stevens dismissed the thought and brought himself back into position. "Just remember what I taught you. Keep your barrel level, hold it tight at your shoulder and loose at your fingertip. See the officer's epaulettes?" Stevens gave Collins his target.

Collins looked around. "I see it."

"Good. Aim lower. Make that your target. And... relax."

What Stevens didn't say was that this would be nothing like shooting empty hogsheads back on the farm.

Stevens shut his eyes for a moment and suddenly, they were both back there. Emma was, too, in the house, frowning from behind an opened window-frame. Then she smiled for them, if only for a moment.

"Breathe. Relax. That's what you've been saying for the last few minutes. I understand."

"Sure," Stevens said. They were standing on Collins' small family farm, attempting to put the derelict acre to some use. "Aim right below the target. Your natural inclination is going to be to buck up when the musket fires," Stevens said. "You have need to expect that and not overreact, but it comes with experience."

"This isn't the first time I've used a musket. I've hunted before."

"And that was the smallest, sickest-looking deer carcass I'd ever seen."

Collins soured, but Stevens went on, "Also, things tend to move away when you try to shoot them."

With that, Collins took a shot, as if trying to prove a point. The target was a stack of old hogsheads piling around the farmhouse. Wooden staves had rotted, broken, or gone missing, the metal hoops long since rusted. With the crack of the powder, birds flapped wildly out of the trees and fled the area. Collins failed miserably. The birds had been in more danger than those menacing barrels.

Stevens shook his head. Collins studied the hogsheads, and Stevens watched his scowl deepen when he saw no damage. "Well... reload and try again."

Collins' raised his eyebrows as his eyes sunk—a mixture of surprise and failure crept on his face. He wasn't improving. What should've taken seconds to reload the musket—an older, worn one passed down by his father—took minutes instead.

Stevens leaned in and watched Collins until he couldn't stand it any longer. "Here, here. If you're serious about joining the regulars instead of the militia, you better learn to shoot and reload. How on Earth did you make it through the Old Line?"

"I had you," Collins said, "and we spent most of our time standing around, remember? There wasn't enough money for shooting."

"I remember. They probably regret that now. Hand me the musket and watch closely." Stevens took the weapon, checked to make sure it was properly loaded, then shook his head and sighed heavily—he removed the ramrod from the barrel. Collins shrugged off the mistake.

Stevens aimed and fired. A chunk of wood flew off where the center of a painted red circle had been. It had been more luck than precision, as the old musket didn't shoot straight, but he'd keep that to himself. Collins bristled.

Then, Stevens reloaded the musket in practiced fashion, clearing the barrel, jamming the cartridge in with the flipside of the ramrod, tearing open a pack of powder with his teeth and filing the pan, throwing the paper behind his shoulder, and spitting the corner out of his mouth.

The whole process took just a few seconds, and he was ready to fire again. Stevens squeezed the trigger, and the flint sparked the powder on the pan, discharging the cartridge and firing the musket. This ball hit a barrel at the farthest edge of the field just right and low of the red target.

"That is how you do it," he said, puffing out his chest just a little bit. Most people couldn't shoot as well as he could. Then again, most Colonials had no reason to fire rusted muskets or old blunderbusses that hadn't seen use for twenty years. That was the difference. "Let's keep practicing."

The display must've motivated Collins because his next few shots actually splintered wood and the reloading went quicker. *Progress.*

Stevens had heard rumors of a special unit of riflemen forming to go north. It sounded like a much better idea than simply strolling into a pub and joining with the militia. He just had to get Collins shooting well enough to blend in. Besides, if they ever *did* see battle, all Collins had to do was fire at the big cluster of redcoats in front of them. *This might work.*

He couldn't have been more wrong.

That imaginary cluster of redcoats in front of them was now a reality. Stevens could make out individual bayonets even through the fog. He hadn't realized the redcoats relied so much on those metal teeth. Truth be told, they terrified Stevens. It seemed such a gruesome way to fight and die. So much more personal.

The British officers yelled, "Ready bayonets!" All color drained from his flesh, his head became light, and pinpricks of terror trickled down his face. He felt as hollow as the fog. Collins remained just as grey and still.

Why hadn't they been told to fire? They had distance on their side, and it was the only thing keeping those bayonets away from him. Several long moments passed in slow, dreadful, silence.

The British officer called out, "Charge bayonets!"

Bloody hell, this is really happening. This wasn't some damned dice game. Stevens held his breath. Everything had gone wrong.

Finally, Major Morgan dashed by behind them. "Fire!"

Stevens' instinct to fight kicked in. Collins, on the other hand, seemed poised to run. Stevens reached to steady him. He looked down the line. None of the other men broke and fled. They were in this together. Instead, they both raised their muskets, aimed at the officer... and fired.

The Pennsylvania longrifle cracked as the black powder exploded. All five hundred of Morgan's men fired at the oncoming British. The sound hit them all at once. Stevens' ears rung, and it took a long moment to recover his senses. When he regained them, the British officer was no longer there.

"By God's wounds, I got him!" Collins' outward jubilee belied the terror that crept back onto his face. He repeated himself, this time with a voice full of raw shock. "I got him... He's... dead."

The British charge stopped. Stevens surveyed the scene: every redcoat with an officer's sword or sash lay dead just before the tree line.

The redcoats studied the carnage, forlorn and silent. Then, they looked up. Rage-filled eyes pierced the fog. Somewhere, in the distance, voices shouted. The redcoats resumed their advance.

Stevens realized he and Collins hadn't taken the time to reload, and the longrifle took longer to reload than a Brown Bess. Then he realized that only a moment had passed—there hadn't been time anyway. He grabbed his friend. There was no response. He shook him lightly. "Uh, Henry, time to move. Those redcoats aren't slowing down."

"Brilliant idea." Collins turned around, his cartridge pack flung wide and then slapped against his uniform spurring him forward. All the other men of Morgan's five hundred did the same. They all turned and ran against the oncoming British bayonets.

Major Morgan bellowed behind them. "Stay in formation, don't run, we've hurt them, boys."

Rubbish. Amidst all the whoops and hollers of the oncoming British with their bayonets, Stevens didn't think they'd hurt them at all. They didn't get very far before redcoats reached them. Hand-to-hand fighting broke out piecemeal in the trees. A few redcoats fired their weapons in loose order. To his right, two men from Virginia fell, one shot, the other run through by a bayonet. Stevens' eyes went wide in horror. He couldn't imagine what Collins was feeling. He didn't want to.

The leaves were slippery, and the fog didn't help. They both slipped and slid across the wet ground in their desperation for distance. They would have to turn and fight. Until now, Stevens didn't think it could get any worse. *This is worse.*

A redcoat closed on them, and Collins fell. He rolled onto his back, but the redcoat was already over him.

Collins was weak and untrained in hand-to-hand fighting. The redcoat, on the other hand, was lean beef packed into a coat. His bayonet raised, ready to pierce straight through Collins' heart.

Stevens swung his longrifle out, and the extra length of the weapon gave him just enough reach to hit the redcoat on the shoulder. It wasn't much, but it knocked the soldier back. Collins kicked the man in the groin. At this, the soldier howled in pain and doubled over. Collins clambered away, and Stevens pulled him back on his feet.

Luckily, the redcoat did not give chase. Instead he raised his musket, giving them both a chance to put a few feet of distance between them and the redcoat. Stevens ducked behind a tree. He hoped Collins had enough sense to do the same thing. The redcoat fired and Stevens exploded in fear for his friend's life.

If Collins died, Stevens could never tell Emma. *I could never look her in her eye again.* And what would happen to him? Would he disappear into the woods one day like his father had done, shortly after his mother died? That happened right before he and Collins had joined the militia a long time ago. Collins was his anchor to this world, his only real contact to civilization.

He never begrudged Collins for marrying Emma. He never held it against him. Stevens had never been honest, never told anyone how he had felt about her. And Collins was too much in love himself to notice. That was his fault—he was too passionate.

Stevens reloaded, though it took longer on the unfamiliar weapon and in such an environment. It had been a while since he'd used one. Now that he'd used one again, Stevens found he preferred the simplicity of his worn musket instead. He finished and raised it at the redcoat, firing the widowmaker and finishing off his work from earlier.

Collins emerged unscathed from behind a tree. On the side, a ball had gouged out a large chunk of bark. They both looked at the hole.

"He missed."

Stevens suppressed a smile. "Luckily, you're thinner than the tree." He looked around and saw more redcoats poking out through the foliage. Their bayonets caught rays of the sun. He took a single, hard breath. "Let's get to the fallback position."

They had to fight in close-quarters twice more before reaching the relative safety of the hasty fortifications. A large ring of *abatis* had been placed around the main breastworks. Major Morgan positioned his men in front of it at the edge of the forest surrounding the farm. Now, they scrambled to reach the cover of the trees and behind the fortifications. Sharpened branches of the *abatis*, or felled trees, jabbed and poked them as they made their way around them to the entrance. Stevens was suddenly thankful for the tireless work of the miners and sappers who had seemingly put this up overnight. If Stevens didn't know any better, he would call it a miracle.

The men arrived in poor condition: low on ammunition, their longrifles already beginning to clog. They were not joined by a great deal of their brothers-in-arms, either. *Where is everybody?*

A moment later, Major Morgan rode up from the front to the fortified position. Maybe that was why Stevens liked Major Morgan and General Arnold so much—they often fought right there with them. But, this was not the general he knew. It was difficult to tell through the fog, but he looked disoriented, as if coming out of a deep hibernation. He looked around and asked in a low voice, "Where are my men?"

"Come on," Stevens urged. They made their way carefully over to the general, keeping obstacles between them and the redcoats. "We are here, sir."

The general looked down at them. Moments later, Stevens heard other men from the five hundred sound-off just loud enough to be heard in between bursts of musketfire. Morgan's hard jaw softened, visibly relieved.

"Well then, what are we waiting for?" Morgan's horse took off at a canter, his voice raising as he went down the line. "Let's show those bloodybacks how well we shoot."

"More?" Collins asked, turning his head toward Stevens. "I thought we were done."

"I'm not sure it works that way." Stevens set about cleaning his longrifle and reloading it. He encouraged Collins to do the same. "We're going to have to fight our way out of this, or Emma's going to get a letter. You don't want that now, do you?"

"Bloody hell." Collins shrugged but set to work. They finished reloading, and Stevens was surprised to find that Collins finished first. *Brilliant. He might live yet.* Then, they both stood and aimed their muskets through the sharpened abatis. Stevens spotted a trio of quietly approaching redcoats and pointed them out to Collins. They both fired.

His target crumpled. Another redcoat let out a scream, grabbing his right arm as blood and bone ripped through skin.

The last redcoat, seeing no opportunity for heroism, took his wounded mate and dragged him away. This is how they should've been fighting all along. Putting a barrier between a decent marksman and a bunch of redcoats was a good idea. Putting a fence in between many good marksmen and the redcoat army would win a battle.

Of course, it wasn't as if the British lacked good men. Someone kept the pressure on them. After all, the British lost most of their officers just a short while ago. They should've been disorganized and confused, but the redcoats still came on strong.

Major Morgan rode out from the fortifications and commanded them all forward. "We got 'em, boys! Let's push them out of the forest." Morgan sped toward the enemy and took two redcoats down with his hunting sword, swinging it down on the collarbone of each redcoat, breaking bone and dislocating shoulders as he rode onward.

Stevens looked up in disbelief, not entirely sure that they had got anything, let alone the redcoats. But the general seemed convinced, and he'd just put on a smashing show. *Once more unto the breach we go, then.* Collins crept alongside him, hesitant to leave the protection of the fortifications. Stevens didn't blame him one bit.

They made their way around the abatis, over fallen branches and wet leaves, crunching and splashing as they advanced. The redcoats proved difficult to dislodge, and progress slowed. As they moved, harassing fire coming from within the tangle of trees stopped them. The British fought piecemeal in the forest. *Since when did the British fight like us?*

Perhaps they had changed their tactics since the days of the French and Indian War. In camp, he had heard rumors. One rumor about the British general, John Fraser, said he was as clever as General Arnold. Maybe smarter. Maybe that was who they were up against. Stevens' spine shivered.

Or maybe the Hessian general. *Baron von something-Hessian.* Stevens didn't remember. He had heard in camp that the baroness was with him, nursing soldiers at a home not too far away. Stevens heard there were worse ways to end the battle than to be wounded and land in her care.

As if on cue, their progress stopped. Too much fire came in at them from behind the trees. Once again, they found themselves outmatched. They had to turn back. Again, their retreat mirrored their hasty flight from earlier. The difference was there were far fewer men from the five hundred than what started out with them this morning.

NINE

Freeman's Farm
September, 19th, 1777.

GENERAL Arnold considered the last year of advances and withdrawals with the British as mere stepping stones to this. If he succeeded here, perhaps he could challenge Gates in a bid for control of the entire army. Hannah would be proud.

But the British were not cooperating.

Though he was surrounded by busy men walking through the tent, looking dutiful and active, Arnold felt alone. His men were going through the motions, awaiting his word. Not one of them thought things through, and all of them were too eager to please.

The wind picked up now, blowing away the fog, but likewise whisking away maps and notes, and dislodging tents and camp equipment. As soon as Arnold had things clear and straight on the table, a gust of wind disheveled it again.

Arnold slammed both hands, palms wide open, on the table to hold still his thoughts and gain some clarity on the situation. Others stopped and stared at him, and when Arnold didn't speak, they continued about their business, such as it was.

He still had no idea what happened to his militia unit. Burgoyne continued to pound Arnold's line. Everywhere, his men met resistance. Burgoyne, Fraser, and the Hessian Baron von Reidesel, were formidable opponents, but their will to fight faded along with their numbers and supply line. All of Arnold's spies pointed to this as their last gasp. Unless they were resupplied, the British forces in Quebec province were finished.

But, this was not how an army on the brink of defeat behaved.

Arnold studied his maps, but the situation hadn't changed. Fierce fighting echoed from the river to his left flank in the forests. The British should've been focusing their efforts on the left. The only other thing that could explain it was if Major Morgan and Dearborn were taking on more than they could handle—if they were, against the odds, holding back the brunt of the British attack by themselves.

Arnold pondered that. Perhaps. Morgan was capable. One of the best. It was entirely possible. But he had to see for himself.

A burst of wind tore through the tent and whisked away papers and knocked over equipment. Aides and generals alike went chasing after maps and held down tent flaps. Arnold sighed. He couldn't work. He couldn't think. What the hell was going on out there?

His horse, a black stallion, neighed and snorted outside. *Warren is just as restless. Perhaps he is right. I'm not getting anything accomplished in here.*

Arnold had a hunch, a kernel of an idea, but he couldn't prove it. The wind died down, and Arnold cleared his throat. Everyone stopped. "Who do we have available closest to Morgan and Dearborn?"

"General Lattimore, sir," a staff officer responded.

"Very well, stretch our line thin there, and pull him and his men toward the left flank."

No one moved.

His immediate subordinates always angered him the most. Arnold traced a finger on the map from the Hudson to the tree line. "This is all a feint."

"Is this correct?" Eleazer Oswald asked. "Reports don't indicate it." Arnold was taking a gamble, and as usual, Oswald called him on it. If Arnold were wrong, it would be more than just this battle. Everything that led to this point would fail. All wasted. Ruined. His army would lose, and the British in the north would link with the British in the civilized parts of the Colonies further south.

If I'm wrong.

"General?" Oswald asked. "Are you sure?"

"Absolutely," Arnold turned away from the table. He grabbed his belt, wrapped it around his waist, holstered a pistol, and grabbed his sword. Officers' swords were mostly ceremonial, but his was not. Oswald stuck close to Arnold with a deepening look of suspicion. His staff chattered and flapped like hens, at an utter loss as to what to do. Arnold ducked out of the tent.

Oswald followed him out. "If you're sure, then where are you going?"

The wind blew right through him the moment he reached his horse. He answered his aide. "To see if I'm right."

"I should have known."

"Just follow my orders. Get Lattimore down there." Arnold mounted his horse.

"They say you're reckless," Oswald pointed back to the tent. The flaps opened as some of his staff came out.

"They're not the men whose approval I seek."

"What if you're killed?"

"Erect a statue of me. Right there." Arnold pointed to an area in the clearing below them. He didn't wait for a response. Instead, he spurred Warren on and swooped down the bluffs into the unknown.

Hannah once said on the field Arnold could become a great man, either in battle as a leader, or in death as a hero. Arnold saw a third possibility Hannah hadn't considered: he could be wounded. Not just shot and left with a painful reminder and a scar, like last time at the walls of Quebec, but ripped apart and put back together in a way that made him an invalid. And the crippled had no place in society nor in history texts—they remained the scars of war, the visible reminders of the pain the country endured, wrapped and bandaged, then forgotten. Benedict Arnold pushed those thoughts away and rode to Major Daniel Morgan's position.

Morgan had an interesting history with the British. He didn't like them with very good reason. A veteran of the French and Indian War, Morgan could've gone the way of George Washington and joined with the British. He was just as capable as Washington, but a dispute with a senior officer resulted in a bloody nose and lashings.

The British officer's nose would heal, but the five hundred lashings Morgan received in punishment scarred him body and soul. And so it was Morgan had five hundred men under him, one for each of those lashings. And each one of those men would do more than give a redcoat a bloody nose.

Arnold rode into the thick of things. On his right were the breastworks where some of Morgan's men made a stand, firing in loose order as they could at the British. Unfortunately, there were more redcoats than they could handle. A few of them made it up and through some of the breastworks and attempted to route the Colonials from behind. Arnold couldn't do much for them. He hadn't brought reinforcements, though he had seen to it they would arrive. However, they might arrive too late. He didn't have but two shots with him—one from his officer's pistol, strapped to his side, and the one pistol he kept in his waistcoat for emergencies—and his hunting sword.

He intended to bypass them but found he couldn't. Instead, Arnold pulled back on the reins of his horse and directed him toward a group of redcoats. Warren plunged into the group. The redcoats could've easily bayoneted the defenseless animal if they had acted quicker. Instead, they dove out of the way.

Arnold unsheathed his hunting sword and drove it onto a redcoat's clavicle, shattering it. The other two men fled back to the British lines. Another redcoat, standing off a ways, lifted his flintlock at Arnold, but before he squeezed the trigger, Arnold pivoted Warren around and took to the protection of a maple tree. The redcoat fired, hitting the tree and showering splinters into Arnold. Dirt and bark embedded into the right side of his face, but he was otherwise unharmed.

The soldiers around Arnold rose and gave him a quick cheer. One of them chased down the redcoat who shot at their general. The redcoat was alone and without a shot. He could've fought with his bayonet, but when he saw the American come after him, he dropped his firearm and ran. The American flung himself onto the redcoat, knocking him down and sending them both sprawling into the wet leaves.

The American rose first and sat on the redcoat, sending a hard right into the soldier's jaw, then another, this time to the nose. He raised his fist once more. Even from up here, Arnold could see blood running over the redcoat's face. Arnold rode out to him, even as muskets continued to fire around him.

"Desist." Arnold did not even need to lift his voice. His soldier stopped the attack. Arnold continued, "This soldier was just doing his duty, as I expect each of you to do. We have some serious work to do." Arnold addressed all the men, "We have the entire British Army to pummel before nightfall. So, push forward.

Bind this man, leave him here, and move on. We'll be at the British lines by nightfall, boys. By nightfall."

The soldiers looked around. One of them spoke up with a nervous voice. "You'll be leading us, sir?"

At that moment, hoof beats of several approaching horses and the drummer and fifers of another unit hit the air.

"Yes," Arnold replied. "With them." Fresh troops approached. "Reinforcements are arriving. If you shall excuse me, I must ride off to meet them." But, before riding off, he caught a few grins from his men.

A short time later, he caught sight of Major Morgan. The major was, for whatever reason, not on horseback. He stood ankle-deep in mud and leaves, his white uniform a mixture of black and red. Arnold wasn't sure if the blood was his. Tomahawks hung from his belt, and his rifle remained shouldered around his back.

He watched as Morgan's sword, not a hunting sword, but an actual sword, plunged into the belly of a redcoat. Morgan drew it out and charged at another, slicing into the man's shoulder. Blood spilled from the wound, blending in with the red uniform, invisible to Arnold from his distance to the fray.

Two other soldiers accompanied Morgan. One looked like a former frontiersman, rugged, with defining stubble, aiming at a tree in the distance. Arnold looked at the same tree but saw nothing. The soldier fired, and a redcoat fell, still holding on to the British equivalent of a sniper's rifle. Arnold did not see where the man landed. *Impressive.*

The third man, tall and skinny like his rifle, poured out cover fire. But, the reload time of the longrifle was slow, and there were too many enemies. Arnold rode to them. He took out his pistol and fired at an oncoming redcoat, dropping him to the ground with a splash into the mud. Morgan finished off another adversary with his sword, but a redcoat had perfect aim at the major and was too far away for Morgan to close the distance with his sword.

Arnold tossed his used weapon aside and reached into his waistcoat for his personal pistol, knowing he was too late. The redcoat looked ready to fire. Morgan grabbed one of his tomahawks and in a smooth, gentle motion, flung it at the redcoat. It hit him in the center of the chest, embedding itself blade-first into the soldier. He fell back and collapsed against a tree, dead.

Morgan wiped away a brow full of sweat and blood and looked up at Arnold. "About bloody time. I expected to see you much sooner."

"I thought you could handle it on your own." Arnold said.

"Not today. I'm feeling old."

"Horse?"

"Dead." Morgan looked old. Old and grizzled. "So are a lot of my men. Good men." He contorted his shoulders and his back as if each one of the men he had lost stung him anew with the crack of a whip. "You look like you've seen some action." He pointed to the dirt embedded into Arnold's cheek. "Did you put that on just for me?"

Arnold ignored him and briefed him on the situation. "You had five hundred men, as well as elements from Dearborn's unit, and it appears you've been fending off the entirety of Burgoyne's and Fraser's forces here."

"Felt like it."

"I think the Hessian had the rest of our line pinned down."

"Makes sense. With a bit of artillery and a few sharp-eyed *jaegers*, I can see that. Of course, his sharpshooters aren't as good as mine."

"I didn't mean to imply they were. I just saw one in action. Bloody good show," Arnold smiled. "I've pulled Lattimore off the line. He should be here shortly."

Morgan took several deep breaths, and focused on the trees.

"So, it looks like the party is going to be here?"

"More or less. I'd like to press out of these woods and reach the British lines by nightfall. That's the weakness of Burgoyne's plans. If we can just give one more strong push here, he will have nothing to fall back on."

"Then what are we waiting for?"

Off in the distance, coming from their lines, Arnold heard the drums and fifes of more soldiers. Soon came the footfalls and the voices of Lattimore's men calling out movements.

"How do you wish to proceed with your men? Are they able to fight?"

"Every last one, sir," Morgan said. "We're not very well-drilled; it'll take a while to form. Time I don't want to waste. There's only a few hours of daylight left."

"Then we will lead and see who follows."

The sun hung low in the western sky and the wind still tore at them. An aide came up to Morgan on horseback and delivered the animal. The aide dismounted, and Morgan gingerly pulled himself up and thanked him.

"Do me a favor, sir," Morgan said.

"Yes?

"Ride a little closer. Keeps the pressure off me from the snipers."

"Maybe you shouldn't wear all white."

"Weren't you the one who used to wear a red British jacket?"

Arnold ignored him. He was normally the cynical one, but he didn't hold a candle to Morgan. Instead, he spurred his horse and said, "See you at the front."

Arnold rode past the men he had left earlier at a slow trot. Behind him a ways, the redcoat remained bound. They'd made progress, but not nearly far enough.

"If you want to fight with me on the front lines, you're going to have to catch up." Arnold bellowed and spurred Warren on as they broke out into another cheer then peeled themselves away from their positions and followed Arnold into the forest.

Stevens and Collins stood silent and in shock as Arnold left toward the sounds of musketfire. Morgan lingered just long enough for him to say, "Come on, boys, we can't let the general have all the fun, now can we?" He spurred his horse onward, then he was gone.

Stevens was not someone easily overwhelmed by titles or authority. But, he had to say he was impressed with General Arnold. And the general had rode off into battle ahead of them all, not a sight he ever expected to see.

He was about to tell Collins, but saw his friend had taken off down the hill after the general. Stevens shrugged. Nothing had changed. They were still outnumbered, they still had little ammunition, and they had not had time to clean or reload their weapons. *This should prove interesting.*

TEN

Freeman's Farm, Saratoga, New York
September 19th, 1777.

THE autumn breeze helped cool Corporal Martin Stevens from the unusual warmth. He wiped perspiration from his brow with his flax linen sleeve, which was itself already soaked. Times like these made him glad he didn't have to wear the heavy wool blue and buff coats of the regulars—not that they were in ready supply anyway. The men in Morgan's unit all pretty much wore what they came in with. It wasn't as if the continentals were a real army anyway. A real army would've made sure they were better supplied.

Stevens checked the black powder in his powder horn and saw it remained empty. His .50 caliber rounds were gone too. No ammo had miraculously appeared in the five minutes since he last checked. He took off the horn and bag and flung them to the ground, shaking his head.

Stevens then tossed his long rifle. It bounced against the trunk of a thin maple tree and landed in a soft bed of leaves. With any luck, he'd come back for it, but it wasn't worth the added weight to carry it now. He had to reach Collins before he did anything else ridiculous. Stevens looked out through the trees to see Collins, still off a ways, running toward the front after General Arnold. Thankfully, he slowed after his initial dash.

With the added weight removed, Stevens caught up just as Collins took cover by the trunks of the trees.

"Good of you to join me," Collins said, stealing a glance behind him. He looked out of breath, and he cocked his brow. "Where's your rifle?"

"It's worthless. So is yours," Stevens said. "Bit surprised to see you in one piece."

"Yeah, well, I might've gotten a little overzealous. But at least I still have the one shot left."

"No you don't. You ran off unarmed." Stevens took note of Collins' rifle. "Your flint's too worn, and by now, your barrel is clogged. You won't get another shot from it, at least not now." At least he'd gotten some experience with it. Collins could now shoot the damned thing. There was that. If only Collins could've put that same patriotic zeal into farming.

Collins asked, "So what do I do with my rifle?"

"Leave it." Stevens searched around, then pointed to a spot a short distance away. "Follow me and keep your head down."

They made it to the clearing where several Continental regulars lay dead in the dirt. Stevens took little note of them. Near each corpse lay what he sought. Among the red and blue uniform coats were several Brown Bess flintlock muskets. He picked one and handed it to Collins. He took another for himself, but frowned at the weight of it. The attached bayonet unbalanced it and made it much heavier to hold and aim. *How am I supposed to shoot with this?*

Stevens separated the bayonet from the flintlock by twisting and pulling it off. About the only good use for a bayonet he could think of was to cook meat over the campfire, a practice frowned on by the army. He didn't know why. He jabbed the sharp, triangular blade into the damp earth. It stood there, erect, as an eerie memorial to the fallen soldiers.

He took two full cartridge cases from the dead. "Consider yourself resupplied." His heart weighed heavy, but need trumped all else.

Collins nodded.

A low groan came from the corpses. They both turned their head in surprise. Shivers raced through Steven's skin. His heart skipped a bit. The groan grew louder.

Then, he heard heavy, uniform footfalls from behind their position. The bushes not too far in front of them rustled as redcoats fell back through the low foliage.

The groans grew in frequency and strength. Collins asked, "What are we going to do?"

Stevens looked through the remains and discovered wounds from bayonets, one from a musketball to the chest—bits of the rib cage were torn away, and he could see part of a heart.

That was something else to consider, the larger caliber musketball of the Brown Bess was brutal.

Stevens heard more noises nearby. He stopped and glanced up, but the sounds had stopped. He was about to suggest that they leave when Collins found the wounded Colonial soldier at the other end of the felled unit. At first glance, he appeared unharmed. His chest remained intact, and it rose and fell with each groan.

"Here, help me get him up."

Stevens reached over and took the man's shoulder while Collins took the opposite side. They sat the man up. The wounded soldier had enough strength to remain upright. "Is it over?" he whispered, his voice weak.

"Not by a long shot," Stevens said.

"Good. I might still have a chance to fight."

Stevens wrinkled his brow in surprise. He hadn't expected the near-deserter to say such a thing, particularly in such a curious accent. It sounded Prussian, but Stevens couldn't place it. And the man looked sick. He wanted answers. Stevens handed over his canteen.

"No, thank you," the soldier said. "I've got my own." With that, he took out his own canteen and took several large gulps.

Stevens took the time to check the man over. He was covered in sweat, though he had laid still in the shade of the trees. His uniform was disheveled, and his breeches were caked in mud. The whole area smelled of human feces, emanating from the man before them.

"Dysentery?" Collins asked, his tone knowing.

"I'm afraid so," the malodorous man answered before Stevens could respond. "I forewent seeing the field surgeon this morning. I couldn't bear the thought of my men fighting while I rested behind the lines on a cot." He dabbed sweat from behind his ears and continued, "I must've passed out. Lieutenant Arntz, Dearborn's regiment. Bit of Prussian ancestry in me, I'm afraid. It's not a helpful trait, given the circumstances."

Prussian made sense. While there were traces of it in Arntz's accent, he took considerable effort in masking it, taking care in the words he chose. It seemed off. Perhaps he was trying too hard. In any case, the lieutenant sounded suspicious.

Musketfire erupted nearby. Stevens thought they might be friendly, if his fellow soldiers didn't accidentally shoot him instead. He pointed up the hill.

"Well, sir, you can either go back there and explain yourself to those soldiers up there and take your chances at not getting shot," Stevens pointed down the opposite way, "or come with us and most certainly get shot at. Your choice."

Before Arntz had a chance to answer, Collins spoke. "Where's General Arnold?"

Stevens thought of that earlier. Despite the general's earlier bravado, it was clear that General Arnold was nowhere near the front. Perhaps he had already won the battle single-handedly. Perhaps it was all for show, and the general was back in comfort and safety while they were out here, exposed.

Whatever his cynicism regarding the general, Stevens realized now was not the time to argue with Collins. Instead, he said, "He probably went down the line, pulling people like us down here."

"General Arnold is here? Out here? Has he lost his mind?" Arntz asked. He picked himself up. An untimely breeze provided Stevens a whiff of the officer. The stench most certainly came from him. "I feel better at the moment. I shall join with you."

Stevens took a long hard look at the man and then turned to Collins. "What do you think?"

"Of course."

Stevens had his hands full with Collins. Adding the extra burden of an officer, a sick one at that, could prove fatal. Still reluctant, he gave in without argument. There would be time for a discussion later—if they both survived to have it. "Let's go."

Arntz stopped to pick up a flintlock as they prepared to make their down the hill. Stevens took it from him with a scowl. Arntz raised his voice in protest. "What do think you are doing? Don't I get a musket?"

"Not until we find someone who can vouch for you," Stevens said.

"I'm a lieutenant."

"Not right now, you aren't."

Arntz smiled. "Clever. I like you."

Stevens led the way, followed by Arntz and then Collins. They made steady progress through the forest at a much faster pace than they had moved so far today. Men from their unit and others linked together and decided that it would be much safer to stay in the forest as long as possible. This time, they remained in the woods and headed north toward the farmhouse, past the south field, where they started that morning.

Someone else from Dearborn's unit recognized Arntz. Stevens sighed in relief and handed him a musket.

"Much appreciated." With his guttural accent, it still sounded odd. However strange, Arntz resumed command, though he wavered on his feet.

They soon arrived at the edge of the treeline overlooking the north field of Freeman's Farm. Directly across the field ran the Hudson River and to the south, along the treeline, stood General Lattimore's men. He had taken position where Stevens and Collins had been that morning, only now, the sun faded instead of rose.

Even with this organized counter-offensive and fresh spirit, the redcoats continued to offer stubborn resistance. Even in defeat, the British were well disciplined and tough. They wouldn't stop fighting. Stevens frowned at that. With the low-hanging sun and the cover of the treeline breaking into open grass, he knew their progress would end. They hadn't gained an inch of ground. *All those men dead and for what?*

Looking out at the British position on the field in front of him, he didn't think they would move much more tonight, if at all. Stevens frowned again. What faced them seemed impossible—two raised mounds of earth stood high above them.

These redoubts were shaped like horsehoes, and the British could fortify themselves within while freely pouring fire out over the sides. Interwoven branches formed into baskets and filled with mud supported each tall, earthen mound. Sharpened tree branches jutted out of the outer-walls at odd intervals while felled trees lined around the base. Those redoubts had not been there before. In fact, he thought that they might have been built today. Stevens swallowed hard. To attack those fortifications meant many more people would have to die.

"Can't we just sit them out?" Collins suggested. "The river is to their backs. Aren't they running low on supplies?"

"We can't do that," Arntz said. "They *want* to cross the Hudson, and they need to link with the bloodybacks sitting on their thumbs near Philadelphia. Or, those blokes could come here instead. Either way—"

"We're dead," Stevens said.

"Well, I was going to say the cause of liberty is finished, but I suppose your concern is more immediately justified," Arntz said.

"So we can't ignore it." Stevens shot Collins a scowl.

"They're not going to let us," Arntz said. He still didn't look any better. He breathed heavily. "General Arnold did not bring us out here to stare at the stars." Between his accent and his breathing, it grew difficult to understand him.

Stevens looked around. More men gathered along the tree line, forming upon the three of them. It felt as if one of them should speak or act. Arntz was probably the highest-ranking among them, but his health disqualified him. Collins certainly couldn't. That left him.

The sun was setting, and the wind continued, cooling his sweaty skin. Stevens looked down the line—no one else appeared of the treeline. The redcoats kept their fire pouring from the redoubts, forcing them to stay low. Stevens supposed that once General Lattimore engaged his men on the field, he would advise Arntz to do the same, but it was not a choice he could so easily make. He had no desire to send men to their death. This was not his fight. *Where the hell are General Arnold or Major Morgan?*

Artillery opened fire. The thunder of cannon. At first, Stevens and a few of the surrounding soldiers threw themselves down on the damp forest floor. His heart raced, but he remained focused long enough to pull Collins down with him. Arntz was on his own.

Stevens didn't know who had fired or which direction the cannon faced. But, as the smoke drifted from General Lattimore's position, Stevens realized it was their side doing the shooting. Sure enough, the small arms fire from the redoubts slowed as the redcoats inside took cover, just as he and the men around him had done.

The cannonballs didn't have much effect themselves, he noted. One buried itself into the raised earth of the redoubt in a large, protracted explosion. Dirt sprayed high into the air, showering the field.

Doing damage was not the point, Stevens realized. That was what mortars were for, but they weren't in use. The noise of the cannon, combined with the acrid black smoke filling the air, and the suppressed fire coming from the British positions, was enough to provide the soldiers limited cover. And that meant just one thing—

"Arntz, I think they mean to send us out over that rise, sir," Stevens said. His chest tightened, and his breath quickened. He looked down at his feet, unsure of where they would take him.

"Indeed," Arntz said. He didn't look any better. "Start getting the men up." He lowered his voice. "I might need your help getting over there."

Stevens found himself nodding even though he had wanted to protest. He couldn't be responsible for— "Okay, Henry, time to get moving," he said instead to Collins.

General Lattimore's troops raced out onto the field. He could make out vague forms and movement through the smoke. Those soldiers had much more of the field to cross than they did, and his heart sank.

"Ready?" Arntz's weak voice did not carry. Stevens was about to repeat it when the sound of hooves came from behind.

"Those cannon are for you, boys!" General Benedict Arnold said with a triumphant holler, as if the battle were already won. He rode in, gallant and imposing on his night-black stallion and blue and buff uniform, though Stevens told himself he would not be fooled. A moment later, Major Morgan rode behind him, his all white uniform stained and muddy. The pair looked as if they'd been fighting the whole British Army by themselves. Stevens did a double-take. *Perhaps I could be fooled...*

"Head for the furthest redoubt, boys," Arnold said. "It's built higher than the other one. If we take it, we take 'em both!"

The general then did something Stevens did not expect: General Arnold, followed closely by Major Morgan, launched himself out of the forests and into the field ahead.

"Let's go, let's go! We can't have the general doing all the work now, can we?" Arntz called out. His voice found renewed strength. Soldiers came alive, up and running out of the forest and headed for the furthest redoubt.

Collins took off ahead, glancing behind him as if searching for approval before running off. He'd grown a little smarter, but he hadn't curbed his zeal to fight. Stevens grabbed Arntz in support, and the pair made it out of the tree line and onto the wide open field.

Musketfire opened on them. Dirt and grass flew and rained back down, and the wind kicked it back up again. Bits of dirt stung his eyes, and the heavy smoke from the cannon made it hard to breathe.

"I cannot... I can't... leave you all... behind," Arntz said through heavy breathing. He felt slick, and his odorous stench had not subsided. He'd get them both killed, but still, Stevens hung on, pulling the lieutenant behind them and following

General Arnold's path to the redoubt. Stevens realized he was the daft one.

It seemed as if General Arnold took up most of the redcoats' attention. That was fine by Stevens. It kept the pressure off all of them, and it allowed more Colonials to close the gap between the field and the redoubts. Clever, but Stevens suspected it would get the general killed.

He looked ahead through watering eyes. Collins was long gone, though he could almost see an outline of him in the distance. Ahead were the two generals, firing once on horseback and weaving between both redoubts as if taunting the British. How either of them remained alive was beyond Stevens' understanding.

Arnold's horse reared and jerked about seventy yards from the closest redoubt. Stevens had never heard a horse shriek so violently. It shook and bucked and tried to run as if trying to wrangle away from death.

General Arnold held on. Stevens didn't know how, or why, for the general went down under the horse when the animal gave out and collapsed. It fell heavily on him. The general hit the ground hard on the back of his head, pinned by the horse in the middle of battle.

Soldiers from Dearborn's unit, and what was left of Morgan's riflemen, sprinted to Arnold's location. Some of the wiser riflemen held back and picked off redcoats who climbed out of the redoubt in a useless attempt to reach General Arnold first.

Stevens looked at his musket and wished it were a longrifle—and he regretted taking off the bayonet. His close-quarters weapon was worthless at such a long distance, but without a bayonet, he frowned. Stevens took Arntz and made for the redoubt himself.

He had kept an eye on Collins, as much as he could, through the fray, though lost him when the general went down. He scanned around and saw Collins a moment later. A redcoat took aim at the unconscious figure, but Collins fired first. The larger caliber ball of the Brown Bess shredded into the redcoat's chest and dropped him dead. Collins reached the general and pulled him free. By then, several others had come to his aid, and Major Morgan placed himself and his steed between the redoubt and the general.

The sky turned a dark crimson. The wind died with the light, and, if not for the sounds of war, it seemed as if it would turn into a still, cool evening. With those red rays of sun, Stevens and Arntz made their way with the determined soldiers swarming the British stronghold. The fighting hadn't ended, and the lingering uncertainty of their general's condition added to their resolve.

Arntz no longer needed support from Stevens. Under his own power, he climbed headlong up the redoubt, in between pointed logs and through sharp abatis. He used those defenses to boost himself to the rim of structure. Relief flooded Stevens to follow someone else, and for once, tried to stay close within the twisted branches.

A figure approached the *abatis* with a lit torch. Stevens' stomach jumped, and he swallowed hard. If the branches were lit, he and other soldiers would be caught within the flames. He groped for any sort of handhold, something he could use to pull himself out of harm's way. He found a crevice, and the fingertips of his left hand dug in. He strained to pull himself up, his legs kicking away sharp branches, his feet tangled. He almost broke free, but as he did, a redcoat peered over the mound, Brown Bess aimed, bayonet inches away from Stevens' right eye.

Terrified, Stevens dropped back down into the abatis. Branches cut superficial wounds into his skin, tearing his clothing. He wanted to scream at the sudden pain but couldn't find the air to do so. Instead, he lay there, unable to pull himself back up. The redcoat with the musket took a moment to find his aim. Stevens looked away to see the figure with the torch attempting to set the branches aflame.

But the wet wood would not catch.

Stevens took that moment to find his breath. He was still under fire. The redcoat looked down at him and, for a moment, their eyes locked. Stevens had an immediate sense of familiarity, that this soldier didn't sign up for this, either. He didn't look like a career soldier bent on killing Yanks. He was just some poor fool who might've gotten too drunk at the wrong pub at the wrong time. Killing Stevens so close and personally would burn into that soldier's conscience, just as Stevens' conscience burned. None of it was personal. They were all victims of timing and circumstance.

With that, Stevens struggled to keep his eyes open and locked on the redcoat's while he braced against the shot that would surely send him to hell.

Arntz grabbed the redcoat's arm. The redcoat jumped but responded swiftly, sizing up the new opponent. He pulled back and stabbed with his bayonet, plunging the blade into Arntz's shoulder. The lieutenant cried out but did not let go. Instead, the two became connected and intertwined like the branches below, but the redcoat's momentum gave Arntz enough leverage to pull him out and over the rim of the redoubt.

It also knocked Arntz loose, and the two fell into the abatis, just as Stevens had done moments ago. He pulled himself clear as the two of them hit the spot he had vacated. Thankful to be alive, he looked down at the two soldiers. Americans swarmed the redcoat, and he disappeared underneath them. Arntz bled heavily, though it did not appear to be life-threatening. But, if he left where he lay, he would either be shot by the redcoats, or trampled by his own men.

Stevens thought for a moment—he could either rejoin the efforts to take the redoubt, or pull Arntz to safety and face possible repercussions for abandoning the attack. If every soldier stopped to care for the wounded, it would have a serious impact on the battle. The practice was frowned upon—unless you were a general, of course. Common soldiers sometimes got the attention of a camp follower in the aftermath of battle. Sometimes.

Arntz had saved his life—that made the decision easy. Stevens made his way down to him, and like Collins had done with the general, took Arntz by his good arm and pulled him out of the branches. From there, he helped him to his feet.

Major Morgan appeared ahead of them. Stevens went pale and stiff as he caught sight of him. He hadn't made it a hundred yards before Morgan tipped his broad-brimmed hat at them both. "Bloody good show, boys. The night is ours."

"By your leave, then, sir." Stevens nodded in relief, and the pair made their way back while the continentals continued to flood into the enemy redoubt.

It wasn't long before Stevens and Collins met. Collins had delivered General Arnold to the infirmary while Stevens had done the same with Arntz. The air around it hung low with copper and decay. The sky turned from red to dark violet, and the first stars shone visible on the horizon. The moon would be full and bright, but for now, it cast pallid shadows within the darkened forest. The calm after the storm, though not the end of it. The British had been pushed back, but not beaten. The battle would resume when daylight reclaimed the land. Stevens wondered how Collins would sleep that night, knowing how poorly he had slept the night before.

"General Arnold?" Stevens asked.

"Alive and well," Collins said. "Though he seemed to be in incredible pain. Something to do with his left leg. I was there when the surgeon made his examination. It didn't appear to have suffered from a musket shot or serious injury."

"Bloody miracle, that is."

"You don't subscribe to miracles."

"I know one when I see one," Stevens said, placing a hand on his friend's shoulder as they walked through the woods toward camp in the south field. "He should've taken a ball. More importantly, you could've been shot, bayoneted or captured."

"But I wasn't."

Stevens stopped him. "You must know I'm displeased, but I'm also proud of you. You've surprised me."

"Taking General Arnold to safety—"

"That's not what I meant. You have found a passion, however misguided. I hardly thought it possible, but you've abandoned what's important."

"What do you mean?"

"Your loyalties should be back home with your wife." Stevens continued walking. "But, you've come into your own as a soldier, I'll grant you that."

"What I do, what I have done, is for them. For something far greater than my own life."

"That's zealotry speaking. There's no yoke around your unborn child's neck."

"The British would enslave us through legislation, through laws. It is because we cannot readily see it that makes it all the more unjust."

"And by the opposite measure then, you must consider that the illusion of free will does not grant choice."

Collins did not respond, and Stevens chose not to belabor the point. They continued in silence.

The two made their way back to their unit, where they reunited with whom they had lost contact. They might've been victorious, but they didn't look it. They were bloodied and worn, and so few of them remained. Stevens' stomach twisted. He didn't know if it were anxiety or hunger—both forces pulled at him equally.

The newer camp bustled—those with strength pitched in wherever they could. A youth no older than fourteen busied himself by stacking all the muskets in tepee formation. Stevens and Collins handed theirs over. Beside the muskets sat three hogsheads. Stevens looked inside one—it contained cartridges for muskets and spare flints. The other two held supplies for the longrifles. It reminded Stevens he had yet to retrieve their discarded weapons. He looked outside the camp to the forest behind him.

Miners and sappers dug quick entrenchments and urinals and felled trees. Other soldiers and camp followers wandered the field, collecting the wounded and piling up the dead. A quartermaster in a wagon made the rounds, passing out grey blankets to a lucky few. Stevens and Collins were not among them.

More importantly, several soldiers were busy shoveling out an earthen kitchen so they could prepare food. Collins joined their efforts. Keeping a campfire hidden from the British was a good way of avoiding artillery fire on your location during dinner. Stevens would've assisted as well, but he had other things to do.

"Where are you going?" Collins saw him leaving.

"To retrieve our proper firearms."

"Need help?"

"Thanks." Stevens shook his head. "No. You stay. I'll be back shortly." Stevens could hunt, capture, and prepare a variety of game animals such as deer, elk, and even snake. It fed him, but he was by no means a cook. Collins was, provided someone else gave him the meat. His stomach tightened once more, this time in clear protest of hunger.

A light wind rustled through the near-bare branches of the maple trees as Stevens re-entered the forest. He made slow progress at first while his eyes adjusted to the darkness and had to be careful to keep from catching his foot on a tree root, or slipping in mud—or tripping over corpses.

Once his eyesight became accustomed to the dark, Stevens had little trouble retracing his route from earlier, though he had a bit of a distance to traverse. Of course, he made much quicker progress through it than he realized. It helped that no one shot at him this time. Soon enough, he recovered both rifles. His powder horn, however, which he had thrown aside in frustration, proved more difficult to relocate.

Movement in the distance caught his eye. He didn't hear anything. Whoever or whatever it was remained quiet. Again. Though still silent, the shadows from the moon betrayed it. Stevens thought it was an animal. A soldier out here on business would've made sure to make noise, just to avoid these types of encounters. Stevens didn't know what else to do, so he called out, "Who's there?"

It was a daft question, and he immediately regretted asking it. He should've just crept toward the noise silently. If it were an animal, it would scamper away once he got too close. If it were anything else... Stevens took a rifle and held it out. It was empty, of course, but the figure out there wouldn't know that, he hoped. His heart beat faster as he crouched low and snuck forward.

The silhouette moved as if seeking darkness. It retreated into the shadows, and a twig snapped. Stevens shot up and leapt toward the figure before it had a chance to escape. He made his way around a tree and caught sight of him. There in the foliage stood a man in plainclothes—a fine linen shirt and waistcoat with an animal skin wrapped around him like a cloak.

"You there. Who are you?" Stevens asked, rifle pointed at the man.

"No one of importance, I assure you."

Stevens came closer. The man's closed palm held something. "What have you got there?"

The man ignored the question and instead said, "I am Marseilles De Plume, a Frenchman from Quebec, long before the British took it over. I am no friend to them."

"I never said you were." Something still had alarm bells ringing in the back of Stevens' mind.

With that, the Frenchman coughed. He brought his closed hand to cover his mouth. It moved, and a moment later, the man swallowed hard. With a dry, raspy voice, the Frenchman said, "Please, I am in search of the road toward Albany, I have relatives there, and I've lost my—"

Heavy footfalls emerged from the forest behind him. A moment later, two uniformed Continental soldiers stepped out and joined them. The noise must've alerted them.

"What is this?" one of the men asked.

"Caught him up here, not making a sound, sneaking around," Stevens said. He kept his empty rifle on the Frenchman. "I think he might have swallowed something."

The same man answered, "We can take it from here. We'll set him up in front of the commander and have a nice chat, won't we?"

Steven's lowered his rifle and cocked his head in curiosity.

"I think you just caught us a spy."

"Fantastic," Stevens said. It wasn't his concern. Finding his supplies was. "Fancy either of you know where I can snag a spare powder horn?"

Stevens returned to a silent camp with both rifles and fresh supplies. He crept over bodies once more, but thankfully, these merely lay asleep. When he arrived back to where he had left Collins, he found him fast asleep, too. For some reason, that comforted Stevens. Next to Collins was a place made out for Stevens to rest. Collins had acquired a blanket for each of them. *Impressive.* In the middle of the bedroll sat a small bowl of stew. Stevens smiled at that.

His body ached, and he stumbled as he lowered himself down on the ground to rest, but it was now his turn not to sleep. Instead, he waved the late-season flies off his bowl of stew and ate it. It soothed his belly, though it was mostly flour. Then, when he had his fill, he went to work cleaning and preparing both rifles for the long day they had ahead of them.

"General Arnold, sir," a voice called out to him.

Arnold awoke, though he remained groggy and barely aware. He thought the voice sounded familiar. "Oswald?"

"I'm sorry to wake you, sir," Eleazer Oswald said, "but there's something Burr wants you to see."

Arnold forced himself alert. His leg still throbbed in tremendous pain, though he had been informed there was no lasting damage. It just hurt like the devil. He had been a reckless fool.

He considered lying there, delegating the task to someone else. Rising and walking would hurt—he wasn't sure he was ready yet for such pain. *Perhaps in the morning.* He shrugged and gingerly made his way, applying as little pressure as he could to his left leg. If his aide and Aaron Burr wanted to speak with him, then there was a matter of great import. He moved as quickly as his leg would allow, following Oswald out of his tent.

Aaron Burr had something of a reputation for being a bit of a scoundrel. Then again, so did Arnold. That hadn't stopped others from putting their faith in him. Arnold trusted Burr, perhaps more than anyone outside of Hannah. Burr left the comforts of Philadelphia and the Shippen family to follow Arnold to into the frozen wilderness of Quebec, just as Oswald had done. But, it was Burr who left and returned with reinforcements when all seemed lost—when Arnold lay cold in the snow, near death—a fresh musketball in the left leg outside the walled city.

He found Burr, a big, broad-shouldered brute with a rough, unshaven face, sitting on a barrel and holding a large hunting knife out in front of a man, bound to a post.

"What do we do with him?" Oswald asked.

"Discourage him from learning law," Arnold said. "Burr makes a much better soldier, don't you think?"

Oswald looked confused, but Burr chuckled.

"I went to school to become a Presbyterian Minister, actually," Burr said in a gravelly voice. "But I went and joined the devil's work."

"As a soldier?" Oswald asked.

"No, I took up law instead." The bound man laughed, but Burr put the knife under the man's chin. "Quiet. Nobody was addressing you yet. You'll get your chance to squeal."

And that was another reason Arnold liked Burr: he could make a joke at his own expense and make you regret laughing. "Who is he?"

"A spy," Oswald said. "At least, we think. He says his name is Marseilles, a Frenchman, but the soldier who captured him swears he saw the man swallow something."

Arnold looked the Frenchman over. He didn't look threatening, but the man in front of him could hold secrets that could kill or save hundreds of Arnold's men. Or, he could be exactly who he said he was. There was no way to know. "What has he said?"

"Nothing," Burr said, "at least nothing convincing."

"We won't know who or what he is until whatever he swallowed passes through his bowels."

"Or we could simply cut it out of him now."

At that, the prisoner went rigid, and life drained out of his face, but he did not speak.

"Give him a steady supply of laxatives," Arnold said to Oswald. Then, he turned to specifically address Burr. "I want to know what's in his belly by the time battle recommences on the morrow. By any means necessary."

Burr grinned. "Happily, sir."

"With any luck, this might be the second mistake Burgoyne as made today," Arnold said, returning to his tent. "And they may both prove to be his undoing."

"What was his first?" Oswald asked.

"He failed to kill me."

ELEVEN

Freeman's Farm, Saratoga, New York
September 20th, 1777.

STEVENS awoke in a swampy fog. Events from yesterday swam around him, assaulting his senses. Morning hadn't arrived, and he was still tired and very cold. He didn't know why he'd woken. Left to his own volition, he'd be asleep. Better yet, he'd be asleep in a bed with a heavy blanket and a fire beside him—or an auburn-haired woman. Instead, Collins lay nearby. He, too, seemed to have been startled awake. Noise he couldn't put together filled the camp. Everyone else was awake, too. Through the murk of his muddled head, he began to piece together what was happening.

Off in the distance, an explosion split the night air.

The fog in his head dissipated and he came clear. *Artillery. The British are attacking.*

Apparently, the British didn't need sleep. Somehow, through the night, they must've repositioned their artillery, and they now brought it to bear on the improvised Continental camp.

They hurried over to their weapons cache and grabbed their longrifles.

"Here, Henry, I cleaned it for you."

"Thanks," Collins said. "How was the stew?"

"Good." Stevens shot him a quizzical look and raised his eyebrows. "Thanks?"

"Just making casual conversation. Thought getting shot at was a well-worn habit by now."

"All in a day's work, aye?" Stevens grinned and grabbed his necessary belongings, strapping a powder horn around him and supplies needed for the attack. Bits of uniform items and broad-brimmed hats littered the ground. Once equipped, he soon found himself in the midst of a growing crowd, handing out supplies and allaying fears.

Some of the men hailed from Morgan's original band of five hundred, but they held nowhere near that number now. Most seemed to be Dearborn's men. Stevens sighed at the realization that this was supposed to be Arntz's unit.

Major Daniel Morgan arrived, riding through the fog toward him. The major was dirty, with leaves in his grey hair as if he had slept in the dirt with his men. Stevens approved.

"Get your boys formed, Corporal," Morgan said.

My boys? This, Stevens did not approve of. He took a step back and looked around. He didn't want to be in charge. They were out here to help Emma, not to be career soldiers. Keeping Collins and himself alive was all he cared about.

"I see no one else in charge of your unit. You did all right out there yesterday." Morgan didn't waste time arguing. "You are it." He then left before Stevens could argue.

Well, that didn't go well. He had no choice. With that, he did the best he could forming his new unit and then listened for orders as the British continued to rain down black powder and hot iron.

The fog hadn't receded during the quarter-hour or so he estimated they'd been awake and under fire. In fact, now he could say for certain that the fog had grown thicker. Their line stretched either way for as long as he could see through the thickening mists. Fortunately, he just had to worry about the handful of men around him and not the entire line itself.

Major Morgan's voice came from behind. "Let them come to us. Keep your distance and stay out of their range. Pick them off one by one and make each shot count."

They could avoid the range of small arms fire with some maneuvering, but the British artillery had no problems reaching them. As if on cue, the artillery opened fire, a sudden and intense barrage, that reeked of desperation. Stevens' men dove to the ground. They weren't supposed to do that in ranks, but Stevens didn't argue. He found himself flush and wet on the damp ground, looking out ahead.

Stevens noticed the redoubts on either side of them. Something about them had changed. Both sides now stood the same height, fixing the mistake the British had made yesterday. The opening was now on the American side of the lines as well. Gone was the opening on the north side. In its place stood large mounds of earth and fresh-cut logs raised outward to match the rest of the entrenchment. Cannonballs pounded the structure, but the freshly-dug earth held shape.

Already, he could see the line clambering for the safety of the redoubts before it happened, falling back against the British advance. With the shock and ferocity of the unexpected British attack, Stevens knew the line would break. It was just a matter of when.

Redcoats and mercenaries broke through the fog and into their line of fire. The riflemen were no good at close-quarters—they learned that the hard way yesterday. Major Morgan was nowhere near them, and Stevens couldn't hear the company commander over the shouts and noise of the firefight. Instead, he listened for the tell-tale notes from the fifers and drummers who carried orders on down the line through different drum beats and notes.

"What are we waiting for?" Collins asked, hunched over, eyes steady on the redcoats, more than ready to pick up the rifle and fire.

Stevens watched as rifles rose at different intervals on the line without direct order. But that didn't seem to matter. "Ready," he said. They all raised their rifles and took aim.

Black powder cracked down the line. When the first echoes of the rifle-fire died down, the drummers changed tunes and gave the order to shoot.

"Fire!" Stevens' unit discharged their rifles. Their fire was disjointed and not nearly as effective as the morning before. Black smoke poured out. Through the smoke, several redcoats stopped their advance, but more kept coming.

The line broke, just as it had done yesterday morning. Major Morgan rode behind them then. "Stay, boys! Stay in formation, every step back is a step of ground we must retake!"

What the general said made sense, and Stevens agreed with it in theory. In practice, the redcoats continued to advance, closing the distance to where they could fire back effectively or push them off the field altogether with their bayonets.

"Keep together," Stevens ordered.

"We've got to get out of here," a voice among his ranks called.

Stevens nodded in agreement. There was heroism and then there was common sense. He opted for the latter. "Where to?" he asked aloud.

"The redoubt."

To Stevens' surprise, it was Collins' suggestion. His friend pointed to the redoubt on the right, the one Stevens had climbed last night. He knew the redoubt was already manned and full, probably of Continental regulars, but other riflemen broke and headed for them. The redoubts would have to hold his men, too, at least long enough to regroup and reload.

"All right, let's go." If he hadn't decided to fall back, Stevens knew his unit would've broken and fled into the woods. This way, at least they were still on the field... sort of.

When they reached the inside of the fortification, Stevens knew he'd made the right choice. Lattimore's Continental regulars crowded into the enclosure. They stood on platforms constructed at the edges of the walls and poured out fire on the redcoats below. From this perspective, the British didn't have a prayer. *How had they taken the redoubts yesterday?*

The sudden influx of soldiers disturbed the hard work of the soldiers inside. Several regulars tried to push them back out. Stevens held his men back as much as he could, but other soldiers began fighting among themselves.

"Ignore them. Reload your rifles." His unit obeyed even as artillery crashed around them. A few moments later, Stevens heard approaching horses.

"Desist," General Arnold called to the brawling men. When the soldiers saw him, they stopped fighting and cheered instead. Most soldiers believed he had died or taken serious injury from the fighting the night before. The cheers went loud, hats flew, and whistles and hollers filled the air. Stevens pictured the British outside scratching their heads.

Behind him, Major Morgan rode up and glared directly at Stevens.

"Corporal, your men should be formed and firing, not cowering behind a wall of dirt."

"Major Morgan, their failure is ours," Arnold interrupted. "Besides, I have need of him and his unit. As you can see, they were the only riflemen who bothered to reload."

Morgan nodded. "Very well." There was no rant, no rage to his voice. A lesser man, subordinate to Arnold, might have protested. He pulled several units out, but left Stevens and his men.

"Corporal, take your men to the edge of the redoubt. I believe you'll find the target causing so much of our troubles this morning." Arnold dismounted and headed up the edge of the rampart with Stevens and his unit.

Stevens peered out over the edge of the redoubt. He didn't see anything through the smoke-filled air. Off in the distance, fog shrouded the enemy soldiers, and people were still shooting at them. He ducked.

"Look again," Arnold instructed. "Straight ahead in the distance. It's General Fraser."

This time, Collins and his men joined him. Stevens focused near the rear of the British lines, but he saw no general.

"On horseback, near the front," Collins said.

It took a moment to register that, but then he scanned ahead of the line and saw a white horse and an older man in a buttoned-up red coat with ribbons on his chest and a straight spine. It had to be the general. "I see him."

"Fantastic," Arnold said. "My men's lives are at risk. Please remove him from the field."

"I got him," a voice at the end of the line said. The soldier fired and missed.

"Corporal, in the future, I would encourage you to fire as one. You have lost the element of surprise." Arnold's face reddened, but he did not raise his voice. Slowly, his dark-toned skin returned.

"I apologize." Stevens saw that a man near the general, also on horseback, seemed to pull Fraser off his horse, as if dragging him to safety.

"It's all right. It appears the good general is keeping still for a moment longer. Besides, I'll wager fifty dollars you can take the shot yourself, Corporal Stevens."

Stevens turned. The general knew his name. It surprised him, and so did the reward money. That was quite a handful of cash. Emma could use that—

Stevens lined Fraser within both the front and rear sights of the Pennsylvania longrifle. The general was about a hundred-and-thirty yards out—past the range of accuracy. He took a deep breath and squeezed the trigger. The hammer fell, striking the flint and lighting the black powder in the pan. The rifle shuddered and kicked back in a controlled explosion. A moment later, the British general fell dead.

"Bloody well done, Sergeant Stevens."

He knew my name... and he called me sergeant?

His own line gave a mighty whoop, interrupting his thoughts. Everyone with a musket or rifle seemed to fire at once at the redcoats. Morgan had reformed part of the line, and his riflemen took carefully aimed .50 caliber shots at the British line, cutting through more officers and dropping them dead in the muddy, emptying field.

The British stopped their advance as unit after unit broke to aide their fallen commander or immediate officers or to take cover from the sustained fire. Only the artillery seemed willing to engage, but the rounds did not come as quickly or accurately.

Stevens took a deep breath.

Collins turned to look at him, congratulating him by striking him on his back saying, "Well, looks like you just became a hero."

Shit. What the hell did I just do?

"General Arnold," a voice called out. Arnold turned and saw his aide, Oswald, approaching on horseback. "I have urgent news."

Arnold clasped Sergeant Stevens on the shoulder in congratulations and, with a smile, he mounted his white horse and rode to Oswald.

Before he could say anything else, Oswald said, "I must stop finding you out here, sir."

"My men need me up front." Arnold could hardly hear him, let alone have a conversation with him.

Through the noise of artillery and musket fire, Oswald countered, "And look what just happened to the British General."

"He's dead because I was here," Arnold replied, but he nodded in understanding. His aide was right, of course.

Oswald shook his head in confusion and asked in a loud voice, "Should we perhaps adjourn to the rear so we can talk?"

A cannonball shot out the edge of the redoubt, spraying dirt and rocks down at the men. Oswald and Arnold covered themselves with upraised elbows while debris rained down on them, but fortunately, the cannonball bounced to the far side of the redoubt, and no one was seriously injured.

"I concur."

A few moments later, Arnold heard his aide more clearly over the noise of battle, and Oswald wasted no time. "We retrieved the contents of the spy's stomach."

"So he *was* spying?"

"A courier, to be more precise."

"And what did you find?"

"This." Oswald produced a small musket ball from his pocket. He handed it over to Arnold's gloved hand.

Arnold took it and discovered its weight surprised him. He shifted the peculiar item suspiciously in his hand.

"It's hollow," Oswald explained. "There's a notch in it where we found a bit of parchment."

Arnold examined the ball and found the hollowed out notch. Sure enough, a note rested inside. "Have you read it?"

"Burr did. Then he sent me to find you. It seemed urgent."

Arnold carefully retrieved the note, fumbling a bit with his gloved fingers, but he eventually succeeded, un-wadded it, and read the note for himself. "Oswald, where do you think we'll go once our business here has concluded?"

"Wherever we're directed, sir. Wherever we're most needed—"

"North," Arnold said. "We have unfinished business to the north."

Oswald nodded in silence.

"Send out a white flag, immediately."

"Sir?"

"And allow Burgoyne's men to retrieve their fallen general. He'll be a hero. Make sure our men don't interfere." He thought for a moment. "Have our colors present. Full honors." Arnold hoped his voice didn't betray a sudden pang of jealousy. *No matter. With this victory, my history will be written soon enough.* "There will be no more death today."

Oswald cocked his head and shot Arnold a questioning glance.

Arnold crumpled the note, then held it out in his outstretched palm. He watched it blow away in the autumn wind before answering his aide. "Burgoyne will surrender soon."

Off in the distance behind Arnold, a large, sturdy oak tree stood in solitude among the thin maple trees of the forest. It was a beautiful tree, with wide, climbable branches and plenty of nooks and knots for critters of all types to call home, the type of tree one should fasten a rope-swing on so children could swing and laugh and play about. If there were a lake nearby, it would make a perfect place to swing out over and splash down in the cool refreshing water on a hot summer's day. But this was not the case. On this oak grew one sturdy branch among a dozen or so, and on this particular branch, there hung a rope indeed.

But, on this rope had been tied a noose. And in that noose hung a body with a gash in its midsection. Entrails hung out, a pile of bloody bile and organs dripping onto the ground.

The body of the French courier swayed in the breeze.

TWELVE

Philadelphia, Pennsylvania
October 24th, 1777.

L T. Colonel George Washington was never one to waste the
morning hours of daylight. Every morning at Mt. Vernon, he
was up and on his horse, covering every acre of his estate and
readying each day's tasks. Out in the field while on campaign, he
found himself doing the same—riding around camp, greeting his
men, and carefully going over each task with them.

But, this morning, he found it harder than usual to rise.
His routine had broken, being subject to the constant whims of
his superiors. General Gage was the latest culprit, setting a date
to meet with Washington later this morning. It arrived too soon.
Washington's chest burned at the thought of seeing Gage again.

Not even the cool dawn could alleviate the feeling as
Washington left his Hessian encampment at Germantown and
made his way down the road. Shortly thereafter, he rode past
burned-out structures of rebel homes on his way toward the
recently captured city of Philadelphia.

General Howe had reclaimed it not more than a month ago,
his victory tainted by the news of General Burgoyne's surrender
in the north. Perhaps, if Howe had gone to reinforce—

Washington focused on the city ahead, a testament to the
shared kinship with the English who had sprouted a thriving city
out of the thick woods of the wilderness. Washington had been
in the city before, long before the war, and he marveled at how
close in appearance it was to small hamlets near London while

accenting the best parts of the New World within its cobblestone streets and red brick buildings.

Like any enduring city, it was not without its own natural defenses. Two rivers surrounded Philadelphia: the Delaware to the east, which divided Pennsylvania from its neighboring Colony of New Jersey, and the smaller, more crossable, Schuylkill River to the west. The city grew from its stately buildings and High Street near the Delaware, and sprawled westward until it met the Schuylkill and blended into forest. To the north was Germantown, a few miles away, where Washington had ridden from. To the south lay farms and fields. It was this quiet, agrarian life that made the bustling hub possible. It made Washington wonder how long it had been since he had seen the fields of his own estate.

He stopped his horse on the outskirts of the city. A momentary surge of bewilderment coursed through him. He couldn't recall how he had gotten here. It felt as if he had slept from Germantown and awoken at the city. Something must have disturbed him. He scanned ahead but saw nothing.

The cool morning air cleared his head, and Washington heard a commotion. Voices argued, and it grew louder. He pulled his cloak around him and decided his meeting with Gage could be postponed. Besides, he was early. He was always early. He nudged his white horse off the road and up to a small ridge.

Below him and to his right lay two small paths carved into the ground by wagon wheels. Down the makeshift path huddled a gathering of farmers. He counted about a dozen, dressed in worn woolen linen of various brown shades, dirty and poor. Since the war, there was too much disruption to maintain the food supply. As a consequence, people went hungry, soldiers and farmers alike.

A contingent of carts mixed in with the disheveled workers, but no animals stood by to haul them. Each wagon held a modest mixture of vegetables: potatoes, radishes, and some carrots. An unhealthy harvest, like the gaunt aging men and women carrying them, but it was more food than he had seen in one location in a long time.

Several soldiers on horseback yelled at them, ordering them to stop. Washington didn't know why. Out of curiosity, he headed toward them. One soldier sat astride a brown horse, holding both reins in his hands and instructing the line of farmers to do something, to which there was disagreement. The other three soldiers confused him in that they carried Brown Besses, not a weapon one carried on horseback. The muskets were equipped with bayonets, but they weren't pointed at the crowd. Yet. Washington broke his horse into a canter and rode for the group of soldiers.

When Washington drew closer, he grabbed for his hunting sword, his chest puffing up and face turning red. He understood the nature of the conflict, and it angered him.

"What is going on here?" Washington asked, hoping his assessment of the situation was incorrect. A moment passed in silence as the perplexed officer looked up at Washington and then carried on, ignoring him.

Undeterred, Washington asked again, "Speak. I wish to know your mind."

The officer answered, "It is no business of yours, Lieutenant Colonel. I have my orders."

The young officer matched Washington in rank, but most of his experience must have been spent in a soft embassy somewhere pleasant. Maybe The Bahamas. *I wonder how much coin that cost?* Regardless of rank or orders, Washington stared the whelp down with silence. Finally, the lieutenant colonel stopped and explained himself.

"We are requisitioning this food for our men. The farmers here are in no danger so long as they heed our orders." The colonel spoke in the usual air of aristocracy-turned-soldiery. Joining the army remained the best way of proving oneself a man—provided you survived the experience. Buying rank and posts out of harm's way was a luxury only the rich could afford and a cheat of the system. Seeing this officer here proved to Washington the Crown was pooling all its resources for a war they had vastly underestimated.

"Tell me, what is your name?" Washington asked. "And why are you stealing food from these people?"

"Colonel Benjamin Taft." Taft held his head tilted to one side. Whenever he talked, it rolled down some more, giving the impression of condescension. *Or maybe he really was just better than everybody else.* "And we are not stealing food as you ignorantly imply. I am carrying out my duties as any British officer would. Our job is to win this war. Ergo, we need to eat. What about that bothers you?" He didn't wait for an answer. "I have given you my courtesy. I am sure the governor of Philadelphia would be equally displeased to hear of your interruption."

Washington glared. "This food belongs to them. Let them take their food to market." He placed himself between the farmers and the soldiers. "If your men find themselves in hunger, or the quartermaster should requisition it, then by all means, go and purchase food."

Taft's temper flared, and his voice rose just as a child's might. "I can tell by your accent you are one of them. A Yank. Who are you?"

Washington had grown tired of this conversation, but answered him nonetheless. "Lieutenant Colonel George Washington, of Virginia. And I am on my way to see the governor now. I would be happy to inform him of this encounter."

At the mention of Washington's name, a collective cry came from the crowd. They stared at him, their eyes burning. Several women picked up radishes. It looked likely they would pelt him. One woman cried out louder than the rest, with traces of venom in her voice, "Murderer!"

The soldiers went to work. They ran down the line on horseback, brandishing their flintlocks over the crowd. "Quiet! Quiet down, all of you," they said.

"Ah, Colonel Washington." Taft paused. "Yes, I do know the name. Now I know the face. I am surprised that someone with your ruthless nature would be so alarmed over such matters as this. You, after all, did lead a raid on a religious holiday that resulted in the cold-blooded killing of General Hancock. And you talk to me about impropriety? Indeed, you are a walking contradiction."

Washington wanted to pummel the boy. He'd finally found someone he disliked even more than Gage. The meeting with him would be a cinch compared to this. Still, the colonel wasn't entirely wrong. Maybe that realization hurt him the most. He ignored it and pressed his argument instead. "We can't just take what he want. We are supposed to be protecting these people."

"Most of these people here have husbands who have killed or attacked our men. Those husbands would happily place a musket ball through your head. In fact," Taft waved his white-gloved hand over the handful of farmers, "I daresay one of these housewives and widows would gladly end your life now if I let them." Taft placed his hand back on the reins of the horse and continued, "The very food we seek for our men would go to aid the rebels if left unchecked. Winter is coming, and it will be the army that better supplies itself which will determine the outcome of this contest. So you see, Colonel, these people should be placed into service for our needs, if I were to have my way. They picked up arms against us, they threaten us, and they have killed our men. Surely, you understand this."

Washington's voice grew louder. "We must take great care not to sully our reputation with such acts. Were you not part of the attack against the rebels at the Paoli Tavern?"

"Sadly, I missed that encounter." That did not surprise Washington. "But I know what happened there. Rumors of a massacre of rebels have been greatly exaggerated. Of course we gave quarter to the soldiers we took prisoner."

Washington smiled. He had him. "And that is precisely my point. Never underestimate the power of propaganda. So long as one soldier was butchered, our reputation diminishes, and our cause is harmed. How can we restore peace when the populace does not trust us? Your attitude on display here is precisely the reason we find ourselves in this conflict. You look down on these people, our own kinfolk, as if they were of different blood. We may be embroiled in battle, but these men are still our brothers—virtue dictates that we treat them as such. If, perhaps, we did not lose sight of this long ago, we wouldn't be fighting each other in the first place."

"I have little time for lectures and history lessons. The Crown's forces have work to finish. My orders come from the governor. If you say that you have a meeting, then I give you leave to discuss this matter with him. Good day." With that, the colonel cocked his head again as if dismissing a child, then started off, goods in tow behind him.

Washington looked over the group of farmers as they took their goods into the city, not to sell, but to be taken away. They returned looks of hate as if he were the devil himself. His heart gave a pained throb. He wanted to help them, but they judged him by his one unforgivable act. The colonel was wrong, they were all wrong, but Washington couldn't convince them.

One thing was for certain: he would not discuss this with General Gage. This was his fight, and he had lost. With a kick to his mount, Washington headed back up the ridge and into the city of Philadelphia—a city that couldn't have been taken if it weren't for the gains made by him and his men as a result of the Christmas Day and Paoli Tavern Massacres. Somehow, that thought didn't make Washington any happier.

General Gage had, rather ostentatiously, set his office in the Philadelphia Town Hall, where the Declaration of Independence had been signed. He probably found some measure of humor in it. Washington did not. He was surprised to find the wooden steeple hadn't been burned down and the rest of the building demolished brick by brick. If men like Colonel Taft had their way, he was sure it would have been. And the missing bell would've been melted down and made into sword hilts. Maybe they were right.

When the Colonials escaped the city, they had taken almost everything of value with them—including the damned Liberty Bell. Only the outer shell of the city remained. The rest lay hollow.

Washington wove his way through the city until he reached Chestnut, then dismounted in front of the hall. An orderly waited to take his horse, and Washington entered a large, white doorway and found himself in the vestibule. Washington frowned, disoriented by the surprising amount of space.

"How may I help you?" another orderly asked.

"I am here to see General Gage." He knew if he had continued straight ahead and turned right, he would arrive in the assembly hall where the Declaration was signed. He wondered if he would've signed such a document under any circumstances. It would've meant treason—and death by hanging. He couldn't. Washington remained a loyal subject of the Crown. "I know it is up the stairs..."

"If you will follow me, sir."

The two walked the dark staircase, and the air grew close and stuffy. Washington was sure Gage would have been more comfortable in the Graff house, or Franklin's home, or another residence down the way. However, that would not suit Gage's style.

They made it up the staircase and down a narrow hallway with the same type of floor as the staircase. The boards squeaked and bowed with every step until they reached a door. There, Washington waited while the orderly discussed his arrival with a secretary. Washington settled in an uncomfortable, high-backed chair for the long wait ahead.

The immediate response surprised him. General Gage looked the same, though grey hair and age had overtaken him. Or perhaps he no longer wore a powdered wig. Washington didn't know, but the most telling change in his features was Gage no longer appeared burdened. Indeed, Gage floated and fluttered about the room with an exuberance of energy which belied his rank and status, his eyes wide and joyful, like a child's on Christmas morning.

"Come, come in!" General Gage beckoned. "I want you to have a sit, er... seat. Would you like some rum? Really, I am probably insulting you. We have so much rum. We keep confiscating it from smugglers up and down the coast. Would you like some brandy instead?"

Sun spilled into the room with curtains thrown open and it bounced off the white walls. It lent the large office an air of openness. Dark but glossy varnished tables sat in a row down the middle of the room, full of paperwork, maps, worn books, and a globe of the known British world. General Gage beckoned Washington toward a large dark wooden chair with brass tacks holding down a crimson leather backing and seat cushion. Instead, Washington stood in confusion.

"Benjamin Franklin sat in that chair," Gage informed him. "He is off in France now. I would have his head rather than his ass imprint if I could. But, it is something, is it not? Go ahead, sit." Gage walked over to the middle of the glossy tables. Crystal decanters, each with a different shade of an amber liquid, covered half of it. He poured a glass from one of them, seemingly chosen at random, and handed it to Washington, sitting at the edge of the chair. Washington briefly wondered if the drink were poisoned. Then he considered drinking it anyway unless he received answers soon.

"We have never been friends, General, yet you dote upon me like a long lost love. What exactly should I take from this?" Washington asked.

"I will speak more plainly." Gage stopped, pulled out a chair across from Washington and dropped himself into it. Brandy rose like a geyser from the glass and spilled over the rim. Gage paid it no heed and sat the drink down in front of him, the alcohol etching a ring around the glass into the varnish of the table. He gave Washington a slow, blank stare, and his cheeriness evaporated. "I find myself too old to quarrel, especially with someone whom I've recently discovered I have much in common. Your actions, George, are why we are in this room in the first place. You have proven quite indispensable."

Washington took a sip of brandy. His lips sucked inward as the libation hit his throat and empty stomach. He honestly had no idea why Gage was still in the Colonies after he failed to quell the rebellion before it grew to such proportions. He had a sinking feeling Gage was about to share—which frightened him more than any rebuke. With the way this day was going, he decided he might need another drink... or two.

"I am being sent to pasture," Gage said, looking relieved. "Cashiered, as it were. I am ready to leave, but before I do, I must insist I bury the hatchet with you."

Washington wanted to ask why it had taken so long for them to recall Gage, but the last part of Gage's words surprised him. Bury the hatchet? *What... in my skull?* "You have my attention."

"Good," Gage said. Then he asked, "Do you even know why I have held such animosity toward you?"

Washington sat back in his chair and thought long and hard over the question, just as he had done many times before. But, for every time he had mulled the question over, he had produced a different answer. In truth, he didn't know, but he answered with his best guess anyway. "I've heard rumors among the soldiers. They say you blame me for the battle in the wilderness. Not the one where Braddock was almost killed, but the mission I was on a year before that."

"Yes, I have heard those stories. You killed that French diplomat, or rather, your companion. What was the savage's name? Half-King, was it?"

"That's not how the event transpired—"

"Started this whole bloody mess, did it not? The French declared war, we fought them here and in other parts of the world, and we won. But war is expensive, coffers ran dry, and a wild land that had been left alone by the Crown for generations was suddenly tasked with paying their fair share."

Washington put down his empty glass when Gage finished. "So you place the blame of the war on my shoulders?"

"Absolutely not. The war would have started with or without you. Don't think too highly of yourself. One man does not have the power to change what will be."

"No, General, that is untrue. A single breath may alter the wind."

Gage laughed. "You were always a romantic, George, with a poem in your heart and the rules of chivalry at your breast. And that, sir, is why I despise you."

Washington shot forward in his chair but did not rise. Instead, he stopped himself, counted coolly in his head, and remained silent.

"You had this life of yours handed to you. You were nothing but a wild Yank. At best, a boy of some means in relation to this savage place, but of little consequence to the civilized world."

Gage had no idea he had just hit upon exactly why the Colonies were in open rebellion, but Washington let the moment pass with whitened knuckles as Gage continued.

"Fairfaxes brought you under their wing after your father passed, and you have been riding the coattails of the aristocracy ever since..." Gage took a long hard swallow of liquor, draining the glass, "...even after you betrayed them." The empty glass hit the table hard.

Washington stood. The heavy, wooden chair fell back and crashed to the floor. "What is the meaning of this?" Surprise filled his voice, and anger boiled at the edges of his words. He had never been so close to challenging another man to a duel—

"I was with you at the Monongahela River. We fought together throughout that whole campaign. You know this." Gage had stood up from his chair, too, albeit somewhat more gracefully. "Did you not realize I saw the letters?"

"What letters?"

"Your love letters to Sally Fairfax."

Washington's face went pale. He went to sit back down and almost fell before realizing the chair was no longer there. His knees went weak and his skin felt dry. The air was incredibly thin and stuffy in the room.

"Lord Fairfax gave you everything, but that was not enough for your wild heart, was it? You wanted his wife, too, that young beauty."

"I never touched her."

"You did not have to. He was hurt all the same."

Washington drew back, catching his foot on the damned chair. "You told him?"

"Of course. Why else do you think the Fairfaxes moved back home to England so abruptly? Rumors of war? No." Gage remained still, silent for a moment. "After all that, he still wanted to protect you, to keep you from making a dreadful mistake."

"Why did you tell him?"

"I had heard you were to be offered a position not within the Colonial Militia, but within the King's Foot. I wanted to stop that from happening. And, do you know what? Even after I told him, he still paid for your commission." Gage placed one palm on the table and leaned over. "That man believed in you." Gage stood erect, but pointed at Washington. "And after all this time, he turned out to be correct."

"I don't believe this," Washington said. He picked up the chair, moved it out of the way, and refilled his own glass with amber liquid. It was a poor choice. He sat the glass down in disgust and edged himself back into his seat. "If that were true, what has changed your mind about me?"

"As I've said. Old age, forced retirement. The failure to do my duties has given me pause to reflect on other mistakes." Gage refilled his glass from a different decanter. "And one other thing."

"Yes?"

"While we were at Braddock's funeral in London a few years ago, I noted that you did not once call upon the lovely Sally Fairfax."

"I am happily married to my best friend." He didn't say he often felt as if Martha was his only friend. Sometimes, it felt as if it were Martha and him versus the world.

"Yes, even so." Gage paused, and breathed out as if letting go of a heavy weight. "I was jealous of you, George. I did not believe you had a right to wear that uniform." He looked at the floor. "I was wrong."

The thing about burdens was that, once someone let go of their own, it became incumbent upon others to pick it up. The words weighed heavily on Washington. He wished he hadn't been told. There was no relief for Washington within Gage's newfound approval.

"Is that why you brought me here? To alleviate your guilt? To make an apology twenty years too late?"

Gage sat. The air in the room seemed to start circulating again. "No, Colonel, but after today, your new duties will keep you busy. I doubt we would have much time together to sit and chat about our past. That is the thing about it: We don't stop to think about the past until we realize that we have no future."

"And what future do I have? What duties are expected of me?"

"Look around, Colonel. Do you not see where we are?" Gates paused for a moment, as if expecting an answer. "Right in the bleeding heart of the Colonial Capital." He tapped the table and looked around the building where a handful of traitors had begun a rebellion. "In any other war the empire has known, do you know what this should mean?"

"Yes." Another rhetorical question.

"But is the war over?"

Washington shook his head. He saw where this was going. "The rebels are very... unconventional."

"And you would know that better than anyone, wouldn't you? That is why you have become such an indispensable man."

"Have I?"

"Your letter to Burgoyne." Gage flipped through a nearby stack of papers and retrieved a worn, yellowed letter. "It says here that your advice to 'let the forest fight for them' was helpful. It hurt the Yanks up north, though not enough to prevent Burgoyne from surrendering. That is his fault, though, not yours, but it proves my point. What you are doing, what you have done, crossing the Delaware—it has not gone unnoticed. That is why I have sought you out as my replacement."

"You want me to take over your duties as military governor of Philadelphia?"

"There is much more at stake than that, but, yes. Precisely. General Howe will most likely be recalled soon, but you did not hear that from me. I believe that Lord North and King George are reevaluating our conflict with the Americans."

"The Americans? Are we calling them that now?"

"Either that, or bloody Yanks. I think these people have irrefutably proven they are not British. Any blood they had in them of ours has long since spoiled."

Washington frowned at that but pressed his concerns back. "So they are not Colonists in open rebellion of the Crown?"

"In light of Burgoyne's defeat and France's involvement in affairs that do not concern them, there may be other ways to end the war or new theaters to explore. I have heard rumors that Parliament may send out a delegation next year. But, for now, we wait. And you maintaining control of the city and regaining control of the Delaware is a crucial step to solidifying our position. A feather in your Yankee-doodle cap, if I might say."

Or a stone with which to sink myself if I fail. "And what are my duties, as governor?" He ignored the Yankee slight. Gage could talk all he wanted; they were hollow words.

"Maintain order, keep supplies in our hands, and safeguard the city against attack." Gage sat up, gesturing to the stacks of paperwork while maintaining eye contact with Washington. "If there is any cruelty to my intentions, it is in the truth that your duties are far more taxing than you can imagine." He stopped and grew serious. "Philadelphia is not the bastion of loyalism King George believes it to be. Rebels hide in plain sight and walk down the same streets as you and I. They look like us, talk like us, but they are not. They are the friends who stab you in the dark when you think yourself safe in bed. Trust no one, particularly your colleagues who wear the same uniform. They are especially dangerous."

Gage got up once again and refilled empty glasses. The room had grown brighter as the sun rose further in the sky. It felt a little early, even for Washington, to be this inebriated so close to the mid-day meal. And it wasn't altogether unwelcome.

"There is more," Gage continued. "Rumor has it..." Gage stopped and leafed through a small stack of letters. He skimmed one. "No, it is confirmed." Gage looked up. "Benedict Arnold is being transferred here."

Washington looked up with a puzzled expression. "Who?"

"The general who took down Burgoyne. We have no idea why he is being sent here. The reports do not say. General Gates has been pulling units down here since shortly after the formal surrender." He let another sly smile escape. "Whatever the reason for his being here, he is your problem, not mine."

"Wait, when do these orders take effect?"

Gage looked around the table for a moment for a piece of paper, then threw his hands in the air. He stood and went over to search the papers at the end of the table. After shuffling through a few stacks, he grabbed the one he was looking for. "Here it is. Thought I had it out ready for your arrival. In any case, you will see the best part of the news. I have not told you yet, so read for yourself." His cheerfulness returned, and Gage handed the paper to Washington with a smile.

Washington took the paper and looked it over. He had to read it twice to comprehend it. The document was signed by both

General Howe and Lord Barrington, the British Secretary at War. It looked legitimate enough.

"Congratulations, *Colonel* Washington. Of course, you have not had enough time in your previous capacity, so we are treating it as a field promotion, but you can drop the *Lieutenant* bit now. There will be a celebration, of course. And drink. The command wants us to commemorate the capture of Philadelphia, my retirement, and your promotion. Your first task, conveniently enough, is to organize it all, in the middle of a war. Enjoy."

Washington ignored Gage. Something flitted about the edges of his mind. He had little use for galas. Washington tried to make some sense out of it. Gage was leaving, finally. He had known all along about his romance to Sally Fairfax, wife of Washington's benefactor, and Gage had tried to sabotage his career for it.

Then, perhaps out of spite, Gage promoted him and gave him the key to Philadelphia? What was going on here? Certainly, there were machinations at work he could not see, especially if the changing of the guard were true. *If Howe were really leaving as well...*

Then, there was the matter with Lt. Colonel Taft from this morning and the improper display of authority—

"Your Excellency, I beg your pardon. I have an urgent matter that I must attend to." He hoped that he wasn't too late. He stood, and so did the general. Washington picked up the paper and rolled it, placing the roll within a pocket of his waistcoat as he walked to the doorway, not asking permission to leave. "I will return in just a moment. I know we have much more to discuss." Gage looked surprised, but he did not bar Washington from leaving, motioning with his hand his approval to depart.

After making his way to the stable and collecting his horse, Washington rode back the way he had come through the bustling city streets. People continued about their business as if in denial that there was ever a war. People coped with change by sticking to routines. They paid no heed to him. Frankly, they had no idea who he was, and most would probably be unhappy to discover his identity.

The noon sun poured over the brick buildings and cobblestone streets. The otherwise cool morning transitioned into a warm day. Washington breathed in fresh air as he wove through the city, anticipation burning like fire in his chest.

It took him longer than he wanted to find the man he was after. The farmers he met earlier this morning were nowhere to be found in the Farmer's Market. Instead, the three soldiers he had seen had taken their place along with their carts of food. They had stolen it and now were selling it themselves. Taft was nowhere to be found.

He had to suppress his anger in his voice as he talked to several soldiers in the market to track down the wayward colonel. His patience paid off and in short order, and he made his way down Chestnut Street, past Fifth, and turned down a small alley onto a row of tightly packed houses. But for the red brick, it looked like almost any other street in England.

He found Taft in cozy accommodations in the middle of a row, no doubt a residence of a former rebel. Washington rode up just as Taft walked out onto the steps just outside the framed red wooden door.

"Lieutenant Colonel Taft," Washington called out from on top of his mount.

Taft looked up, shielding his eyes with his right hand against the bright rays of sunlight. He said nothing.

Washington didn't stop for pleasantries and instead cut right to the point. "You will compensate those farmers for their food at the price your men were selling it. Then, you will clear out your accommodations at this residence and submit yourself for discipline."

"Who on the bleeding cross do you think you are?" Taft's jaw dropped, but anger soon replaced the look of shock on his face. "Had your little discussion with the governor, yes? Ran off and told him like a sniveling schoolboy?" His words cut sharp, but each came out with a little more apprehension in his voice as if realizing something had changed since their first encounter.

"I did no such thing. Keep to this line of discourse, and I will add each word you utter to the number of lashings I'll unleash on you." Washington edged his horse ever closer to Taft, so he now towered directly over him. The sun shone directly behind Washington as he said, "I am the new governor, and I will be making some changes."

THIRTEEN

Wissahickon Creek, sixteen miles north of Philadelphia
November 27ᵗʰ, 1777.

"YOU summon me, and the Earth quakes and shatters. I arrive, and the night sky lights up in waves of blue and green," Major General Benedict Arnold said. He sat astride his white horse, riding to meet General Horatio Gates, Commander-in-Chief of the Continental Army. The bitter night air dictated that both generals wore heavy grey cloaks, which flowed over their mounts. The horizon lit up as if an electric green ribbon had been thrown across the night sky.

"Relax, General," Gates replied, his voice deep, and his words carefully chosen despite his age. Gates styled his greying hair as if it were a wig, and his small, sunken eyes usually hid behind a pair of gold spectacles. Those were absent now, but when he put them on, he resembled an old granny. Granny Gates. "The ground has shook before. It is rare, but it is not unheard. The natives have spoken of such things before." Gates turned to Arnold, glaring. "And the lights you see are the Aurora Borealis. It's unusual for them to be seen here in Pennsylvania, I'll grant you, but I'm sure you've seen them up north before. Do not portend omens out of the natural laws of science."

"I have seen them before," said Arnold. Gates had been correct about that. "But your natural laws of science cannot sufficiently explain them for my tastes." It was hard to believe he felt threatened by this man. They had both read the same books, but Gates somehow saw the world differently. Too differently.

Arnold, however, knew better. "And the men will believe what they want to believe. They have faith."

"It is... misplaced," Gates countered. They continued riding through a small ravine where a thin creek flowed. Patches of grass dotted the path, but most of it was brown. The broad-leafed trees surrounding them lay barren, but the forest remained thick. Gates made his way down the fortifications of the Colonial line. Philadelphia lay just over a dozen miles away to the south.

"Have you finished your notes?" Gates asked.

"I just arrived."

"I, myself, have just returned from examining some of the British defenses," Gates said. "It looks like it will be a long night of writing for the both of us."

Arnold shook his head. "I think you may find me out here, underneath the lights." He was not surprised to hear the rumors were true—Gates loved his papers. Seeing the general outside his quarters surprised Arnold, though. The commander was a shrewd tactician, but he often remained so far behind the battle lines, he might as well have been on the moon.

Arnold sighed. It was time to put away the niceties. "General, why am I here, exactly? And why did you recall some of my finest boys last month?"

Gates stopped. A cloud blew out of the horse's nostrils when it snorted in displeasure. It would much rather be in the barn with some fine hay, Arnold guessed.

"Is the majority of the business north of here not yet concluded?"

Arnold sighed. Of course that was rhetorical. Burgoyne had surrendered months ago. As far as Congress was concerned, there was no more war in the north. They were so short-sighted.

Gates continued, "Why would I not seek to strengthen our position here? I recalled Major Morgan and his men because of their expertise."

"You recalled my men because you lost your last engagement. Germantown was a failure. You seek to—" Arnold forced himself to stop. Gates had lost most of his battles, but it was no use pointing that fact out. If he continued... "The British hold Philadelphia," Arnold said instead. He turned his horse so he now faced Gates. "You need my men, but what you really need is me."

"I have no need for such... *accoutrements* in my army," Gates said. His voice deepend into a growl. "The British defenses are formidable, and my mind is set. We have already found a suitable location for winter quarters near an iron depository. Tomorrow, we make for Valley Forge."

"The British are here, now, right in front of us!" Arnold irritation flared. "I have arrived. I am here to fight. Take back this city!" He was not just some decoration on Gates' uniform. His accomplishments were his own. Gates had already tried to take credit for Burgoyne's surrender. Had Gates been present, he probably would've succeeded—

"You have arrived because I've arranged for it."

"I'm here, as you said, because you need the best."

"No, not at all. You're here so that you may answer your inquiries. There are outstanding expenditures and unaccounted receipts. They must be reconciled. Your duties as Northern Commander have interfered with them long enough."

Arnold stopped for a full, silent minute. The lights continued to bounce back and forth in the sky. That wasn't why he was here at all. "I've become a threat to you, haven't I?"

"A threat? Hardly." Gates returned a look of indignation. He moved along the ravine again. Green light bounced off the water in the creek. "I understand you were passed over for promotion in the face of several court-martials. I have successfully petitioned Congress to rectify that... incongruency. John Adams has awarded you your back-seniority, your rightful rank." His voice rose. "Congratulations, *Major General*, on your victory at Saratoga. Your rank is now only surpassed by Charles Lee and myself." Gates' voice went stern. "If I were to see you as a threat, why would I have done that? You simply have other matters to attend to elsewhere. I'm granting you leave to do so."

Arnold remained silent, lost in thought. He did not know why Gates had awarded him his proper rank. But, there was something Arnold did know—Gates' deceitful nature. Arnold decided to test just how full of the Devil Gates was. "Receipts and expenditures will still be here when the war is over. I will stay and offer my assistance here, and when we are through, I would like leave to resume my command in the Northern Department."

Gates let out an exasperated breath, but he remained cool and composed. "That was the expected response. You are as stubborn as you are foolish. You may stay as you like, accompany us upriver to Valley Forge. Make a place for yourself at the camp. But, you will have no men. No one under you. You will have no command or duties. You will be a general without an army."

"I will stay," Arnold said without hesitation. "I will not disappear the same way you cashiered General Schuyler."

"Schuyler? You believe you warrant your name to be spoken in the same breath? Do you not think I could topple you just as easily as I toppled Schuyler? He was a well-connected and respected gentleman. Schuyler? I outmaneuvered Charles Lee. I conquered Congress. There is no one better suited to lead this army than I. If I were your enemy, you would know it." Gates slowed his speech and lowered his voice. "I will have your respect. We will win this war together. Afterwards, we will have a new aristocracy, and I will be its apex. If you do not follow me, then your name will crumble and fade in the wind. If you join me, our names will live long after we are gone."

"I am doing just fine without you, General."

Gates sighed, his breath misting in the chill air. "You look at me as if I am the villain, but there are no villains here. I am the best choice to secure victory. Liberty is a noble purpose, one you are well suited to carry out as my right hand."

So there it was. Arnold smirked inwardly. They had always been enemies. This exchange had made it formal. "I'm glad to hear it, since we'll be spending so much more time together." Arnold spurred his horse. "Good evening, then. I'll accompany you on the morrow as you begin your... retreat." He rode off before Gates could respond.

Arnold wondered if it was beyond reproach to challenge his senior to a duel. That would be the quickest way to end their dispute, but he pressed the thought out of his mind. He had much more urgent matters to consider. Now that he was back with Daniel Morgan, he had old friends to find and plots to scheme. For the foreseeable future, he was stuck here with General Gates—at least until either winter came and went or he found a way to capture Philadelphia on his own.

"I was this close to Washington," Sergeant Martin Stevens said, showing everyone around him with his thumb and index finger spaced thinly apart, just how close to George Washington he had been. They all huddled by the fire. Collins sat to his left and a healing Lieutenant Arntz flanked him on his right. More of his comrades gathered on the far side of the fire. They all huddled under threadbare blankets, but they were the fortunate ones.

"An' you didn' kill 'im?" a voice asked, "You didn' kill that bloodyback bastard?"

"Had I known, I would have," Stevens lied. Killing someone was no easy task, and at the time, there had been no reason to do it.

A moment later, horse hooves hit the hard ground nearby. They all looked up to see a white horse appear out of the forest and into the clearing of their camp. The rider came closer. Stevens recognized him and held back a skeptical frown.

"It's General Arnold," Stevens said. "Everybody up."

"Easy, boys. I'm just on my way to find Colonel Morgan. Do you know where he is?"

"Not directly, sir, but we are his men," Arntz answered. "You are in the right area, at least."

"Good, good." Arnold seemed lost in thought. He hadn't made eye contact with any of them. In fact, it appeared that he was about to ride off when he abruptly looked back and stared directly at Arntz. Arnold asked, "Lieutenant, weren't you with Dearborn's men?"

"Yes, sir, I was. Our units combined shortly after we arrived. Begging your pardon, sir, but Colonel Morgan threw fits. I've never seen him do that before, sir."

Arnold chuckled. "Yes, I suppose that would do it. Gates is an... never mind." Instead of correcting himself or riding off, Arnold surprised them by dismounting. "You," he said. "Sergeant Stevens?"

"Yes, sir."

"I thought that was you. Good shooting. I never got a chance to formally thank you, what with General Burgoyne's surrender and then Gates whisking you boys away." Arnold then did something rather odd, Stevens thought. He sat down on a log by the fire. "Well, go on, sit down. What were you boys discussing?"

They sat. A moment of awkward silence at first hung between them, but Collins broke the quiet, chill air. "We were just talking about Stevens here. He used to ferry goods and people across the Potomac. On more than one occasion, he ferried for George Washington at Mount..."

"Vernon," Stevens offered.

Arnold pursed his lips downward in thought. "Is that so?"

"I met him more than once. But mostly it was his wife, Martha, or Lund Washington, his cousin, who managed the estate. I used to run hogsheads of milled corn and flour and salted herring down the Potomac for them." Stevens also didn't say that he'd spent time as part of the fishing community on the river, hunting in the nearby woods, nor did he mention that he had been there as a means to escape his feelings for Emma. Some things were better suited for silence.

"My sister, Hannah, manages my estate for me in my absence. I'm sure she and Lady Washington would have much in common. Managing a large estate is challenging. Somehow, she makes it look easy."

Stevens said nothing. Having lived a solitary life, he knew nothing of estates outside of working at Mt. Vernon. He hoped his silence did not tip his hat, but he did not know what to say. Arnold seemed distant, as if filing away what he had heard. "I see, well, I did not come here to speak of such matters. In fact, I did not mean to trouble you at all this evening. I was on my way to visit with Colonel Morgan."

"No trouble at all, sir," Arntz said. "We're pleased to have your company."

"Nonsense. No one likes to have their superior around. But, in any case, I have had a most interesting discussion with General Gates just now. I have need to put my receipts in order. And it occurs to me, after crossing paths with you this night, Sergeant, that the fifty dollars for shooting General Fraser is still outstanding."

Arnold went to a saddlebag and retrieved a small, fabric pocketbook. He thumbed through a thin stack of currency, took several bank notes out, stopped and put them back in, then withdrew them once more. He put the money into an envelope and turned back to the men.

Stevens was sure he wasn't supposed to have seen any of that, but the bright green lights revealed many things the darkness was meant to hide.

"I have it for you now," Arnold said.

Collins stepped up beside Stevens and in a low voice said, "This is fantastic. We haven't been paid in months."

Stevens turned to his friend and frowned.

Reluctantly, Stevens took the envelope containing the fifty dollars from Arnold's hands and immediately handed it to Collins. "There. This should go to Emma and the baby. She can purchase a crib or cloth, or whatever is not on her British boycott list."

Collins' mouth dropped open. He gave a ferocious smile. Stevens tried to smile back. Instead, he just stood there in awkward silence with his lips cocked into a dumb grin. Fortunately, this time General Arnold broke the silence.

"A baby?"

"Yes, general, I'm having a baby!" Collins said.

"Well, you're a bloody fool, running out in the field like that to my rescue with a baby on the way," Arnold said. "If it's all the same, I appreciate your efforts very much. I may not be standing here today if it weren't for you," he looked at all of them, "and the bravery of you all."

There was a round of nods and appreciation. Someone added more wood to the fire. It crackled and grew, mimicking the flickering of the sky.

"When is your child expected?" Arnold asked.

"Well, sir, that's the problem," Collins said. "I had been thinking that the baby wouldn't be coming until after my enlistment expired at the end of the year. He's supposed to be born come January. But, a letter said the baby could come sooner." Collins lowered his head. "I would like to be there for that, if the Lord wills it. I'm not breaking my oath and abandoning my brothers here."

"That's a good patriot," Arnold said. "I can tell there is something different about you. You have fire in your heart, and that's why our cause will be triumphant. Still, we are fighting for our families, are we not? We cannot abandon them, either." Arnold took a moment to think. "There may be something I can do for you, Collins. We will wait and see, but there may be something yet. I have need of such men as you, my friend."

He stopped, then looked around and walked over to Lt. Arntz and shook his hand. "Your wound does not go without your country's appreciation." Arnold went around the campfire, personally addressing each man. The action impressed Stevens— and that somehow worried him.

"You have all made my evening. Thank you," Arnold said, then returned to his white horse. "Now, if you'll excuse me—"

A woman screamed. They all turned their heads toward the woods beyond. A moment later, they heard laughter in the woods. Arnold climbed onto his horse. "Stay here. I'll investigate. Good evening to you all." With that, he dashed away into the forest.

Stevens thought about following, but they were on foot, and he would already be there long before they caught up to him. He wasn't sure what type of help they would be. Instead, he sat back down and watched the jumping flames of the fire and the bouncing lights of the sky.

Though he had been impressed with General Arnold's bravado and ability to connect to them, he still felt as if there were something he hadn't said. Stevens thought of himself as a rational creature. The earth shaking and eerie lights in the night sky did not trouble him. But something about General Arnold's arrival tonight filled him with an ominous sensation of things yet to come.

The crowd consisted of mainly Gates' men. He knew because he recognized none of them. Still, they were soldiers, and Arnold had his rank, if nothing else. *What the hell are they up to, anyway?*

Arnold rode through the thick forest of pine and oak. The Aurora Borealis still shone brightly, illuminating his way. Then, he saw the answer. Sitting high on his horse, Arnold could see over the crowd. There, amidst ill-uniformed soldiers, was a Negro woman. She lay on the cold dirt, tied to a tree behind her, her hands raised above her head.

She wore a silk blue dress, which was odd. Her hair was neatly kept and tied back. She wore earrings and silver bracelets that caught the reflection of the green from the night sky.

Her dress was torn, but in what manner it had been ripped, he did not know yet. The dress rode up her legs from her struggles, revealing smooth ebony calves down to her kicking feet. The dress was ripped across her chest too. Her right breast was mostly exposed, prickling in the cold night air. The Negro woman was still youthful, though past the point of being used solely to produce offspring, if she were a slave. No impropriety had appeared to befall her—yet. He could use that to his advantage.

Arnold rode closer. Soldiers lacking jackets, with threadbare shirts and patches of worn leather strapped to their feet, took notice of him and then continued. The young, tall soldier leading them had wild white hair and held a long, stripped branch.

"Where'd ya get that dress," the soldier asked. He drew her attention to the switch. "Did'ya kill your masters? Did'ya slit their throats in their sleep and rob 'em?" He put his face near hers and grabbed her chin in his fingers. "Look at me!"

"Desist," Arnold said.

Nothing.

He raised his voice. "Desist!"

The soldier looked at him, then turned away and struck the Negro woman in the face with the switch. She inhaled sharply as her face twisted left on impact. Her cheek swelled, and blood oozed from an abrasion. Tears ran down her face, the salt surely stinging her wound. But she said nothing.

Arnold tightened his hands on his reigns, his face reddening. It had been a lousy evening, and it was getting worse— none of these people knew who he was. He thought he was past that. He sighed and rode to the white-haired soldier. "You there. What are you doing?" Arnold asked. "Who's in charge here?"

"Me," the youth said with a bit of arrogance. He gave Arnold a careful once-over and saw his rank. It didn't seem to faze him. "General, is it? Who are ya?"

Arnold shot him a glare and took in a heavy breath of cold air. "Major General Benedict Arnold. You may have heard of my victories, or at the very least, have heard tales of my wrath."

The youth went as pale and white as his hair. Bits of green light cast an eerie pallor across the white skin of his face. "Begging a thousand pardons, sir. I did'na know ya. We were just doin' our duty."

"Like hell you were. Now, let's try this again, shall we? Who's in charge?"

"I... I am, sir." The last word came out strong and clear. He turned away. "Hey, boys, this here is Burgoyne's Bane." Hollers and cheers went out. Emboldened by the shift in conversation, he asked, "What'er ya doing down here, sir?"

I have the same question. Instead of answering, he called to the soldier, "Disperse your unit, then answer me. What is this Negro's crime?" Arnold's skin cooled and returned to its normal, dark tone.

The soldier nodded in agreement, then turned to the crowd. "Ya' heard the general. Nothing for your eyes to witness here. Leave, all of ya." The crowd mumbled beneath their breath. "There's still gills of rum yet to drink, so get goin'.'" The crowd of ill-equipped, hungry, and cold soldiers disappeared through thick woods.

"Now, explain," Arnold said. "Who are you?"

"Sergeant Whitehall, sir."

Whitehall, white hair. That one was easy. Arnold filed the name association away. "What happened? Be quick. And speak proper."

"Yes, sir." His voiced slowed. "You see, me and my boys, we found her coming into camp off the Old York Road. Probably sneaking back into the city to tell Howe and Washington all about us," Whitehall said. "We was... *were* trying to find out, we were interrogatin' her when you came upon us."

Arnold sighed. "Did you try just talking to her?"

Whitehall returned a blank stare.

"Cut her down and tie her to the front of my horse. And retrieve her cloak, if she has one." He waited impatiently. "Your duties here are rendered," Arnold said when Whitehall had carried out his instructions.

"Aye, sir."

"And sergeant... If I catch you whipping anyone else again, I'll make sure to have my boys show you how a proper beating is done. Just be sure to bring anyone else you find out on these roads immediately to your superior and let them handle it."

"Yes," His eyes cast downward. "Yes, sir, Your Excellency."

Arnold paused for a moment in thought. "No... have them brought directly to me. I passed the Black Horse Inn on the road down here. You shall find me there. I'll have coin for you if you do."

With a courteous nod, Whitehall walked away.

Arnold had his horse begin a slow step. He made it a few feet when the rope holding the Negro woman went taught. Arnold stopped.

"Move along."

The woman returned a glare and pulled back on the rope with both hands. The horse began to back-step toward her.

Arnold shook his head. He turned and gave her a wry

smile. "Stubborn?"

She remained silent and did not budge. Instead, she wrapped her fur cloak tightly around herself but shivered in the cold nonetheless.

"Very well. You can either walk or be dragged." Arnold started back through the forest in the direction he had originally come. He would have to meet with Daniel Morgan some other time.

Still, she remained standing there. The rope went taught again. Arnold did not wish to drag her. "Would you rather that man beat you again? Do you wish me to recall them?"

Her first step came hesitantly. Subsequent steps were more willing.

"That's good. Thank you."

The pair continued along for some ways through the forest toward the king's road—that would have to be renamed, of course. They passed the time in silence. Arnold had much to mull over. It had been a spectacularly awful night. He realized he didn't want to think about it any longer. Instead, he turned to her. "Your name?"

She didn't respond.

"We can pass the time in silence, or we can converse. Maybe understand each other. I did save you back there, if you remember."

"Abigail."

"Ah, you do speak. And spoken well. You must have some letters or education about you," Arnold said. There was silence. "Whitehall was right about you in one regard—you certainly are a mystery."

"I am no spy."

"That's what all the spies say."

Abigail looked at him with a raised eye.

He laughed. "It was a joke. Are you from the city? Philadelphia?"

"I was."

"Interesting. What were you doing?"

"The new masters in the city, they don't even look at me. They don't even know I'm there. I'm not there to them. So I come and go as I please."

It was Arnold's turn to be confused. "I have heard of freemen, but never a woman who was free. What happened to your masters? You must have had them."

"They were taken away."

"Yes?"

"New masters did not like old masters."

Arnold grinned. *That was one way of putting it.*

"Home?"

"Burned."

And that explained it all. Well, most of it anyway. She could still very well be a spy, but her story was not an uncommon one. As he traveled past Germantown just this afternoon, he saw the remaining hulls of houses, burned and destroyed—all in the name of retaliation. General Howe had not stayed his hand. Apparently, neither had the governor of the city, Colonel George Washington. He expected better from his fellow American.

Usually, burning things down was his job. They said, mimicry was the greatest form of flattery. Arnold turned back to Abigail. He still had many more questions for her. "You consider yourself free?"

"No one troubled me until tonight. Until now it felt..." she seemed at a loss for an unfamiliar word, "...good."

Arnold nodded. He could understand that. "You left the city. Where were you going?"

"Anywhere. That's the point of being free, is it not?"

He winced. Arnold looked back down. He was starting to like her, but once again, he needed to focus on business. Only this time, he had the upper hand. "And the city? How was it when you left?"

She turned her head back sharply. "You want me to spy for you?"

"I may," Arnold said. "I may have other uses for you. I cannot tell as of yet. For now, I simply want to know. Do you return to the city often?"

"As I've said, they don't see me. I enter and leave when I may."

Arnold smiled. He may have found another use for her, one that would benefit him a great deal. There may yet be a way to outmaneuver Gates. If he could find a pipeline into the city, perhaps he could find a weakness. There may be patriots there he could call upon and rally like he had done before the war with the Sons of Liberty. He would find a way to crack the walls of this Jericho and march triumphantly into Philadelphia. And he could do it all here, under Gates' nose. That was the best part yet.

They neared the two-story inn. Smoke poured out of the chimney, warm and inviting. He dismounted, though his left leg protested. He bit his lip in pain, careful not to show it, and grabbed Abigail by the arm. She looked nervous.

"There's going to be a celebration. It has been in the making for weeks," she said. Perhaps she was showing just how useful she could be, but Arnold already knew. "All they're waiting on is for you and your soldiers to move further from the city. Then they'll dance."

Arnold floated now, and ideas of all types filled his thoughts. Instead of entering the building, he sat down on a bench outside it, and sat Abigail beside him. "Do tell me more about this celebration," he said, smiling.

"I'll tell you more when I'm safe and warm."

"Well, until then, let us look out at the lights." He stared skyward. "Aren't they heavenly?"

"They're like nothing I have ever seen."

"What do you think they mean?"

"I don't know, but they fill me with strength, with purpose. They're a sign from God." The answer surprised Arnold. He would've guessed something else. She looked at Arnold and returned the question. "What do you think it means?"

"I don't know, either, but I think it's meant for me." Arnold continued to stare in silent fascination before continuing, "Everything truly significant has come from the heavens."

PART THREE

"Associate yourself with men of good quality if you esteem your own reputation; for 'tis better to be alone than in bad company."—George Washington.

FOURTEEN

Philadelphia, Pennsylvania
December 24th, 1777.

BY now, Benedict Arnold had grown accustomed to having a pistol waved around his face. What made it dangerous this time was that his heart was involved. She stood behind a British officer on the stairwell of her home. From several steps below, he could see past the pistol to her position above him. He could still see her soft morning-blue eyes and short golden hair. It was too late. He had already fallen in love with her...again.

The pistol waved, bringing Arnold's attention back to it. The man holding it from a few steps above him was her suitor. If the weapon was any indication, Captain John Andre didn't seem too pleased to make his acquaintance.

To be fair, Arnold had fallen in love with Ms. Peggy Shippen first, a long time ago, before the captain even stepped foot into Philadelphia. She had been too young then—though she had grown into a young woman now—shapely, soft, and sensual. If he had not married his first wife, Margaret, to seal a business arrangement, he would have waited to marry Ms. Peggy Shippen. He should have.

"Benedict, please, do what Mister Andre says," Peggy said, her voice filled with worry. "Go with him to his headquarters. I don't want to see you hurt." Even now, she was half his age, but Arnold found he would've jumped out a balcony window had she asked it of him. That was the problem. Captain Andre, he could handle; Ms. Shippen, he could not. He should never have snuck into Philadelphia and invited himself into her home. A sense of foreboding doom rose in his chest.

Then, came a knock on the door...

Valley Forge, Pennsylvania
3 Hours Earlier

When Benedict Arnold was a boy, he was always in trouble with the local constabulary. He possessed a mind for mischief and an untamable spirit—he had to fly free. Tonight was no exception. General Gates couldn't keep him chained in camp without anything productive to do. There was a war on. As the sun lay low in the clear, cold, western sky, Arnold and his compatriot finished going over the details of the night's excursion.

"Are you ready, Collins?" Arnold asked. He had thrown a lot at the soldier at once. He wanted to make sure it had all sunk in. They stood outside a small stone-and-mortar home not too far off from a miller's much nicer and larger home, one General Gates had taken over for himself. The Schuykill River ran behind them, and the majority of the winter headquarters of Valley Forge lay to the west.

Christmas Eve was, of course, a cold one. Snow clung to the ground in patches where rain hadn't cut through it. They both wore cloaks. Arnold had loaned Henry Collins one of his. Arnold held a fresh brown package with Hannah's handwriting under his arm and waited on Collins' reply.

"I... think so." Collins looked wide-eyed but also eager. Good. "It's just that when I came by tonight, as instructed, I had no idea—"

"Be ready for anything. Your life can change in an instant."

"Yes, sir," Collins said, seemingly unsure of how best to respond.

Arnold saved him the trouble. "You thought I was going to bring up your wife, your family." Arnold gave a practiced smile. "Relax, dear boy, I have not forgotten. Though I do apologize for getting back to you so late. It's in the works."

"But, my enlistment ends next week, on the thirty-first, sir."

Arnold had prepared for that. "I assure you, after tonight, you'll understand everything. And I promise, you'll want to continue your service."

Collins returned a raised brow but said nothing. He seemed a little more at ease. Also good. Arnold would need someone calm and collected by his side if he were to pull off tonight's plan. He smiled, genuinely this time. Not since Honduras had he felt this alive.

Arnold asked, "I assume you've ridden a horse before?" Collins followed the general around the corner to the stables behind the tavern. A striking black horse waited for Arnold alongside a smaller white horse for Collins. Both were saddled and ready to go. Tavern Negros brushed them down and gave them a last minute snack of oats and hay—commodities already in short supply. He looked at Collins.

"Well... sir," Collins replied, "it's been a long time."

"You'll recall it well enough. Besides, it's only half an hour's journey by horse," though the terrain would be unknown and the light dim under the growing cloud cover. "It's an easy journey. At most, you'll have aches in your legs where you didn't know you had muscles."

The two mounted their respective horses, though a servant had to help Collins. He gave a sheepish grin. Arnold shrugged. It didn't matter, so long as the boy didn't fall off midway on their journey.

They rode down the half-frozen, half-muddy path. Collins remained silent, focusing on controlling his horse. Arnold smiled to himself. This was the easy part as they still rode through the American encampment. Pretty soon, they would be behind British lines.

At the edge of camp, they passed through Aaron Burr's position and left Valley Forge without incident. Burr's men had been expecting them and let them pass with a nod. Then, Arnold left the road and entered the heavy forest. Collins hesitated, but convinced the horse to leave the path.

A while later, Collins stammered out a question. Apparently, the boy had grown comfortable enough in the saddle to focus on riding and talking at the same time. *Unfortunate.*

Collins asked, "Sir, why did we leave the road?"

"We can't just ride into the city, my dear boy, now can we?" A cool breeze caught hold of his words. It gave Arnold pause to think. If they were to win this war, it would be with the sacrifice of the enlisted man. Collins did well. He had perhaps even saved Arnold's life. He reminded himself why he had brought the boy out here in the first place, though he kept that close to his chest. Collins was doing well—at least well enough. Arnold turned back to face him.

"Well, no. I knew that," Collins said from behind a sheepish frown. He tried to catch up to Arnold, but the horse moved faster than expected and slipped on a piece of ice. Collins lost his balance and slowed the horse, which stopped completely. Collins kept going and nearly fell from his saddle. He recovered, and Collins returned to his normal gait and distance from Arnold and continued his thought. "What I meant was, I assumed we would leave the road closer to the city."

Arnold faced forward once more, but raised his voice. "Remember, we're following Abigail's route and map. She has crossed through the British fortifications in and out of the city many times. The path she laid out for us is the route we'll take in."

On her first few forays into the city as part of Arnold's spy network, she alerted Sergeant Whitehall, who in turn alerted Arnold. Now that they were entrenched at Valley Forge, Abigail met with Burr first before being brought to Arnold.

Their meetings were... intense. Arnold didn't know if she enjoyed it, but she allowed the encounters to happen. Afterwards, she told him what she knew, and he gave her coin. Then, she was off again. Maybe she enjoyed the freedom he gave her. Maybe she was plotting to kill him. Arnold didn't think so. He was the best thing to happen to the woman.

It had taken a while to contact patriots still living inside the city. First, Arnold had Abigail contact known acquaintances. Through them, he eventually discovered there was indeed a Sons of Liberty association operating inside the city. After several weeks, Arnold contacted them. All they lacked before had been leadership and coordination from the outside. Arnold was more than happy to provide both.

Abigail also explained what she knew of tonight's ball, to take place right after Christmas services, more of a changing of the guard and less a Christmas celebration, but it was extravagant— entirely propaganda to show their strength. While the Americans remained freezing and hungry, the British celebrated, holed up, safe and cozy, in the American city. Arnold wanted to see for himself.

So here they were.

Collins interrupted his thoughts. "What if it's a trap? What if she's setting us up for capture?"

Then tonight's excursion will come to an abrupt conclusion. Arnold shook his head. Most probably, they would be hung as spies. Arnold was too dangerous to be kept alive. At the very least, they would languish in deplorable conditions onboard a British prison ship where they would wish for a death that came all too slow. But he said none of that. "We'll be treated well as hostages until a suitable trade is arranged. Then, we'll be paroled and sent on our way. Happens all the time. Why, General Charles Lee was captured and paroled." Arnold also didn't tell him his own aide, Oswald, had been captured and released. But neither of them had been sneaking into an enemy stronghold.

Collins rubbed his hand around the front of his neck in a nervous gesture.

"Relax. It won't happen so close to our own lines. We're still safe. For the moment." Collins sighed with relief. "We'll probably be captured closer to the city, wouldn't you say?" He envisioned Collins jerking back in surprise. Arnold smiled again.

As they rode, they passed the remains of homes among the woods, each one blackened, charred, and nothing but the strongest corner of the structure or its chimney remained.

"What happened here?" Collins asked, his tone hushed and reverent.

"Retaliation." Arnold replied. "For every attack on the British while Philadelphia laid besieged, they destroyed another home. It's the work of our Virginian, Washington, as far as I can tell. It has to be." He had no evidence to support that, but he went off rumors and his own gut feeling. *That traitor.*

Before long, they reach their old lines, the ones Gates vacated and retreated from almost a month earlier. Most of their entrenchments remained. Arnold sighed. They had given up a valuable position. Gates paid more heed to the landowners paying for the war and losing their homes to the British than to the enlisted men and officers losing their lives.

They passed the place he first met Abigail, then the two rode on in contemplation, following her directions. Ten minutes later, they reached the Schuylkill River. Arnold stopped and studied the crude map. Abigail had no letters. She drew and explained things to him that he wrote down, but otherwise, this was all he had to go on. He looked around and edged his black horse down to the edge of the bank. The river cut across the forest, a scar on the land.

"Sir?" Collins asked. "How are we supposed to cross?"

"There's a way." Arnold didn't know either. He moved downstream at the edge of the river. He didn't think it shallow enough to ford. There had to be a crossing somewhere, but he also knew that no visible bridge would still stand.

Collins sat still, perhaps glad for the chance. But, then he said, "Look," and pointed to the edge of the water, upstream from Arnold. "There. It looks like part of a wagon wheel."

Arnold rode to examine it closer. When he arrived, he saw what appeared to be the remains of a wagon, washed away by the river. But, on the edge of the bank lay two stones placed a wagons-width apart, marking the crossing. Arnold smiled. The whole thing was invisible unless you knew where to look or stumbled upon it by accident as Abigail had done. "Right you are. Good eye."

Arnold prodded his horse into the river, toward the first wagon. As expected, he found a series of them submerged, flattened on top, and hitched together to form a bridge. Both sides were known to do this, but he guessed the British placed this one for small foraging expeditions. The British always relied too much on natural barriers instead of manpower. But, the hidden bridge and lack of sentries at this crossing suited his purposes.

Collins followed, though fear struck his face as his horse sank to its knees as it forded the river. He made it across, threatening to spill over in half a dozen places. It amused and worried Arnold at the same time. But they proceeded without incident and traveled some distance further into thick forests, approaching the city itself.

Here, the British defenses would naturally be thinner, but no less deadly. There were no longer any manned redoubts to worry about, just foot patrols, but they could still be spotted. Abigail was a Negro and a woman, not usually worth a second look. They were not. To minimize their chances of being caught, they had to walk from there.

Arnold dismounted in a way to cause the least amount of pain in his leg. The bruises were healing, but the muscles remained stiff and weak, particularly in the cold. At least it would eventually heal, but it still took some effort to hide the pain from Collins.

Collins needed no help in dismounting—he let gravity do the work and fell from the saddle. With an unfortunately loud crunch into snow-covered grass, he hit the ground and shortly thereafter arrived at Arnold's side.

"I'll tie the horses. Then I'll change," Arnold said. "Wait here, and stay low. Keep a watch out. From here on, you'll need to keep quiet. Take this." He handed Collins a spare pistol from his saddlebag, along with a crimson cockade. Collins fastened it onto his cloak, disguising himself as a loyalist.

Arnold had an ulterior motive for going into the city tonight—several, in fact, none of which he told Collins. He'd find out soon enough. Arnold removed his thick grey cloak. A chill went through both his brown jacket and waistcoat, then through his bones. Arnold shivered, but removed them both anyway. He shivered again, hung his jacket over a branch, and retrieved the package Hannah had sent him.

Arnold always thought he looked better in red. Inside the package was his old, worn, red coat, the one he wore throughout the Ticonderoga Expedition, the same one he had worn when he met General Schuyler. It felt like so long ago. The jacket had been tailored to him, the gold trimmings and circular patterns still bright and striking. It fit more snugly than it had before. He tugged on the edges, but it did not stretch. He frowned. It would have to do.

Next, he put his large grey cloak back on. Of course, with his darker skin, Arnold should have thought to go as a Hessian. That might have worked better, but there was no time for that now. He had a ball to attend.

Finished, he signaled to Collins, and the two of them crept from the forest at the city's edge into the city itself. If approached by British sentries here, he may or may not be challenged to provide a password, one that he would not have. If this was a trap, if Abigail had set him up, it would be sprung here. When they reached the lit city sidewalks, they would be safe.

Here, anonymity would aide them. Only a few British officers would recognize Arnold, and Collins was just another loyalist. There were no canvas portraits of Arnold, and he had not had his picture in the paper in Philadelphia. He sighed at that. Besides, no one would be looking for him on the shadowy cobblestone steps of the city. If approached by a talkative redcoat wishing to chat, Arnold knew he could indulge them with idle conversation.

Thick clouds filled the sky, and the moon let out slivers of light in between them. Arnold couldn't pick out footfalls or voices of anyone approaching from the din of nighttime noise. So he walked carefully, ready to react to any trap or ill-timed sentry.

Their own steps sounded loud and dangerous. Arnold found sweat building underneath his gloves. His boots snapped the occasional twig and crunched on the rarer dry leaf. Each step felt like a crawl as the pair made their way to the relative safety of the street that seemed just out of reach.

The muddy streets were empty here, and the few hovels that were not burned or destroyed sat lifeless in the dark. Further down the road, shuttered windows let out a bit of candlelight. The realization that other people were close by filled his veins with a cold, flowing ice that melted away as resolve replaced alarm. He hoped Collins felt the same transformation.

When they made it, Collins blew out a deep breath. Arnold almost chuckled. They made their way down the muddy road, then turned down the first cobblestone street they met.

Here, the streets had names. More people were out of their homes and about the city walks. As they turned another corner, heading south toward the center of town, a couple out for a late stroll passed them by: an elderly gentleman, wearing a sensible dark brown jacket and tan waistcoat with a cloak like Arnold's. He escorted a younger, rosy-cheeked lady in a fur coat and a gaudy pink gown with ruffles. Her gown's outer layer was raised to reveal an equally hideous petticoat underneath. Neither took notice of them as they walked by in quiet conversation.

He forced himself to keep walking and not to look back at Collins. He didn't want to give anything away or to accidentally cause Collins undue alarm. Their steps faded, and Arnold's heart resumed beating. He grabbed Collins by the arm. "Are you all right?"

"I... think so, sir." Collins, surprisingly, had strength in his gait. He seemed just as calm as Arnold, maybe calmer. Perhaps because he didn't know the full circumstances of their danger, nor did he know all the exciting things they were about to do. Ignorance was bliss. "My heart has never beaten so fast, but I think I feel good. I don't know why."

"It's the patriotic blood in you, boy," Arnold replied. "Does marvelous wonders."

Arnold came to a street he recognized and turned down it. From here, he could make his way to Walnut Street, then cut across to High Street, the artery of the city. Tents and shops and market corners lined the road. There were a few steep hills in the city, and most of it sloped gently down to the Delaware River. It was here he would find what he sought.

As the pair continued, he took casual note of his surroundings, careful to avoid looking too conspicuous but mindful of things that might be important later. Here, closer to the heart of town, lamps illuminated the walks. All of the four-sided Franklin streetlamps burned. This was the first city in America to adopt street lighting. The Franklin fellow had his hands in many pots. That reminded Arnold, he still owed Ben money for supplies purchased in defense of the north.

Shadows flickered against the cobbled pavement and on the doors of apothecaries and clothing boutiques. Some businesses, he noted, were boarded or left vacant with shattered windows and rubbish strewn about. He assumed those stores belonged to patriots. *Shameful.*

From here, he could see the outline of the newly-named Independence Hall. Everyone appeared to head toward it. Arnold and Collins joined them along the busying street. As they approached, they received a few wayward looks from British soldiers and a few from ladies taking a turn in the cold evening with their suitors. Fortunately, nobody glanced at them more than once.

Further down High Street, smoke from a large fire and the sound of a large orchestra at play filled the air. The sounds and smells cut through the chill night and broke all pretense of an occupied city.

"What's going on?" Collins didn't know about the celebration.

Arnold lowered his voice to a whisper. "While you starve, they celebrate. See what they would have you suffer while they remain in your capital?" Arnold gestured ahead. "Come, let's take a closer look."

Collins seemed hesitant, but followed.

It seemed as if every resident in the city gathered at the small square as if no war were going on around them. People tended to respond to crises by sticking to routines, Arnold knew, but this was beyond ridiculous. To them, this was simply another Christmas Eve.

Arnold hung his head in disgust and walked up the front steps of a large red brick home that might have belonged to Franklin. He didn't know, but he noted that it wasn't burned down. Even the British liked big Ben. A holly wreath decorated the door.

Collins stayed on the street. From the top steps, Arnold could see over the crowd into an expansive canvas pavilion set up in the square in front of them. It was too large and loud of a ball to be held inside a home, even on a dark, cold Christmas Eve. Decorations hung throughout. Near the center of the square stood a large Christmas tree, trimmed with golden chains, angels, and red balls.

At one end of the square roared a great bonfire. Arnold was too far away to feel the warmth, but he could hear the crackle of wide, green logs even at this distance. The orchestra broke into, "Adeste Fideles". *Oh, the irony. Come, all ye faithful.*

At the other end was a stage and podium. People filled the stage: soldiers in uniform Arnold wanted to avoid. Standing at the podium was someone Arnold thought he recognized, wearing the traditional wig, red jacket, and buffing of the King's Foot.

Everyone in the Colonies knew George Washington. That was the price of being a British puppet, the price of getting a crude but recognizable, print of your face in the papers and publishing your campaign journals. Washington was tall, muscular, and commanding. He had a rough face, whittled away from childhood pox and carved with middle-age and a pronounced lip due to dentures that didn't quite fit. Rock candy had damaged his teeth. And of course, there was the infamous red sash he had worn for over twenty years given to him by General Braddock. *Everyone* knew Washington. *That bloody traitor.*

Washington accepted bursts of applause as he continued his speech. Arnold was curious but too far away to hear. So, he left the height of the stairs and made his way to Collins.

"Come on, I'm getting closer." He grabbed Collins by the cloak and pulled him into the crowd of civilians.

"What? No," Collins protested.

The boy forgot his formalities. Understandable, but it could get them killed. With a purposeful edge in his voice, he faced Collins, whispering into his ear, "Listen to me. You must do exactly as I say. You are my aide. I am a major. We went over this. Keep yourself composed, and you'll be fine." Arnold took a step back and said a bit louder, "I swear on the king's crown." The last part was a joke, but Collins did not return a smile.

They squeezed their way through the crowd of people. Ladies wore thick brown furs over evening dresses of proper yellows and greens. Tight bodices tucked away unflattering bits and popped out those that were, much to Arnold's approval. He had to stop himself from staring on several occasions.

The majority of the men wore uniforms. Those who didn't, the Philadelphia loyalists, whom Arnold despised, wore fine linen waistcoats of brown or black with intricate stitching. They all wore English wigs. No one wore blue.

Finally, they reached a place just outside the pavilion where Washington's words carried. He was well into his speech by this time, but Arnold got the meaning of it. Most of it had to do with giving thanks, the usual fluff all public servants used when they had nothing to say.

Washington seemed the perfect mixture of contradiction, both authority and servant, brooding and charismatic. Arnold had the impression that Washington both despised and loved this evening's affair. Finally, Washington ended with the words, "Our Country, England, will stand united with its American brothers." Applause once more. Fittingly, the orchestra broke into a celebratory tune, one Arnold didn't recognize. The formalities finished, the crowd on the podium dispersed, heading off-stage into the pavilion below for refreshments and dance.

No one looked at Arnold or Collins as they breezed right in. Majors were too common to be noteworthy. He turned to see how Collins fared. He looked warm and sweaty, but one could pass it off from the large bonfire that emanated heat in and around the tent.

Plenty of other people of note surrounded them, far more significant than Washington. But for some reason, his eyes kept drifting back. He watched as the Virginian descended the podium. Arnold kept his distance but locked both eyes onto him. Washington shared words with everyone along his path and before Arnold knew it, Washington was a bare twenty feet from him.

Washington looked up, right at him, and stared. Arnold couldn't be sure what that meant. The uncertainty scared him. He doubted Washington even knew his name. In any case, the general seemed to be heading straight for him. Arnold's heart stopped, and he swallowed hard. It was time to leave, but to do so at this moment would be obvious. Washington continued his approach.

Then, the orchestra struck back up. It was a waltz, a rather new and scandalous dance, one that Arnold knew very well. Washington stopped. He took something out of his breast pocket, examined it, and then went in search of someone. A moment later, he plucked a lovely lady from the crowd. Apparently, the governor was very familiar with the waltz, too.

But the girl, the one Washington had his arm around... she looked familiar.

Arnold's face grew red at the thought of Washington's hands all over her, even if Arnold strained to place her face. She seemed older than the person he remembered, which recalled a memory from a long time ago. The daughter of Edward—

Someone tapped him on the shoulder. *How rude.*

"Excuse me, sir?" Collins said. Irritation colored his voice. "Major?"

"Yes?" Arnold faced him and was surprised to see Collins standing next to someone in uniform.

"This gentleman would like to address you, sir."

Arnold had to mentally shake his head clear and adjust to this new threat. Fortunately, Collins had been present to intervene. *Well done.* The address was a bit off, but anything worse just then would've gotten them hung. He took success wherever he could find it.

"Merry Christmas, sir. Chilly weather we are having tonight, yes?"

Arnold kept his composure. He made up for inward fear with an outward display of bravado. He looked back over at Washington and thought about his response. Then, turning back, he said with a raised voice, "It certainly is stiff."

The young officer went on, ignoring the strange reply, barely pausing. "Pardon me for asking, but do you know where I might find a General Westburg?"

Arnold squinted at the lieutenant, much younger than himself. He was pale, English, and well... English. They all bloody looked alike in uniform. He supposed that was the point. Then, he replied, with some intentional annoyance lining his voice, "I have no idea where you can find General Westburg." He looked over at his aide. "Collins, do you know?"

"Sir, I do not."

"Indeed. There you are, Lieutenant. Cheers." Arnold took a measured look at the dance, plotting his next move. Washington had drifted closer.

"That's quite all right," the young lieutenant said, "because General Westburg does not exist."

Arnold frowned. If that was some sort of code, some sort of test, he doubted very much he passed. All he could do now was to pass it off casually and see where the evening took him. He looked at Collins, nodded with encouragement, and plunged himself into the dance, but not before he said, "And that's precisely the reason why I have no idea where he is."

A moment later, he was face to face with Colonel Washington.

"Your Governorship, may I please cut in?"

Washington turned a perplexed brow, but recovered. "Of course."

It wouldn't matter if Washington gave any approval or not. By the time the dancers shifted, the lady was in Arnold's arms and Washington was left standing alone. The transition wasn't as smooth as Arnold would've liked, but the benefit of these aristocrats was that they were too gentlemanly to protest. In any case, before long, Washington was in hand with another pretty damsel.

Arnold kept a close eye on Washington, the lieutenant, and Collins while he waltzed with his partner. He was in the belly of the beast and his heart raced—for more than one reason.

"Mister Arnold? Is that you?" His dancing partner asked with a soft voice, though it held an edge. "I know you!" Her eyes widened, and she smiled in surprise.

Her eyes triggered Arnold's recognition. Even still, his jaw fell, his knees weakened, and his heart beat out a song. There, in front of him, was indeed Peggy Shippen, his first love.

Arnold looked Peggy over. She was beautiful. Her morning-blue eyes were her best feature. Her breasts, pushed together by her tightly laced bodice, exposed a pleasant display of cleavage. Her green silk dress flowed elegantly from her plunging neckline to the floor of the pavilion. Arnold was a tall man and she was shorter than most women. She made him feel large and powerful.

"Peggy."

"It is you," she gasped. "What brings you to back to Philadelphia? I thought you were in Hartford. Wait... You don't fight with the British, do you? Maybe I am just being forgetful. But I thought you had something to do with Saratoga?"

Even from an early age, her father engaged his children with politics and education. Even the girls received an education, a position he was not unfavorably disposed toward. The new republic would need strong, educated mothers to raise its sons. Therefore, he had found early on that he could talk intelligently with her.

He also found himself being more open and honest than he should have. "I have my beliefs and I fight for them." Arnold changed the subject before he revealed too much. He asked her, "What about your father? What of his beliefs?" Arnold winced. *That was incredibly daft to ask.*

"The rebels have done nothing for my father. You know what they do to patriots in the city. How many homes have you seen torched? He has done what he needs to survive."

Cowardice. But the sins of the father were not hers. "And you, what do you do to survive?"

"I do not need to survive. I flourish."

Indeed. She was a woman after his own heart.

"And is the rest of your dance card empty?" Arnold asked as they continued their dance.

"What type of question is that from a gentleman?" Peggy took a step back. Immediately, he felt the loss of her body heat. It panged him that he had hurt her. "Are you not married?"

Arnold frowned and answered as best he could with a smile. "Come now, you know I am no gentleman." Then, with a lowered voice, he continued, "Margaret passed on, almost eighteen months ago."

"I am sorry. She was a nice woman. I was happy for you." Peggy reached in to pull him closer, and her hand grasped his more tightly. They shared a long moment in each other's eyes— then she abruptly recoiled.

He wasn't sure if it was because she saw through his ruse, or if he had been too aggressive, or if it was something else. But Peggy tensed and stepped back once more. "Yes, I have been escorted here by someone. John Andre. He's discussing politics with men outside the tent. He doesn't yet know I could talk his ear off."

"Or maybe that is exactly why he is off somewhere else?"

"Ouch. You tease." Peggy smiled. "Do you know him? You might have served with him."

Arnold didn't know the name. "Anyone would be a fool to leave your side."

"You are sweet, but he's a busy man. He's the one who organized this whole *mischianza*. He did a lovely job." Then, she gave a long pause. After a deep breath, she confessed, "We are engaged to be wed." She stopped once more, unsure of whether to continue, then said, "It's not official. Actually, I am not supposed to know, but I do. You can't keep a secret from me." Then she stopped dancing and stared at him. "Like you. There is something about you and the fact that I cannot place it concerns me. You seem so perfectly suited here, yet out of place at the same time."

"Maybe it is just that I am so struck by you. You look amazing."

The orchestra stopped. Peggy's eyes shut, and an icy wind blew through the pavilion. Her pale soft shoulders grew cold. Her golden hair stopped bouncing. She looked at him, through him. She knew, but she didn't seem to know how to respond. Maybe her feelings were torn. "Please, I am very cold and a little tired. I am going to go now." She curtseyed in preparation to taking her leave. "Thank you for a wonderful dance. It was so good to see you again." With that, she walked out of his life once more.

Now it was Arnold's turn to stand awkwardly alone. He politely begged the pardon of those around him and took a few steps away, playing it off as a matter of course. Then, the orchestra struck up a more modest minuet.

Shortly, he returned to Collins. Collins didn't waste any time and said, somewhat frantically, "We've got to go. Our friend is bringing company, and I'm pretty sure it's not more women for you to socialize with."

Arnold turned sharply. "Emboldened, are we?"

"A little. This gets the blood going. I apologize, sir, it's just that—"

"Don't be," Arnold said. "I knew I liked you."

Collins nodded politely and smiled.

People inside the pavilion now studied them. Other redcoats were on their second and third glances. Peggy had departed, perhaps to retrieve her suitor. Time for them to exit the stage while they still could.

Now that he had his pleasure, it was time for business.

FIFTEEN

Philadelphia, Pennsylvania
December 24ᵗʰ, 1777.

BENEDICT Arnold couldn't help but be a little displeased with how his reunion with Ms. Shippen had ended. There was something there, he thought, something unresolved. He wanted desperately to know what it was.

This was neither the time nor place. He and Collins had just left the pavilion tent. Of course, he stopped by the buffet table to stuff a crab cake in his mouth and drain a glass of sherry. He offered one to Collins, who politely refused with a somewhat panic-stricken expression, so Arnold stuffed the second one in his mouth as well before moving on.

He tightened his cloak against the cruel winter outside the relative warmth of the pavilion, and Collins did the same. Arnold had no idea how the patriots in threadbare shirts, lacking proper shoes and blankets, managed in Valley Forge. Winter promised to be brutal. Tonight, black clouds threatened icy rain.

Arnold's feet kept drifting toward the Shippen townhome on Society Hill near the Delaware. The fact that his next destination was nearby didn't help as he wasn't exactly sure where. They stopped some distance from the celebration surrounding Independence Hall. He turned to Collins, hoping his confusion did not read on his face.

"Where are we going, sir?"

Arnold answered with a question of his own. "Have you ever been to this city before?"

Collins shook his head. "Just twice, on my way from Annapolis to New York, there and back."

Arnold nodded in reflection. "When the war is over, go out and travel, my dear boy, live life, show your child the wonders of the world. So often people stick to their routines and corners; they forget the world around them. What a difference it would make if we were not ignorant of our own neighbors."

Collins looked confused. "I don't follow."

"The British," Arnold clarified. "They ignored us for so long, and we forgot about them. We grew apart because we kept to ourselves."

Maybe that was why Peggy withdrew. They had lost sight of each other. They had become strangers. He hoped he could bridge their connection from the past and rekindle that flame. He looked at the street in front of him and recovered his bearings... he hoped. "This way," he called to Collins.

A while later, they came to what appeared to be an abandoned home. He compared the address with the one from memory—Abigail had given it to him earlier this week where she often left or retrieved letters. Now that he was here, however, he had no idea what to expect.

It could be a trap. There could be a hundred soldiers inside. Or, he could be meeting with someone from the Sons of Liberty. There was too much risk involved. "Shall we?"

The pair reached the front door. Arnold circled the grounds twice, thankful the light blue building constructed from wood—not stone—was detached from its neighbors, but barely. He saw nothing unusual or suspicious. He returned to Collins, who stood on guard.

"Now what?" Collins asked. "Do we knock?"

Arnold cocked his head. "Knock? Don't be daft. If we're going to be spies, we might as well act the part."

"Spies? You didn't say anything about being spies!"

"And yet, here we are."

"I don't want to be a spy. What on Earth did you bring me here for?"

"I needed the company." And a good lookout; someone to watch his back. Someone Arnold could trust. Collins threw his hands in the air as if resigned to his fate.

Arnold undid the latch to the door, and pulled it outward. It creaked as he opened it, revealing a dark interior. So far, nothing happened. "Stay here. Keep watch." Collins nodded, and Arnold stepped inside the dark home to whatever awaited him.

Despite a calm, still moment, Arnold's eyes did not adjust to the darkness. He saw vague outlines of what should be furniture—a table, several chairs, a fireplace and mantle. The room was bare, except some candles and a few leftovers from previous occupants. A torn portrait hung on a wall in a cheap wooden frame.

He made his way to the table but found it empty. He checked again to make sure, running his gloved hand over the surface. Nothing. He didn't want to risk lighting a candle. The house appeared vacant, but light risked waking any refugee inside or alerting anyone paying attention outside.

After another moment of stumbling in the dark, Arnold realized he had no choice. He made for the mantle, stubbing his toe on the brick fireplace floor. He ran his hand over the mantle, stumbling first across a candle and then a peculiar steel and flint striker resembling a pair of shears. The strikers he used at home were made from polished brass and fine wood, shaped more like a pistol.

It took a moment to get the apparatus to flick correctly. Then he took a piece of tinder and held it under the striker. Sparks flew and caught on the cloth. Arnold used that to light the candle on the mantelpiece. A lot of work for one candle. It was so much easier to always have something burning.

Arnold looked away from the candle, lest the small flame blind him. He went to work, searching the house, every corner, dusting away every cobweb. He searched everywhere twice, the second time with the candle in hand. He came up empty. Arnold's heart raced. He was starting to believe this might indeed be a trap.

The door opened, and a gust of cold wind threatened to extinguish the candle. Collins stepped in and shut the door behind him, latching it from the inside. Arnold took a deep breath and calmed his nerves.

"Collins, what in blazes are you—"

"Did you find what you're looking for?" He was cold. His cheeks burned red. Arnold forgave him the slight. The truth was, he could use an extra pair of eyes.

"An envelope, large." He motioned with his hands to show a width of about six inches apart. "I cannot ascertain its whereabouts."

"How obvious should it be for us to find it? I mean, is it supposed to be hidden?"

"I've looked around the room, and I've come up empty. So if it's here, it's not for wandering eyes. See for yourself."

Collins circled the room. Arnold rested against the fireplace mantel.

"I'm sorry, sir. I see nothing."

"Hmm. Indeed," Arnold said, resignation in voice. "Then we're done here, I'm afraid."

"Sir, have you checked for loose bricks?" Collins asked, pointing at the fireplace.

"Twice."

"If it's not there," Collins said, also with resignation in his voice, "then of course it's not in the fireplace cupboard."

"Fireplace cupboard?"

"The cupboard beneath the floor beside the fireplace. For storage." Collins motioned to the floor beneath Arnold's right foot.

Arnold looked back in surprise. He had never heard of such a thing. He bent down and pulled the board free, revealing a wooden interior. There it was, a brown envelope.

"How did you know about the cupboard?"

"We had one built when I had a brick fireplace like this one put in."

"You had money for that?"

He wrinkled his nose. "The fireplace was expensive; the cupboard was not. And it was practical. Nevertheless, it's surprising how quickly money disappears."

Arnold cast his eyes down at an empty bottle of rum on the fireplace mantle, lost in a memory. "You have no idea," Arnold said. "No matter how much you have, you'll always manage ways to squander it."

He took out the pages, not bothering to shield them from Collins' eyes. As he expected, the papers were blank.

"There's nothing there," Collins said, clearly confused.

"Invisible ink, and a damned waste of time. What spymaster, upon seeing this, wouldn't apply the correct medicine to reveal its contents? I would never bother to waste my time." He almost said that spies were cowards, sulking in the streets rather than taking a torch to the city, but he stopped himself. They may also prove quite useful. Arnold shoved the papers back in the envelope and tucked it away in his left boot. He would have to determine how useful they were later.

But first, he had to see Peggy again.

"What are we doing now?" Collins asked. They left the vacant house after extinguishing the candle. The wind blew as they exited, and a few drops of rain splashed on the cobblestone walks before them.

"One more errand." They headed south, toward the rushing sounds of the Delaware.

By the time they reached Fourth Street South, the light rain fell with a little more strength. Before long, it would become a downpour. Arnold smiled. Washington's celebration would end prematurely.

The Shippen family didn't actually live in Philadelphia, but because of Edward's posting as judge and mayor, they owned a townhouse in the finest part of the city. The two-story home was in the standard red brick, featuring the same white wood trimming around its windows and door that graced every home in the neighborhood. It stood in the middle of the row, nestled between other houses of similar elegance. Arnold would never have found it in the dark if it weren't for its defining feature: its half-dozen, low, thin steps leading to the door, announcing to the tax collector that this home belonged to the wealthiest family on the block.

When they reached the bottom of the steps, Arnold turned to Collins. "I need you to stay here. It's too dangerous to go inside."

"Where are we?"

"The girl I was dancing with?"

"Yes, I recall. I was left with not so pleasant company."

Arnold ignored the last comment. "This is her house. I'm going inside to pay her a visit."

"Her home? Going inside? Are you—" Collins' voice cut off, but his raised eyes and outstretched palms completed the thought.

"Of course. I thought that was rather obvious by now." Arnold gave a sly wink. "I should have you speak with Eleazer. The stories he could tell. All exaggerations, of course."

Collins shook his head, but a trace of a smile escaped him.

"So, please, stay here."

"Won't that look suspicious?"

Arnold considered it. "I won't be long. If I'm not back in fifteen minutes, give a good knock on the door, would you?" He smiled and turned away before Collins could respond and started down the long row of townhomes toward the rear of the building.

Arnold was breathing heavily by the time he reached the end of the street. He still had to turn the corner and head the same distance back the way he had come down the alley behind the homes. He was getting old, his thirty-seventh birthday just over a fortnight away. Perhaps he should've asked Collins for more than fifteen minutes.

Along the way, he chastised himself for not counting homes so he would know which one belonged to the Shippens. Fortunately, their home had a second story balcony on which he had discussed business propositions with Edward over the years. He looked up at the row of townhomes and breathed in a sigh of relief. None of the others had one.

When he reached their home, he saw a flicker of light from the furthermost left window upstairs on the same side of the building with rising smoke from a chimney. Peggy had indeed made it back.

He eyed the balcony and white lattice-work, laced with dying, frostbitten ivy, and judged it an easy climb. His left leg protested, and Arnold found himself out of breath by the time he reached the top, but he reached the wooden railing and pulled himself over. He stayed there for a moment, letting his sweat dissipate in the cold, soft, rain, shaking his cloak off a moment later. He ran his hands down his uniform, composing himself and then tested the large-windowed doors leading inside. The latch opened. After all, who secured the door on the second story?

The door opened outward, creaking as it went. Arnold winced. Eventually, the doors opened wide enough for him to slip through. He stood and slid past the door, but not before his waist hit it, causing the hinges to squeak again. He frowned a little, but otherwise froze. He took a quick moment of complete stillness. Once confident he had not been discovered, he stepped fully inside. Small drops of rain plinked against the glass.

Darkness shrouded the home, even with its many long windows. The curtains had not been drawn for the night. He occupied a spot on the upstairs hallway, overlooking the front door. To his right was the stairwell that led to it. To either side were doors leading to different rooms. Arnold followed the flickering light coming from beneath the closed mahogany door to his left.

Arnold had not heard anything yet—no voices, no creaking of the floorboards. The house was silent. Then, there was a loud cry, a shrill gasp of excitement from a girl which echoed through the door and filled the upstairs hallway. She was... giddy, her voice full of mirth, which was joined with that of another woman. They laughed. Then came the distinct low tone of a male voice.

The male voice was not her father's. This would not do. Without a second thought, he burst through the door.

"What on God's green Earth?" Captain John Andre wore an expected look of alarm. It was fun to see, nevertheless. He knelt with a gold and garnet ring held out in a white-gloved hand. Peggy and her sister, Elizabeth, sat holding hands on a teal, velvet-backed sofa. The two girls looked up. Elizabeth smiled, but Peggy seemed annoyed.

"Proposing to Elizabeth?" Arnold said to the stranger on one knee. Then, he winked at Peggy and slid his voice into a sarcastic octave. "She is the eldest, you realize. Therefore, you couldn't possibly be seeking Peggy's hand, could you?"

"What... What is the meaning of this?" Andre stammered. He hid the ring in his pocket. "Why are you here? Wait. Who are you?"

Arnold walked around the room as if it were his, looking over the lavish decorations. The fireplace was bright and hot, and candlelight danced on brass sconces and candelabras throughout the room. "Is that anyway to address a superior officer, Captain?" He came to a large cabinet filled with liquor bottles. He picked out one he had shared with Edward before and swirled the reddish liquid around inside, then casually poured it into several small crystal glasses.

"Mr. Arnold, what are you doing here?" Peggy asked. The fire swirled shadows and light across her chest and shoulders in a seductive dance. Arnold's skin crawled.

He walked over to the girls. Elizabeth took the drink offered by Arnold with a quizzical expression. While she was older and also attractive, she was not Peggy. "I saw the Captain here had the unfortunate displeasure of being outnumbered by two women to his one. I sought to remedy the disadvantage."

"Are you implying I was amidst anything improper or deceitful?" Andre was fully dressed in his uniform, from white wig to polished black boots. His left hand rested on his prop of an officer's sword.

"If it passes your English code of honor, then it is certainly chivalrous, I'm sure."

"My English—" Andre looked Arnold over. Confusion crept into his eyes. "Major or not, I could have you brought up on charges for slander." Andre turned his back on Peggy and asked, "Who are you?"

Arnold handed Peggy a drink, ignoring Andre for the moment. Peggy took it, her fingers accidentally touching his, sparking a smile on her face. Arnold returned the smile, then pulled himself away, turning and handing Andre a glass. If the soldier held a drink in his hand, he couldn't hold a weapon. But, Andre declined. "What is your regiment, Major? Where is your—"

"Mr. Arnold is no Major, John," Peggy said.

The captain looked over to Peggy for answers, the confusion he held burning into anger, his face turning red.

Peggy explained, "This is Benedict Arnold. We first met here in this very room several years ago. He was enamored of me and I of him, though Father thought I was still too young, and Elizabeth had not yet garnered the attention of her cousin. Otherwise, Father would have married us off."

"As your father would say," Arnold downed Andre's rejected glass, "guilty as charged."

Peggy and Elizabeth chuckled, as if this were part of some elaborate, inside joke.

Captain John Andre, though, did not laugh. Instead, he pulled an officer's flintlock from inside his waistcoat and pointed it toward Arnold, his face now flushed in anger and perhaps some embarrassment. He said, to Arnold's astonishment, "I know exactly who you are, General."

Arnold smiled even wider. Despite walking about in plain sight all evening, he had gone unnoticed. Finally, someone in this city recognized him.

Andre took a step closer to Arnold, walking him backward out the door he had come in. "Ah, the American Hannibal," Andre said. "I find I dislike you."

Arnold continued his smile. He was beginning to like the man. Perhaps they could share a drink together some day. After Peggy was his, of course, and America decided its own fate. "What have I done to cause this intense feeling, Captain? All I have done this evening is interrupt your proposal. I didn't even know of you before my lovely waltz with Peggy."

"You *waltzed* with him?" Andre asked. Apprehension filled his voice, as if he didn't want to know the answer.

"Well, I was waltzing with Washington—"

"That womanizer?" Now, Andre's voice was incredulous. "Stay away from the governor, and Arnold, too." He shook his head in disbelief.

All four of them now stood, and it was becoming a little crowded. The rain outside came down harder—they could hear it with the door to the balcony open.

"Captain, you still have not answered my—"

"Silence!" Andre waved the pistol in front of Arnold's face. He turned to Peggy as if she had been the one who asked. "Indeed, this man has tried to kill me."

Now, it was Arnold's turn to be confused. "Have I met you on the field? Were you at Saratoga? Quebec?"

"Saint-Jean. My first overseas command. It was supposed to be a simple posting, cold, but not altogether unmanageable. Then you sacked Ticonderoga, just downriver from us, without provocation. We were sure we were next. I even saw you spying on us from out on the river. We were only a few hundred, but we vowed to hold our position at all costs, fighting to the last man if we had to. Why would you attack your own countrymen? What made England so terrible that you would kill men like me to escape it?"

Arnold paused, for he didn't have an answer, at least not one that would satisfy Andre. But he could at least drive a wedge between him and Peggy and perhaps survive the night. "So, your answer is to kill me in cold blood?"

Peggy gasped, her mouth and eyes going wide. He didn't know how Peggy felt about him, but he doubted she wanted to see him dead.

"I will do what I must," Andre replied coolly. "If I don't kill you before I deliver you to Colonel Washington, I'll have you swinging on a gibbet by dawn. You will not be the death of me."

"You cannot hang me. I am no spy." Arnold pointed to his red uniform jacket. "According to your code, I am in uniform, albeit an older one, but one that saw service after this war started. If I am in uniform, I am not a spy. Your rules, not mine." Arnold tapped his red coat with one hand and held on to the railing with the other as he descended the stairs. He was still walking backward, taking the steps slowly and looking up past Andre to Peggy and her sister above her. "So shoot me here and now or take me to the constabulary where I might be turned in and promptly paroled."

Andre frowned and took a step down, shrugging as he did so. "Don't be daft. This is war. I don't care what you're wearing."

"Ben, please, do what Mr. Andre says," Peggy said, her voice filled with worry. "Go with him to his headquarters. I don't want to see you hurt."

She called me Ben. Ah, so Peggy does have feelings for me. Arnold was awash with warmth. His job here was done.

A burst of knocking came from the door. Three knocks. The first one was faint, while the others which followed it came on strong. Everyone gasped in surprise and looked to the door.

Everyone except Arnold.

"My apologies, ladies," Arnold said. "This may get ugly." He grabbed the barrel of the pistol from Andre. His grip was strong. Good. Arnold pivoted as hard as he could, but he didn't need to use much force—he had all the leverage in the world. From a step lower than Andre, Arnold grabbed at the pistol and pulled down and across. Andre didn't let go in time.

With a wide-eyed gasp, the captain tumbled down the stairs.

Arnold jogged up, brushing closely against Peggy, whiffing her perfume and breathing in the fragrance on her neck. "Ladies, excuse me. Peggy, expect letters from me shortly."

She smiled and placed her hand on his shoulder.

Arnold made it up the stairwell as another round of knocking came once more, this time much more assured. Arnold threw himself outside through the opened balcony door, a deluge of hard rain striking him all over.

He found he still had the damned glass from earlier in his hand. It came in handy, as Arnold looked around, searching for options. He knew time was short before Andre recovered and came up after him.

Arnold took the glass and threw it in the alley below. It shattered into a thousand shards in the direction he had come just fifteen minutes before. Then Arnold grabbed hold of the edge of the roof and pulled himself up onto it, straining and gasping as he went. He was not as young as he was before and not as spry.

Finally, he reached the top of the angled roof, climbed it, and started over on the other side. He heard a door open and turned to see behind. Andre burst out at street-level, most likely from the rear servant door, and bolted down the alley past the broken crystal. Arnold took in a quick sigh of relief, but then frowned. He was not out of the city yet.

Henry Collins *really* didn't want to knock on the door.

Reluctantly, he brought his fist up, held it there for much longer than he should have, then knocked, lightly at first. At the realization that the people inside were already aware of his presence, he knocked again, this time with more authority.

I've knocked, so now what the devil am I supposed to do? Stand here in the rain?

Then he heard a loud thudding sound, and someone or something tumbled down and hit the door from the other side. He froze, shrugging his shoulders. He didn't know whether to throttle the general or admire him. This was the last thing he had ever expected, to be caught up in his world.

The white door in front of him flew open. An officer, dressed in full uniform, but disheveled with his wig on crooked, glared down at him.

"What do you want?" the officer demanded.

Collins was at a complete loss for... well... everything. He was sure General Arnold would've had a smart remark, or a good solution. But then again, if it wasn't for the general... "Uh..." Collins returned a blank stare, hoping for something. All he could think about was the rain.

Nothing. Then, "Merry...uh, merry Christmas?"

The officer looked at him, then through him with piercing, white-hot eyes. "Stay here!" With that, he slammed the door and disappeared. Collins heard heavy footfalls, then the sound of a distant door opening, then... silence.

There was an abrupt whoosh of air, as if someone had fallen into the bushes. He turned to investigate. Someone had. Thick drops from leaves sprayed into the air, and loose bits of shrubbery scattered. A dark figure lay prone, momentarily stunned. He got up and started after Collins.

"Well, that's one way to get down," General Arnold said, brushing leaves and twigs and the remains of an orb weaver's web off his cloak. He grumbled something about getting older and then said something even more incoherent about chasing away a suitor for Hannah. Finally, he raised his voice. "Come on. We haven't much time."

General Arnold looked calm, as if nothing had happened. Collins had no idea what had gone on inside, but the fact that the general had just jumped off the roof suggested it was not a slow evening. Yet, everything seemed perfectly normal to him. *Admire or throttle?* Now was his chance.

He chose neither and asked, "What about that... the soldier? Is he going for help?" He had forgotten the respects, but at this point, he didn't think it mattered.

The general ignored him. They moved as quickly as they could down several blocks, weaving through the rows of townhouses, away from the river and further into the farms, near where they first entered the city. They were careful not to run, instead lengthening their stride as they hurriedly walked. Arnold limped a little on his left leg. Collins wondered if he had wounded it during the fall, or if that was from an earlier injury.

Despite the injuries and the cold rain, they made a narrow escape.

When they had placed several blocks between them and the townhome, Arnold answered Collins' unspoken questions. "We're safe enough, or rather, as safe as we were before. That man you met was John Andre, and he thinks himself too much of a gentleman to tell anyone I was right in front of him and escaped." Arnold slowed. The rain made it hard to see. Puddles formed as the cobblestones gave way to dirt. They sloshed their way through them.

"We are just two citizens out walking," Arnold continued. "To the Loyalists in this town, we're every bit like them. We can use that. In a fight, press any advantage you have. That's the difference between fighting with virtue and fighting to win."

Collins disagreed. "They think we're savages. Won't that make them right?" He didn't mention the rain and that it might be hard to explain to a sentry why they were out on a stroll in inclement weather. Not to mention the envelope stuck in the general's boot. At the moment, he certainly didn't *feel* too virtuous.

"It is too late to change what the British think of us." Arnold stopped. "All we can do now is show them our patriotism, our zeal. They'll respect us and treat us as equals once we beat them, whether it be on the field of battle or in the halls of diplomacy." Arnold stopped for a long moment. Collins had no idea what was running through the general's mind.

"Then, that is exactly what we will do."

"Exactly," Arnold smiled. "You understand why I brought you here with me tonight?"

Collins shook his head. He'd been wondering that all evening, giving up on finding out when he stood cold and wet in front of Ms. Shippen's residence.

"I wanted to impress upon you the need for you to stay with our cause. You have what so many other soldiers lack, even your friend. They lack conviction, a sense of true purpose for what we're fighting for. I need you to share that zeal with your brothers. It's instrumental to our cause." He stopped as if correcting himself. "It *is* our cause."

Collins thought about those words for a while and let them sink in. He wanted to fight and win this war single-handedly, but he also had other responsibilities. On one hand, he wanted to get back to Emma, who would be giving birth any day now. On the other, this was General Arnold, standing tall in front of him, personally asking him to stay. It was a tremendous experience. He didn't think anyone else would even understand, not Stevens, not even Emma.

They came to their horses they had left earlier. The steeds were still there, undisturbed, bothered little by the rain, grazing gently for rare tufts of grass. Arnold climbed with a bit of effort and a heavy sigh. This time, Collins mounted his without difficulty. They made the crossing of the hidden bridge without incident.

Arnold turned his black horse around. "Where do you think you're going?"

Collins shot a confused look back at Arnold.

"This, dear boy, is where we part ways." He rifled through a pocket and produced a slip of paper. "As you know, I transferred you under me as an aide. I did this for one reason—so I would have leave to offer you this." He handed Collins the paper.

Collins took it. He couldn't read it in the darkness and the rain.

"Congratulations, Corporal."

"Corporal?"

"Yes, Corporal Collins. The other reason I brought you with me tonight was a practical consideration. Your home is on the way from here. On my horse, which I am lending you, you should arrive in a matter of days."

Collins stared, at an utter loss for words. His mouth worked, but nothing came out.

"No need to thank me. I owe you thanks enough. You have been of tremendous assistance, and I will never forget that." They continued, and this time Arnold rode with him, heading south, with the Delaware River to their left. "Spend some time with your wife and child, but I want you back on the first of March, not a day after. I'll provide an enlistment bonus out of my own pocket. I know that fifty dollars you received from your friend isn't worth nearly that much now with inflation, so it's my way of making it up to you. And I want my horse, cloak, and pistol returned, of course."

"Absolutely. Yes, sir." Collins beamed.

"We have a general, a Prussian, who promised to get us into fighting shape. Come back and instill your zeal into our training. Help us become the army that can defeat the British. Inspire others to fight as you have done. At the end, you'll be a patriot and a hero to your country and your family. There's no greater blessing than that, is there?"

"No, sir!"

"So, I have your word?" Arnold asked. "You will return?"

"Yes, sir. I will."

"Very good. Thank you for your assistance this evening, and Godspeed." With that, Arnold turned his horse around and headed in the opposite direction.

For the first time in a long while, Collins found himself alone. It was raining, it was dark, and there could still be enemy patrols further south, but none of that mattered. Collins rode off, warm and with a smile on his face.

Corporal Fredrick Bakker shivered, and his right foot ached. Though it had been a year now since the surgeon had cut off his two smaller toes, he still felt them wiggling every time the wind blew or the rain came or he stepped wrong. Especially on a night like this.

In total, he had spent several months in recovery. First, recovering from frost bite and the amputation, then because infection had set in. That took another several weeks of recovery. He had spent so long away from the war he no longer felt any attachment to it. Bakker thought he might return home and see his mother again. He no longer felt ashamed of being a criminal's son; the service he rendered should more than compensate for that. He could marry.

Thoughts of women filled his head. Their soft touch. Their warm smiles. He had never known a woman intimately, something he very much wished to rectify. Wearing his soldier's uniform and his wounds would most certainly help.

However, he found himself thrust back into his old unit. His commander, Maximillian, was as charming as ever. They were stationed in Philadelphia now, and the weather here was as unpleasant as anywhere else he had been in the wilderness: too hot and humid in the summer and too cold in the winter. They'd also done a fair bit of fighting since.

Things now had returned to quiet—and cold. And wet. Bakker grumbled. They weren't *really* in Philadelphia, not the city at least. The Hessians were stuck in the outskirts, in the mud, while the British were nice and cozy in their beds. *Let them guard the redoubts*, they said. *Let them fight*, they said. *They are paid for it*. Bakker was getting sick of hearing it. He hadn't seen the money, and he was stuck here like the lot of them.

Rain fell, and the lean-to he had built failed the task of keeping him dry. At least, he was sitting. Maximillian stood a bit of a ways off but still within earshot, his company both a blessing and a curse. He yelled to get his attention.

"Do you have anything to smoke?" It was cruel, he thought, to be so close to such a ready supply, yet so far away. America might be the land of tobacco, but it was so expensive, no one here could afford to smoke it. To the Americans, it was like lighting bank notes on fire.

"I already gave you my last bit, you ingrate." Maximillian smiled.

"Holdout." Bakker returned the grin. What could he say? Nights like these on sentry duty made them friends. Who knew, maybe in the morning, they'd still like each other. But probably not.

Bakker heard a rustle through the leaves. Off in the distance, he could swear he heard a horse. He leaned back and relaxed. Wild horses roamed these parts. He'd come across it before, and it didn't strike him as worrisome.

Something about the noise bothered him. The horse sounded focused, ridden rather than out for an evening graze. That concerned him, but the cold and rain concerned him more. Maybe Maximillian could check it out.

"Do you hear that?" he asked.

"I don't hear anything," Maximillian said. "If you did, you should go look."

Bakker convinced himself it was just a horse or another animal out for food. His spot on the log was the only thing dry. He did not want to get his trousers soaked when he sat back down. His foot would start hurting again if he tried walking on it. "It's probably nothing."

Maximillian grunted. "I could do without this rain."

"So could I," Bakker said. He shivered. Fortunately, they only had one more hour. He leaned back once more, rubbing his hands over his shoulders and arms. "So how about that leaf?"

Corporal Frederick Bakker would never know General Benedict Arnold of the American forces slipped by not more than one hundred yards away.

SIXTEEN

Valley Forge, Pennsylvania
January 14th, 1778.

MARTIN Stevens found being a sergeant made him no dryer or warmer than the soldiers under his command. In fact, he found himself often left with bloody knuckles, cracked from the cold, after a hard day constructing log cabins. He would be the one heading back to his tent in the snow while those he helped enjoyed the warm fruits of his labor.

That his enlistment had expired two weeks ago was of little consequence. The soldiers here were freezing, sick, or dying. They needed anyone able-bodied enough to pick up a log or hunt and trap for what little game remained.

Most days, he was too busy trying to stay alive to think about much else. When those rare occurrences of silence came and there was food enough in his belly to think—mostly when everyone else was away at Sunday camp sermons—Stevens found his thoughts drifting to Emma, her baby girl, Jane, and of the life he could've had if things had been different.

He received news not two days ago via letter inviting him to return. Stevens hadn't informed the new father he was still at Valley Forge and had no plans to leave until the camp was in order and some two thousand log cabins were built.

Besides, there was no place for him there. He didn't know his way around a baby. He would just be in the way. In fact, there was no place for him anywhere. He could be on his own, alone in his cabin in the woods, or he could be here, helping those around him survive the winter.

He sighed, and a thick foggy breath formed. Frost clung to his beard and his ears and nose were numb again for yet another day. His home was here for the time being. Responsibility weighed heavily on his shoulders. Duty was a curse.

Today was Benedict Arnold's birthday. It didn't feel like it, and no one had brought it up. Gates knew. It was written down on one of his papers, but it didn't make the General Orders. Nor did Gates personally come by on this snowy day and wish him well. That would've been an interesting conversation, one he would've relished. Arnold sat at his desk, hunched over a letter. One day, he knew, everyone would celebrate his birthday.

He wrote each word with careful precision, going back and re-reading the lines and often scribbling them out and starting over. He wasn't as sure-footed with poetry as he would like, but he knew his letters to Peggy were a damned sight better than the poems Andre wrote her.

No doubt.

He focused so intently on the letter in front of him that it barely registered when his door opened, a draft blew in snow and ice, and Abigail entered. She didn't utter a word and disappeared behind him.

Arnold did notice, however, a while later when she disrobed. It was routine. Once she was warm, she would remove her garments, and he would have her. But not this time, and not since he had returned from the city last Christmas.

A line had him stumped, his thoughts focused on the ink and parchment in front of him. For Peggy, the thought had to be perfect. A moment later, he carefully formed each letter and transferred his brilliance to paper. Then he read it again and frowned. It was horrible. All the while, Abigail stood naked.

"Are you coming?" she asked, annoyance latent in her voice, tucked away from years of bondage but there all the same. "Or are you going to ignore me again?"

Arnold heard her, but did not respond.

She placed her arms around his shoulders, her breasts pressed against the flesh of his neck. He hardly felt her, focused as he was on the letter, but she stopped him by grabbing his wrist.

He spoke softly. "Not today, Abigail."

Abigail recoiled. "I'm not your whore!" She pulled on her

garments—an expensive cotton dress, dyed yellow, and several layers of warm wool atop it.

Arnold smirked inwardly. He was pretty sure she was his whore. He had her and paid her. Textbook definition.

"You defile me and then reject me? I'm a woman. I have feelings."

Arnold set his quill down, his latest letter to Peggy finished. Well, mostly finished. He would like to write another draft. He turned and stood up from his chair, knees popping and back stiff. At least his leg was healed.

"You're a runaway slave," Arnold said, his voice low. "I could have you whipped and sent away. Your masters, if they're still alive, would most likely reward me." Arnold moved from the desk to the other side of the room and sat on the edge of the bed, motioning for her to join him. She did not. "I haven't done so for several reasons. You're more valuable to me in my possession than in theirs. And, you've been useful." Arnold stood and walked over to her. He whispered, "I've treated you more than fairly, and I have paid you in silver and gold for *all* of your services."

"What makes you think I won't run to the British the next time I'm gone? What loyalty do I owe you?"

"None. But you have loyalty to this." Arnold took out a small coin and showed it to her. "The British may send you north to supposed freedom, but then you would have none of this."

"That's not my purpose." She casually pushed the coin aside, dismissing it and looked away as if in search of a memory.

"Then, what is?"

"To live. To have purpose of my own creation. To tell my children they're free in this land because I've helped make it so."

"You have family?" Arnold asked.

"A husband. The babies ripped from me when I was young aren't mine. I don't know them. But I'll find my husband, and one day, we'll have a family of our own."

"Where is he?"

"He belongs to Mount Vernon."

Arnold looked confused. "I thought Washington didn't break up slave families?"

"He doesn't, but he's not there. I've seen him in the city with my own eyes. It wasn't he who bought my husband away."

"I'm sorry to hear that. The work you do helps make sure that you'll live in a land better than the one the British would offer." It wasn't a lie, but it wasn't the truth either. "They offer you falsehoods to tear your people against us. It is the same lies they told the tribes, and we both know how they were treated afterwards. Their lies hurt everyone."

Arnold walked to the desk and handed Abigail several letters. Two of them were in tan envelopes and one of them was in pink. "Take these two to your regular drop. The pink one to Peggy. Just slip it in the mail slot, as you've done before, if you would be so kind."

"More letters for her?" Abigail sounded flustered and hurt. "I'm not doing this just so I can be caught by the soldiers with your poetry on me. Last time I went north out of the city to escape, I came across you. Perhaps next time I go south, I'll find my husband again."

Arnold took several gold coins from his purse. "Here. This is twice as much as I pay you. I have no complaints from the spies inside about coin, so I know you've been paying them. You have no reason to be either honest or loyal, yet you have been. So I must think you have some honor, some code. I urge you to keep to it just awhile longer. At least until we're away from this blasted city. Who knows, maybe someday soon, I'll take you to Mount Vernon myself."

Abigail answered, her eyes locking with his. "I'll do what you ask. But there will come a day when I'll slip quietly away, and you'll never see me again."

"I can ask no more, but remember your place. Your people live to serve."

Abigail shook her head. Her eyes became sharp and focused. Anger laced her words. "My parents were not born servants. That's something you have done." She looked down at her hands in front of her. "My mark is my own skin. I need only look at myself to see my bonds." After she spoke, she seemed to cool. She took the letters, hid them within secret compartments in her coverings, and sulked through the door, slamming it shut behind her.

The wind blew in snow and ice once more, and when she was gone, he felt cold and alone. He dismissed most of his conversation with Abigail, though it sparked a solution of sorts to a problem that had troubled him since he and Collins rode past the burned-out husks of homes and into the occupied city.

It just might work. Galvanized to his course of action, Arnold unlocked a drawer on the desk. It held a secret compartment of his own design built for him several weeks ago. After raising the false bottom, he removed the envelope he retrieved from Philadelphia.

He had already applied heat to the pages to reveal their secrets. The bulk of it consisted of a map in several pages that had to be placed together. Hastily drawn and not terribly accurate, it showed the city. Certain buildings and homes had been crossed out. He was sure those were places where loyalists lived or worked, but he didn't know why some of the homes were marked and others not. None of the other papers had shed light on this matter. His requests to learn more had gone unanswered. All his contacts inside said was that they waited on his word to begin.

Arnold threw the envelope and all the papers in the fire. He had committed most of it to memory, and he was tired of looking at them. Whatever the Sons of Liberty were planning, he could do no more until he set his own ideas into motion.

He had the seedling of a thought, but it needed to be fleshed out and required someone younger and more up to the dirty task of carrying it out. It might be time to pay his friend, Aaron Burr, a visit. George Washington had a birthday sometime next month, and Arnold had to prepare a gift for him.

SEVENTEEN

Little Hunting Creek, Potomac River, Mt. Vernon
February 22ⁿᵈ, 1778.

SERGEANT Martin Stevens was supposed to be leading this expedition. He briefly wondered how he had come from being a simple, solitary outdoorsman to rowing a bateau on the crisp waters of the Potomac River. He crowded into the twenty-four-foot long craft with two hogsheads worth of supplies and three other men: Lt. Colonel Aaron Burr and two brothers, each a lieutenant. As the sole enlisted man among these educated officers, he wasn't so much leading the expedition as he was showing the way. Stevens kept as far to the corner of the boat when he could.

His shadow shrank against the deepening purple sky—a few stars flickered with Venus on the evening horizon. The other men on this journey may have been officers, they may have even been well taught "in the finest halls of education in New Jersey, ergo, the world," but they still held onto the appearance of a band of ruffians.

Colonel Burr was gruff and ill-mannered, and always had his hunting knife in hand. The two brothers—Stevens couldn't remember their names—spoke crudely of the last time they had been with a woman, and what they would do the next time they were with one.

Burr told the same story of how he and General Arnold had faced peril at every step of their journey on the Kennebec toward Quebec over and over. The stories were for Stevens' benefit, he guessed—the brothers had been there. Whenever any of them complained of the cold or of muscle fatigue on this journey down the Potomac, Burr repeated the tale and then said, as he snuffed a thumb-ful of milled tobacco, "This is nothing."

Stevens paddled softly, often taking a long rod out to steer the bateau. Sometimes, parts of the Potomac would turn green, usually in spring after the surrounding farmland had been fertilized. But tonight, in the winter, the waters were black, deep and dark, the edges frozen at each bank.

The slow, rhythmic motion of each stroke put Stevens in a near trance. He pretended he was back in time with his father. He gazed over the ripples and the green shoreline that all seemed to melt into one surreal moment. He was either hunting in the forest near the river or trapping something to eat. Or he was taxiing strangers and supplies around the river. But in his silent fantasies, no matter how far he traveled, he could never outrun thoughts of the woman who ensnared his heart.

"How much further?" Colonel Burr asked, slapping him out of the past. Burr asked it too many times on the long journey. Whenever they passed a great estate, he or one of the brothers would ask, "Is this it? Is this the house we are going to burn to the ground?"

Mount Vernon wasn't just a manor. It was a series of buildings, farms, and mills spread over a large estate. There was no way to burn it all. He had tried to explain this to Burr, but all Burr ever said was, "The general says you know the way around, so you are leading us to it." He never had a choice in the matter, but it was work no one but Stevens could do, and so he found himself here, near Little Hunting Creek on the west side of the Potomac.

"We're coming up to it," Stevens answered, recognizing some of the landscaping and docks not too far from the main home of the estate. He recalled the home was simple by comparison to some of the grand manors they had passed on the river. Still, by Stevens' standards, Mt. Vernon was palatial. Though he had doubts about the companions he accompanied on this mission, George Washington was the true enemy, and he'd have no qualms about burning the governor's home to ashes.

Earlier, Stevens mentioned the idea of landing just north of the estate. There was a small inlet and creek where they could beach and make the rest of the short distance through the woods, around the house. It would minimize their chances of detection, he argued.

Burr, to some surprise, agreed. He even smiled. "I knew there was a reason we brought you here. You're not just an anchor, after all." Stevens didn't bother reminding him if they hadn't brought him along, they probably would have set fire to half a dozen of the wrong homes, leaving Washington's intact. But, there was no point in arguing.

Stevens' shoulders ached from the constant rowing, and his freezing clothes clung to him, offering no chance of escape from the cold. The bateau hit the frozen ground of the creek and relief poured over Stevens. The men shared moans of respite as they dragged their wet, soggy selves out onto the riverbank.

"Is it safe to make a fire?" one of the brothers asked. They both looked toward Stevens, rather than Burr, who also cast a sideways glance at him.

"No. Not here, unless it's an earthen kitchen to hide the flames." They nodded—they had to dry off before finishing their journey. And eating would be nice.

While Stevens and Burr rolled the two barrels from the shore to their camp, the two brothers constructed the kitchen. Once they arrived, Stevens cracked open the first hogshead as Burr sat and supervised. Inside were several torches, remarkably still dry. Along with the torches was Stevens' Kentucky longrifle. He looked at it curiously. He'd packed it, but at the time, he didn't believe it would be useful. Burr had urged him to bring it. Now, after spending time with them, Stevens wasn't so convinced his longrifle would go unused.

The second barrel stunk of decay even before Stevens had finished removing the lid. He slammed it back down again, coughing and stepping back, waving the smell from his nose. The concoction inside looked like a meat pudding left out in the rain, but it smelled like decaying flesh and molded bread with a whiff of clumpy yellow milk thrown in for good measure.

"Well... looks like fish tonight," one of the brothers said, waving a hand in front of his nose.

Though Stevens grew anxious about the night's activities as the evening wore on, at least now he was dry and fed. This might be his last meal in a while, and who knew what would happen between now and then? He put his clothes back on—brown breeches and rough flax linen shirts—and covered himself with a threadbare grey blanket he wore as a cloak to keep warm. The others wore similar outfits, but out of finer and warmer linens. The brothers, unfortunately, wore identical brown waistcoats, jackets, and overcoats, which worsened the problem of identifying them. Burr, rather ostentatiously, wore his full uniform on tonight's covert mission.

Stevens scratched at his scruffy chin and face. The Prussian general back at camp had insisted that they all shave. Stevens had lost his beard. Now, it was daily drills, all day, every day. In truth, he was glad to be taking a break from the constant drilling, and he looked forward to re-growing his beard—though his face kept itching. Maybe he'd keep it clean-shaven when he got back.

"Let's break and make for the forest," Burr stood up and took an unlit torch from the hogshead. "Stevens, we'll follow you."

Stevens attached his hunting knife and materials for his longrifle, as well as the weapon itself and made for the forest.

"What about the boat?" the taller brother asked, after collecting a torch for his brother and then grabbing the last two for himself. Stevens stopped and waited for the answer.

The bateau was constructed out of very green pine and glued to an oak frame. It was barely afloat to begin with—it wouldn't make the journey home, which was fine, as it would be too dangerous to travel by water afterward. They would have to make the journey back to Valley Forge overland. And, of course, their provisions for that journey had spoiled.

"Leave the boat," Burr answered. "Let any hapless fool who uses it to chase us away sink in it. Did I tell you about the *bateaux* we used on the Kennebec...?"

Burr launched into a monologue, and Stevens lost himself in thought. He wondered how Collins was managing with Jane. He hoped Emma was well. In a little under a week, Collins would be back, and the two would start another season of war together. He looked forward to seeing him again, to hearing stories of Jane. This year would be the last, Collins promised in his letter. And this time, Stevens would do a better job of keeping him to it, if they survived the crucible of conflict first.

Even though he failed to win over Emma's heart, he could still do his part to make sure the world in which Jane was raised in was better and safer than it was now. So, Stevens embraced the soldier growing inside him and resolved to make it through the war to be there for Collins, Emma, and baby Jane.

He would teach the young one to hunt, to fish. It didn't matter that she was a girl—all people should know how to survive on their own. He would try to teach her that even when right and wrong were blurred, there was an innate sense that could direct you. He would teach Jane to listen to that voice and stand up for it—it was a lesson even he had a difficult time learning.

Standing up for what you believed in required confrontation. That was not Stevens' way. But to secure the future for the next generation, you had to confront those who would tear down what you had built. That lesson guided him now. Soaked at first and now dried by fire, Stevens went out into the woods with a renewed sense of purpose.

Guided by the light of the stars, the three men followed Stevens through forests of oak, elm, and the occasional walnut in what was the River Farm north of the estate house. The ground was soft against their feet, leaves still damp from the continual winter that besieged them for so long now. At least most of the snow here was gone.

The cicadas of spring had not yet invaded the sanctity of the evening hours, nor had buzzing clouds of mosquitoes. The sound of the lapping river to their left would have made this a pleasant night, if not for the cold and their masked intentions.

They were well on the estate, though they had seen little evidence of the place aside from the occasional horse-beaten path. After the hour-long hike, his followers were restless. Stevens knew the thick forest would give way to an open field soon, and the main house would be in plain view. But for them, all they knew was tree after tree.

Stevens sympathized and opened his mouth to reassure them when he heard something ahead in the thick foliage. A voice behind him whispered, "What's that?" They all stopped. The river washed away much of the ambient, natural noise of the forest. But this sound was not made by the flitting of insects.

The voice behind him said, "There it is again. It's coming from over there." The younger brother, pointed to a natural hollow on their left where several trees and shrubs had made an enclosure. It was hard to make out in the dark, but he could have sworn he saw a bush move slightly against the wind.

Then he heard it.

A low moaning at first, vaguely familiar but definitely not the first sound he thought of in a forest, yet every bit as natural. The moaning increased in exuberance and vigor, coming rhythmically, almost musically. The symphony continued to mount toward climax, and the bush shuddered more violently... and then the men behind him broke out into snickers.

"Boys, I think we just stumbled onto a treasure chest, ripe for plunder," Burr said.

Stevens didn't know how to react. The foliage went still, and voices hit his hears, though he could not recognize the words or even if they were in English. So, he was not the least surprised to see a Negro man emerge from the bushes, completely naked. The Negro stood tall and powerful in front of them, but fear filled his eyes.

A female voice called from inside the foliage, and the slave turned to respond, revealing a patchwork of razor-thin scars running along his backside. When he spoke to the female, he rose himself up, as if in pride. But, when he turned back toward Stevens he could see the man slink back down again.

Burr and the brothers kept looking past the man into the bushes behind him, hollering and catcalling, and generally drawing attention to themselves.

The black man spoke to them in a language no one recognized. He tried again, "You... no tell?"

"We won't. Just passing through. Go back about your... business," Stevens replied. He didn't know if that was the right response, or even if it was his responsibility to engage the Negro. Judging by the sneers on the faces around him, followed by several crude gestures, his response had been less than satisfactory.

"You... no tell?" the slave pleaded again.

"Sure... we won't tell. We just want what you're having," a voice said.

Stevens looked around at the three men and then back toward the Negro couple. They were no threat to Stevens and his party. It was unhappy circumstance that their paths crossed.

Somewhere in those bushes was a naked woman. Black or not, slave or free, his unsavory companions were not the disciplined type to pass on such an opportunity. That voice inside him, the one that sounded like his father and told him right from wrong, screamed.

"Sir, what about our mission?" Stevens insisted, turning to Colonel Burr. "You were adamant this had to take place on the twenty-second. It's getting late and soon we'll be out of—"

But it was too late. The older brother had already drawn his ivory-handled knife, flat on one side and curved near the point on the other. "We got time, don't we, Colonel?"

Stevens tried to warn the Negro but the slave did not understand. Instead, he tried to run, but Burr and the other brother stopped him and threw him face-first to the ground. Burr drew his knife, raised the man's head off the ground, and ran the knife around his throat. The man made no sound.

Burr wiped his knife off the bare man's buttocks, leaving behind a crimson smear. The other man removed his cloak, placing a knife in his mouth by the handle as he did so. Stevens hadn't been able to save the man, but if he were going to act, it had to be now.

He would've reached the brother first if the woman hadn't emerged from the bushes just then. She was beautiful, probably in the height of womanhood at twenty or so, with long hair and slender legs of dark cream. She had taken time to put her clothes on, but they hung loose around her body as to not cover much of anything.

She turned to him, ignoring the approach of danger and screamed at the sight of her lover, slain and bleeding on the cold ground. A moment later, rough hands shoved her to the dirt beside him.

Already, the man was on her, his knife held as if to remove her garments. The others headed toward her. Stevens grabbed the brother's wrist at the hand holding the knife, only to be pushed aside by a powerful arm. "Sod off. You'll get yours in soon enough."

Stevens grabbed, more forcefully now, the brother slightly younger but stronger. The man struggled, but Stevens was determined and had the element of surprise. He twisted the arm behind the brother's back and drove his right foot into his ribs.

The older brother looked up from the ground in shock. He recovered, keeping a firm hold of the knife, getting to his knees and lunging out at Stevens. Reflexively, Stevens dodged, grabbing ahold of the man's shirt and using the momentum of the lunge to swing him back toward the ground a few feet away.

Before the brother could stand upright, Stevens grabbed his own hunting knife. But, now the shorter brother stood before him. The Negro girl struggled to her feet. Stevens couldn't take them all on, nor did he intend to die to save a slave. So, he did the only thing he could do, the only thing that would end this and resume the mission.

Burying his shame deep within him, Stevens raised the knife upward, grabbing onto the slave girl. She grabbed onto him, as if in a hug. But instead of finding arms of protection, she found betrayal. The girl gasped in horror, her eyes springing open, wide in shock. They bulged outward, the whites reflecting the faint illumination of the stars as her spirit made its way to a better place. Or so Stevens told himself, though he did not believe such a place existed. Blood spilled down his hand.

"I'm sorry," he whispered, as she slumped out of his arms, embracing her lover on the ground below.

The men stopped and stared at him, unable to appreciate the situation.

He looked up in as much shock as they were, but for a different reason. There was a long moment of silence. Finally, he said, "She was keeping us from our mission." That was not why he had done it and hoped the lie sounded convincing. Later, during sleepless nights, he would convince himself of the lie as well. It had been for the best, he would remind himself.

It was for the best.

"Are we ready to move?" Stevens asked, a little bit more resolute.

Burr had the look of a child who just had a toy taken away, but he said, "The sergeant's right. A bit of sexual release would've done us good, but our task tonight is much too important, too noble for us to concern ourselves with our needs." The two lieutenants glared at Stevens but remained silent as they listened to the colonel. "I fear we may have lost the element of surprise. Gentlemen, light the torches. Stevens, lead the way." Then Burr lowered his voice. "You and I will have words later."

"Come on," said the brother who Stevens attacked earlier. "We didn't come all this way to watch the sunrise over the Potomac. I won't kill you until after we're done."

Stevens couldn't tell if the man was serious or not, but the brothers walked abreast of Stevens and said nothing else. At least they were back on track.

Their torched burned brightly in the night sky. If the earlier disturbance hadn't alerted everybody, then this would. The bright flames of the torches made it difficult to see what was ahead.

The night-blindness slowed them down, but they soon arrived at the edge of the forest at the tree line surrounding the north end of the estate. The small but imposing homestead sat perpendicular to them and parallel to the river in the shape of a large horseshoe. From here, they had a partial view of the main house and its two wings, obstructed by several outbuildings, some of which held slave quarters and stables. On the other side of the home, on the outside of the horseshoe, stretched a clear field and a breathtaking view of the Potomac River.

The house ended abruptly at the field and lacked a back porch, but signs of construction lay all around. Indeed, Stevens recalled the house and surrounding property undergoing a constant state of demolition and rebuilding at all times during his stay.

And now, it would undergo one final demolition project.

"For this to work, the timing has got to be perfect," Burr said. Then he addressed the older brother. "Remember, Mathias, you and your brother go to the far wing. Stevens, you take the closest wing. Once your building is caught aflame, fall back and support us. You're the one with a firearm, and I hear you're a good shot. Make it count if we need you." Burr continued, "I'll take the main house, but remember, according to Stevens here, none of these three main buildings are connected, so if we're going to get them all, we must be quick and thorough. General Arnold wants it all to burn."

"And Stevens," Burr said afterward, in a whisper, "put that knife away."

Stevens returned a blank stare. Slowly, he looked down at the knife, still wrapped tightly in his hand. He couldn't believe he was still carrying it. The slave's blood had already started to thicken, some of it now dry and flaky. In between his fingers, he felt it, sticky and thick. He loosened his grip on the leather handle, and the knife slid easily out, falling to the soft earth. Loose mud clung to the blade, burying the remains of the slave woman underneath.

Burr and the brothers had already left Stevens alone with a lit torch. He breathed in the quiet night air, hoping for some absolution, knowing that his course of action tonight was right, from saving the slave girl to avenging the burning of patriot homes and the death of John Hancock at the hands of George Washington.

Stevens reached the nearest window. People stirred inside, though nobody came running out at them yet. He took the torch and used it to break the glass in front of him. Next, he made sure the thick velvet drapes caught on fire. He repeated this process twice more, and then, in the last window, he threw the torch in.

Already, his building blazed. Orange flames flicked out like the tongues of a thousand serpents. He could smell the wood burning. It matched the smell coming from the building next to his and the building on the far side. Now, the whole estate burst into an uproar. People ran out onto the grounds, mostly slaves, though there a few whites sprinkled among them.

It was time to fall back and provide support. If any of the estate hands offered resistance, Stevens had his rifle ready to assist, though he believed they would be long gone before anyone had a chance to react.

He made his way back toward the tree line at the topmost edge of the horseshoe, where he could watch all the activity occurring at the front of the house. In the light of the blaze, he had no problem seeing the silhouettes of figures running past the fields. He saw first the brothers at the opposite end of the horseshoe, but then they disappeared, most probably returning to the rendezvous point.

Something didn't quite add up. There were more people here than he had anticipated. He wondered if the noises from earlier hadn't put everyone on alert. He wondered how they would make it through the throngs of slaves unheeded, and he nervously considered that they may not make it out of here without getting caught. His heart pumped hard, but all he could feel was ice in his veins. *Something's wrong.*

Already, Stevens could feel the heat rising from even the tree line. Both side buildings were fully engulfed in flame, but the main house showed a trace of fire as if someone inside were attempting to quell it. Stevens didn't think anybody was there. Martha was rumored to stay with her husband, and the manager, Lund, lived in a home outside the main residence. But someone was most definitely inside.

Bits of ash spread out in the air like broken pieces of memory. Then, just as before, everything happened faster than he could react. Everything he knew burst into flames. *Had General Arnold known Martha was here, or was it a horrible coincidence?*

The possibility of betrayal burned in his eyes. This was not the mission he agreed to. He had looked up to General Arnold. He respected the man, changed his views on the war and wanted to be a better soldier because of him. But, if the general had indeed sent them on a mission which put an innocent life in danger, even in the setting of war, it meant Benedict Arnold was nothing short of a monster.

Everything Stevens had feared from the very beginning came into vivid focus. The river glistened in the reflection of the flames. Shadows danced around him like devils.

He didn't see it at first. Burr had stopped moving, as if his feet were frozen in place to the ground. An older lady, greying hair, small, but stubborn, emerged from the burning home, holding a Brown Betty, aimed directly at Aaron Burr. That lady, whom he had seen many times making his runs, was Mrs. Martha Washington.

She yelled something loud but unclear. Her faded nightgown billowed out slightly in the air, flames licking it but not consuming it. Burr had no weapon Stevens knew of, so he had no way to defend himself. That was Stevens' job, one of the main reasons he had come. He could have easily taken aim and fired at Martha. It was his duty.

Before tonight, he did not think himself capable of killing an unarmed, matronly, woman. But before tonight, he hadn't thought himself capable of stabbing a slave in the heart. He had taken the life of that girl who had done nothing wrong. An innocent. Martha was armed. She was an enemy to his cause, even if she wasn't a soldier. Burr remained still.

Waiting.

Slowly, Stevens brought her into his sights.

Martha gestured with the rifle, making small, defined motions with the barrel. Burr's hands raised. Stevens could tell by the way Martha stood she meant business. He could also tell Burr planned to do something stupid. And Martha saw it too.

Burr's hand shot down into his waistcoat. Martha pointed the gun at Burr's chest, hunched over its sights. Stevens reacted, Martha still in view of his longrifle.

Stevens took in a quick breath of air, held it...

And fired.

EIGHTEEN

Outskirts of Philadelphia, en-route to Valley Forge
March 1st, 1778.

SHE had been born on the 28th of December, hours after Henry
Collins arrived. Little Jane. His wife was already in the sweats
and agony of labor. Fortunately, for Emma's sake, little Jane was
a fairly small baby with a small, soft head, born bald, wrinkly, sort
of furry and named after her maternal grandmother. She shrieked
for her mother's breast, but had a hard time suckling, and she
made such terrible messes and cried in erratic bursts throughout
the night since her birth.

He recalled just after Jane's birth and the screaming had
subsided—the muck cleaned off, the umbilical cord cut, bloody
piles of bedding removed and disposed of, and Jane suckled—that
Collins let go of the fear that had gripped the back of his mind.

She was the most beautiful baby Collins had ever seen,
and his wife the fairest. He could've sworn Jane smiled at him
through closed eyes. He realized how lucky he had been. Emma
survived through both pregnancy and birth. Their daughter was
healthy. He knew all too well he could've easily lost them both
during the sixteen-hour ordeal.

Had he known what Emma would've had to endure, had
he known of the sleepless nights and the tireless days that a new
baby would cause them both, he never would've stoked the fire
that night or the night after. If he had known that Emma's mother
would practically move into their small home and correct him on
every technique he used to try and quiet Jane, he would've sailed

to Spain and joined a monastery—something even his Catholic-hating reverend would've approved of.

But, when Jane was quiet, sleeping on his chest while he creaked back and forth on the old rocking chair, he knew he was the happiest and luckiest man alive, a truth universally acknowledged by every new parent. And it was the greatest feeling of all.

He asked himself many times on the road back to Valley Forge why he parted ways with that feeling. He kept telling himself he was duty-bound to return. He was a corporal now, and that position meant more responsibility and trust. After all, he did promise General Arnold that he would return. Not least of all to return the cloak, pistol, and horse.

Nothing would've stood in the way of him staying with his family—other than his word. He doubted the continentals had the time or means to round up every last soldier who chose the warmth of their family and their stove over the coldness of the winter all alone under the empty, black sky. He had even heard whispers that General Gates offered amnesty for returning deserters. Even he seemed to understand.

His friend's enlistment had expired, but Stevens had renewed once Collins had written to inform him of his plan. At the very least, he felt compelled to return to camp solely out of his bond with Stevens. Stevens was only out there because of him in the first place. It wouldn't be right to abandon him. Family is connected by blood, but friends are connected by loyalty.

The farm had never looked better, even in the dead of winter. Emma was plenty capable of taking care of herself, pregnant or not. He had seen inklings of this just before the war, when Emma had been asked to boycott British supplies by their reverend. She put everything into it, even organizing a group of the other local wives, creating lists of self-banned goods and enduring long, laboring workarounds to ensure local families didn't go without.

But now, it was something else. When Collins returned, he found the small family plot in working condition. The fields were maintained, if not in use during winter. Tools were absent from where he had laid them against the tobacco house. The fence was mended. He found out later that they had produced some tobacco that year, more than the wild crop that grew despite his best efforts at ignoring it.

The fifty dollars Stevens had been awarded paid off a few debts and allowed them to keep the farm house until next season, when Collins was hopeful that a new crop would keep things going, and he had his enlistment incentive from General Arnold to also look forward too.

Even though the fifty dollars had devalued in the passing months, they had managed to buy a crib secondhand from a neighbor and some material to make garments and blankets. They were a long way from being out of debt, but Emma had saved the farm. He tried to picture Emma, greatly pregnant, hoeing the fields. He couldn't. Then again, he couldn't imagine him doing it himself, either.

Therein rested a deeper truth for leaving his family. He had to do something. His survival had only been through the grace of others. His family was fine, to be sure, but it took the combined efforts of Stevens' heroics on the battlefield and Emma's strength at home to achieve it. He failed to see where he fit in.

Emma said she loved him. He honestly didn't know why, but he was sure he could give her a reason if he could refocus himself. He thought joining the war effort would make him a better man. He wasn't sure if that was something you could start doing—being somebody—but he had to try. So far, it hadn't worked.

It had been a rough few days on the road. On one hand, he had finally grown used to riding. On the other, he failed to find a group of other returning soldiers to travel with, and going alone was always dangerous even without the war. He was constantly on the lookout, not for redcoats—but for his own people. His biggest fear was to be lynched by loyalists, those who knew him and what side he had chosen. As he grew closer to Philadelphia, the more dangerous it became.

That was not to say Philadelphia was filled completely with loyalists. Sure, there were quite a few, from what his own experiences with Arnold last Christmas had shown, but the unwritten rule seemed to be whoever held the guns commanded the loyalty.

In Philadelphia's case, those guns were firmly pointed at him and his camp. He didn't think that would last much longer, and when he and General Arnold marched to liberate the city, those same loyalists would wave a different flag—the nine-striped, red-and-white Sons of Liberty flag the Americans had adopted for their own.

The cold bit him as Collins reached the last bit of road safe to travel so openly. Philadelphia would be coming up on his right along with the Delaware and Schuylkill Rivers. He wondered if the hidden wagon-bridge was still there. But, he obviously had no intention of taking it and crossing into the city.

He felt older and wiser, more confident. General Arnold had done him a tremendous favor. His child had, too. He felt, as a father, he could tackle the world and sculpt it into the type of place safe for his child.

Collins was about to bypass the path that would take him to the city where once he had been scared witless. Since then, however, he found he wasn't so fearful after all. Even Emma had noticed and smiled at him as he stood tall against the fire, holding his child, cooing softly in his arms. But, through the trees, something in the sky caught his attention.

Collins spurred his horse through thick, bare woods, toward the Schuylkill River, in hopes of getting a clearer view. When he arrived at the clearing at the river's edge, he confirmed his suspicion. Above the city hung several wispy lines of grey smoke, feeding into a large pillar, rising into the sky, not the results of so many chimneys all stoked and lit at once.

Philadelphia was on fire.

Collins kicked his white steed and let out a sharp command as he crossed the hidden bridge and entered the farmlands outside of the city.

NINETEEN

Philadelphia, Pennsylvania
March 1ˢᵗ, 1778.

Colonel George Washington rarely smiled. Oil paintings and busts he commissioned depicted him well—stoic, with a stiff military bearing and a mouth that neither smiled nor grimaced. His thin lips wrapped around premature, rough dentures of ivory. His smile, if he had one, was held together with wires and rhinoceros horns. In truth, it hurt. The wires dug down into the soft flesh of his gums. They bled after every meal. The ivory felt unnatural against his tongue, pressing hard against his real teeth. Not a day went by that he was not plagued by pangs of toothaches and sore gums. It drained the will to show a smile.

After the news he had received over the past few days, he did not think he would ever have cause to smile again. His slave, Hercules, came through the rich, red door of mahogany, carrying a silver tray. On it sat breakfast tea and the Philadelphia Gazette. Hercules sat it down on the desk before Washington and walked away without a word.

Washington brought his personal servant over from Mt. Vernon when he took over as military governor, vacating the lavish offices of Independence Hall for far simpler ones in a three-story red brick home on High Street. His wife, Martha, was supposed to have moved into the home with him, as she so often resided with him on his postings in the Colonies. But not this winter. She stayed behind, fearing for the home they had worked so hard to build together, as if she could protect it alone through pure force of will. He would have demanded that she come stay with him, but Philadelphia was not safe, either. They were under constant threat of attack.

Now, Martha was dead.

Rumors of what happened that night circled around him and the city. People whispered behind his back. They said his slaves had escaped. Hands had been murdered. His house was ash. Washington did not care about that. Homes could be rebuilt, but families could not. When stepping into this position, he knew he risked his estate. He could have never guessed the rebels would be so bold as to bring harm to her.

Now, Washington awaited word from an official courier he had dispatched not four days ago. He had to know for sure. Unfortunately, at the time, he selected a rider noted for his speed, not his silence. Now, he hoped that would not be a mistake. The city was already on edge. Upon the courier's swift return, Washington expected, hoped, that the rumors of his wife's death were untrue, that she would be returned to him unharmed, and that the city's citizens would settle down. Until then, he dismissed the gazettes; they would say anything to hawk papers and rile spirits.

For the time being, he threw himself into his work, hoping that would help his nerves, but he discovered that it did not. He had to know. Newspaper clippings, open journals, and diaries he so meticulously kept neatly organized on shelves lay in scatters. The candle on his desk burned down to its brass base, and trails of cooled, white wax crept outward like phantom fingers reaching across the wood. The courier would return today. Washington didn't have to wait much longer.

His aide arrived, opening the door partway. When he gained the courage to enter, the plump young officer stepped inside. He was new to his posting, and Washington couldn't remember his name. He flew through aides and would continue to do so until he found one who suited him. This one had managed the job for a fortnight. Washington stared past the ensign from behind perched spectacles. Gloomy sunlight found its way through the tails of threadbare cream curtains hanging over rods to make the most of the low winter light.

Washington continued to flip through files, all research on Benedict Arnold, a man with whom he was altogether unfamiliar. Burgoyne's Bane, the papers called him. The American Hannibal. Washington found the name the natives had given the rebel, Dark Eagle, interesting. A most impressive title, far better than the scramble of consonants the natives had given to Washington in earlier days. There were whispers that the rebel general may have had something to do with the fire at his home, though Washington doubted it—nobody could be that devoid of honor. He shifted his attention from stacks of newspapers in front of him to the boy, hoping he hid his apprehension. Judging by appearances, the news was grim.

"Your Excellency," the orderly announced, fat fingers intertwined in apprehension.

"Yes?" The problem with his aide was not the youth's girth. It was that he would not speak loudly and with confidence. That could be taught and learned—if Washington could find the patience.

"There is some news—"

"Martha?" Washington asked. *Get to the point. Tell me what I need to know.*

"She," the aide stumbled after Washington cut him short. Dark brown eyes cast down to the floor. Finally, he said, "She is presumed dead, though we have..." the aide quieted, infuriating Washington further. Washington motioned heatedly for the aide to continue, which he did, in a voice even harder to hear than usual. "We have not recovered her body due to the extensive damage caused by the fires."

Washington took a deep breath. His heart pumped fiery blood down to his fists and feet, but his eyes felt wet and sunken. He took off his spectacles and threw them on the desk. He recovered and sat the spectacles down with care. Martha had given this pair to him last year upon his forty-fifth birthday.

"The messenger spread the word as soon as he returned to the city streets." In a rare display of poise, the aide's eyes finally faced him instead of at the floor. There was hope yet. He clarified, "People on the streets said he shouted, 'The house is blackened, ash trees to ashes! The lovely Lady Washington has passed!' to anyone who would listen, that damnable fool."

Washington winced. As governor, Washington had a duty to the city first, before he could mourn Martha. But, he couldn't help let out a little anger. "Bring me this rider at once!"

"Sir, there are already mobs forming in the streets. Riots seem the natural course of events, if not diverted." The aide cast a curious glance outside, then made for the nearest window, straining to make out any detail through the thick, blurry glass. "Have you not... Did you not, umm, hear the noise, sir?"

Washington hadn't noticed anything on his morning measure of the city. The streets were quiet, shops buttoned... *or were they?* The more he thought about, the more he realized he couldn't remember anything from this morning. The last thing he recalled was leafing through the stacks of papers on his desk, when Hercules entered with his silver tray. *Had I slept at my desk the whole night, or was I so lost in thought, my memory dulled?*

Commotion came from the city now, faint and distant through the brick walls and double glazed glass. This disturbance was recent, perhaps unrelated. *A bread riot?* Something manageable for someone else to deal with so that he could shut it all out.

The noise grew. He would have to act. "Never mind about the rider. I will deal with him later. Prep my horse, and let us investigate further." He would have frowned, but it would have hurt.

"Very good, sir," the boy huffed, a worried look swept across his face. Clearly, he did not enjoy the thought of exercise, but he continued, nevertheless, as was his duty. As was Washington's duty. "I will meet you outside."

Washington found he did not all together dislike the boy. The aide's plumpness was a symptom of the problem they all faced: they had grown comfortable and lax behind brick walls and beside hot fires, passing the winter months with nary a thought to the war outside. When they did discuss matters of conflict, it was couched in terms of, 'later,' 'spring,' and 'perhaps when Clinton decides.' They had lost their urgency, their initiative. It was as if the war was over, defeat in hand, yet no one bothered to tell the high command. But the war remained, and now, it struck out against their families.

Washington had just lost his wife, his home, everything that made him a Virginian. And it was all his fault for going to war in the land that was once his home. Washington crossed the Delaware. He killed General Hancock. If Washington could have taken it all back to be with Martha again, he would. He would have decided to have nothing to do with this infernal war. He would have resigned his commission and lived in quiet on the bank of the Potomac. Now he didn't even know if he belonged in America anymore. This was no longer his home. There was nothing left for him here.

When Washington opened the window to the three-story brick house and stuck his nose out, he caught a whiff of smoke. His throat dried, and his eyes wet with tears. *The mobs bypassed rioting and proceeded on to torches.* There was something wrong with this. It was too soon... too calculated. He smelled something far more foul at work. He had realized some days before that his home burned on his birthday. The message was meant for him. He thought back to the notes on his desk. The name, Benedict Arnold, floated to him like a piece of ash, hanging in the sky. He had dismissed the name at first. A coldness, a cunning, something sinister he could not quite explain settled around Washington. *Benedict Arnold, this is all your doing, isn't it?* The redness and the rage in Washington's eyes and balled fists matched the fires burning around him in the streets below.

Private Frederick Bakker hated sentry duty. He resented the British regulars and their warm, cozy beds, kept safe in the city. Bakker's underpaid and underappreciated vigilance, kept the rest of them warm while he remained out in the cold. For weeks now, the sun remained shrouded in a constant shade of grey. Today had been no different, except that today, he was the lucky one. While the British regulars were scrambling, filling buckets and pouring them on fires, burning in their warm wool uniforms, Bakker remained on sentry duty, quiet and uneventful. He almost laughed.

Even from this distance, he could tell the firefighting failed. The combined work of the King's Foot amounted to little more than a stalwart hero cutting off a hydra's head. As the British fought the flames, the fire raged and grew with more intensity. Buckets of water hissed as they turned to steam. Everywhere, that great hiss filled the streets. Smoke, ash, and soot blanketed the streets.

Bakker tried to enjoy this. He was a long way from his sentry post, having wandered in, drawn by the flames like a moth. When he reached a small stone wall that provided a good perch to gaze upon the burning city, he took a part of his uniform coat and used it to soak up a bit of water from the ledge. Then he sat, his back toward the open field behind him, facing the city. Smoke billowed past the rooftops. The cobblestone roads endured a flurry of footsteps as soldiers and citizens dashed to and fro.

A voice rose up to quell Bakker's hopes of a show. "Private Bakker, move it."

Bakker faced the sound. It did not belong to a commanding officer, but rather, a comrade on sentry duty down the line. Bakker remained sitting. He wanted to ignore it completely, but after a long pause, he answered. "*Ja?*"

"We must go in the city and assist in putting out fires. Go and tell Maximillian on down the line, and have him pass the message. Get down into the city and help out in any way you can."

Bakker turned his head back and lowered it. "*Scheisse,*" he swore and then stood with deliberate slowness. His feet hurt, and they were still damp. As if they would ever dry anyway. It was a never-ending winter in the Colonies, which would grow to a wet spring and a humid summer. You were either wet and cold or wet and hot. Either way, you were miserable.

In any case, Bakker glanced at the towering inferno ahead and thought to himself that it was about to get a whole lot hotter and wretched. He started on the cobblestone path that cut across bent blades of grass, then muddy tracks. He explained their orders to Maximillian, who also swore, then turned back around and headed toward the blaze. All the while, Bakker had a continual thought rubbing at the back of his brain. He had heard what happened to Washington and his home. *Were those same people here, burning down Philadelphia?*

Major General Benedict Arnold had just written the greatest letter of his life. Even though he sent it off to his beloved Peggy hours ago, he still went over the resplendent poetry in his head, making sure his thought and intent had been properly conveyed in the message and marveling that it had.

There was no way Peggy could resist falling for him, and her letters back toyed with that idea. She wasn't explicit, she couldn't be, but he knew it had to be true. The thought warmed his heart in the cold March mid-day. Though the sun was out, blankets of thick grey clouds dulled it. There was a bite to the air, but Arnold didn't feel it for the song in his soul.

The letters to and from Peggy were a lovely distraction. When he thought about them, he didn't think about how his plan to rattle Washington might have very well gone up in smoke. He worried about Burr and the mission. It was past time for their return, having left just over a week ago. Now that he had reacquainted himself with Peggy, it didn't seem such a bad thing to stay near the city forever.

And it wasn't as if General Gates was ever going to do anything. Leave, attack, or surrender, it didn't even matter to Arnold anymore. Just bloody *do* something. They hadn't even set up siege lines. All Gates did was hibernate in winter quarters. The Commander-in-Chief had hardly stepped outside his home or escaped the warmth of his fire. The army just sat here, rotting from the inside in the frostbitten air, save for the constant drilling on the parade field.

To be fair, Arnold acknowledged the continentals lacked the men and knowledge to properly execute a siege around a major city. Arnold reminded himself he had once camped his army outside the walls of Quebec, and it hadn't ended well. Arnold unconsciously rubbed his leg where he had caught a bullet. He was determined to play the game better this time.

Despite this, he worried. While it wasn't a complicated plan, it had its risks. And at this point, no news was bad news. If something had happened, news of it would've spread like wildfire. He had only heard whispers and read a few unconfirmed reports in the papers. This morning's Philadelphia Gazette had the same 'eyewitness' testimony. Perhaps Mount Vernon burned, but if he accepted the paper's version of the story, the estate was smote down by God himself.

Well, perhaps that wasn't too far from the truth.

Once he received word that all had gone according to plan, he would send word via Abigail to the Sons of Liberty to proceed. They had a plan, one he was not yet privy to, but he was sure it would light a fire under the chairs of those who had sat frozen all winter.

The sound of approaching hooves drew his attention as he stepped out from his room into the grey March day. He looked up in time to see three dragoons approaching. Arnold did not recognize two of the soldiers on horseback, dismissing them from his mind. The third was a friend Arnold had long known: a tall blond with short hair and gold eyes, a charmer who possessed a smile that could woo the coin out of men's pockets and the virtue out of a lady's heart.

"General Arnold," the dragoon called out to him.

"Captain Horner," Arnold answered, "I haven't called for your men yet." The captain had served together with Arnold in Connecticut. Well, not served, but the captain assisted Arnold in the Sons of Liberty, back when the group was nothing more than a disguise to cause mischief among the neighbors and protest the demands of the Crown. Now, the Sons of Liberty were fast becoming a symbol for the new nation to rally behind. Its nine-striped red-and-white flag flew over battlements and whipped in the wind along with every regiment's colors.

Captain Horner answered, "We'll be ready for you at a moment's notice for sure, but that's not why—"

"Are you sure?" Arnold asked. "You and your dragoons will accompany me into the city. They will need nerves of iron to carry out a mission such as this." The captain was loyal to Arnold, not to Gates, but loyalty was not the issue. It would be a brave thing they had to do.

"Running into an enemy stronghold? Sure. General Gates had us run across the entirety of the British line to draw fire once, just so he could get a feel for the enemy position. Running into Philadelphia and rattling our swords seems just as daft. We'll do it for you, sir."

"Very good," Arnold considered. The dragoons need not attack. They needn't do a damn thing. They just needed to be seen within the city, to prove to the misguided loyalists there that the British could be pricked. To prove they were not safe, nestled in their beds. The greatest armies often fell easiest when shown their own vulnerability. Arnold continued, "So why are you here?"

"General Gates bids you to speak with him. Sent us as a way of bringing you."

Arnold's eyes went wide in confusion. His brow furled in thought. Then he asked with a sly smile, "Am I in trouble?"

Captain Horner returned the smile, but his was better. "There are only three of. Unless the general thinks that low of you, I'd say we would be outmatched."

Arnold scoffed. *Quite the charmer.* "Very well, I'll ride with you without protest." Arnold mounted his black steed and rode with the dragoons toward General Gates' lush accommodations at the furthest edge of camp. Here, Arnold was the black sheep of the four riders, with their white horses in the soft daylight.

When they arrived, Arnold said, "Stick close, if you would

be so generous. When I return, I shall want a friendly ear." He dismounted as Captain Horner turned to the others. They all nodded in agreement. "Thank you. Thank you all. I shall have need of you soon. I'm waiting on word from Burr, then I'll unleash you like the hounds of hell on the sleeping city." *I wonder if Gates had somehow received word before me.* Arnold was confident this meeting was precisely that. It was the real reason he wanted the captain close.

When Arnold opened the door to Gates' winter abode, he was accosted by a sudden rush of warmth. No, Arnold thought. The air in here was not just warm. It was hot. A nearby fireplace, one of two burned bright with flame. Both were lit, and it felt like a summer's day inside.

Arnold wondered if Gates knew how many barefoot soldiers had perished this winter. Of course, Gates would have the number written down somewhere in a ledger or report. But he wondered if Gates had stepped outside, had visited the graves, had taken a turn through camp. Or, if Gates had stayed inside, wrapped in a blanket by two hot fires, hunched over a writing desk all winter, as he was now. More men died from dysentery, disease, hunger, and cold here than killed in battle. Did he know? Or were they just a number on some parchment?

Gates didn't waste any time. He barked from beneath the blanket in a shrill voice, as if he were one of General Charles Lee's little dogs. "What have you been up to?"

"Keeping to myself, of course," Arnold answered. He hadn't even been offered a chair, so he took one anyway. "As I recall, you stripped me of my army."

"Seems to me you've found other ways of keeping occupied. I gave you a chance to get your outstanding affairs in order. Not only have you squandered the opportunity, I think you're up to further mischief."

Arnold wanted to know what Gates believed. More importantly, he wanted to know *how* Gates learned of it. The commander was cunning, certainly, but just how clever? "I do not take your meaning."

"Then simply give me a general account of your activities of late."

Damn.

"If I could take Philadelphia by myself, I would do so, even without an army. It's what I do," Arnold capitulated. His face reddened, and most of it was not due to the heat in the room. Arnold felt like unfastening his brown waistcoat or removing his brown jacket, just to take some measure of relief.

Gates sighed, his expression weary. "Washington's estate house was destroyed. I know you know that. It's been in the papers. What I want to know is why you thought doing this would benefit you."

"I'm sorry to hear of the governor's loss. What happened at the estate is a tragedy. Even if Washington is not on our side, the destruction of a man's home is not gentlemanly," Arnold smiled. He hoped he had not been too quick to answer, or too clean. "You couldn't possibly accuse me."

"This has your signature on it." Gates squared his shoulders and leaned forward. "You have scorched the earth before. During your retreat from Quebec, you spared no field, no crop. What you cannot have, you deny to the enemy. These are the actions of a savage. Of course I suspect you. I knew it as soon as I heard reports that the city of Philadelphia is ablaze, just half an hour past."

Arnold was speechless. His face went pale. *The city... ablaze? Is that what the Sons had planned?* They had not waited for his signal. But if the rumors in the papers surrounding Martha's murder were true—something he had nothing to do with—then Arnold could see why tensions ignited so prematurely. Something else tore at him from the back of his mind. Something important. It called to him in a champagne voice.

"You would sooner destroy an American city than allow the British to hold it for a winter?" Gates' harshness broke the soft spell.

Arnold's composure broke. He could not handle his superior's daftness any longer. It was Arnold who had done the noble deeds, it was Arnold who had acted. "I would sacrifice half the Colonies if it meant some sort of victory!"

Gates scowled, ignoring the content of the outburst. "I'll understand your mind yet. I ask again, what is a general with no army doing? Sneaking in and out of camp, requisitioning supplies and soldiers for aides, yet I see no aides about you? Should I suspect something far more sinister than a simple waste of resources? Treason, perhaps?"

Arnold seethed. He wished nothing more than to rise up and challenge Gates, here and now. He'd shoot the commander right in the heart, but the voice in the back of his mind kept calling to him. He pushed it aside and answered smoothly, "What I do is my business."

The map, Arnold realized, wishing he had never thrown it in the fire. It coalesced in his mind, but not as clearly as he would've liked. He visualized homes crossed out. It started to make sense. He would bet his entire fortune, small as it now was, those homes and businesses were the ones on fire... unless of course the British were doing some burning of their own in reprisal.

"It is my business what you do, Benedict. You still answer to me. You will be held accountable—"

Peggy!

Before Gates finished another word, Arnold flew out of the chair.

He heard Gates yell, "If you dare leave this house, I'll have you drawn up on charges of insubordination and treason. You'll face a court-martial!"

Arnold had already bolted out the door. The sudden drop in temperature from the heated room to the bitter cold outside had no effect on him. He recalled quite vividly that the Shippen townhome had been crossed out. Peggy—his Peggy—was in danger.

"Ready your boys," Arnold said to the dragoon captain. "Meet me at Society Hill."

"As you command, sir."

Arnold tore off on his black steed even before the captain finished his respects.

TWENTY

Philadelphia, Pennsylvania
March 1st, 1778.

PEGGY Shippen sat in a comfortable chair in the drawing room, a stack of letters perched precariously on her lap and thoughts swirling around inside her heart. Her oldest sister, Elizabeth, and her two middle sisters, Sarah and Mary, sat in the room with her. A Murano glass lamp burned next to Peggy atop a hand carved side table, etched with leaves and cherubim, stained in a dark almond oil. A handmade doily, yellowed from age, separated the oil lamp from the table. Everything was in its place, pristine, as if it were a temple to European gods rather than a drawing room.

Peggy and her sisters wore the latest fashions because it was the English thing to do. So, because it was the thing to do, here she was, dressed in expensive pink silk. Sarah teased her every time she wore the dress. "Pink Peggy," she called her. Sarah and her other middle sister dressed in gold cotton gowns. Elizabeth wore purple.

They were dressed for reading in an ornate, fancy room designed for just that—because that is what the English aristocracy would do. Broad windows, curtains spread wide, offered them a view of the street. Outside, she thought she heard noises, louder than usual. But up here, tucked away, she was lost in a world of her father's creation.

Peggy picked up the most recent letter she had just received from the stack in her lap. While the poetry was pretty poor, she admired it for its intensity and sincerity. Still... it *was* bad. She loved it anyway, because the words were written just for her.

Although she loved and admired her father, Peggy knew he controlled her life, and she resented it. Unfortunately, she had no choice but to obey. He would decide upon a proper arrangement for marriage. He had passed on Benedict Arnold so long ago. It remained to be seen whether Andre would win her father's approval.

Her engagement to Andre was far from final. While those things were not yet sorted, she felt no reason why she could not indulge in a few fanciful letters from a man she could fantasize about being with—for the time being. She remembered Arnold from her youth. Apparently, she had made quite the impression on him. Yes, if she could marry outside of those rigid and expected English traditions, then she could see herself with the brash but roguish Arnold. If the timing had been better, if things had been different...

At that moment, a figure barged into the room, as Arnold had done so dashingly more than two months past. She gasped along with her sisters. Sarah let out a small shriek as the man entered. *Could it be?* But it wasn't Arnold. It was Andre, his overcoat flintlock out.

The hinge snapped and the door cracked into the plaster wall behind it. He didn't seem to notice. Instead, he looked right at Peggy and made for her, a worried look dissipating to one of relief as he approached. *Perhaps there was a bit of brashness in him as well.* That made Peggy want to smile, but for the seriousness of how Andre had entered.

Peggy straightened in alarm. Her sisters looked to her, but she turned to them and mouthed, "I don't know." She forgot about the letters in her lap, including the one in her hand.

She was about to speak, but Andre spoke first. "Miss Peggy, we must get you and your sisters out of here, now." He lowered his voice to a whisper. "It isn't safe."

She realized, then, the raised voices she heard earlier weren't just idle talking. Peggy rose, the letters spilling out over her lap and onto a maroon and gold woven rug. She and Sarah hurried to the window to look out before Andre could stop them.

Even before she looked out, she could smell the smoke. It smelled just like any other day, like so many chimneys with fires raging in their hearth. She reached the window and took in the scene. These were not chimney fires, and the smoke and grey ash billowing through the streets was not chimney smoke. This was deliberate, and as such, it transformed the normally crisp smells of smoke into a malodorous and maleficent veil.

The outlines of people in fine attire ran and shouted. A man out of place ran into a nearby building and returned a moment later with a small bundle of blankets under his arms. *Was he a criminal looting the home or a hero rescuing an infant?* She couldn't tell, but there were others with weapons, breaking glass and looting supplies out of shuttered shops.

Peggy gasped, and her grip tightened on the curtains. She asked, "Where would we go? It's dangerous out there." She looked to Andre. "We should stay. You would be much safer up here, with us."

Andre stepped into the middle of the room, where the scattered letters Peggy had dropped earlier lay strewn. "We cannot stay—" Andre reached down and picked them up. "What are these?"

Peggy didn't realize until now she still held one of those letters. She considered herself as one in control of her emotions. She knew how to act and play the part; she'd done it her whole life. But in this instance, she had the misfortune of being caught off-guard, and her initial response of hiding the letter in her hand behind her back betrayed the calm demeanor that came immediately afterword. "Nothing at all, Mr. Andre. Just some letters to pass the time."

If she hadn't jerked back the letter in her hand, it wouldn't have piqued Andre's curiosity, so she told herself. He scanned the letter in front of him, and his face dropped. "These aren't the poems I've written you," he said, filing through them.

He looked up, Peggy's eyes met his, and there was sadness and anger behind them. "These are all from that damnable Arnold fellow. Why would you have these?" Andre finished picking all the letters off the floor, running through each one, until he looked at the last lonely letter held by Peggy. "Is that a letter from Arnold as well?"

Sarah grabbed the letter from behind Peggy's back and read part of it in a loud abrupt voice. "'Would the stars sparkle with such might, as the light from your face, for I can see heav'n bright'r in your eyes than by gazing at the wond'rous night.'" She giggled. "This one is definitely from Mr. Arnold. I hadn't read this one, but it's just as funny as the others."

"Sarah! How could you?" In the back of her mind, Peggy realized her sister did not understand the seriousness of the situation, but that didn't keep Peggy from turning to anger. She had no idea Sarah had been reading her letters, too. *Has everyone read them?*

"What are these?" Andre asked, interrupting Peggy's thoughts as if hoping for a different answer. "What are you doing with them?"

"They are just letters. They are nothing."

"Then why do you have them? Why were they on your lap just now?"

"They give me something to do." Peggy thought quickly. "As Sarah said, they are awfully funny and nice to read."

"Why would you read them? It is obvious Arnold is infatuated with you. Do you not see that?"

"Yes."

Andre took a step back and let out a huff. "I was going to ask if you enjoyed the attention of having two suitors, but I see that not one of these are the poems I have written for you. So I shall ask if it is his attention alone that you enjoy." Andre looked out the window, smoke blew past the glass.

"I—"

Andre cut her off. "I thought your father had arranged for us to be together. Do you not wish to be wed? is there no love between us?"

"It is not not really about love, is it?" Peggy responded, her words filled with annoyance. "What is wrong with being courted by more than one suitor? I have not yet heard my father agree to any formal arrangement, and you've not asked me."

He seemed perturbed. With another huff he explained, "I am in the transition of seeking a major's billet. It is expected that I take a wife."

"Any woman would do?"

"It's not like that," Andre said as he blew out a long breath. "I need a proper match, and you are the shining jewel of the city. I would be the Chief Intelligence Officer of the British forces in America. Prestigious indeed!"

Shining jewel? She was a jewel, but not one to be set in another's crown. She wanted to say that. Instead, without thinking, she blurted out something that would hurt him, an attack on his manliness. "A spy? You would make a horrendous spy. You would get caught and hung before the year is out."

Her sisters laughed.

"Why do you treat me so?" asked Andre.

That was a bit too harsh. She took a few verbal steps back. "Come, come. If we are indeed to be wed, we cannot take each other so seriously all the time."

That got his attention. "Are we to be wed?"

"That is not for me to decide. If my father says we are to be wed, than we will."

"And if he refuses?"

"Then we will not."

"It's that easy for you?"

"I am a woman in a man's world. I am resigned to it. I will play my part. I have my lines to speak. That is all."

"You are vexing," Andre's eyes grew big and he cast them to the carpet like a puppy that had just been kicked. "I do not understand how you could keep these letters. You are the best thing that's happened to me, but this damned Arnold fellow has been haranguing me ever since I arrived in Quebec. And now, of all the women in the world, he chooses you. It will not stand. It cannot. Can't you see Arnold does not love you? He hates me."

Peggy laughed. She tried to stop it, but it just happened. It wasn't so much the letters, but rather who they were from. She knew the laughter would be taken wrong, especially with an audience full of women. Andre looked at her and soured.

"What is the matter with you? I did not come here to match wits with a woman; I came here to save—" Andre remained silent for a long pause and turned to the commotion directly outside the window. He looked as if he'd continue the tirade, but then his face grew concerned. Almost simultaneously, they all smelled it.

Smoke.

Andre said, "We will continue this at some other date. First, I must get you to safety."

Despite the danger, Peggy was curious. "What is going on?"

"Those da—" He stopped himself, as if embarrassed at cursing out of anger. Then he continued, omitting the word, "Those rebels whom you so enjoy are systematically burning down homes belonging to loyal citizens of the King. Your father is very much loyal. Ergo, you are in danger. It appears this house has already been attacked. We must go. Follow me."

Andre still gripped the letters. He was nowhere near a side table. He could have dropped them on the floor, but Peggy noted that he stuffed them purposefully within his boot as if planning on using those against her when the argument resumed. She frowned.

Then, instead of reaching for her hand, Andre once again retrieved his flintlock, loaded and cocked, and held it ready. The five of them went out into the second floor hallway and down the stairwell. Two servants followed.

Part of the ground floor was already ablaze. Curtains and the fabric material on the sofa had caught. Thick smoke filled the room. Peggy coughed. She could barely breathe. The front door was already wide open, as if the downstairs servants had already fled, leaving their masters upstairs to a different fate.

Peggy clutched the banister, covering her mouth with her fancy English dress and descended the stairs, grabbing a sister's hand by the wrist and dragging her down with them. Andre cleared the stairs, sweeping his pistol side to side in case of any intruder or would-be looter.

He stopped for a moment, but Peggy didn't know why. Andre grabbed a pair of curtains from the wall, ripping the rod away from the plaster. The fire was small, and Peggy could see Andre attempting to smother the blaze, but it spread faster than it was being snuffed out. They had no choice but to evacuate to the dangerous city streets outside.

"Come on, but be careful when we leave," Andre announced. They all exited the exquisite home, perhaps for the last time. Peggy was wary, concerned that whoever started the blaze would be outside waiting for them.

Sure enough, as they stepped out into the gloomy March afternoon, she saw someone in front of them, though it was impossible to tell through the smoke and ash if it was friend or foe. Smoke stung her eyes and obscured her vision ahead, but she could still see Andre and her sisters as they stopped in apprehension. A glint of recognition darted across Andre's face, and then his eyes turned cold as if in anger. She'd seen that face once before. Could the figure be that of Benedict Arnold?

It couldn't be. Was Arnold behind all this? Did he set fire to their home? Or was he here to rescue me? Her mind fell between flashes of anger and something else. Was it love? Whatever she felt, Peggy did not get the chance to think on it longer.

Andre aimed his pistol and fired.

By horse, Corporal Henry Collins was less than an hour's ride to the freezing wastes of Valley Forge. Philadelphia loomed in front of him, a pyre of smoke rising in the sky. The flames drew him. He no longer held any fear of the redcoats. General Arnold had seen to that. He was just a civilian, same as everyone else here, and he knew he could walk openly through the city, easily and freely—especially with everyone's attention turned to the fire.

A smattering of farmhouses sat on either side of him, and a small church lay ahead. Collins cut across the lawn of the church's cemetery as he neared the first cobblestone streets of the city. *Strange.* He hadn't noticed the church before, but that had been in darkness in the rain while his heart beat a hundred times faster than it did now. Collins felt calm and cool with little fear in his step. He would report back to General Arnold what he saw in the city, or if the city was under attack, join in the fight to liberate it.

Already, the streets billowed with smoke. At that proximity, he heard the chaos—the flickering of flames, the wails of those trapped, and the footfalls of would-be rescuers, racing on the red cobblestone roads with full buckets sloshing about.

When he arrived at the edge of the city, he made for the only cover he saw, crouching behind a cheap, wooden wagon in major disrepair—a wheel sat by it, separated at the axle. The cart itself was empty, and some of the lumber had been torn off. He peered around the cart. Water puddles rested every few feet along the streets. Higher up, water dripped from the eaves of several nearby buildings. Water mingled with waste in the street, creating brown rivers running down the roads.

There were few people nearby, but most of them looked occupied, their attention on the city. Someone glanced back and caught sight of him. The man looked confused, but turned his attention back toward the blaze. Collins ducked and then cursed himself silently. He was foolish, he realized. He looked more suspicious hunched over, hiding, rather than upright and out in the open. He forced himself to stand, wrapping his borrowed black cloak around him as if that would help hide him.

Now, he felt fear.

He made sure the crimson cockade was firmly attached to his coat, as he walked down the city streets. Lines of soldiers and citizens alike snaked around him now, passing buckets of water. Those at the beginning of the line filled them; those at the end dumped them out onto the fire. Empty buckets passed back and forth, replaced by full ones.

Collins wondered what had caused the fires. They seemed sporadically set with no single focal point. He saw no signs of battle, and only individual homes or shops had been set ablaze, along with the rare townhome where the fire from one building had spread to the next.

Walking into the city gave Collins an odd sense of confidence. His fear subsided, and he considered whether he should help on the fire line. After all, the city wouldn't be in British hands for long.

A British officer ahead called out orders. He looked around and spotted Collins. Collins' heart jumped, then sank into his stomach like a lead ball—his confidence eroded. The redcoat shook his head in disapproval, but for what reason, Collins did not know for sure. Collins turned away as casually as he could and went down a different street, out of sight of the soldier. Time for him to leave.

The townhome across from him leapt alive with flame with little warning other than a brief instant of smoke pouring out of an opened window. A shadow rushed from the home, through the smoke, and out of Collins' sight. He went to pursue the shadow, but before he could, he heard a woman's voice scream something unintelligible.

Then he saw her, a young Negro of twenty or so dressed in plain clothes for so fancy a neighborhood. Coughing in fits, she ran toward him screaming, "Help, baby in home!"

Instinctively, Collins approached the woman, grasping her arms. "Where's the baby?"

"I dun'no. Is so dark, I could no see baby. I left master's baby playin' in the corner, but baby no there now." Though the Negro was not the baby's mother, tears streamed down her eyes all the same.

Collins looked around. He was the closest one to the home and the person the Negro had come to. Of course he would risk running into the burning building, but he worried he would not find the child either—or, if he did, it might bring unwanted attention his way. But it didn't matter. He'd expect a stranger to do the same for Emma and Jane. "I'll find him."

A look of dismay crept onto his face as he hurried into the burning building.

General Arnold raced toward the city, the mouth of his steed dripping with foam. Before long, Arnold came across the hidden bridge. He edged down toward the riverbank, but the horse seemed reluctant to cross. The Schuylkill did not flow more rapidly than it had before, but all the same, the horse refused to be coaxed.

Arnold had to get off his horse and step into the river himself. He grabbed the animal by the reins, and encouraged the horse to follow him. The water was cold, and the wagons shifted under their own weight. He had to take it slow and steady, but his patience grew thin. After being ridden so hard, the horse wasn't in the mood to carry Arnold across the water. Horses, like people, could be annoying bastards.

Finally, they made it to the other side. Budding trees surrounded them. He still had to traverse fields and farmhouses before reaching the city. It appeared an impossible distance off. He was about to re-mount when he caught sight of a riderless horse he recognized: his own, on loan to a Corporal—Collins if he remembered correctly. It had been a few weeks.

But why would it be here?

Arnold hoped he had not filled the boy's head too much. Perhaps he had unwittingly rubbed off on the boy. Collins was going to get himself killed or captured. Arnold mounted, no longer caring about the horse's exhaustion, and spun into the city.

Now, he had two people to save.

Collins exited a few moments later. He coughed, wiping the stinging smoke from his eyes, but generally, he was fine. And so was the thick bundle of blankets wriggling in his arms.

"You dun'it! You save the baby!" The Negro woman ran up to them. "Ever'one, look at this here hero!"

Collins would prefer they didn't. Besides, he hadn't done anything heroic. Collins had found the baby right off, hiding under a table, chewing on something no doubt picked up off the floor. He seemed nonplussed about the fire, almost casual, but he had screamed and shook when Collins picked him up, wrestling and kicking and finally going limp to get free. The baby had to have been under a year old, but he looked older. Collins had used blankets to grab him and protect them both from the fire.

Now that the blankets were removed and they were in the obscured light outside, he could see him better. The boy was big with blonde hair and blue eyes and a few teeth, and he was heavy, especially compared to his little Jane. The boy almost broke free again, but not before Collins was able to hand him off to the Negro.

"Thanks to you. Thanks to you," she said.

Collins looked away, stepping back and shaking his head, anger in his step. The Negro had no children. A parent would have gone back in. And then it hit him and it him hard, as if the burning building itself had collapsed on top of him. *I left my child while the world burns.*

Fury filled him. It wasn't that he was in over his head in enemy occupied Philadelphia. It was not that he had chosen to go to war, leaving his family behind in hopes of making a better world. No, his world was already better. And it was the small, stupid things—like staying up all night with his daughter asleep on his chest because she could not sleep alone—that had made it better.

Now, he realized his errors, happy that he was still alive. He coughed a little more. The tears falling were no longer from the smoke. *Time to leave.* Unfortunately, his actions had earned him unwelcomed attention. People with buckets approached as if Collins should join their line at the head, brave as he was. He did not want to be here. He could not be. *Damn.*

A figure whipped past his eyes. Collins caught sight of the shadow again. It loomed just ahead and to his right, the direction he had picked for his escape. The figure stopped for some reason and looked right at him. He saw pale eyes. They spoke fury. Abruptly, the man took off down the street toward the Delaware.

Anger welled up inside Collins. That had to be the barbarian who started the flame. No one should put a child at risk like that. No one should ever hurt a child. Not even in war.

Collins went after him, blood pumping fire into his legs. He was surprised to see himself catching up to the man, but the figure seemed winded almost at the outset. Then the man disappeared again.

He caught sight of the man as he turned the corner. Collins found himself a few blocks down from where he had been, in the middle of an empty road. He stopped and froze the moment he recognized where he was. *Society Hill.* This was Peggy's street. And there were Peggy's steps, where he had stood last Christmas Eve.

Collins heard a crash, the sound of broken glass. Then a thud as something crashed inside the home. He looked up and saw the figure toss a lighted torch into the home. His heart skipped a beat. Rage built up in him, but this was not the place Collins wanted to be. Then, he saw the flames and smelled smoke.

The figure did not see him, and Collins could tell he was finished with his task of setting fire to the Shippen home. The man was about to turn around, but there was no place for Collins to go. He could either retreat or confront the man who had set fire to at least two homes—one of which had a baby in it. Collins would have fled a few months ago, but now...

Collins let out a cry, and lunged at the man, knocking him backward. The man stumbled to the ground with a groan, the hard, uneven surface of the street doing more damage to the man then Collins' lunge. He sat up as if to confront his attacker.

From here, Collins could see the man clearly. He was large, broad faced, broad-shouldered, though one of the shoulders was wrapped tightly in bandages, his arm in a sling. Even through the waistcoat and wrappings, Collins could tell the shoulder underneath was badly damaged. It looked larger than the other one and let out a purplish hue under the white shirt. It was either a fresh wound or one that refused to heal. Despite his wounds, there was a toughness to him. Thin, sharp eyes and razor-thin eyebrows glared at Collins in a stare that sliced right through him.

The man recovered from the ground beneath him and let out a kick that tore through Collins' abdomen, causing him to heave uncontrollably. He sucked air as the man regained his footing, wasting no time with a jab straight at Collins' face.

Collins tried to block with an upraised hand, but the momentum went right through it and carried his own hand into his face, effectively hitting himself. The world went bright white then black for a split second, but Collins managed to return a jab of his own.

The blow sent the man back, and Collins felt the edge of victory, but the older man was beside him, sidestepping out of harm's way. Before Collins could react, the man landed a hard blow to Collins right temple, enough to topple him down. He couldn't control the fall, either. He just collapsed on the cobblestones, which hurt like hell when the other side of his head smacked into them.

He might have been eager to confront the man, but that didn't mean he possessed the strength or skill to defeat him, Collins thought remorsefully. He'd just been beaten by an older, one-armed man. Then, Collins remembered his pistol, the one Arnold had lent him. He reached for it, but then the man towering above him spoke.

"I wouldn't do that if I were you." The voice was rough and commanding. Then the man asked, "It looks like we're on the same side, you and I. So why the surprise?"

Collins tried to shoot off a look of confusion, but his face was already starting to swell. So he just sat there instead in silence and listened.

"You're a Yankee soldier. I spied you and the general back here at Christmas. Looked right at both of you during the dance. Followed you to the blue house. Don't know what you're doing back here again, you stupid bastard, unless you brought your army this time." The wounded man looked around. "But I see nothin'."

"And what are you doing, that we'd be on the same side?" Collins challenged, his anger compensating for the pain at his temples. "You might be General Arnold's contact, but the way I see it, you were setting fire to babies."

"Houses. Not babies. Houses. You got that baby out, didn't you? I saw you, I did. Safe and sound that Tory is. Gonna grow up nice and strong and hate us Yanks. The army should be doing the same thing, torching the place, instead of setting out there in that field with your damned thumbs up ya arses. If you can't keep Philly, you damned well shouldn't let the British buggers keep it, either."

"So you're going to burn it down?"

"Aye, aren't we a sharp one, eh?" The man stood tall and confident. "It's all planned you know, on account of that

Washington fellow. Had his house burned down to the ground, you see. But it wasn't supposed to happen for a few more days. Rumors spread faster than truth, I suppose. Proper news takes time. We just received word of that this morning."

The man's face showed an unexpected weary sadness. "Then the fool redcoats took torches to some of buildings still left standing that belonged to a few of the patriotic types. Beat us to the punch. Don't know any names, but for the Franklin fellow, John Andre will be terse that his own side burned his living quarters to ash." He huffed and remained silent for a moment.

Smoke filled the air, and ashes from the nearby fires intermingled and twirled in the air. "Well, use your own damned eyes to see the rest of the story. So you see, we're on the same side after all. Better check next time before you knock a wounded man to the ground." With that, he extended his good hand down to Collins. "Best be moving."

No, Collins thought. This couldn't be how the world was. Aflame. Ash falling. *His* side with torches, burning it all. His thoughts drifted back to the baby he had carried out of the building, to his own child at home. He couldn't wrap his sore head around it. *This old spy can go to hell,* Collins swore silently. "We're not on the same side."

The spy withdrew his hand. "Have it your way, but these folks here are Tories, and they've made your life as a soldier in the field a living hell whether you know it, or like it. They'll be running out of that house any second, so you better get moving, on account of they won't be nearly so kind to you as I was."

Kind? Collins wanted to laugh, but he couldn't. He hurt.

He picked himself up off the road, the pistol still in his hand as a swirl of smoke and ash surrounded him. As the man raced away, the white door to Ms. Shippen's home opened.

"Run! This way. Follow me," the spy said, darting down the road and disappearing around a corner.

Collins knew the man was right. Now more than ever, he needed to leave, to get out of this hell, before Ms. Shippen saw him.

But it was not a lady who exited the home first. It was a man in plain clothes, with others behind him. Collins froze. It took a moment to register, but through the gloomy sky and thick smoke, he recognized the glimpse of that face. It had burned into his dreams for a fortnight after Christmas. This was the British officer who opened the door that Christmas Eve.

Collins didn't know why, but everything seemed to become molasses. He tried to move, but everything he did was not quick enough. Since his legs refused him a means to escape, he did the only other thing he could...

He raised his pistol, but Collins never got a chance to fire.

There was a single sound. A sound louder than anything he had ever heard, louder than even the cannon. There was no pain. Somehow, in an instant, he just knew that he had been shot.

But in that instant was an eternity's worth of life and wisdom coalescing in and out of reality before him. In that last eternal moment, he looked upon the truth. Collins had held everything important to him already, and there was no reason to go out in search of it.

He was somebody. He was somebody who mattered to his daughter. To his wife. To his parents and family. To his friend, Stevens. Those simple relationships were the important things that mattered above all else. It was a simple lesson, but one which took him a lifetime to learn. In that moment, stretching onward toward the stars, he felt warmth spreading across his heart.

He looked down and saw his daughter laying there, asleep on her stomach across his chest. Her warmth next to his. The rise and fall of her back as she breathed softly. Her breath. Her small hand grasping his finger. He was happy. He was content. Everything that mattered was right here. Emma smiled at him. He smiled back.

His last breath blew out of him, and blackness closed in.

TWENTY-ONE

Philadelphia, Pennsylvania
March 1st, 1778.

CAPTAIN John Andre stood there, aghast, completely detached from the scene before him. There was a man, dead. The face was recognizable but not who he thought.

That is not Benedict Arnold.

The smell of black powder hung in the air and bit into his nose. The smoke from the barrel faded against the carnage of the city as small, white flakes of ash fell to the earth. It wasn't the first time he'd fired the flintlock he carried in his overcoat, he thought, but it was the first time he'd killed a man with it.

And the wrong man at that.

He tried to push the thought to the back of his mind, but the corpse in front of him defied his attempts at denial. The white ash drifted to the ground, burying the body in a curious juxtaposition of soft snow as hellfire raged all around them.

He had come here to see his future fiancée to safety, and he was in the middle of that task now. The man had simply gotten in the way. With that, he realized that he had more work to do. If this wasn't Arnold, then he still didn't know if this was a concerted attack on the city by the rebels, or if it was the work of a few turncoats working in the city alone. He heard the clatter of horseshoes on the cobblestones heading their way. There could be more of them, he realized. He had to get the ladies to safety.

But first...

Andre knelt before the body sprawled down in front of him and closed his eyes. Ash pooled on his eyelids and caught in his eyebrows like a feathering of angel dust. The man looked as if he were at rest. "You were in the wrong place at the wrong time," Andre whispered, as if that would put wrong to rights.

"Come on, quickly now," he called to the four ladies. He looked at them as he stood. Elizabeth and Mary held each other. Peggy seemed cool headed and composed. Sarah, on the other hand, clutched at Peggy and wailed at what he guessed was the sudden loss of her home, the corpse lying in front of her, and the inferno swirling all around.

The hoofbeats grew louder, so Andre had no choice but to leave the body in the street. A thin blanket of ash already covered him like a blanket. That would have to do for the present.

Andre shuffled Peggy and Sarah down the way. He looked around, but in the ash and carnage, he couldn't discern the best route before Peggy brushed the others aside and stepped out in front. "If we are heading to the river, it is this way."

Andre smiled in spite of everything. Moments like this made him love her. He could almost forgive her Arnold's letters. In truth, he knew she didn't need saving; he had used the fires as an excuse to see her again.

Then, his smile faded. That wasn't true, he realized. What would have happened to her with that soldier? Andre's lips turned downward, and his heart grew hard. He raised himself up, with sanguine strength, and started down the road.

They made it a few steps when he heard an angry voice call out, "Murderer."

Andre recognized the voice just as hoofbeats crashed down behind him. He spun and looked up, but got an eye full of ash. His eyesight blurred, with the form of a large man on horseback towering over him. Something very heavy and hard landed on his head. It erupted into a cacophony of throbbing agony surrounded by flashes of light and dark. Through the pain, Andre recognized the real Benedict Arnold. A second after that, he collapsed to the ground.

Corporal Frederick Bakker had been passing buckets for a little over an hour, but it felt like his entire life. It had appeared a simple thing to do, so he jumped at the chance when he came upon a fire line forming to save an old house near Fourth South and High Street.

At least he wasn't near the fire itself, nor was he perched high on a ladder, dumping buckets of water on the rooftops while homes burned from below. Bakker was grateful for that—he could just as easily watch their hard work from down here while sticking to passing buckets, although his back ached with the constant twisting motion. He hadn't imagined buckets of water would be so heavy, or that there would be so many. He wondered how much longer this could continue. Looking around at the smoke filling the sky, he guessed it might go for some time. He wished he was back on duty again, bored and cold.

His prayers for a reprieve were answered when an angry-looking British officer bellowed at the soldiers in the line. Some of them, like Bakker, were Hessians on sentry duty, now tasked to put out the blaze. Bakker only knew the name of a handful of the British officers. This wasn't one of them, but he knew, essentially, the lowest-ranking British officer outranked any Hessian, which meant he had to listen. So he stopped and put the heavy wooden bucket of water down at his feet. The man next to him gave Bakker a coarse look and picked it up before realizing the line had all but stopped.

Bakker's English was still near non-existent, except for the few curses he had learned, so he had no idea what the man said. The officer let loose a few foul words, some of which Bakker knew. It told Bakker they weren't being rewarded for their hard work. Bakker groaned in frustration. The pale-skinned British officer yelled even louder now, his face turning cerise and sweaty.

After that, a few men, all Hessians, melted out of the line. One of them, Maximillian, tapped him on the shoulder. He spoke in Prussian, "He wants to know why we left our posts. He is angry." Bakker had understood that much.

His sergeant continued, "He also says we are putting out the wrong fire. He says not to worry about this one. He says this home belonged to a man named Benjamin Franklin and that the officer himself had set fire to it earlier. He wants us all to leave this fire and make ready our defenses for attack. Governor Washington's orders."

Bakker shrugged inwardly. The owner of the house wasn't his concern. Neither were the fires burning down the city. *What difference did it make?* Bakker had a hard time distinguishing between the people living in the city and rebels living outside. They all looked the same to him.

He didn't know who Franklin was, either, but apparently he was someone who didn't want the British here. It was a shame because now, he had lost his home. That was something Bakker could commiserate with, his thoughts drifting to his mother's home in the bustling streets of Kassel. Bakker gave an empathetic nod toward this house, now in ashes, then turned and asked, "So, what now?"

"Back to where we were. Sentry duty. Come, let's go."

Bakker smiled and followed Maximillian. It was the best news he'd heard all day.

"I should have killed you, Andre. You have no right to live." General Arnold spat at the figure slumped on the ground, dazed and semi-coherent. "Had I known you were going to kill Corporal Collins, I would have made sure to take Saint Jean and leave your corpse laying twisted in its wake. Now, I will have to settle for having you hung."

Arnold dismounted his horse and walked up to Peggy. Without meaning to, he took hold of her wrist and yelled, "What happened?"

Peggy, for her part, slapped Arnold with an unexpected burst of frustration. "The house was on fire. Andre came in and escorted us out. Your man there was outside the door when we came out, pistol in hand."

Peggy glared at him. Sweat from the heat of the flames dampened her skin, making her anger all the more real and fiery. She tore her wrist free and stepped forward, forcing Arnold to step back. "The real question is whether you destroyed my home or not. It did not even occur to me that this might have been something by your design until you swooped in. Now, here you are. Did you mean to save me? Or did you mean to hurt me?"

She gestured at her sore wrist from where Arnold grabbed her. Then she looked at her home, completely engulfed in flame. Then, she gestured to the city and the rain of red hellfire all around. "Did you mean to cause all of this?"

"I never meant—"

"The real question," Peggy cut him off, "is whether *you* killed your soldier or not."

Arnold took another step back, at a complete loss of what to say. He looked over at Collins, then walked over to him, knelt down, and put his hand on Collins' shoulder. When he was sure no one was looking, he slipped off the loyalist cockade from Collins' cloak. He patted the soldier's chest. Then, Arnold stood, resolute, and said, "No, Peggy, of course not. I had no idea any of this would happen. I didn't even know my friend was here..." In his mind, Arnold finished the thought. *I thought he was at home with his wife and newborn.* "I came against orders to find you. And yes, to save you. I didn't realize this... *monster*... would be here."

"This *gentleman*," Sarah interjected, "and he happens to be marrying her."

Elizabeth spoke. "He knows. He was there."

Sarah looked confused. Peggy still looked angry and hurt.

"You're not still marrying him," Arnold asked, "after what he did?"

"You mean," Peggy said, "after what *you* did?"

"No..." Arnold's sword clattered to the street. His tanned skin went pale as ash continued to rain down. Fires crackled in the background. Wood snapped and popped as it was consumed. "What about my letters?"

"Letters? Are letters enough to kindle a heart during an inferno? We are from two separate worlds, Mister Arnold! You are a Montague while I remain always a Capulet. It has to be your world that burns or mine. *Our* world will never be."

Arnold's throat went dry, but not from the heat of the fire. He saw Andre stand but couldn't deduce his intentions. Arnold wanted to dive at the man and throttle a confession out of him. *It was Andre's fault. He killed Henry. Couldn't Peggy see?*

He knew Andre's only weapon was his faux officer's sword, as his pistol was fired and empty. There was little Andre could do. But what Andre did next surprised Arnold more than any pistol Andre could have pulled.

He yelled, "The city is under attack. The rebels are here!"

A moment later, General Benedict Arnold heard a series of hoofbeats. It sounded like the whole British Army racing down the street toward him. His heart skipped a beat as he looked around for an exit. Fires and people and movement everywhere blocked any route of escape.

Andre looked at him, gloating in his victory. "You shall make a nice prize indeed. If that will not land me the hand of the fair Peggy and my major's billet, then I shall want nothing more of the King's Foot."

"My hand is my own," Peggy said sternly, making sure voice was heard. "Nor did I ever need rescuing."

"But, isn't that sweet?" Sarah asked. "Both of them came to your aid."

"Quiet, both of you. Don't you see? We've lost our home. There's a body lying dead at our feet, and still you squabble. That is pathetic." Elizabeth, the eldest sister, put an end to the discussion. Her eyes drew moist with tears. "We must be going."

"We have nowhere to go," Sarah answered.

The hoofbeats drew nearer, and Arnold heaved a sigh of relief. Those soldiers belonged to him. Of course, the dragoons shouldn't have been so close to the center of the city. Something wasn't right.

Two dragoons encircled Andre, pointing sabers at his throat, while Captain Horner approached Arnold. "We heard the shot and thought you were dead. I am glad to see we were wrong." Horner pardoned himself first in front of the ladies, tipping his hat.

Horner looked down at Arnold. "We must be off. The redcoats are already starting to reorganize. Our time to escape is drawing thin."

Then the captain turned to Andre. "And it appears you are coming with us. General's orders. We are to bring back Arnold as well as any one soldier Arnold may be 'associating' with. My apologies—" The captain, glanced over at Collins' body. His voice cracked, then halted. "Never mind. I take back my apology if you had anything to do with this." He pointed to one of the two dragoons. "See to it that the captain is bound." He dismounted, taking a large flag out of his saddlebag. It was the same flag he had carried for years, first as a Son of Liberty and now as a soldier. He walked somberly toward Collins.

The flag was the same all members of the Sons of Liberty carried: thick flax linen, no cotton, with five red strips running lengthwise across, giving the distinction of nine red and whitish-yellow stripes. It was a hasty covering, yet this flag had an elegance to it that seemed fitting to wrap a fallen soldier in. Collins' wound stuck to the sheet and stained part of the white stripes red.

Horner and the third dragoon carried the body and tied it to his horse. Then, they all mounted and made ready to depart.

The four ladies stood there, alone. Their home, and the homes attached to it, now lay as a cindered char of ghastly horror, its skeletal walls a memory of what it had been just an hour before.

What a difference one moment in time could make, Arnold thought.

Arnold tore his gaze from Collins and turned his attention toward the girls. They had to flee the city before they wore out their welcome or, like Andre, they would be captured. But he had to say goodbye to Peggy one last time.

Peggy and her sisters stood fuming, but they remained silent and mournful. Arnold approached from the safety of his horse. "Capulets and Montagues, eh? If only Shakespeare could have used you to capture the beauty of Juliet." He looked at her and smiled, but she did not return it. "I've always preferred Julius Caesar, myself. At least, the first part anyway. Once again, I apologize for the intrusion. And I am sorry for the loss of your home. Will you accompany us back to camp?"

"Go to Hell."

"Yes, ma'am." He looked around. It appeared they were already in it.

"What will happen to him, to Andre?"

"Most likely he'll be taken to Albany, spend a few weeks as a prisoner, then be exchanged or paroled. Then, it will be back to England for him unless they hang him for murder. But, when he is gone, I'll be happy to take care of you."

"Then, I suppose I will fight to free him," she replied, ignoring him. "Then I may move to England." She stared at the cloud of ash where her home once stood. Her golden hair, dampened with perspiration, framed her face. "I have nothing here."

Arnold wanted to correct her, tell her they could ride off together, right now, and that all the he had to offer was hers. Instead, he nodded in empathy. "You'll be heading to the river?"

She nodded. Her sister responded in kind.

"Then, I kindly take my leave of you all." Captain Horner and his dragoons had already left, taking Andre and the body of Collins with them. Arnold bowed and rode off, anger seething. Now that his back faced Peggy, he could let it out. On one hand, Peggy was a nuisance. He wondered what other kind of trouble she could have caused for him. For a moment, he was glad to be away from her. On the other hand, he was glad she was safe. She seemed so lovely. His heart beat out a protest as he rode away from her.

Private Bakker was happy to head back to his post. The smell of the city drifted behind him, and thinning smoke still obscured objects in the distance. Ash still fell around him. Some of his unit reformed, but instead of going back to their individual posts, they formed ranks together for reasons he did not know. He attempted to keep the smoke from bothering him, but his eyes stung, and sometimes, tears leaked out. His eyes were red from the near-constant rubbing. He'd be glad when he reached the city perimeter and away from most of the smoke, if not the ash.

He and a few other members of his regiment formed beside Maximillian. Whoever was in charge of the city was restoring order from chaos. Units reorganized, and the people fought the flames back. Soldiers began to patrol the streets in ranks, like a proper, disciplined unit. Bakker approved. *Let others fight the fires.* It wasn't his city, though he still wondered who started the fires and if he or his unit would run into them.

It was then that he heard the familiar beat of hooves from behind him; they sloshed through the brown rivers that now ran over the streets. While Bakker and the Hessians had to trudge through the sludge, officers apparently never had to walk, splashing as they rode past. He prepared to cover his face and as much of his uniform as he could so he wouldn't have to spend half the night cleaning it, before he realized that there were far too many horses coming in behind him. *Damn pferds*, he cursed at the beasts as the first horse and rider passed.

Bakker dove out of the way of the horseman. He tore right and slammed into a red-bricked building, breaking the impact hard with his right shoulder. He pushed himself away, and his rifle slid down his shoulder. It would have splashed into a puddle had he not caught it by the strap. He looked to his side, where Maximillian fared little better. Then, he turned to the damned officer who had nearly trampled him underfoot, and his jaw dropped. The horseman was not wearing a British uniform. *Was it an American?*

It couldn't be.

But there before him, racing full-on, were several horsemen wearing the uniforms of the enemy. Bakker reeled back in confusion. *Was the city under attack?* He didn't think it was, but he couldn't explain why a group of dragoons had just come from *behind* him. Maximillian called out in Prussian, "Fire!" Bakker groped desperately for his rifle.

Arnold had not caught up with the rest of the dragoons; the three of them slowed down for him. Still, even slowing down, he trailed several yards behind the trio. One of the riders had also let it slip that Gates waited for Arnold back at camp. He didn't look forward to that meeting, but he knew it was time for a reckoning. He wouldn't be easy to discipline.

Arnold worried that his plan had fallen apart. Still, he had accomplished nearly everything he set out to do. Governor Washington felt the heat. The British must realize by now that Philadelphia was too difficult to hold.

When the British retreated with their coat-tails between their legs, it would prove a boon to the rebel cause and crush the idea of the invincible British. What's more, Philadelphia wasn't as remote as Saratoga. Everyone in New England would know Arnold had a hand in this. He would triumph over Gates.

Arnold could see all of this in his head. He could see Gates understanding this, too, giving Arnold all the leverage he needed to smooth things over, like he had many times before. He was too important to the cause. Arnold even thought he could see a way to honor Collins and his horrific sacrifice. He could put it to good use. Collins' death, Arnold reasoned, would be for a greater good.

What Arnold didn't see, particularly through the grey smoke and ash that clouded the streets, was a group of Hessians up ahead. He noticed their presence when they dove out of the way as the three dragoons rode through them. Captain Horner had just about run them over, sending the Hessians scattering out of the road like ants after a mound was kicked.

They recovered too quickly for Arnold's liking. He heard an order, barked in an unfamiliar language, but it didn't sound promising. He gathered the reins of his horse and urged the black stallion onward. The horse responded but couldn't move any faster. Besides, it wasn't safe to gallop over cobblestones. Arnold was already pushing his luck at the pace he was going.

A moment later, the world became a confused, spinning mass hurtling wildly out of Arnold's control. Muskets fired a few yards away, and they all seemed to point at him. The sound was deafening. Arnold thought he might have been hit but had no time to consider it, for all too soon, he knew his poor horse had been.

The horse let out a scream, then dropped down, dead. Arnold kept going. The momentum of the sudden stop threw him in the air, away from his saddle and into the brown water pooling on the stone street. He splashed hard into the wet road as his right shoulder shot out in pain. Everything continued to spin and the world went white.

Bakker had been told, on more than one occasion, he fired his weapon too high. He belonged to an elite team of soldiers, and though he did his soldierly job, he was ordered to improve. Bakker typically did what was required of him and little more. He didn't think that made him any worse—or better—a soldier. Why would anyone else do anything different?

But seeing the rebels tear through the city caused him to swell up in anger, as if his very pride had been attacked. So, Bakker took a firm grip on his rifle. He saw a target, a large and imposing man, impossible to miss. He made sure that his rifle was lower than he normally held it, so that it would compensate for the upward recoil during firing. The large rebel was squarely in his sites.

Bakker fired. Then he cursed.

He knew he had hit his target. Or rather, he would have hit his target. But, someone else had also fired, but they had hit the horse instead. The rebel flung from the saddle into the street.

Before Bakker could respond or reload, two dragoons had stopped and recovered him, while a third horseman placed himself between the Hessians and the other dragoons, brandishing a sword in one hand and a small firearm in the other. Bakker didn't know if the dragoon still had a shot. He didn't want to find out. The blond-haired dragoon smiled. *That was strange.*

A moment later, the three dragoons charged off again, each horse burdened with an extra rider as they made their escape. They couldn't possibly catch up to the dragoons on foot. Bakker was disheartened. By all rights, that rebel should have been dead, he thought. He just wished someone hadn't shot the horse. At the very least, he should have been in Hessian hands. Instead of celebrating with an extra gill of rum tonight, he'd be out in the cold again.

He went back to reforming with his regiment, talking about what had just happened, putting on some false bravado, and secretly wishing for this *furchtbar* war to be over.

The first thing General Horatio Gates noticed upon the dragoon's return were the horses. They were slick and wet, their mouths covered in foam. This, Gates understood. They rode hard and quick like lightning out of the city. They had to, or else they would have been caught.

The next thing Gates saw caused him to crush his reading glasses in his right hand. He didn't even know he had done it until pain cut through his palm. He looked down to see blood from where the glass had shattered.

Even though the same number of dragoons that left for the city had returned, each of the three riders bore something extra. General Gates saw the body first, covered with a flag of nine stripes, several of which were stained dark crimson. Blood.

One of the riders carried Benedict Arnold, who looked like he had lost a fight. The right side of his face was swollen and purple, like so many summer grapes. His mouth was shut tight, though blood trailed out between his lips. His right shoulder seemed slumped, lower than the left, as if it were hanging there, dislocated. Gates wondered if he had been injured attempting to flee the dragoons and silently wished the dragoon captain had shot him instead.

Arnold, what terror have you wrought on us? Have you actually gone and done something so daft when you knew I was watching? You've made my task much too simple.

Then he saw the final rider and Gates at last felt relief. There, hands bound and a forlorn look on his face, was a simple man in simple attire bearing the air of aristocracy and the look of an officer. Gates knew he would find his answers, the truth, with this man.

"Bring that officer to me," Gates called to the dragoon as they reached the two-story stone structure serving as the command post. Gates had waited impatiently outside the whole time. Two dragoons dismounted and pushed the prisoner down to his knees a safe distance away from the commander. To the prisoner, it would appear that Gates had complete control. Theatrics, of course. But, most of life was appearing as if you knew what you were doing.

Gates started to ask, "Who are—"

"Captain John Andre, sir, and I won't say a word about my kidnapping to my command if you'd kindly escort me back to the city."

"Is that so?" Gates bit his tongue. *Kidnapping?* "Before we discuss anything further, I should remind you I am still a general, even if I am not your General. Such disrespect shall not be tolerated."

"You can either trump up charges or release me. So, kindly please, make your decision." Then, Andre tacked on, "sir."

"Very well." Gates motioned to the men standing next to Andre. "Search him."

Andre's eyes bulged out in protest. "There is no reason, I am not armed. I have nothing on me. In fact, I threw away my only weapon." Andre again inadvertently looked toward the body wrapped in the American flag. Two dragoons went to work, searching Andre, tearing through his clothes and each pocket.

Gates caught the glance. He asked, "Is that work yours?" He nodded toward the body. "What happened?"

Andre remained silent.

"Answer!" Gates received no reply.

Then, Captain Horner pulled out several sheets of folded papers from one of Andre's black boots. He handed it to Gates and said, "I didn't see what happened, but I assure you that Arnold is innocent in anything that may have happened. Perhaps this will provide some answers."

Gates rummaged through it, skimming through as much as he could. "Letters? Love letters?" Each of them was addressed to someone named Peggy and all signed by Benedict Arnold. Gates didn't know what to make of it. He was prepared to make false accusations against Benedict, but these... these were a godsend. They could very well be the real thing. "Is this some kind of code?"

Color seeped from Andre's face, he went white as a winter's dawn at the sudden implication. He knew what Gates meant. Even if they were not spies, it suited Gates' purpose. It was more than ample.

Gates looked over at the slumped form of Arnold. He jerked his thumb over at him as he asked Captain Horner, "Is he dead?" He didn't think so, but didn't hurt to ask. A slow rise of his chest dashed the last of his hopes. A quick search of the unconscious Arnold revealed a loyalist crimson cockade hidden in a pocket. Gates said to the air, "Benedict Arnold, you are a traitorous bastard. Captain Horner, bind him and bring him inside."

Andre came to Arnold's defense. "Sir, Arnold is many things, a rogue and a scoundrel, but he is no traitor, and those are not treasonous notes. They are misguided attempts to distract my intended." Andre's voice cracked. Gone was the indignant man who had stood before him moments ago. "This may all be Arnold's fault, he may be a wretched soul, but he is no spy."

"Nonsense. You come to his aid because, if he *is* a spy, then so are you."

"A spy? I am no spy! If you think me a spy then you are bereft of sense. What will happen to me, to Arnold? He is one of your highest-ranking generals, and I have connections in the General staff, including General Clinton himself. You can't simply claim him a traitor. You cannot declare me a spy based on terrible love letters."

Gates could almost see the thoughts running through Andre's head. He still looked pale, but his color returned, his eyes wide and black.

Gates answered, "There is a corpse over there on that horse. The city of Philadelphia is in flames. I catch him with you, and you have letters with his name on them. There is something amiss, and Arnold may hang for it. If things go poorly for you, you may be swinging right beside him."

Gates motioned to the dragoon commander. "Fetch this spy a shovel. I want him digging a grave for the soldier these two killed."

Andre's face flushed, and his jaw tightened. Arnold shared the expression as best he could through his injured face as he was taken inside. Gates returned the glares with a smile. He looked at Philadelphia in the distance, the grey smoke fading into white. A bitter wind picked up and blew through the cold March air. The British would have to abandon the city before too long.

Arnold had accomplished that; the dissipating smoke testified to it. When they left, Gates would be there to crush the British forces and end the war.

It was almost over. Victory was assured. Gates had prevailed. He had triumphed over Schuyler. He had swiped command for himself from General Charles Lee. He had found a formidable opponent in Benedict Arnold, but not even Arnold had been a match for him.

By summer, Gates would deliver independence to America. For Gates, it wasn't just about securing victory, it was making sure *he* secured it. While the losers busied themselves assigning blame, the victor raised statues. From the Pharaohs of Egypt to Julius Caesar, generals stood among mortals as gods, not just on the battlefield, but in the halls of leadership. Because of that truth, Gates knew this new nation would also need someone strong to lead it. *Why shouldn't that leader be me?*

He could think of no reason. He smiled again as he followed a defeated Benedict Arnold inside the command center and closed the door behind them.

PART 4

"Good God, are the Americans all asleep and tamely
giving up their liberties, or are they all turned philosophers, that
they don't take immediate vengeance on such miscreants?"
--Benedict Arnold

TWENTY-TWO

York Road, Towson, Maryland
March 2ⁿᵈ, 1778.

SERGEANT Martin Stevens had never been sicker in all his life. It was still early in March and cold, with winds whipping through budding tree branches. Even so, Stevens shook with fever. His skin slicked with sweat while his throat was hoarse and parched. He knew he needed to drink, and his thirst for water was vengeful. But there was nothing he could do about it. He lacked the muscles needed to move him to a source of water, and his canteen was long since empty. All he could do was lean against the smooth bark of a poplar tree and move his breeches down just far enough that he did not soil himself. Despite the effort, he still smelled of refuse. The ground beside him was wet and slimy with waste.

Stevens had spent most of his lifetime in the wilderness. He had learned to track, hunt game, and speak haltingly in several tribal tongues. He made a living providing those skills as services to those who had long since forgotten. But now he needed help for, if he just laid here, he would die.

He wasn't sure how he had picked up the disease. Perhaps it had been squirrel meat, partially undercooked and sitting raw in his stomach. All Stevens knew was that he did not wish to die of dysentery.

He struggled to remember exactly where he was, which native tribes were nearby, and whether they were hostile or friendly. He could seek help there from one of their shamans or be warmed and dry inside a mud-and-grass hut. But he could not remember, and he could not move.

There was much he still had to do if he survived. He had to get back to Collins and ask about little Jane. He missed his friend. He was duty-bound, not by his uniform, but by friendship, to discover General Arnold's true intentions. Stevens still struggled to understand what the war was really about, and if he was on the right side or not. His upcoming confrontation with the general would tell him what he needed to know and whether he should take Collins and flee.

General Arnold would want to know what happened. Burr, and possibly the brothers, had been captured. Stevens had fired wide, not intending to hit either Burr or Martha. Somehow, it was one of the few times he missed. From his position, hidden within the tree line surrounding the burning estate, he grazed the outside of Burr's left arm. But the explosion of black powder had the intended effect—Martha's shot went high in surprise.

Stevens saved Burr's life and spared Martha's, even if in the end, Lund Washington and a few others had descended upon Burr as he lay in the grass, bleeding. Stevens didn't know where the brothers had gone, and he had not run into them since. He had to assume they had been caught as well.

He could do nothing for them, or at least, nothing logical. So he escaped into the wilderness with the intention of heading back to Valley Forge on foot. His words were their only salvation now. If Arnold was the villain Stevens thought he might be, then Stevens needed to rescue Collins before something happened to him.

But right now, he lay helpless next to streams of his own excrement.

Stevens was about to pass out again when he heard voices coming from the forest, away from the road which he followed but kept himself hidden from. He didn't fear British soldiers. They kept to the cities and their supply wagons. He wasn't too worried about civilians as he had little of value on him. But he feared meeting with the brothers he had left behind at Mount Vernon, the brothers who threatened to kill him.

But these voices were Negro, or at least—as the voices became clearer—they sounded like slaves. George Washington owned many slaves. With the estate gone, it was entirely possible many of them used that opportunity to escape to freedom. If the voices did belong to slaves trying to stay hidden and off the main roads like he was, if they came across him, they would most likely kill him, lest he be tempted to turn them in for a reward.

The voices carried a thick accent and broken English. Two of them—both male—came closer.

Stevens scrambled to pull his breeches up and tighten them against the flesh he had lost since he joined the war. He had lost more in the last several days since he had been inflicted with the brown flux. His skin crawled with fear and unease, and he was thankful for the burst of energy his heart gave him, but did not know how long it would last. With the blood pumping hard through him, Stevens raised himself up and put his back behind a thick trunk several trees away.

He didn't know how long he could stay hidden, especially in bright daylight in the bare forest of March, given his weakened condition. Nonetheless, he braced himself despite his dry throat and held back a burst of flux.

The voices came in clearer now, if not as understandable through their speech. They were close enough that he could guess what they were saying.

"What we gunna do? We have nuttin' now," one of the voices said.

"We had nuttin' before. Now's no different. All we need is His love," the other answered.

"But you saw what dey did to her? To him? To our home? Dey are monsters. What we gunna do if we runs cross un' of dem folk?"

"Dey are monsters, true. But dat was not our home. And dem' folks dat did it will be judged by God."

"After I's kills 'em first."

Hearing speech so radically different from what he was used to jarred Stevens. He tried to translate it, despite protests from a throbbing head, but eventually, he understood the rhythm of it, finding it quite poetic. But even poets had been known to kill. Stevens scrunched lower and tried to remain hidden, hoping they would soon pass.

Instead, they both stopped. One of them sniffed the foul air and said, "It stinks."

Stevens began to cough, a violent eruption of spittle and yellow acid. He spilled over, out from behind the tree and looked at the two Negros, several feet away. Just seeing them reminded him of the young slave he killed. It was the last thing he saw before he passed out in front of them.

Stevens awoke to a sip of cold water caressing his lips, the cool moisture refreshing his tongue. The two gaunt Negros, wearing ripped clothing, bearded with unclean hair, kneeled over him. One of them must have refilled his canteen. His buttocks were bare, but he felt clean as he lay on a bed of soft grass away from his earlier filth.

"And who are you?" the Negro asked. He asked once more before Stevens recovered his bearings and translated what they were saying into something he could better understand.

"I say we kill him," the shorter and brawnier of the two said. "That's how this ends. We either kill him or he kills us. I'm not goin' back to no farm."

That prompted Stevens to speak. "I am a soldier." He hesitated before continuing. "I have to get to my camp."

"A soldier? What are you fighting for?" the same man spoke. He didn't give Stevens a chance to answer. "For freedom? I don't see no chains on you."

That is what Stevens had said, originally, when he sat down with Collins to play backgammon. Now, those words had come back to him. He wondered if the slave was right.

The other one asked a question now, the taller one, with uneven patches of hair growing from within his beard. He held out a hand as if to motion the other man to remain silent. The shorter slave obeyed without complaint. "Where is your camp?"

Stevens again hesitated to answer. He didn't know anything about these Negros, nor their intent, but they had brought him water and cleaned him. They could have left him to rot or killed him. That ought to count for something. Reluctantly, he answered the question, "Pennsylvania. About a hundred miles northeast of here."

"Ah, so we have here a Yank. No blue clothes. No musket. Off to fight hisself and die because another man say he should." He clapped the other, shorter man hard on the back. "He don't know he's a slave, too." He finished with a laugh.

The laugh unnerved him, though he did not know why, yet there was little he could do. They had taken his rifle and knife when he passed out. Even if they hadn't, even if his strength recovered, he was now at their mercy. The world had turned upside down. Very strange indeed.

Stevens pushed back a little. "And what do you know of the war?"

"I's knows that we all suffering. I's knows that you white folk full of shit. Fighting to be free," the shorter slave spat. "The British are good marsters, and you all complain'. But what of us? We not gettin' free of our marsters, of you. Nobody freein' us from our chains. Yet, we are the ones truly enslaved."

The bearded man turned to the other scrawny, shorter fellow and said, "My friend awoke to find our marster's home aflame. In the woods was his lady cousin, killed, found lying next to a man she loved. Now, my friend must live with no food, no shelter, and one less member of his family. Does your story compare to that?"

Stevens tried to scoot away, his face paling. Slowly, he stopped and drew a deep breath. The Negros looked him over carefully. "N... no. It does not."

The one with the patched beard seemed confused. "Hmm. What do you know about Vernon? Why you so far away from camp on the same road as we?"

Stevens thought how best to respond. He knew he should stick as close to the truth as possible but blurted out, "Nothing," before he could think. He looked them both over. They remained silent. He continued, covering it up, "I heard Mount Vernon burned down. Did you belong to Washington?"

"We don't belong to nobody!" the smaller man yelled, standing over Stevens. Again, the other man held him back. This time, there was defiance in his eyes, but he stopped nevertheless.

The bearded man spoke up, "We both worked there—"

"We don't work there no mo' on account it's been destroyed. Now we left with even less than we had before, which was a pot of cold soup next to nothin'." He embedded Stevens' hunting knife deep into a dead tree and tore off a branch. He threw the branch onto a nearby pile that Stevens had just noticed for the first time. "If I find the folk who dun it, who killed my cousin, I will kill 'em—even if it did give us means to escape."

Stevens turned away, anxious to change the topic. "What are your names? Where will you go?" He tried to calm his pounding heart through inconspicuous breaths. This was the best he had felt in days.

The one with the patched beard identified himself as Jarosa. The other one remained silent and refused to give his name. Jarosa spoke. "My wife works in a home in Philadelphia. We see'in if she is safe. Perhaps my old master will take me and this one on."

Stevens' mouth almost fell open. The answer surprised him. Many questions ran through his head, and the idea that the Negro was married surprised him. He had never considered slaves might have families. "You are seeking another master? Why don't you run away?"

Both slaves laughed.

That confused Stevens even more.

"You don't know a lot, do you? There is no place for us to go. You don't understand. There is no freedom just for steppin' outside a farm. This entire place is a prison to people of color. We have to go way up north for that type of freedom, but then we would have no money, no food, no job, and no learnin'. Those things don't fall off trees, now do they? It's a far cry from being free to being safe. And this is the only life we know, the only life God has challenged us with."

Jarosa stopped and went back to his task of rubbing a stick in between his palms into a notch of another branch. Next to it sat a tiny bed of kindle. Sweat poured from each temple, beading at the tips of the hairs of his beard near his ears. "Besides, I have a wife, and my duty is to her. Master Washington always tries to keep the married 'uns together. But, he gone on account of the war, and Master Lund needed a slave who knew 'bout grist-milling, and I's his man. Wife had to stay there. Two or three times a year, he gives me papers to visit." He said this as a tiny ember emerged. It caught on the tinder, and Jarosa carefully blew, igniting it. The firewood the other Negro had gathered was ready and it soon lit. Stevens nodded with an air of respect—slave or freeman, not even he could make a fire without flint.

Soon, the fire roared and later, Stevens' breeches were returned to him, cleaner and dry. "Why did you stop to help me?"

"Because you looked in need of help," Jarosa said. By the light of the fire, he looked up from a book.

"You know your letters?"

"Only in this book." He pointed down to it. "But this is the only book that matters. Now get some rest. We will try and have some food for you in the mornin'. We will get you well again and back to your camp. It is close enough on the way to the city."

Stevens blew out a deep sigh of relief. He thought he might survive this, if they did not find out the part he had played in their lives and if he could overcome the sickness coursing through his body. They would still kill him or leave him to die if they found out. It was all relative. To Burr and the brothers, that slave girl meant nothing. To these two Negros, it mattered deeply, but his own death would not.

What Stevens should focus on, he considered, was what the slave girl meant to him and how he should confront General Arnold. He hoped Collins fared better. Stevens hoped that this delay would not make him too late.

TWENTY-THREE

Mabie's Tavern, Tappan, New York
Ides of March.

THERE was little light in Benedict Arnold's ground-level cell, where he had been detained for a fortnight already, along with Captain John Andre, in a red Dutch-brick home, repurposed and expanded into a tavern. Arnold had been a rising star, a general well on his way to glory and the redemption of his name. Now, he sat incarcerated, his fate in the hands of his enemies.

But his mind remained free to roam as he lay on a knotted cot, an empty bottle of rum next to him. His mind kept roaming to a time when his star began its ascent, just after his meeting with General Hancock, several years ago. Then his mind wandered, to a darker period and place.

Darkness loomed when Colonel Arnold and the boys in his bateaux reached the northern bank of the Kennebec River and into the promised land of Quebec. Burr, Morgan, Oswald, and the few hundred other survivors were beyond exhausted.

They froze. They starved. They became dangerously lost with maps intentionally meant to lead them astray. They met with disease. They endured desertions and betrayals. Every planned bit had gone completely wrong. Their stores had been destroyed by the elements. Their transports had been constructed so poorly, they had to rebuild them on the journey.

Soldiers loyal to the cause, if not to Arnold, had fled. Female camp followers had picked up arms and taken the place of their fallen husbands. If Colonel Arnold could not seek help from the Abenaki tribe that inhabited these lands, this would be the end of his invasion of Canada and the capture of Quebec, if not the end of their lives.

From Arnold's perspective, he could scarcely believe they had made it so far. Letters of encouragement from General Hancock and Congress echoed his thoughts. But, if he didn't get resupplied, re-armed and his regiment back to strength, it wouldn't matter. The march would have been for nothing, and the men who had perished on this journey would not be remembered. Arnold would just be a footnote in history.

He could not let that happen.

As the darkness set in, during the fading moments of twilight, a small figure, hunched and old with weather-beaten skin, approached them. Arnold hoped it was the native chief meant to meet them. He desperately hoped his note-bearers had succeeded in making contact. The figure moved closer and clasped his arms around Arnold's shoulders as if in a hug. Then, he stood and said, "Man with raven feathers, man whose name is Dark Eagle, is welcome here. But, your journey, a dark path, is just beginning."

Major General Benedict Arnold felt his journey had reached an end. His end, it seemed, was in a tiny tavern room for what amounted to his jail cell. At least the food was good. The drink was better. His vision blurred, and he stumbled aimlessly around the barren room until he collapsed back onto the cot that was worse than some of the ground he'd slept on. The pain from the injuries incurred during his harsh horseback fall had faded, though the wounds he had suffered earlier still plagued him. It lessened a bit thanks to the medication he found at the bottom of the bottle. But, now his head hurt, and he felt hot and stuffy, despite the March cold.

Over and over in his mind, he churned over how he had been betrayed. By Gates, for attempting to take credit and sullying Arnold's name. Congress, passing him up for promotion repeatedly. By everyone who ever doubted him, including Captain

Croskie. Ingrates, all of them, even if they proved right in the end. *Perhaps I will come to an end as my father did. I'd rather drink myself to death than let them see me hang.*

Nobody appreciated him, his sacrifices, or the work that he had done. Arnold had single-handedly taken on the whole of the British forces, and he had nearly won. Now, he languished in jail on charges that Gates could never prove. Nothing mattered.

His real aggravation was not with them. Sweet Peggy chose a British fop over him. That pain stabbed at him through his heart. Like Brutus, her cut was the deepest.

So, over and over again, the Dark Eagle ran through all of the betrayal he endured in his mind. He started to open a new bottle when anger overtook him. He threw the bottle at the wall. It shattered into several large pieces, and rum ran down the red brick wall, thick as blood. Arnold had never quit before. He would not end up like his father.

By heav'n, I will have justice.

Colonel George Washington hadn't slept since the day of the fires. The same day he had discovered that Martha was dead. Her death was his own fault. He understood that. The war had needed a decisive and quick end, but he had been apprehensive about his role in the war and how others saw him. He had held himself back. But now, he didn't care what they thought. All he knew was the Yanks had to pay, and the red uniform jacket he wore would give him the best means to do just that. The best way to do that was to win the war by any means possible. For starters, Washington had to re-instill discipline within the British ranks. He had to forge a force that he could use to wipe out the rebels.

To that end, he stood at the same spot in the square, where at Christmas, he had promised Britain's reunification with her Colonies. However, instead of a large pavilion tent and the pleasant company of the city's socialites, he stood with a large mass of civilians and soldiers. A large, low dais, which smelled of fresh pine, stood before them. The stage might have been built a few days ago, but weeds already shot up from in between the boards. Spring was coming. No. War was coming.

On the stage, the previous defendant, a bare-backed man charged with looting and missing several Sunday services, was unchained from a tripod. The tripod was fashioned out of spears of cold iron which now ran hot with blood. He was carried across the stage, head down. Sweat poured across his scalp, matting his brown hair. Blood and bits of skin trailed down his back. "Now, go and rub salt in his wounds. He is free of his transgressions," the announcer said from atop the dais.

That would hurt like hell, Washington knew, though the process was meant to prevent infection. It wasn't enough, however. The soldier's pain and subsequent lesson had not been enough. As he had been doing over the last few cases, Washington interrupted the announcer. "No. Double lashings."

The announcer nodded, long past disagreeing with the governor. The lashings continued. Cries hit the air. The soldier on the stage had long since passed out. The cries came from the audience, and that was fine with Washington. It was an object lesson for them. Finally, the soldier was dragged away—his back a beaten and bloody mess of puffy raw meat and welts.

"Next is Captain James Tyler, Fortieth Regiment of the King's Foot," said the announcer, a British colonel—tall, lanky, with an equally thin face. He looked as if he could walk through a tight alleyway with room to spare. His uniform was pristine, new perhaps, and his wig was white and over-powdered. His frown, which caught Washington's eye, wrinkled into his old, sagging face, as if folded and pressed there throughout the colonel's entire life.

He spoke softly but sternly, like a schoolmaster. Reading from a black book held out in his hands, he continued, "Bring forth the condemned so his sentence may be carried out in front of God, his peers, and the city." Captain James Tyler was marched out onto the stage, and color drained from his face. "For charges of disorderly conduct, for which Captain Tyler has been determined guilty, the punishment is twelve lashes." The announcer said it in a way knowing it would be doubled by Washington.

Captain Tyler had set fire to homes in the city during the morning of the Philadelphia Conflagration. He came onto the stage near naked but for a pair of light breeches. He remained silent, but his eyes betrayed fear and humiliation. Humiliation was a bedfellow of fear. However, Washington had found it much more effective. Even so, Tyler was awarded a light punishment. They all were, Washington thought, but floggings had been capped at twelve. If he could have, he'd triple the number, but with General Clinton in attendance, Washington thought it best to punish these offenders on stage with only twice the legal limit of lashings.

The flogging commenced. Washington felt every scream. Each time the nine knotted leather cords bit into Tyler's back, there came a loud snap, then a shockwave which made Washington's skin crawl. He knew what was coming next. A scream. They all screamed for the first several blows before their bodies gave out and they succumbed to the pain. Then it was whimpers.

"Please... make it stop..."

Washington derived no joy from this, but it was necessary, he told himself. If this had been done before, if they had kept to discipline and rained hellfire on the rebels... Martha might still be alive. *What the fear of God will not do to keep the soldiers in line, the cat o'nine tails will. I will use these soldiers and my uniform to make things right.*

The screaming stopped. Shortly after, the whimpering died, too. Captain James Tyler came down from the tripod and soldiers carried him off the stage.

"Now go and rub salt within his wounds. He is free of transgression," the announcer said gravely, giving Washington ample time to interrupt, which he did. The lashings re-commenced until Tyler was taken down and carried away. "Next, we have..."

The cycle repeated.

Later, after a long day of discipline, the crowd started melting away. It was almost silent but for the birds chirping in the budding trees and burned-out boards, chalked and ashen, on the remains of nearby walls. Washington was about to head back to his three-story red office and home, untouched by fire, and to a half-empty bottle of rum, when General Clinton approached him, fighting against the current of people heading away.

When Clinton reached him and they exchanged respects, he asked, "Are you sure this was the best course of action to take?" Clinton sounded like a New Yorker, no doubt from his childhood in the city.

"We've grown soft, and as a result, war came to us," Washington responded. He had prepared for a question like that. "We lost the initiative against the Yanks. Today will remind us of who we are and our purpose, sir."

"You misunderstand me, Colonel," Clinton said sternly, though he did not raise his voice. His face remained passive and cool behind big, black eyes and bushy, black eyebrows which contrasted starkly with his white wig and the shine of his leather buffings on his uniform. "Discipline is needed. My concern was you carried it out in public and doubled their punishments in direct defiance of the law. But, it is of no matter now. It is too late to change it. You are in perhaps a better position to gauge the best course of action. At least the citizens here saw it carried out by one of their own."

Washington winced. "One of their own, sir?" *That stung.* What was worse, Clinton didn't even realize the barb. *Every Colonial sees me as a traitor. Every King's man sees a Yank. But I do not care what they think of me so long as I can do my duty.*

"Yes. Certainly," Clinton said. "As a Yank, you have served us brilliantly, I must admit. Most of us have had our doubts about you. Some of us thought you might even turn. However, you continue to serve well, despite your misfortune." A spring breeze blew an ill wind. It would have been a warm day, but wind alone that caused the chill. "It's true what they say. In battle, there is little a single man can do to affect its outcome. However, you seem to be the pesky bugger that proves its exception. General Braddock once told me how you organized a retreat in the wilderness long ago, a retreat Braddock himself had barely ordered when you rode out, flux-ridden, rallying the troops, organizing their withdrawal. Braddock never told you this, I know, but your action most probably saved his life and the expedition that day. And it launched your career."

Clinton took a step toward Washington and continued, with one upturned cheek, "Now I see it wasn't for naught. I've seen how you've handled yourself here. I saw the results of your Christmas attack. Most lately, I've seen for myself what you salvaged of the city as governor. You organized the city defenses during the rebel raid, or whatever that was, all under the pressure of hearing the news of your home and your wife meeting a most unfortunate fate." Clinton paused, his eyes turned down, head nodding. "Once again, I offer my condolences to you. No one should suffer the loss of their wife."

"Thank you, sir. It has been a trying time." Washington knew Clinton could relate. Perhaps that was why Clinton had taken Washington under his wing as of late.

"I lost my wife a few years ago," Clinton replied in a whisper. "Set me back quite a bit. I recently found my way again. Have you heard the rumors?"

"That you are to replace Howe?" Washington wouldn't waste any time beating around the bush. There was much work yet to be done.

"I imagine it won't be long now. People in England know. It is odd, is it not? It's as if they hold the future but cannot tell it. We here must wait for the ship's sail and a westward wind. If the ship does indeed hold orders for me to take command, I will remember your hard work and keep that in mind for further campaigns." Clinton's wide eyes narrowed as if to emphasize his point. "Although, you and I have some matters to discuss."

Washington remained silent. Curiosity filled to the surface but remained hidden behind stern skin.

"Walk with me, Colonel, and we will discuss the future," Clinton said, "or at least, one possible future." Clinton turned around abreast of Washington and they walked, but to where, to what destination, and to what path they would take, Washington was unsure.

The two wandered past near-deserted streets where charred wood and blackened brick lay in piles. Workers shifted through the ash and debris. It had been over a fortnight ago, and yet one could still smell the smoke. At least the strong scent and sickening taste of roasting pig, where men and women had been caught up by flames, had finally left the roof of his mouth.

Clinton stopped to speak to every common soldier he crossed paths with as they toured the city. This made sense, Washington thought, as Clinton was a soldier first and a general second. Clinton often commiserated in the misery of his soldiers' lives. It had endeared his men toward him. Washington tried to emulate this as often as he could—sleeping out under the same stars his soldiers did on the same hard, frozen ground, just as Clinton did.

Finally, Clinton returned his attention to Washington, and rather abruptly, he let loose words that Washington could not expect. "You should have been punished, you realize," Clinton said, his voice raised as they resumed their tour of the destruction. "This was your city, and you let it burn."

Washington turned sharply, but there was nothing he could say. Part of him knew Clinton spoke true.

"But no one will discipline you or say anything because of your personal loss. To be fair, they saw how quickly you restored order out of the chaos. It is some skill you possess. I, for one, am envious. I do not hold you responsible for the hurt caused by the Sons of Liberty on this city, but others might, including the loyal subjects who saw you punish everyone who deserved it out in the public square. Everyone, except for one man: *you*."

"It is true. I hold final respons—"

"Quite. There is more to it than that, as you know. You are one of the few people who know the whole story, but we cannot deny what so many people witnessed." He stopped for a moment to let out an exaggerated sigh, "Rebels, in this very city."

I had Benedict Arnold right here, and I let him slip away. It boiled Washington's blood. He felt his face heating with an uneven temperament. He knew he could explode into anger. It was rare, and he most often kept it tightly packed away, hidden under so many layers of humility and self-doubt, but it was there, even more present of late. *Now is not the time to let it loose.* Besides, Washington thought, Clinton was right.

"This was certainly the work of General Arnold," Clinton said, spreading an arm across a vacant lot where a once proud Tory home had stood. "According to the Shippen girls, he was right here, not too far from where you are standing and where Captain Andre was abducted."

Washington had no doubt that Arnold was behind the attack on Philadelphia. He glowered, knowing also Arnold was behind the attack at Mt. Vernon and Martha's death. Washington had done his research. It was Arnold's style—he scorched anything he couldn't possess. *That damnable Yank.*

"And what of Captain John Andre?" Washington changed the subject to cool his nerves.

"Major, now, I am sure of it," Clinton corrected. "His promotion papers are likely in the same ship's hold as my own. He was to be our chief intelligence officer... but perhaps he was daft after all." Clinton shook his head in disbelief. "The Americans say he shares a cell with Arnold. They claim the two were scheming treason. Of course, that's impossible. But, if we come to Andre's defense, then it exonerates Arnold, and that general is better left in a gaol if the Americans are daft enough to keep him locked away for us. Particularly now that the French have so brazenly escalated the war."

"Yes. I'm aware the French recognized the Colonies back in February, but they have yet to send ships or soldiers. They just send weapons and credit. They are likely not sending anyone until General Gates is better tested. He has a dubious track record at best. It is on paper, only. It means nothing."

"Yes, quite, but do not underestimate Gates or the French. Let us hope we beat the rebels before the French decide to land troops. If we do, this whole problem goes away. For if the French do indeed go to war against us, America becomes a much smaller issue as the war moves to a much grander scale. King George and Parliament will have larger concerns and a smaller coffer. Already, there are reports of the French fleet en route to the Caribbean. The French want the territories they lost in the last war against us, but as of now, they do not know how much those lands will cost them."

"Cost?"

"Quite right. This war is all about money." He looked at Washington. "What is your shirt made of?"

"Cotton."

"Is it cheap?"

He shook his head. "No."

"What is that you smoke in your pipe?"

Tobacco. Washington nodded without answering. He saw where this argument was going.

"France may want the Ohio Valley, but it is all damnable wilderness and hostile savages. We want the farms of the south, the indigo, rice, the tobacco, and to a lesser extent, cotton." A crisp wind blew. "Every country in Europe wants their piece of the New World, and New England just wants to keep their cabbage farms. As far as I am concerned, they are welcome to them. If I am indeed placed in command, I might look to end the campaign in the north and seek to start anew in the south. But first, we must regroup in anticipation of what the French might do."

"Regroup, sir?" *Retreat, you mean?* Whenever the British made the slightest move backward, the loyalists fled from their ranks, and the rebels swelled with cheer. "They will use it as propaganda to fill their ranks and increase enlistment. They will see it as victory." Washington's blood boiled again. This was not the hasty general he knew. *We need to hit the rebels hard and end this war.* "While we wait here, the rebel army is out there, training and growing stronger every day."

"Our mission has not changed," Clinton said after a long pause. "We will try and draw out the rebels and crush them. We will have to leave this city, and soon. You know as well as I do that it is no longer a tenable position."

They had been walking for a while now. Washington's feet began feeling sore. He usually did this on horseback. Apparently, Clinton preferred to walk. Another chill wind blew as they crossed the damaged part of the city. Here, war stared them all in the face. In the crowded streets, people begged for food or stole blankets and apples to stay alive another day. There were just too many people without homes.

"It is ironic. Now the civilians are forcibly quartered with the military. That has brought us our share of problems," Washington said, "but there just is not room for all of them. Especially the poor and the slaves. It has also become a breeding ground for all sorts of foul things. We will need to start shipping them to New York."

Clinton acted as if he didn't hear him, his attention drawn away to an area in the distance. Washington looked over as well.

A ways away, an outdoor hospital had been arranged to treat the wounded and the burned. Enough time had passed since the fires for burned nerves to regrow. Now, the whole area heard their cries of pain. Past the field hospital and tents lay another area, cordoned off where nobody but surgeons went. Clinton eyed Washington carefully. This must have been one of the unresolved issues he had mentioned earlier.

"Smallpox."

"Yes," Clinton said. "You understand what this could mean for us if it breaks loose as we try and evacuate the city?"

Washington swallowed hard. "Yes."

"The first thing you need to do is do something about the sick civilians, the homeless, and the soldiers unable to make the march with us. You know the rebels will hit us with everything they can when we leave the city. This will give us the chance to draw them out into the open on a real field of engagement. Let them taste our zeal and bayonet. But we cannot leave if our soldiers are sick."

"Yes, sir."

"When we leave the city, it will be their downfall," Clinton said it as if it were a matter-of-fact, as if it had already come to pass and he was stating it for the record. Another chill wind blew, growing colder. "Others are wary of you, but I want to give you an opportunity to shine in the field, yes?"

Washington waited patiently to hear what Clinton had in mind.

"What I would like to do, Colonel, is offer you the chance to plan our exit of Philly and for you to take the vanguard post."

Again, Washington remained silent. He wasn't sure about this. He wondered about Clinton's motivations for handing him such a plump assignment. *Did he feel sorry for me, because of Martha? Or is this a trick because I am a Yank and it'll be easier to blame me if it fails?* He should have declined the offer. Instead, he found himself saying, "Yes, sir."

Clinton shook his head. "I should, perhaps, make myself as clear as possible. This war may be over soon. Perhaps we will have one or two more chances to end it with ball or bayonet before a quill decides it for us. If you lose this next engagement, it will be more than the loss of Philadelphia hung on your name. We will also lose our edge at the negotiation table. It will reflect poorly on us that we, as you said, are retreating. It weakens us, yes? If we fail, you will be blamed. You will keep your commission, and they won't say anything publicly—but you will be exiled all the same."

I am to be their scapegoat if we are unsuccessful. At least Clinton was upfront about it. Washington thought for a long moment. *This gives me a chance to hurt the rebels. I must not fail.*

"I may not be the commander for long," Clinton said. "There is also word that Parliament is sending over a peace commission to entreat with the Americans. I am friends with one of the members; he wrote to me of this earlier. The commission should be on the same ship carrying our next orders. This is why I know things." He winked. "There is also something else I know. I have been in contact with an old, dear friend recently. He may prove to be useful—an ace up my sleeve, if you will. But I will not say more." Clinton waved his hand in front of his face as if shooing the secret away. "Braddock believed in you, as do I, but the stakes here are high. You must be made aware of them." Clinton turned to depart. "I must be on my way. I expect to hear from you soon."

Washington stopped him. Though he remained soured, he kept calm and controlled as he erased his painful frown. Clinton had dropped quite a bit of weight off his own shoulders and onto his. Washington didn't appreciate it, but he didn't mention it. "Very good, sir. As for the refugees too injured to travel and those stricken with smallpox... I plan to release them into the rebel camps."

"Yes, quite," Clinton said, as if he had already moved to other things. "I am glad to hear it." He stopped as if processing what Washington said. Then, he turned around and smiled, nodding his head in vigorous approval.

With that, Clinton departed. A moment later, Washington was left to his thoughts. His work, his hard work that his life had centered around, went unappreciated. He knew that to the British, he'd never be one of them, though he was in no way different from any of them. Being born in the Colonies was his only sin. He was the scapegoat in case things fell apart.

He sighed inwardly but did not speak ill out loud. He knew he would perform his duty, as long as capable, if for no other reason than this was the life the Divine had chosen for him. He had a lot of work in the coming days, but the work would distract him from other thoughts.

Washington went to close his cloak around him, but realized too late it wasn't there. The day hadn't started off so cold. The birds had stopped their singing as if spring had evaporated. He had this nagging sensation of following a path he was not meant to follow.

It does not matter. By the Divine, I will have justice.

TWENTY-FOUR

Valley Forge, Pennsylvania
March 18th, 1778.

IT had been just under a month since Sergeant Stevens had left, and he was already a fortnight overdue. He had spent those two weeks weak and sick with dysentery. He recovered thanks to the slaves Jarosa and his friend, the cousin of the slave girl Stevens had killed. So far, Stevens had kept his mouth shut, and they hadn't figured it out.

He continued down the forested path near Valley Forge with the two Negros; they were almost there. That meant sentries, at least in theory. Stevens' arrival would be unusual and his companions unexpected. Sentries did not like unexpected surprises, and Stevens didn't want to get shot by his own side.

He had expected to return triumphant with Colonel Burr and the brothers. But now, as far as Stevens knew, he was the only one who had escaped the hushed mission, a mission that he couldn't say he had been on. *Oh, and by the way, I picked up some companions along the way.*

News of Philadelphia reached them from natives who had passed them by and shared their food. The Powhatans told of how it had been attacked, parts of the city lying in smoldering ash. Stevens shuddered. His two guides exchanged looks and eyed him warily. *Was that in response to what we did?*

Since the city was in chaos, the two Negros decided to accompany Stevens to Valley Forge instead, risking the chance they would be pressed back into slavery. Jarosa knew he may never see his wife again if she had escaped the city alive. He had said as much. It was not safe there, however, nor was hiding in the forest. Still, this was their last chance to decide otherwise.

A crack of black powder shot out over them and thundered over the hillside. The three jumped.

"Halt." The command came from ahead. "That first shot was a warning."

Stevens looked up the rise but did not see where the voice had come from. Stevens stopped, and the two Negros looked at him. The bearded one, Jarosa, turned to him and said, "You were at our mercy before. Now we will be at yours."

Stevens nodded. He couldn't make any promises, and for some reason, that saddened him. He responded to the sentry, "I belong here. I'm one of Morgan's men, what's left of 'em. Now with Dearborn, under Lieutenant Arntz."

Several men now grouped together on the hill overlooking Stevens' position. He didn't recognize any of them. "What's the watchword for passing?"

Watchword? That was new. Knowing General Arnold, it was probably 'liberty' or another nonsensical patriotic platitude, but he didn't want to play guessing games. "Uh, yes, about that, see, I'm not going to know any code." He faced upwards and smiled. "Is that going to be a problem?"

At that, the men started down the hill at them. "Tie 'em and bind 'em, boys." He sighed loudly and shook his head. "We got one bad apple, and now the woods are crawling with spies."

Stevens' spirits sank. He turned to Jarosa, warning him in a hushed voice, "Now may be your only chance to flee."

"If we do dat'," Jarosa said, even as he had to pull back his companion, "'dey shoot us all."

Stevens understood, but he wasn't happy. He turned back to the sentry, a tall, lean man who had the look of a proper soldier, not an untrained Colonial, and said, "Would it do us any good to say that we aren't spies?"

Actually, he wasn't a spy, but he admitted he didn't know what the two Negros would do. They had been enslaved by Washington. Maybe that made them more sympathetic to the rebellion. Maybe, they didn't care either way. Even so, he spoke in their defense; they had, after all, saved his life. "Look, these two are with me. Please take us to see General Arnold. I have important news—"

"General Arnold, eh?" the sentry said with a sudden smile. "Well, now, I know you're spies." He winked.

"What do you mean?" Stevens shut his eyes as he found himself on the defensive. If he didn't know any better, he would guess that using Arnold's name was the wrong thing to say, although the sentry seemed more relaxed now. *What happened while I was away?*

"What regiment did you say you were from?"

"Daniel Morgan's."

At that, the guard laughed. He motioned for the two other guards to stop. They lowered their hands and shook Stevens' as he said, "I thought I recognized you. You're the rifleman who shot General Frasier up in Freeman's Farm. Still, strange things are brewin' around here. General Arnold is no traitor, yet he rots in a jail, you see." He shrugged. "Maybe he is, but I don't believe it, though there is still talk of spies. Got the whole camp in an uproar."

"General Arnold...imprisoned?" Stevens became confused. *Was Arnold's actions at Mount Vernon the reason behind it? Does this mean that I might meet the same fate?*

"It's all a shame. The business in Philadelphia. They say they caught the general red-handed as the city was going up in flames, but I think he was the one setting the fires. Good for him. We've been sitting on the frozen ground too long. Still, it's a right shame. Got a soldier killed up in the city, too."

Stevens didn't care about the details, anxious to speak to anyone that might know what in the devil was going on. He had questions. He'd like to see Collins, but he expected he wasn't going anywhere until his name was fully vouched for and verified. "So what will happen to us?"

"Sorry," the sentry said, turning a frown. "I still have to escort you up the chain of command until somebody proper can sort things out. I won't have you blindfolded or nothin', but orders are orders. I doubt you're a spy. I'd stake my next hard firecake on it, but if General Arnold's a spy or traitor or whatever, then the whole world is upside down."

"I... understand." Stevens could have fought, but he would get answers faster this way. "Who are we going to go see first?"

"I'll take you up to my commanding officer, and he'll most likely take you to see Colonel Burr."

"Colonel Burr?" Stevens' eyes went wide. Color faded out of his face until he was as pale as a ghost.

"Just arrived this week, a few days ago," the sentry said, wrinkling his brow in response. Even so, he motioned for the other guards to escort them up the hill. "Come on, let's move." Then he turned back to Stevens. "Best of luck to you. Hope you get things sorted. If not, well, I'll see you when you hang." He laughed at himself.

Stevens did not enjoy the joke. Things had changed since his departure. His respect for General Arnold remained in question. For all he knew, Arnold was capable of being a despicable man, so being a traitor wasn't that much of a stretch. But, that wasn't what concerned him. *Apparently, Burr is neither dead nor captured?*

Collins was the first person Stevens wanted to see upon his return; Burr was the last. Burr would have as many questions for Stevens as he did for Burr, but Burr would not like his answers. His skin flushed, and he could feel the blood rush back. At the least, it should prove to be an interesting conversation. Stevens had heard another rumor from his conversation with the Powhatans, one that suggested Mrs. Martha Washington had been killed. That had left Stevens confused. When he had left Mt. Vernon, Burr had been captured, and Martha had been alive. Apparently now, neither of those things were true.

He was led through camp. On the way, they passed through a throng of thin refugees. They were not here when he had left; that was something else which confused him. *Who were all these people?* They certainly weren't militia. Old men, boys, and women crowded around them. They had to be survivors of the fires. *Why were they here?*

This crowd went way past the usual band of camp followers—civilians who earned their keep and kept the army on its feet. There were no women out doing laundry nor wounded men pulling carts. It was a city outside a city, as if the inhabitants of Philadelphia had streamed out and stayed within the sprouting trees and bushes of the springtime wilderness.

They were poorly dressed, and everyone looked hungry. What was worse, these people didn't have the look of accustomed hardship on their faces. Cold and starvation were new to them. Distraught looks of anguish peered through dirt-caked faces. Their eyes glued to him, as if he had answers for them. He eyed one of his blue and buff escorts, hoping for an explanation.

"Refugees from the city," the soldier answered, looking back at him with a knowing glance. "So many of them lost their homes. They blamed the British, so Washington just dumped them here, pawned them off on us. Of course, we have nothing to offer them, my rations being non-existent as it is."

Stevens remained lost in thought. *Weren't the British charged with protection?* There were no easy answers on both sides of the war. He was about to remark on the situation when he saw a large enclosure off in the distance, out in the open. This enclosure was full of refugees, too, mostly people of color. "And those?"

"Smallpox. Damned Washington sent those over to us, too, hoping to infect us all. He wants to kill us without ever getting out of his own comfy bed. Bloody lobsterbacks, all of them." He spat in derision.

They stopped when one of the escorts interrupted. "I'm afraid your manservants will have to come with me. They'll need screening, as will you once you arrive at headquarters."

Stevens meant to correct the guard, but he thought better of it. It might confuse matters. But, before he could argue, Jarosa's companion yelled out in protest, "Don't you see what 'dey are doing? 'Dey are no Negros walking aroun' back dat way. 'Dey put dem all behin' dem fences!"

The guard could have lashed out and berated the man, but he didn't. Instead, he spoke calmly and said, "I assure you that is not what happened. The Negros in the city were stabled with the cows, and they got sick. You will be taken care of until things are sorted."

"Go. I'll follow up with you later," Stevens said. "I'll will find a way for you to get to your wife." Stevens was unsure why he made that promise or how he would keep it. The Negro was, after all, only a slave. Nonetheless, he meant those words. Now, he'd have to find a way to do it. *At least, I will try.*

Right now, he feared meeting with Burr. He could find himself locked away if he weren't careful. Stevens thought back to the warm spring day a year ago at Collins' house on the small, rundown farm. He could do with a dice game and a warm beer poured for him by Emma right now. Hell, he wouldn't even mind holding baby Jane.

TWENTY-FIVE

Tappan, New York
March 23rd, 1778.

BENEDICT Arnold slammed down his tankard brimming with rum. He was in no danger of over-drinking now. His wounds were almost healed from smashing into the ground a few weeks ago, though his gloved right hand ached as sticky golden liquid spilled over the rim, onto the table and the letter in front of him. He picked it up and whisked a spray of the golden liquid off it, sending it streaming across the empty tavern.

Arnold brought the letter up close to his eyes again, reading each word carefully once more and then tossed it down in disgust. *Congress would invite the French military onto our shores? Into our beds? Revolting.*

America didn't need the help of the French Navy and Army. They could gain their independence without them. If Congress accepted help, America would not be free—not truly. The country would be a puppet state of the French. America would serve French interests. *We would be at the mercy of the very people who butchered and murdered so many of us during the last war. How quickly men forget the ill deeds of others when it suits their purpose*, he thought.

The French monarchy had no interest in liberty. They had no interest in American independence. Their sole interest in the Colonial conflict lay in how it might hurt the British. The French were in it to reclaim their stake in the New World. Nothing more.

John Adams and the entire Continental Congress were blinded by the helping hands offered. While the alliance didn't mean the French intended to declare all-out war against the British, it laid the groundwork. When and where they would land troops was—at this moment—anyone's guess. As usual, it was up to Arnold to clean up this mess.

Of course, given Arnold's current circumstances, he could do little to assist. He languished as a prisoner of General Gates. That much had not changed. However, he had moved upwards in accommodation from the jail cell to the tavern itself. He was technically imprisoned here, but he had free rein of the place. A typical tavern guest gazing over at the deposed general would have guessed Arnold was simply enjoying his Caribbean rum.

But I'm not.

While his general demeanor had improved slightly over the last few weeks, fury still rolled in his guts, his temper controlled just under the boiling point. It helped cool his blood that the charges of treason against him were met with a growing pool of skeptics. Only Benedict's enemies continued the charade. As charges faded and his influence and coins grew around the tavern, so did his relative freedom. He was free to roam around the inside, free to meet with whom he liked, and free to carry out what business he could.

Hannah had already come to see him, informing him of his shipping business. It was all but closed. Debts were mounting. The war had cost him his fortune, which he had earned with his own sweat and blood on the waves of the sea, but his sister managed where she could. The apothecary was still open, and Arnold's sole remaining ship, the *Fortune*—the one not in the hands of the British—made an occasional low-risk supply run.

Arnold's restricted freedom and slow trickle of income against a flood of debt was at least more than he could say for his fellow prisoner, John Andre. The British officer and sometimes artist remained confined to his cell. Whenever Arnold needed to subdue his temper, he looked at the unfortunate Andre. He would likely hang, or be shot by firing squad, though the case against him was equally dubious. The difference was Arnold didn't care about Andre's trumped-up charges; he had wooed the wrong woman.

Arnold needed a moment of refreshment after reading yet another letter about the abominable February French Alliance. He eyed Andre, who sat writing, or perhaps drawing, at a small table. Occasionally, Andre looked through cold bars on the window into the sky beyond. Arnold turned, took a small sip of rum, and moved onto the next letter in the stack of unopened mail beside him.

This letter was from Captain Aaron Burr. Parts of it were written in code inside an innocuous letter, and parts of it in hidden ink, styled after the manner in which Arnold had instructed its use. *Perhaps there was some measure of use for this spy craft, after all.* With some thought and effort into deciphering it, he uncovered its code.

After a long delay, Burr had successfully returned to Valley Forge. However, it was a partial victory. Yes, Washington's home was destroyed—that much Arnold knew—but the next line shocked him. Burr was the only one who made it back. The brothers had been captured and Burr had lost Sergeant Stevens, following an altercation with Mrs. Martha Washington.

What in blazes transpired that night? The letter went on to say that Burr was injured, then captured, but managed an escape. He suspected that it was Stevens who wounded him, but could not be sure, as Martha and Stevens fired simultaneously. One of their balls had grazed his shoulder.

The two brothers had been captured with Burr but were unable to make their escape with him. Now, the they awaited payment for parole. Lastly, and most disappointingly, Lund Washington had eluded capture, and Martha, Arnold knew, had been killed, but Burr's letter had not explained how. Arnold didn't intend for Martha's death to happen. He needed her alive. His attempt at kidnapping someone of importance to Washington had failed.

Arnold wanted to look back at Andre for a quick boost of cheer, but the letter in front of him demanded his focus. He narrowed in on the words, checking to ensure that he had not overlooked any further messages. He was so engrossed that he almost overlooked a man in uniform approaching his table. When Arnold was satisfied he had not misread the code, he looked up.

He jumped in surprise, his blood bursting with shock. There, standing before him, without any ceremony or sign of his arrival, was the Commander-in-Chief, General Horatio Gates. Arnold suppressed his surprise and turned to anger, though he kept the letter in front of him, resisting the urge to jerk it away. *That would not do.* He barked, "What in the devil's name are you doing here?"

"I wanted to see how my favorite traitor was doing today."

"Bah. You could go to hell if the devil weren't afraid you'd take over."

Gates shrugged it off. "Your barbs are of little consequence. Get them in while you still can. I assure you I can pay you in kind. You see, I'm personally escorting the Lady Margaret Shippen to meet with Andre. She is quite lovely." Gates took off his riding gloves and dropped them on the table. Then, he gestured, surveying the place. "It looks like your usual flair for bouncing back has served you well. It looks like you own the place." Gates sat down. "I do admire your ability to survive."

"You can imprison the body, Gates, not the mind." Arnold lifted his drink, gesturing to it. "Nor the spirits." Gates did not laugh. As usual, the humor escaped him. Arnold let out a smile, one of the few that had escaped since his incarceration. "So tell me, General, what of the fair Lady Margaret? I suppose you two have had quite the journey together."

"Oh, we've had a grand time, Arnold. She has spirit. She knew we had Andre, and she refused to leave me alone until I took her to him. We shared a carriage the whole way here. I can see why you were so smitten with her. She has a lovely figure, wouldn't you say?" Gates let out a cruel smile. "Especially as the carriage bounces."

Arnold slammed the tankard of rum down, spilling it again. "You know, her father did a reasonable job of teaching her politics. One of the few women I know who seem to have a mind for it. I bet if you talked to her rather than stare, you'd learn a few things."

"Her father is sympathetic to the British. There isn't much in the way of politics I'd want to learn from her." Gates pulled out a chair and sat silent for a moment. "You know, I would like to have been able to show her father your letters to her. I wanted to gauge his reaction. That's my first thought, you know, that you were passing secrets on to Andre or her father through these ridiculous love letters of yours. I know how you fancy code and hidden ink. I should've given you over to Ben Tallmadge, the spymaster. I did give him your letters, but he found nothing other than poor verse."

"Since I didn't write any secret messages, of course you found nothing," Arnold said through clenched teeth. "So does this mean that you'll exonerate me?"

Gates gave Arnold a long stare, his eyes betraying the truth. "In truth, that's why I'm here, I'm afraid." He frowned and motioned over to a wench to fill a glass. "Madeira, if you please."

Then he turned back. "You know, Arnold, let me be plain with you. Let me just show you my hand, as it were." The fingers on both hands splayed wide. "The French have signed an alliance with us. While they may not be openly fighting on our side quite yet, they've shot a warning to the British. They've already sent a fleet down to The Bahamas. Once the French land troops on our shores, it will all be over. The British in Philadelphia must act and do so quickly before they find themselves cut off." Gates grinned before continuing, "This means that the British will have to reorganize. They will abandon Philadelphia and regroup in Long Island. And when they do, I'll chase them down, somewhere along the road I just traveled, and we'll have our battle that will end the war."

Gates' wine arrived, and he took a blissful sip.

"They're leaving Philadelphia because *I* burned it to the ground," Arnold corrected. "You waited too long to act. If you go after them now, you'll lose. You can't go out and meet them on their terms."

"Ah, like you did at Quebec?" Gates reminded Arnold, pointing to the wounded left leg.

"If things had been different, if we had gotten there just two weeks earlier, we would be inside those walls, and Quebec would be the fourteenth state. That should be a lesson to be more aggressive, not less. Instead, I was injured, and we lost. You can't win against a superior force."

"Superior? That, they're not. I can and will beat them. You overestimate them."

"No, I *understand* them."

Gates shook his head. "I would've loved to see you on the battlefield, Arnold. You're a good general, but you're too ambitious. As fate would have it, I'm in a better position than you to take advantage. In our war, in our time, thousands will have fought and died. Less than a handful will ever be remembered, and fewer still will be glorified. I will be the one history remembers while you will fade away into obscurity."

Arnold waved an arm around the tavern. "My wrongful imprisonment... my dismissal... all of this, just so you can have your name written in a history book?"

"No, not a name in a history book. You think too small. They will carve my face in mountains."

"You'd better be willing to show your face on a battlefield first."

Gates took another long, slow, sip choosing to pass the insult into silence. Then he said, "Insubordinate? Yes, you are. A traitor? Not yet. There isn't enough profit in it for you." Gates scowled. "You also burned an American city to the ground. At least when you razed soil before, it was Canadian."

"Technically, it was all British whether up north or in Philadelphia. It depends on who you ask. I would burn one hundred American cities if it meant the progress of liberty. I would cut out a state on our map, any state, if it meant freedom for the others. Like a mustard tree, liberty only needs a tiny seedling in which to grow."

"There is still a soldier dead because of you."

"I'm a general. There are many soldiers on both sides dead because of me. It's the nature of our job to be harbingers of death. That makes me somber, humble, but not a traitor." It was Arnold's turn with the upper hand. He pressed his advantage. "But, that is not what troubles you." Arnold dug through a pile of papers on the table near him. Not too far down the stack was a newspaper. Arnold pulled it out and unfolded it. "You've said things that you'd never tell an accused traitor. Of course, some of what you've said *is* common knowledge."

Arnold read a snippet from the gazette. "The British have begun preparation for a strong offensive season, with changes to its general staff and movements of several corps. This suggests the British in the burned city of Philadelphia are reevaluating their position. When asked for comment, sources would not confirm that this was in direct response to the actions of Major General Benedict Arnold, the American Hannibal."

Arnold ceremoniously folded the paper back down again and put on a smirk. "Lucky for us, we have loyalist newspapers to spy on the British, though I... didn't see your name mentioned in there."

Gates turned a light shade of red. Arnold kept poking, "You are here to gloat. So, keep your chair, buy me a cheese platter and another rum, and do your gloating. When you're done, I'll go back to my command and win this war."

General Gates stood, shaking angrily. "Once, not too long ago, you were in a tavern like this in Albany. Schuyler bought you a drink and outlined his plan for you. That very night, you discovered your wife had died. Schuyler wrote it all in detail to General Hancock. Honestly, I think that was why Hancock took pity on you and let you have your expedition to Quebec. I encouraged it only because I thought you'd never make it, but of course, you have a horrid habit of surviving. You mourned your wife, made your mark on the field, and now you've crossed into my path." Gates sipped his drink and continued, "You're right, you are no spy. No traitor. Not near as I can prove. And Congress forbids me from holding you here any longer."

Arnold jumped at that and rammed into the table, spilling both drinks onto the floor with a loud clatter.

Gates put his hand up as if to stay him, "But John Adams has given me leave to send you home, on forced leave, until such a time they deem appropriate."

Arnold cursed and stood still. He looked over at Andre in the cell who stared back at him with a wicked smile.

"Of course, by then," Gates said, "I will have defeated the British and ended the war."

Arnold's hands twitched to throttle the commander when Ms. Peggy Shippen walked in. She looked refreshed, entirely different from the last time he had seen her, standing in front of her home which had been consumed in a lick of flames. She wore the elegance he remembered her by, a crimson red dress, velvet and cut low, with her hair up under a small lace cap, barely noticeable from the front. Golden strands of her hair clung to her smooth, slender neck from the long journey in the mild spring air. Her eyes shone even inside the dimness of the tavern as she coyly bit into her lower lip.

He had shunned her when he left her standing there amidst the smoke and ruins, but she was back. All the things about her, all the things Arnold had fallen in love with, shining bright. Looking into the fire in her eyes, that flame was rekindled.

"I apologize, General. I wished to stretch my legs and freshen myself before coming inside," Peggy said. "I heard the noise. Is everything all right?"

"Yes, everything is fine. Just a difference of opinion," Gates said. "There's no need for you to apologize for your absence. It gave me a chance to share a few words with my friend here." Both Gates and Peggy turned to Arnold.

Peggy stepped inside, closing the door, the aura of light behind her gone. "Mister Arnold, how are you not in prison?" Peggy asked. Surprise laced her words. There was a trace of anger in there as well. And... *something else*. What it was, Arnold did not know.

The spell faded. Arnold responded with indignation, "Miss Shippen, is this not a prison? Am I on the field of battle? I have been forbidden to come to the aid of liberty. Now both my country and myself suffer in equal measure, I assure you."

Gates interrupted before either of them could say more, and asked them something altogether unexpected. "Might we all enjoy a midday meal together?" He turned to Arnold. "Stay here, have dinner with Peggy and myself, and we will speak of more cordial affairs. My expense."

Arnold glared, but in the back of his head, he considered how to turn it to his advantage. *Why not? It could prove to be amusing, at the least.*

"Thank you, General," Peggy said, "but I could not, not with John sitting alone in a cell. I couldn't stomach a meal."

"Then I will arrange for him to join us."

Arnold's eyes shot wide in surprise, although it was not unexpected. Rules of chivalry and gentlemanly codes of honor called for such nonsense, but that decided the matter before him. *Yes, I most certainly will stay.*

"Thank you, General Gates. That is very kind of you." Peggy beamed, as if that were her plan all along. A grin emerged. *Cunning,* Arnold thought, as he placed himself between her and Andre's cell as they moved to a larger and cleaner table.

With that, Gates beckoned a server over and put an order in for turkey, cheese, and some bread and drink for them all.

While Gates did that, Arnold found himself alone with Peggy. She turned to him, addressing him as if nothing had happened between them. "There is no need for you to return to war. Neither should General Gates. I told him as much on the carriage ride over. You and I both know that there are other, diplomatic solutions to end the war." She sat as Arnold held her chair for her, then Arnold took a seat himself. A guard outside the tavern came in a moment later with a key to Andre's cell.

Arnold listened intently. Peggy was always free with her advice, and often, he found himself agreeing with her.

Peggy continued, "While you fight, countrymen on both sides are dying. King George has offered, and continues to offer, resolutions to end the conflict. Why, I hear a commission is on its way now to put an end to the war. There is no need for the rebels to involve the French." She finished with some disgust at the last word. Outside of some Parisian fashions, she had no need of the French, either, like anyone who had grown up hearing the horrors of the French and Indian War.

"Peggy," Andre said from inside the cell, "might I remind you that I am, by birth, half French?" Andre represented everything Arnold wasn't. He was younger, late twenties, and he was loved everywhere he went almost without effort. That annoyed Arnold.

Peggy smiled, but Arnold ignored Andre and said, "Ah, Peggy, you are wise beyond your years and your sex. I admire your loyalties, however misplaced, but as to the French, you and I are in agreement." Arnold shot a look of contempt toward the prisoner, then turned back, smiling. "In regard to your diplomats, well, there have been previous attempts. As long as neither side compromises, no agreement will ever be reached. Diplomacy only ever works if everyone has their way, or no one does. It is the way of such things."

Before Peggy could protest, Gates returned. "The food should be here momentarily."

While they waited, a guard freed Andre of his cell and unchained him. Guards still stood at the door and miles of rebel territory outside, offering little chance of escape. If he tried, Arnold would just shoot him.

They sat awkwardly at first, Peggy smiling at everyone. Gates sat there with his arms folded. Arnold grinned. *Yes, this is amusing. Now where's the free food?*

A while later, after cheese, black bread, and cheap white wine had been placed at the table and nibbled on, the turkey came. The serving lady, a rotund, thick-boned woman of at least forty with a large, white cap covering blonde hair, and big brown eyes, brought the turkey out and plopped the cooked bird on a pewter platter. She spoke with a thick Dutch accent, "Now, what would everyun' want?"

"Dark meat and breast, if you'll please," Peggy requested.

"Dark meat, if you please, madam," Gates ordered as soon as Peggy was done.

Arnold slipped in his order before Andre opened his mouth. "Dark meat as well for me, but I'll help myself to a bit of breast afterwards."

Andre turned to Arnold with a glare in his eye. He growled, "White meat, please."

"Listen, it is a small bird. It was meant to feed poorer folk than you. There isn't enough to go around for everyun' to get all that they want," the serving lady said. "This here bird has gone through the ringer, but I'll tell you what, I'll carve this bird up so that everyone gets at least a slice of what they want."

Arnold looked at her, the back of his mind spinning. Something she said sparked with a comment spoken earlier. A connection of sorts struggled to meet. It clicked, and Arnold hit upon a thought. An idea formed, brewing in his mind. He mulled it over, without revealing it to anyone at the table. *Carving. That might just work.*

Finally, Captain John Andre broke another round of awkward silence and interrupted Arnolds' musings by asking the obvious question in front of them. "General," he said, his aristocratic voice returning to him, "I overheard you talking to Arnold. He is to be free. But, what of me? Shall I still be hung?"

Peggy dropped her bite of turkey. Her fork clattered loudly during a long moment of silence.

Gates broke the stillness. "Unfortunately, Captain, your fate no longer rests in my hands, else I'd free you this afternoon and send you on your way with Peggy."

Arnold wondered if Andre could tell a lie when he heard one.

"Your fate could go in either of three ways. There are some in Congress who wish to hold you accountable for the death of Corporal Collins. They've made a hero out of the soldier and cast you as the villain. There's even a song." If Arnold didn't know any better, he would say Gates looked jealous. *Well, if it's death you want...* "You could be held until a suitable trade is arranged." Peggy's eyes gleamed when she heard those words. "You're quite valuable, you know. Everyone speaks highly of you, including General Clinton. That must instill you with no small amount of satisfaction," Gates said.

"I'd prefer I were less of a man and free, at the present," Andre returned.

"There may perhaps be freedom for you yet," Gates said. Peggy and Arnold jerked their heads toward Gates, though it was for a different reason that Arnold did so. "Congress may detain you as our guest until it meets with your rumored peace commission. Do you know anything about that?"

"No, I do not," Andre said. "You must have kidnapped me before Howe or Clinton mentioned it. This is the first I've heard."

"Certainly, the future head of British Intelligence should know something about rumors, especially one as loved and connected as you are to both the aristocrats and high command here and in London."

"Those rumors of peace are unfounded, as rumors so often are. We will win this war with wits... not words."

"Spoken like a poet. Tell me something, Captain," Arnold asked, changing the subject. He had an idea in his head, one that he needed to discuss with Peggy, alone. "How do you feel about Howe leaving? What is your measure of Clinton?" Arnold found himself in unwanted company. *What to do?*

Gates turned and scowled. "As of now, the Captain is our guest, not a source of secrets. I will not allow you to harangue him this way, seeing as you have no authority to entreat with this man in any capacity."

"Yes, indeed, Horatio," Arnold contested, "but our guest here is also a distinguished gentleman. Let us not forget that he is a poet and painter, and well learned. Therefore, I will ask him questions and, like a gentleman, he will respond to them in a manner befitting one."

Andre put the argument to rest by interjecting, "Howe is greatly loved by those who serve him. He leaves us at a time when we most stand in need of his service. However, Clinton is a friend as well as a competent commander. However, I will remain silent on anything else you ask me regarding those two generals."

"Very well, then," Arnold said. With a wry smile, he asked, "What measure do you take of our own Granny Gates?"

"Benedict!" Peggy said, covering her mouth to stifle laughter.

Gates folded his arms.

John Andre, for his part, said nothing.

"There," Arnold said, pointing. "The mark of a true gentlemen. If there is nothing nice to be said, say nothing at all!"

Peggy laughed.

Gates threw down his fork on an empty plate. Steel chimed on cheap china. He stood and placed a hand on a full belly. "My Lady, gentlemen, excuse me," he said curtly. "I have need for fresh air and relief. I will return shortly." Gates turned to a guard at the far end of the hall. "Captain Andre should be returned to his cell for the time being." He turned back. "Mister Arnold, you have leave to depart to your home immediately. Please do so, and give these two some privacy, even if there are bars between them." With that, he left the room.

Gates has shown his true disposition. When confronted, he runs. Arnold nodded. *One down, one to go.*

Arnold excused himself and made for his previous table. The staff had cleaned it except for several large drops of ink that spilled when Arnold nearly knocked it over. He examined the blot. It looked to him like a large bird of prey, wings a-flight, eye and hooked beak cast sidewise. The bird held something in its talons, something Arnold could not make out or envision. Whether the bird was rising through the sky, or descending to the ground, Arnold could not discern from the stationery stain.

His eyes left the ink and moved to the quill and paper in front of him. He may not have had Lund Washington to use against George Washington, but he realized that he now had John Andre to use against Clinton. Arnold needed something small to begin negotiations with the king's diplomats, and Andre would do.

Arnold knew diplomatic attempts with Congress would fail, especially with the French fleet around the proverbial corner, but Arnold's idea would not. It *could* not. His whole fate was sealed up in it. Certainly, a treaty with King George would be a more favorable alternative than bowing to the French. Peggy was right about that.

Arnold knew he was in the wrong business. Generals made war. Politicians made peace. Arnold had come to an unfortunate discovery: victory in battle came by bayonet; victory in war came by words. It wasn't blood that needed to be spilled, but ink.

He could not allow General Gates to win. Arnold could not live in a land that did not know his name. He could not live in a place subject to the French, for all their crimes against the Colonies during the last war. With that, he picked up the mightiest weapon, and with it, wrote.

As Arnold wrote, he stole the occasional look over at Peggy. He would need her help. She stood, her hands through the bars, holding Andre's. Like a poor translation of a Shakespearean comedy, the two held hands and spoke through the bars, as awkwardly and vilely as two forlorn lovers through a chink in a wall.

Occasionally, he eavesdropped. He faintly heard Andre ask, "Have you heard back from General Clinton? Has he been able to secure my release?"

"These matters take time, John. Clinton knows of our plight and is mustering the support to free you. We just need to wait. My father is doing everything in his power to help. He says that when you are released, we are to be wed."

Andre looked at her, his eyes full of hope. "Yes?"

"You never did finish asking," she teased.

"Peggy, will you—"

Her teasing stopped. "No. Not here. Not like this, with you in a cage."

"Yes, my love."

"John, promise me that, if we do wed, you will take me to England with you? You will take me to see the world?"

"I will take you anywhere, gladly. Anywhere but here. This is the second time I've been captured by the Yanks. Last time, I was treated poorly. This time, they threaten to hang me. I've developed a certain disdain for this place."

Peggy smiled. "I must go." They embraced awkwardly through the bars, but it was enough. It was all they had.

Arnold turned away in disgust as he finished the last of the letter. He turned back as Peggy was leaving and caught her eye, motioning her to join him.

He stood as she came over, making sure to place her facing him, her back to Andre, so he could not see them talking. He spoke low and carefully. "My dear Peggy. Please, take a seat." He went to offer her a chair, but she declined it. The two remained standing, on opposing sides of the small square table.

Arnold broke the silence. He was the one who called her over, after all. "The dear captain only wants you so that he can have your father's money. He needs it to pay for his promotion."

Peggy said nothing.

The silence was disarming. "I still love you, Peggy," Arnold divulged, quite accidentally.

Peggy blinked. "And what of it? Your actions are reprehensible, you burned down my father's townhome, and got that soldier killed. Now, John sits in that cell." She pointed.

"I assure you, my loyalties are to my country. Everything I do is to that end. But, my heart belongs to you. You could have my loyalty if you but wish it. Then, everything I do will be solely for you."

She looked up at him. There was emotion behind those eyes. Something burned behind them, but her face remained a calm mask. *Was there nothing I could do to break through that façade?*

"Did you ever love me?"

She answered slowly softly. "Once."

"Do you love me now, even if only a little?"

They stood there in silence for a long moment. Peggy did not answer. She could not answer, at least, not with words.

"Ben, what is that letter in your hand? Is that the reason you invited me over? What scheme are you up to now?"

He slid the letter across the table to Peggy. "Treason."

"Treason, or another love letter to me? General Gates considers it the same thing."

"No," Arnold said, a serious tone in his words "I am betraying my country, and by betraying it, I hope to save it. But I must have your help."

"You certainly are an enigma, Ben," Peggy returned, surprise etched into her voice. "But why should I come to your aid?"

"Because you care for me."

"I do? I am to be wed soon. I will be off to England."

"That is, if Andre is freed. He may not be."

"That is out of your hands." She turned to walk away. "Goodb—"

"Not, if you help me," Arnold said in desperation. "I can ensure he survives if you pass these letters to the men I need to speak with."

Peggy stopped. She stood silent for a full moment, processing what Arnold had said. "You want me to do the very thing that you stand accused of? You want to involve me in your schemes?"

"I can think of no finer person. Your talents would be wasted on a man like Andre. You'd have a much more interesting life with me, you realize."

"Certainly." Again, Peggy stood there for a strong minute.

"Quickly, Peggy, please," Arnold pleaded. "We haven't much time before Gates returns."

Peggy took the long, thin letter, folded over and stamped with wax. She bent over slightly to reveal part of her bosom out of view of Andre, but within full sight of Arnold. He watched in delight as the flickering shadows of candle-flame bounced about them. She hid the letter within. "I might as well put it in full sight of Gates. He didn't stop starring the entire carriage ride here. I hope you were more the gentleman."

"But of course."

General Gates stepped back in just as they finished. Nerves crawled along Arnold's spine. For Peggy's part, she gave no outward indication of fear. *She'd make a fine player on stage.*

"Benedict, what are you still doing here? Are you leaving?" Gates asked with an irritated screech.

"Yes, sir," Arnold returned, putting a hand on Peggy's shoulder in full view of Andre, smiling as he walked past her. "I'm on my way home."

Arnold had always been a nautical man, from the earliest days as a merchant in the seas around Honduras and the Caribbean to his time stalling the British on Lake Champlain. He knew the wind did not always blow in your favor. In those cases, you had to chase after a wind yourself. Now, he thought he had caught the ideal breeze, one that would cause his sails to billow, a wind that would finally sail him to fortune and glory.

TWENTY-SIX

Valley Forge
April 8th, 1778.

A GAIN. What exactly happened?" Aaron Burr asked. His voice did not present an aura of calm, collective patience. He'd been at it for a week now, and Sergeant Martin Stevens repeated his story of the night they burned down Washington's home—save for one detail.

"I've told you before, Mrs. Washington must have fired on you." Stevens grew weary of hearing the same question and giving the same lie. But, assuming he stuck to it, Burr would eventually grow bored. *I hope. And perhaps I'll even learn of how you escaped and Martha died.*

Stevens wasn't exactly in chains, but he wasn't a free man, either. His plans for meeting Collins and fleeing together had to wait. Instead, he spent the past several weeks in Burr's barrack, a small log cabin he had claimed all for himself, recovering from another sickness. If Stevens recovered and could answer questions posed by Burr to the captain's satisfaction, he could leave. So, Stevens shrugged, he was stuck here, sick, for the time being.

One morning, a day or two after his return, Burr had come up to Stevens, hunting knife in hand.

"What's that?" Stevens asked. He thought Burr had brought it for torture. He grew pale, a sudden release of sweat on the back of his neck soaked into his shirt.

"Hold out your hand," was all he said.

Stevens did so, though he was not sure why.

Burr took the offered left hand, took his knife, and slit the back of his hand.

It stung, but the wound was not deep. Stevens jerked it back anyway.

"Hold out your hand again, I'm not done with you yet."

Stevens did so, but was more recalcitrant about it the second time.

Burr held a paper envelope, small and with many creases, the wax around it, flaking off. He held out his free hand, palm up and poured a tiny bit of brown powder into it. This, he dusted into the bleeding cut on Stevens hand.

Stevens jerked it back again, with a contemptuous glare. "What did you just do?"

"Infected you with pox," Burr said, gleaming.

"You mean to kill me, not with a knife, but with a plague?" Stevens recoiled in horror. Those infected with pox did not often survive. Those who did carried scars and sickness for life.

"Kill you? No," Burr said. "Lucky for you, I've just inoculated you. General Gates' orders, on account of that Washington fellow. Sent over those Negros with the sickness you saw on your way here. He's the one who meant to kill us." Burr laughed with a grunt. "Slow us down, yes—a great deal. But, he won't succeed." He turned to stare Stevens in the eyes. "I didn't kill you, but in a few days, you might wish I had. Don't think for a moment that I won't use your fever against you. Maybe then, I'll get some answers from you."

The first day passed without complaint. As did the next day. But, the evening after the third, Stevens fell ill. The next morning, he did indeed wish that Burr had killed him instead.

The pox plagued him for nearly a fortnight, and his body, already in a weakened condition from the flux, was in no shape to fight off this second infection. He writhed and sweat, fevered, and shat himself. Aides cleaned him up, and Burr asked him questions, but Stevens did not die. The inoculation had only given him a mild case of pox, Burr informed him, though he did not believe it.

This morning was the first time Stevens could stomach food, so he broke his fast with a plate of runny eggs over hardcake. Burr interrupted it, coming in as Stevens jammed a mouthful of egg-yellow yolk running down his chin. Yet again, Burr set to asking the same questions. Apparently, Stevens had not changed his story while he was under fever. Or, he had, and this was a test. He could not remember.

Burr stood before Stevens across the table. "I don't recall Martha's firelock going off before I heard yours. I remember standing there, her weapon pointing at me. I was about to take care of matters when I heard the discharge of two weapons." Burr moved to the side of the table, and Stevens slid his chair backward to increase his distance. Burr wagged an accusatory finger at Stevens and continued, "You were supposed to keep this mission together. You were there to protect us, lay down cover fire and the like. Get us out of any sticky situations."

Stevens wanted to yell, *"What did you want me to do, shoot her?"* He did not. Instead he just listened. He'd heard all this before.

"Instead, I find myself a few moments later, on my back, blood dripping down my arm. Now, I'd ask you what that's all about, but I know you aren't going to answer. So, I'll just say what happened afterwards, see if any of that will loosen them memories," Burr said, tapping a finger down on the table.

"After that, the Odgen brothers got a good push-and-shove themselves. Some of the servants must have come down to restrain them. Later, when I awoke, we were together. Several servants were around us, but most everyone's attention was drawn to the fire. I could see we were outmatched, but the brothers started to argue on purpose. They caused a fight, you see. Clever boys. One of the brothers managed to pick up a rock. The next thing I knew, several of the field hands surrounded him, when the other brother pulled out a knife tucked away in his boot. I escaped in the scuffle, and when I did, I could've sworn I saw an old lady lying still on the ground, ash across her face, blood pouring out of a wound near her head. That lady must've been Martha, as I heard she died. I didn't pay any attention to it at that moment because I fled as fast as I could away from there. Later, I swore I ran across you in the forest, sick as a diseased cow, two Negros at your watch." Burr looked down in disgust. "And that was the end of you, 'til you came traipsing back to camp with those same two Negros.

"Now, I've told you my sin. I freely left my friends at the farm. I fled, and I left them all right, but there wasn't a lick I could've done about it. General Arnold says I should let it go, but it still troubles my mind, just as your story does. I suppose it's possible that it was the late Mrs. Washington who shot me. Or, you are just a damn poor shot. Neither of which I believe. If I were a man of ill repute, I might've found another means of extracting the truth from you."

Burr sat down at the corner of the table. "Are you sure you want to keep that as your official story?"

Stevens sat through it all, attentive to the things he had not heard. When Burr finished, he was hopeful that this would be the last of it. "Yes, sir. That's what happened," Stevens said. He'd almost flinched and confessed, but Burr *was* a man of ill repute, and Stevens didn't want to find out what Burr would've done if he'd started cracking.

Burr sighed. "Well, that's the way it is then. As luck would have it, there's need of you in General Charles Lee's corps, seeing as how you've recovered of sorts from the pox. Most of Morgan's men will be down with it shortly," Burr said with a sly grin. Then he added, "General Gates has us moving out soon enough, though we'll be down in strength. He said, 'It's time to put our mistakes behind us and focus on the future.' And I agree."

Stevens thought for a moment. *So, my actions did lead to Martha's death, even if I didn't pull the trigger.* The thought weighed on him, but he didn't have time to think about it now. Burr wanted him back in the field, most likely to kill him. It didn't matter whose corps he was in anyway. At the first opportunity, he and Collins would flee. Stevens grew worried over the whereabouts of Collins, having not heard from him since returning. Stevens had requested to see him. Burr ignored him each time.

"And another bit of news, Sergeant," Burr interrupted. "You have a visitor." Burr stood and opened the interior door.

Finally, Stevens thought. *Collins has come.*

Then Emma walked through the door.

When Emma and baby Jane came in, Burr took his leave. Stevens jerked upright and darted out from behind the table. His brows drew together, and his mouth hung open. *Why would she be here?* "Emma?" he said at last.

"I came here as soon as I heard. They didn't bring Henry's body with them when the soldiers came. Something about wanting to bury him here as memorial. I don't quite understand, so I did the only think I could think of. Jane and I traveled here instead," she said, rambling, as she drifted closer to Stevens, half-hugging him in an awkward embrace when she reached him, Jane still clutched in her free arm.

"Emma, what are you on about?" he asked when Emma was back in front of him. "What happened to Henry?" Stevens helped her to a chair, and she thanked him, sinking into it. Now, a look of confusion swept across her face as well.

"What... you don't know? How could you not know? Were you not there? I found it odd that you were not the one to deliver the news to me. I wanted to hear it from you, not a stranger. I've come up here to learn what happened."

"Learn what, Emma?"

Tears poured down Emma's face, and she rocked Jane back and forth. "I want to know how my husband died. I want to know how he died when you promised to protect him!" she screamed, letting loose her fury. Jane let out a startled cry.

Stevens' heart sank. His knees went weak, and he almost toppled over. The air left him, as if the news of his friend's death were an enormous stone, cold and heavy upon his chest. The room grew darker as the fire died down. It cracked and ripped while Jane and Emma cried. He let loose tears, too.

He kneeled by Emma's side and saw Jane for the first time, cradled in Emma's lap. He tried to soothe her, softly singing a sad song. Jane was gentle and beautiful and looked so much like her father, with blond hair and blue eyes, and a skinny, bony body. She quieted as the room became still and dark. All three of them stayed that way for some time.

The two sat in the silent, dark room until little Jane woke up and broke the silence with a hungry cry. The two looked at each other over the protests of the little baby. There was much that needed to be said and done, but one thing was clear—life would not stop for them, even with as much grief as they carried. Without a word, Stevens rose and exited the room, allowing Emma some privacy to feed Jane. As he left, he wondered if there would ever be a time Emma forgave him, or if he could ever even forgive himself.

It had been almost two months since Emma had first met with Stevens and moved to camp. Since then, the weather had grown hot and humid. Stevens was formally released and introduced into his temporary new unit under General Lee. Stevens, Emma, and Jane visited the memorial and resting place of Corporal Henry Collins as often as they could. They both discovered how he died. They said he died a hero. That didn't matter to them. Collins was gone.

Every soldier Stevens and Emma talked with around the memorial spoke of a sense of loss. They rallied around Collins, the Hero of Philadelphia.

Valley Forge itself was a flurry of activity. As predicted, the British were on the move. Tents struck, drills doubled, and plans made ready. General Von Steubens made circuits around the camp to instill any last lesson he could.

Camp followers organized themselves and packed their belongings. Emma had set up a small tent with them and joined with the other women who did laundry and sewing. Because she was new to camp, work came slowly at first, and she worried Jane would go hungry. However, once word whispered through camp that she was the widow of Corporal Collins, jobs came more readily, as did scrip. Wreaths and flowers would appear each morning outside her tent as they did around Collins' memorial.

Stevens held no real loyalty to the two Negros, but he had promised them answers and found none. He tossed around the idea of not seeking them out, dropping the matter altogether. If he turned his back on them, no one would care.

But when he heard where they were through whispers, he changed his mind. Stevens found them a short while later, right where he was afraid he'd find them. The guards told him to keep his distance, but he informed them he was inoculated and gave them his papers to prove it. Stevens walked right up to the long fence formed in the manner of a corral and demanded to see Jarosa, the slave who had saved his life.

A few minutes later, an old black man, hunched over and coughing, brought out a familiar bearded face. Behind them, Jarosa's friend followed. Stevens frowned. He hadn't asked for him. He looked warily over to the soldiers for reassurance, but they were too far away. Stevens shuddered.

The older man went to leave, but crumpled in a sudden onset of coughing. Jarosa comforted him and had his friend fetch water, which came back in a wooden ladle, the liquid brown and dirty, while Jarosa quoted scripture to the dying man. They finished as the old man lay down on a filthy pile of straw. Jarosa shut the man's eyes and held the lids down with small smooth stones. Stevens watched with sorrowful eyes, helpless beyond the fence.

Jarosa spoke, clear agitation laced in his voice, though it was restrained. "What do you want?"

"I came here because I promised I would."

"And?" the smaller man asked angrily. "You lied to us; you killed us." He turned sharply to Jarosa. "Do no talking with 'dis man."

Stevens expected this, but he spoke anyway, frowning, "I suppose you can't be any more disappointed in me." He looked at Jarosa. "I couldn't find your wife. We can't get into the city, and as you know, she was not one of the refugees who ended here."

"Yes, 'dat we know," Jarosa said. "Thank you for trying. It is more 'den we woulda been told from anyone here. It is good that she is not sick."

Stevens felt relief. He had done all he could and turned to leave. But, there was another reason he had come, something he did not realize until he was here. As he turned back, his heart sank. His arms felt lifeless, like dead weights hanging from his body. His throat began to dry. "There is something else, something else I need to confess."

"Speak."

"You did not find me by accident in the woods. You know why I was there."

"Yes. You smelled like burning wood and your clothes was flaked with ash."

What? "Why did you say nothing? Why did you help?"

"My answer has not changed from the last time you asked," Jarosa said, pointing to the book in his hand. "Because 'dis book says to help."

Jarosa's answer stunned Stevens. He would've stood there in shock awhile longer, but the small Negro stepped up, anger flashing across his face, eyes as red and burning as hot coal. Stevens did not need to be told why. He knew.

"What about Rebekah? Did you kill my cousin, too?"

The questions cut like daggers, as sharp and piercing as the one he had used to kill the slave girl. Her ghostly, wide eyes flashed before his face. Stevens blinked and shook his head, but he could not escape the image. "Yes," he said somberly.

The younger slave dashed toward the fence. Several soldiers, some distance away, turned and yelled, "Stop," as they reached for their muskets. It was Jarosa, though, who succeeded.

"Why you holdin' me back? Why you sidin' with dat killer? He killed her! He killed her!"

"Do not hold anger towards dis' soldier. It was by God's will. He was simply the tool for God's hand."

The kindness in Jarosa's voice disconcerted Stevens more than anything else. He had little experience with Negros. From a young age, he had been taught by the pulpit that slaves had a better life in the Colonies than they would have back in their villages across the dark sea in the Dark Continent. That was that. He'd never considered it further.

However, the horrors of war opened his eyes. He'd killed that girl. He'd almost killed Martha Washington. Collins was dead. He had failed the two Negros who saved his life. *Anger*, he expected from the Negros. That was reasonable. That Jarosa could express calm, amidst all these horrors, was surprising.

Stevens broke down, and a tear escaped. Moved as he was, inexplicably, he kept sharing, more than he intended to. "I have a friend who was taken from me as well. He was in the wrong place at the wrong time, and he was killed for no real reason." Stevens eyed Jarosa, who stood there, listening in return.

"The thing is, my friend wanted desperately to find his place in life. He always thought this war was it. He would come out of if a hero, as a man, as someone people respected. He didn't know that he always was, at least by me. I was envious of his perfect life, his good nature, his family at home. He had everything I've always wanted. I never told him. Maybe if I had, he wouldn't have been there, on that street. He would have been with me, throwing dice and drinking ale." Another tear ran down his cheek. "And the horrible truth is, in a cruel way, he is now the hero he wanted to be."

"We cannot change the path that God has set before us," Jarosa said smiling. "We can only choose how we face each step."

It was Stevens who grew angry. "I'am no instrument of God. My path is my own. Things happen in life that are unjust. Just as it is wrong that you two are here."

The smaller slave spoke up. "You is right, 'bout 'dat, an' I will get out o' here. And I will kill you."

Jarosa put his hand up. "Go. Go with peace, soldier, and do the Lord's will, whether you intend to or not. Just as we will fulfill it here." With that, he took his friend by the shoulder and drew him away. While they spoke, other Negros had lowered the dead man into a shallow grave. That, Stevens noted, was how everyone would end. Neither Negro would leave this camp alive. There was no inoculation for them. Why should there be? *And who will say a prayer for you, Jarosa, and place stones upon your eyes?*

The morning to depart camp came fast and cold. Dawn broke before Stevens was ready. He shook off his groggy unease and mustered in the morning. He had not wished to rejoin a soldier's life, but that was before Emma had joined them as a camp follower. And follow, she would. Without Collins' income, she and Jane had nothing except for what monies she earned herself. Stevens would not leave without Emma, though she was still angry and wouldn't speak with him. Therefore, he led his small unit for the time being, biding his time. He hoped he wouldn't let them down, too. With fake aplomb, he stood erect, taking roll of the soldiers in his charge.

They waited for what seemed like hours, formed in ranks two deep and columns stretched out forever. Finally, they heard the drums they had not heard all winter. The columns moved. The war was on again.

The soldiers broke into a marching cadence, and with steady voices, began to sing a somber song. It took Stevens a moment to recognize the words. Not a usual tune, nor a hymn. As the men sung, others in front and in back joined in the chorus. Stevens felt himself swirling inside a wellspring of sadness, pride, and anger. His friend had died, but he would be remembered through song, at least for the time being, even if for all the wrong reasons. Though he didn't know the words, he listened as they marched off to battle, catching the last bit of the chorus:

Remember thy fallen, soldier and companion,
remember thee,
Collins, our fallen; with this day, we fight to be free.

TWENTY-SEVEN

Near Freehold Township, New Jersey
June 27th, 1778.

COLONEL George Washington rode through parallel ranks of his Hessian soldiers as they marched through the morning humidity, promising another baking hot day. Even with that promise, Washington wore his uniform tight. His red jacket fit just right, his white wig powdered, not a single strand out of place.

Washington continued through a sea of Hessian blue and until he met a wave of green. For the first time in his career, there were British soldiers under his command, even if they were Irregulars. He strode up to his subaltern, Major John Graves Simcoe, dressed in an equally fastidious manner. Though, as a commander of the Queen's Rangers, Simcoe held more distinction in green than did Colonel Washington in red and buff.

Before Washington said a word, Major Simcoe eyed him over. He remained reserved and kept his face blank. Washington felt heat beneath his skin, and it had nothing to do with the summer's sun. *Who are you to inspect me?* Instead, he ignored the slight, as it would delay his duties. With that, Washington asked, "How are your soldiers?"

Simcoe slowed his mount and brought it alongside Washington's before answering. "My Rangers are ready, sir. I trust the Hessians are in order as well?"

This, Washington also ignored, but he would go no further. "Donop assures me they are. I have almost finished inspecting them myself, just to be sure. I see you have done the same."

"Well then, sir," Simcoe said, "it appears everything is in order. Shall I continue my duties?"

In other words, Washington translated, *leave me the hell alone, Yank.* Or, maybe Washington was reading into things too much. His horse clipped uneasily down the uneven dirt and stones, hidden beneath the tall grass as he bounced around in the saddle before regaining control. "I look forward to concluding our business with the Colonies."

"That is something I look forward to as well," Simcoe said, finally showing a trace of kinship in his face. "I am ever at your service, sir."

That he now commanded British troops, and that his British subordinates at least gave him courtesies, was an improvement to his career and standing. No matter his rank or his position, Washington would always be a Yank in British clothing. Even in positions of authority, his subordinates would never let him forget that. Neither would his superiors. Otherwise, Clinton would have informed him of his ace—the reason Clinton felt so confident they would win the battle ahead.

Washington couldn't help but settle into an unease over the approaching storm. He dismissed Simcoe and spurred his horse onward. He still had soldiers to inspect and battle plans to prepare. The ranks of Irregulars ended uncomfortably short, but they were his men to command, and he still had a duty to perform.

As for the doubts lingering in his mind, he knew one thing: the rebels would most assuredly attack, and he was counting on it. Then he would smash them, avenging Martha's death, restoring his honor, and proving his nationality once and for all.

The day had already been as hot as hell, and New Jersey hadn't even dipped its toes into the first full week of summer. Thankfully, the cool late-afternoon winds brought the temperature down. General Horatio Gates wiped his brow and examined the assemblage of generals he had called to council on this eve of battle. A map of dubious origin lay on the table in front of them, with generals of the council bickering over its accuracy and the placement of troops—British and American alike.

Spies tracked the long British column as it exited Philadelphia and made its way to Long Island, New York. There had been a few skirmishes and raids on supply lines already. Still, the British continued northward, unprovoked. Gates couldn't tell if the British were avoiding a fight or choosing better ground. He determined he'd have to provoke the British into fighting them on his terms.

"Poke the snake hard enough with the stick, and eventually, it'll strike," Gates said to the assembled men standing around the table. They appeared unmoved.

"Sir, aren't we the snake?" Nathanael Greene interjected. Greene was a Rhode Islander, a large man in his thirties with a long nose and small, sharp eyes, offset by a premature hairline retreating across his scalp. "'Don't tread on me,' as I recall. We hung that flag with us in the Kentish Guards."

The former pacifist thumbed his Masonic jewel and nodded at the Marquis de Lafayette, who remained present but silent through the long day. "If we poke them hard enough, they'll attack. You're right. But that could be what they are waiting for. They could be hoping we continue to over-extend ourselves. We're already down a third of our fighting strength due to these inoculations against smallpox." Greene shook his head in frustration. "And that's *after* our losses from winter."

It was a pity that Daniel Morgan's men, and several other regiments loyal to Benedict Arnold, couldn't join them on the field. They were recovering from an untimely inoculation of the pox while Gates surged ahead with the others. *A pity indeed.* Gates nodded to himself in victory.

General Charles Lee broke his silence. "They aren't looking for a fight. Greene's right. We are chasing the Lobsterbacks as a seaman pursues a whore. It'll be more than disease that we'll catch, mind you, if we poke 'em with our stick." The raucous older general surprised them all with a somewhat logical voice of reason, even if it were couched in crude terms. He bounced his hips back and forth to drive home the point. Just outside, the shrill barking of several runt dogs punctuated the heated discussions inside the tent.

Gates had heard enough.

"General Lee, you have the advance column. Lafayette, you'll take this flank." Gates drew his finger down away from Monmouth Courthouse and tapped the map, then pointed to several other generals in the tent and gave them their orders. "And General Greene, you'll be held in reserve."

"Excuse me, sir," came Greene's protest, "but what would be the meaning of keeping me in reserve? I'm pretty sure my men and I would be better suited supporting Lee."

"And in reserve is where I need—"

"This is *not* how we should go about it," Lee said. "I've laid out my plan before, and now I find myself reminding you of it once again." As if on cue, General Lee's yelping dogs barked in irritation, clearly backing their eccentric master. "As I said before, if we let the main body be—"

"And I will remind you, yet again, that you aren't in charge here," Gates said. "I appreciate your input, but until the day Congress sees fit to replace me, remind yourself of your place."

"I will remind you of our equal rank."

"And?"

"I have served with distinction in the field. You are, and always have been, an administrator. Have you ever actually been fired at? That should—"

"Excuse the interruption, sirs," Greene said. "We were discussing tomorrow's battle plan. I find it unhelpful that some of our best soldiers are sidelined for this upcoming action—soldiers all loyal to Arnold. I trust that has no bearing on your decision to hold my unit back?"

"Preposterous," Gates said, grabbing his eyeglasses off and eyeing Greene. In truth, everyone in Arnold's command was sidelined for the time being. "I have need of your services in reserve. Never have we come out in force to attack the British. If the battle doesn't proceed as planned, who else will I have who can hold the line as well as you?"

"A committee of overweight wankers gave you command over me. Now I find you won't even take my advice," Lee interrupted, pounding the table once with his fist as if trying to bring the attention of the room back on himself. The older man seemed to sweat a little more than usual. *That's odd.* Lee recommended pursuing small-scale skirmishes along the supply train, which he had been adamant that his unit, and his unit only, should carry out.

Gates ignored the general and addressed everyone in the tent. "So much of our future depends on how we proceed in the morning. I'll be as close to the action as I can, but once the shooting starts, it'll be up to you and your boys to see we achieve victory."

"The boys have been training hard, sir. Von Steuben has disciplined them well, and they are ready. We'll serve wherever and however we can for the cause of liberty," Greene agreed.

"It doesn't matter if your men are ready or for what cause they believe in," Lee said. "We left a large part of our boys back in Philadelphia. They are either too sick to fight, or they are taking care of those who can't, or they are rebuilding the city and assisting the refugees. Put simply, Commander, we don't have enough firepower to match the British."

It was true, Gates thought. So many men were missing off the rolls due to dysentery, smallpox and civil reconstruction. Now that Philadelphia returned to their hands, it had to be rebuilt. That diverted funds and resources away from him. "The soldiers we do have are in the best shape they have ever been. We know how harsh the conditions were this winter, and Washington did us no favors by pawning the sick refugees off to us," Gates said. "But the British are soft and turning tail. According to my reports, our numbers roughly match those of the British." He turned to look at Lafayette. "If we beat them here, then the French will land troops, and we will win the war."

"Then it will be a contest of training, won't it?" Greene said.

"It could be one we very well are not prepared to fight, particularly with these last-minute changes," Lee argued.

"Battle calls for flexibility," Gates said. "That's never changed in all of history. I also never approved your plans. You assumed incorrectly."

Lee turned red and spun around. As he stormed out of the tent, he cursed. "Just send me my orders when they're ready. My dogs need attending."

That was not what Lee said, but it was what Gates chose to hear. The real words had something to do with "bitches in heat." It grew quiet in the tent. In truth, Lee's leaving pleased him. He could deal with the delinquent general later.

Gates broke the silence saying, "I've been out in the parade field and finally succeeded in shaping the mass of rabble into a proper, disciplined army."

"But will it be enough for us to succeed?" Greene asked to no one in particular.

Gates answered anyway. "We'll find out."

With that, Gates dismissed the generals, and they filed out to make their preparations for tomorrow. With the tent clear, and

Lee's damned yapping dogs gone, he could think about how best to handle the chronic insubordination running rampant through his General Staff.

First, it was Arnold, but he was back home in Connecticut. Charles Lee had always been a thorn in his side, but he was so ostentatious and eccentric that no one ever took him seriously. Gates had never considered him a threat, but he was still a capable commander out on the field. So, Gates held his temper. If General Lee performed well, then Gates could forgive him. If Lee failed, then Gates had someone he could blame.

In any case, General Horatio Gates had until morning to get everything back under control. Right now, he had papers to sign.

TWENTY-EIGHT

Monmouth, New Jersey
June 28th, 1778.

THE dawn broke earlier each morning, Corporal Frederick Bakker thought, as the days grew longer and the sun grew hotter. While winter was no easy task, there was fire, hot soup, and strong drink to warm his belly. In summer, there was no escaping the heat, no way to avoid the biting mosquitoes, and no way to stay dry with all the mugginess hanging heavily in the air.

Bakker rose, having slept under the stars over matted brown grass. He had his blanket under him to protect him from bugs, since he didn't need one over him. But the blanket under him didn't help. A large centipede curled up with him. After letting out a startled cry, Bakker grumbled, rolling off the blanket and flicking the insect into the dew-soaked ground. It skittered away.

Then Bakker rolled his blanket, trying in vain to wipe away the sticky wet blades of grass. It was then, he realized, that the grass also stained the knees of his white breeches. *Great. Good start to the day.* He looked back down at the mess. If he left his blanket bundled, he could've used it as a pillow, it wouldn't be covered in grass, and then he also wouldn't have been one of the last people to get breakfast. He ate quickly and gathered his belongings.

Shortly thereafter, his commanding officer rode past in a hurry. Beside him rode a giant of a man, going just as quickly down the line. A brief moment of recognition glinted in Bakker's eye. A little while after that, their unit's black drummer brought his drum to life.

Bakker's feet began to ache, as if his pain was triggered by the damned drums. They hurt every morning as soon as he heard them. He'd barely begun marching, but his feet, particularly his absent toes, somehow remembered each step from the day before.

The land past Philadelphia was gutted with deep ravines, small patches of forest, and large expanses of grassy farmland between fingers of streams. In another life, Bakker could see himself with a hoe, tilling the land and maybe even raising some cattle. It would be a peaceful existence, away from anyone telling him to march at first light, away from piercing bayonets and away from his father's sins—

"You're out of step, Bakker." Maximillian's voice was as irritatingly helpful as ever.

"Got two left feet?" Another soldier from his unit said from behind. Bakker thought his name was Anderson.

No, but I am missing two toes.

"But, what if he's doing it right," Anderson said, "and we're all the ones out of step?"

Maximillian put a stop to it. "That is enough. We have another long day of marching. Maybe more. It's made longer by your racket."

Bakker joined in the conversation, happy to ignore his sergeant. "Did you see Colonel Washington ride past this morning? He wasn't twenty meters away."

"Colonel Washington? Is that the same man who took us across the Delaware?" Anderson asked.

"It was," Bakker replied. "I saw him pick up a horse that night. The beast fell—or it should have. For some reason, it remained upright. It was as if the Colonel had kept the horse upright by his own will of strength. I also heard he carried two giant pails full of water and threw them both at once at an orphanage during the Philadelphia fires."

"Telling stories again, Bakker?" Maximillian said.

"Only what I heard."

"I've heard stories about the colonel," Anderson said. "He slept in comfort in Philadelphia. On a nice soft bed."

"He's been sleeping under the same stars as we have and the same ground since we left Philadelphia," Maximillian corrected. Bakker nodded.

Anderson raised his brows. "Really?" he said, nodding in approval. "I would follow a leader who did that to the end of the world."

"I would follow that person, too, but not toward the pointy end of a bayonet—and that's where we're being led," Bakker said. As highly as he thought of Colonel Washington, he was by no means willing to die for him. Since it was already too late for him to survive intact, all he wanted to do now was go home. Maybe punch his father. Maybe just work a farm in the middle of nowhere. He definitely wanted to meet a girl.

"A bayonet?" Anderson said with contempt. "The Yanks don't know how to use bayonets. They shoot and then they run. They wouldn't know what a bayonet was if it skewered them in the ass."

"They've been practicing all winter," Maximillian shot back.

Bakker reached over and felt for his canteen, grabbed it, then pushed it aside. There was another canteen next to it and he took a long swig from that one, finishing his ration of rum. It had been put to good use, though the liquor didn't mix well in his churning stomach. He'd have to give it a few moments to settle.

Before it could, the drummer's beat changed. Everyone stopped, and faces turned in all different directions in a panic of confusion. Bakker's unit went through several facing movements that brought them from parallel marching ranks into a position to engage them in combat. In a few minutes, they had moved off the road and transformed from one large column to one large row. *Are Yanks nearby? Or is this a precaution?*

Sweat beaded into Bakker's eyes from the heat, of course. He looked to his left, toward Anderson, who now stood beside him instead of behind. He could see his brow was slick with sweat as well. Maximillian was no longer near, having stepped to the rear. Envy filled Bakker, wishing he had applied himself better so that there was a row of Hessian blue between him and musketfire. It seemed safer.

Bakker didn't see anything in front of him, and not knowing made it all the more difficult to stand his ground. At any second, he could meet a hail of fire or a swarm of canister shot. If that happened, he hoped he would not even see death coming. He did not want to end up like one of those fools who bled to death for hours while their screams permeated the air.

While his attention focused to the front, an unexpected noise erupted from behind. Anderson jumped. He took a chance to look back and saw a horse-mounted artillery piece, a three-pound cannon, put into place. A moment later, the drummers marched his unit through another few facing movements to allow a path down which the cannon could fire. Bakker didn't know as much about them as he wanted, except that they made holes bigger than his bayonet or musket balls did. He thanked God those bigger guns were pointing toward the Yanks and not the other way around.

More time passed, and his unit moved up the field under sharp, ordered commands. Like chess pieces, they marched into position. Here, Bakker noticed gullies cutting into the earth and hills and large-leaf trees surrounded and blocked the view. He still could not see anything.

Apparently, somebody else had.

The drummers once again changed cadence. Now Bakker heard the familiar sound of Maximillian as he ordered their company to affix bayonets. He did so and was surprised to find the familiar twist and click of the bayonet sliding into place strangely satisfying. In the same moment, Bakker saw the Yankee Army for the first time since Philadelphia.

Sunlight gleamed off Yank bayonets. The Americans marched in unison in a similar fashion to how Bakker had just done. There were places to hide, and the rebels had yet to fire a shot. They looked like an army.

Bakker swallowed hard.

He shut his eyes for a moment to stop the world from turning. When he re-opened them, he found everything was just as *verkehrt*. He'd seen men on both sides drop their muskets and run. Maybe he would be the one to flee this time. *Only, where would I go?*

He looked left and right at Anderson and then at his other squad mates. He couldn't run unless they did. They would never let him live it down, and they didn't look like they were going to flee. *It is a long swim to Kassel.*

The order to half-step came, which meant now, with bayonets pointed straight ahead, Bakker and his line drove toward the Yanks. It resembled a game of chicken, but here the stakes were higher than silly boyhood games. *If the Yanks don't flinch first...* Bakker dared not finish the thought.

The Yanks should have fired, then fled. Instead, they did something Bakker did not expect: they held their ground. Neither side gave way for the other. They continued their march, now a few dozen meters away from the Yanks. He'd never seen them this up close before. They looked...

They look almost as frightened as I feel. Their faces were pale and sweaty. Bakker wondered how he looked to them. *Probably the same... scared witless.* But, he marched onward, and they did the same. Bayonets glinted against the rising sun. Then the battle began.

The sun had reached highest point, and the day was still not yet at its hottest. Sergeant Stevens couldn't imagine the heat being any worse. On top of that, his stomach growled, sounding like a bear, and his head hurt from the extra rum rationed that morning. His canteen was empty, though there was little time to stop and eat or drink when Hessians and artillery fired at him. He wanted to beat the drummer. Stevens looked around. His unit was much smaller than it had been under Arntz, before the winter... before the war had plucked his friend from the formation.

As he marched, he took care where he placed his feet. Bodies littered the ground. Some wore blue, baking in the raw sun. Others wore darker. They cooked just the same. The sun held no distinction. As his unit marched on in circles, the same bodies came back to haunt him. He sidestepped them as best he could, something they hadn't taught during the winter months training in Valley Forge.

The Hessians, in this case, seemed like a memory. Before, they shot, marched, and ran them off with bayonets whenever Stevens' men drew too close. But now they appeared distant. Unreachable. Like grabbing handfuls of fog.

The drummer stopped.

Stevens thought for a moment. They'd been marching for hours, like a giant game of chess as each side jockeyed for position. To their credit, Steven's side performed remarkably well, but as the day went on, he knew they were being out-maneuvered. They were hot, dehydrated, and exhausted. Their orders either came too slowly, or not at all. Something was wrong, but he was in no shape to figure it out. All he wanted now was water.

Then someone shouted, "They're behind us!"

Stevens sobered. The cloud in his head evaporated like the moisture in his throat. He asked in a raspy voice, "Who?"

Nobody answered. Soldiers in blue threaded past him and his ranks toward the Hessians beyond. He turned back for an instant. In that moment, he could've sworn he saw a flash of green. That didn't make any sense. They had been fighting the Hessians, and the Hessians were in front—

"Retreat... retreat!" came the order.

That didn't make any sense, either, Stevens thought. If they retreated, it would be orderly, as they'd trained. This was chaos.

Shots thundered. A man to the left of Stevens flew forward and landed face-first, the left side of his flax shirt wet with thick, dark red. British Rangers poured out of the trees behind him, some on horseback, others on foot, some in green and others in regular garb, as Stevens once wore as part of Morgan's riflemen. He looked back in the other direction as the Hessians appeared ready to close in.

How'd they get behind us? And how are we cut off from everyone else? It didn't matter. He moved, legs pumping, fast as his feet could fly. Stevens dropped his rifle and ran. *If Burr wanted me dead, then his wish might very well come true.* Stevens made it past a wave of green before collapsing to the ground, burying himself among a soft bed of cool grass.

"Who in God's great name gave the order to retreat?" General Gates flew through the open flaps of the command tent and into the blinding sun. He squinted in response. The tent sat further to the front than he anticipated with only Greene's men in front of it. Now, Greene and his men were gone in an attempt to stay the British advance. So far, it wasn't working.

Gates felt naked and exposed.

Three aides stepped out with him, the only ones still around as everyone else had taken the field. One of three said, "We seem to be falling apart."

"Not helpful." Gates would remember to award that aide latrine duty when the time came. "All this appears to be happening around Lee's corps?" Gates recalled the maps in the command tent.

His brightest aide, Hamilton, responded. "General Lee seems to have let the British slip right past, almost as if he wanted—" Hamilton took a dry gulp of air as the realization hit him. "You don't suppose?"

"Not Lee. Something must have happened. Get a messenger out." Gates paused to think. "But if the rat is up to foul deeds, we need to get word to Lafayette and Greene to make a stand here. I shall go myself." He headed to his horse. It basked in the shade, chewing down lonely pieces of tall grass. Gates stopped and turned to Hamilton. "Perhaps I should—"

"Why don't I go instead?"

Gates sighed in relief. "Find out what is happening. Get back here as soon as you can." He helped Hamilton to his own horse and saw him off just as several soldiers, Continental Regulars by the looks of them, ran through the command area. They didn't stop. They didn't recognize Gates or any of the officers nearby. They ran past. A moment later, a few more men did the same.

"Stop them!" Gates called out. By then, the soldiers and his aides were gone, and he was alone.

A moment after that, General Charles Lee rode up on horseback and squared off with Gates in the center of the camp.

Gates cocked his head in confusion. Charles Lee towered above him, but lurking beneath that exterior lay a crack in his command—his hands shook and his eyes darted.

"What are you up to, Charles?"

General Charles Lee stopped and surprised Gates by dismounting his black beast of a horse. "How many times did Congress pass me over for command?" Lee asked, his voice full of anger.

"What are you on about?" Gates answered.

"Hancock should have never led this army. I should have been in charge, right from the start. I gave up my commission in the British Army to take command of this rabble." There was coldness in his voice. "If I had been in command, none of this would have happened."

"Did you order the retreat?"

"Then Hancock was killed," Lee pointed a crooked finger, bent by age, ignoring Gates. "And you stole what should have been mine."

"You were a guest of the British at the time," Gates reminded him.

"Yes, and they helped me remember my loyalties." Lee laughed, then said, "My men are drunk, terribly hot, and overtired. Now, they find themselves cut off. While the rest of your command tries to rescue them, I've made sure to tell General Clinton precisely where you are."

Gates paused. "You..." There did not exist a word adequate enough to say how he felt. "You fool."

"No, sir. I am no fool. I am an Englishman. A proper officer and a gentleman. I shall not now, nor shall I ever, tolerate insolence from so low as you and your ilk again."

"But, you've killed men," Gates said, shaking off the betrayal. "Our men."

"How many good British men have died? How many?" Lee withdrew his officer's sword and stepped toward Gates. "How many on both sides were going to die before you saw the error of your ways? How many graves would it have taken before you reached out to me in our time of need? Instead, you play games. You supplanted men of exceptional breeding with those of backwater Yanks. You gave Greene, a private before the war broke out, *a generalship*! You dismissed Schuyler and accused Arnold of treason while the real threat to you stared you in your face, yet you never saw it." At that, he took the sword and dropped it at Gates' feet.

Gates stared at it, then looked back up. "And betraying our cause makes you a better man?"

"This is not my cause."

"Then what are you doing here?"

"I came to get my dogs."

The sound of incoming troops caught Gates' attention. He looked up, past Lee. A contingent of Crown forces—Rangers, he thought—headed straight for him. A moment later, more flooded the camp. Bayonets and drawn knives and pistols dotted his vision. A certain zeal filled their step. He could have sworn he saw smiles.

Gates had one chance to escape: convince Lee of the folly of his plan. Carefully, he turned to the turncoat. "You can still be the better man." His voice sounded desperate, unintentionally so. Lee heard it, too. Gates sighed and shook his head, keeping his voice under control. "This is my fault. I should have known better about all of it."

"Indeed," Lee turned to the Queens' Rangers. "He's all yours, boys."

Heat filled Gates, heat that did not come from the summer day. "Your soul will blacken for this! It will be sent straight to Satan's maw. It is not too late for you to end this, Charles. Escape with me now, and we can regroup and fix this. You shall have no more than a court-martial, I assure you. You shall not see a single thread of rope."

"Ah, my friend, but you shall. A pity. You were a good soldier once. Instead, you betrayed your King." Lee flung his hand in the air, unaware of his own hypocrisy and continued, "Can you imagine the statue they will build of me in Hyde Park once the war is over? Once I have delivered the lot of you?"

"Liberty will not die with me."

"Hollow words do not befit you, Horatio." He looked out over at Simcoe's men, awaiting the commander's word. He gave a half-wave to them. "This is your chance to die as a soldier. What do you say? Shall you go out a hero, or muck about with capture?"

"Neither, you daft fool. Look at them. You told Clinton to come here, but Clinton didn't warn them you'd be here. Those muskets are pointing at you, too." Gates saw Lee's face drop as the Queen's Rangers approached them.

Gates could hear a voice ask from among them, "What do you want us to do?"

The Rangers readied their weapons, but hesitation showed on their commander's face. Gates hoped he could take advantage of that to make his escape. The major's voice called out, "Surrender now, or we will fire." A row of Brown Besses, bayonets extended, leveled not at him, but at General Charles Lee.

I must escape. I must warn the others of his treachery. If I'm going to go, now is my only chance. With that, he burst the few feet toward his horse, and his foot found the stirrup.

"Do you want us to fire?" a voice called out from behind. Gates flinched, but there was no response.

Lee spoke out. "Gates is getting away! Don't just stand there. Shoot him! My reward will be less if he escapes."

"My orders are for the capture of the rebel commander. I cannot fire on an unarmed general," the major returned.

That exchange gave Gates all the time he needed to mount his horse. His glasses flew off as he swung himself over. Out of the corner of his eye, he saw Lee take out a pistol from his jacket. "Do I have to do everything myself?" Lee demanded. "Are not even the Queen's Rangers up to the task of us old-war veterans anymore?

Have you all gone soft?"

Gates knew before Lee did what the motion meant. In pulling his pistol, Lee sealed his own fate. Over the chorus of gunfire emanating from the Rangers, Gates could hear the major scream, "Hold your fire!" Some of the balls came at Gates, whizzing by and shattering tree branches. He spurred his horse and made his escape just as the body of General Charles Lee crumpled to the ground.

Sergeant Martin Stevens awoke to find an angel kneeling over him. His throat didn't feel as dry, and he didn't feel as hot. He realized the light was fading. He wondered how long he'd been out. A moment later, he recognized the angel. He called out in a soft, tired voice, "Emma?"

"I was worried."

He shot up on his elbows. "Where's Jane?"

"Safe, with other women, far away from here." She looked at him as she bent back over, a pitcher of water in her hand. "Here, you need more." She lowered a ladle down to his mouth. Stevens sipped. "There are so many of you who didn't wake back up. Not only the ones who have passed on, but ones like you who just dropped."

"How long have you been doing this? Where is everyone—"

"Away from here. A general—I believe it was Greene—came by here and pressed the British back. They seem to have lost interest anyway, for some reason, and are heading back up the road. That's where the fighting is, but they left the lot of you boys here lying in the grass, baking in the sun. As soon as I saw you all needed help... Well, there were several ladies. An artillery man's wife started it all. We just grabbed buckets of water and some rags. It's terribly hot, and you would die without water soon."

Stevens made out the sounds of battle not too far off in the distance. Closer than Emma said it was.

"How bad is it?" He looked up at Emma. Her hair was damp, and her clothes stuck to her. She looked worn, like she had been the one out here doing all of the fighting. He still found her beautiful.

"What do you mean?"

"Wasn't I shot?"

She threw a damp rag at his face. "No. You just went down after being in the sun all day. Your breath reeks of rum."

He rolled his eyes at her. "I just faded out, huh? Just do me a favor and don't tell Coll—" He frowned.

Emma remained silent.

"I'm sorry." This was the first time he'd spoken with her in a long while. Now was his chance. "You shouldn't be here, you know."

There was a moan from a man nearby. He called out in a throaty whisper, "Miss... pitcher..."

"There are other people I need to get to," Emma said to Stevens. "As soon as I saw you, I rushed over, but I need to help out—"

"Stay."

"I can't." She touched his hand. She meant it for support, but even so, it made his heart skip as goosebumps rose all over his arm.

Dammit, I still love her. What's wrong with me?

"We don't belong here. Neither of us. Not with Jane. Not with what's happened to Collins. Look at me. I almost died," he pleaded.

"You drank too much."

"I hardly drink at all. That's the point. Something sinister happened here. I got lucky. And we don't belong here."

She ignored him. "Nobody belongs where they are. We all find ourselves caught up in things we can't escape."

"But we can... we can leave. Tonight. Simply fade away. Forget all the bad things."

"I can never forget Henry."

Stevens frowned. "I didn't mean that. I just want you to be safe. I care—" This was the worst time to say anything. It had almost slipped out.

"There are still duties we have. It's the inescapable truth. We don't do the things we want to do because we have our daily duties to each other. Doing what we want to do requires a selfishness most people don't have."

"Do you have it?"

"I have my responsibilities. You do, too. There are people who need our help. Innocent people caught up in this awful conflict. Just the other day, we sent a lady who had come to us covered in ash and blood to a church to be taken care of. She had lost her memory. How tragic it is to be out here in all this and not even know who you are. We have a duty to help people in this war so they don't have to endure the same suffering that we have."

Stevens looked her over. Perhaps she was right. General Arnold was no longer in command. He'd been the one Stevens feared, and he had survived today's battle intact. Perhaps nothing alarming had taken place. It was all in his head. He looked at Emma, already up and caring for another soul. *Perhaps she's right. If she can still serve others despite all she has lost, I can certainly fulfill my duties.*

Still, something fluttered at the back of his mind as he turned away and headed toward the closest wounded soldier.

TWENTY-NINE

Manhattan Island, East River, New York
July 1st, 1778.

THE gazettes called it a draw. Colonel Washington nodded to himself. If the rebel rags were calling it that, it was a sound victory indeed. He handed back the newspaper to a subaltern and continued riding down Queen's Road, overlooking the East River on his right. The sun was warm, the air was cheery, and loyalists lined the streets.

Washington did not like New York City, a sinful place full of bordellos and back-alley crime, but his mood today let him forget that. He almost forgot his anger at General Clinton. For the moment, he let it pass as their victory at Monmouth burst into rousing ovations by the crowds in the streets before him. Washington and his men arrived at New York as conquering heroes.

Washington followed the officers as they turned down a side street toward the waterfront and stopped at a grassy field before a large home constructed of wood and painted yellow with white trim. Officers filed in and out of the front door. Those coming out carried drinks. Some milled about. All wore smiles.

Leaving his mount with a servant, Washington made his way toward the home. He filed in with several other high-ranking officers and various aides and guests. A few of the officers' wives were there, eliciting a stab of pain through his heart as he stepped inside. The house smelled of sawdust and pine as it was built in the wake of the fire of '76 in New York.

Inside the home, the trim shone wet and glossy with lacquer. The wooden floor bowed without a squeak. All the windows and shades were thrown open, and the white walls and decorative mirrors gave the house a wide, open feel despite the crowd. He looked around for a serving wench and blazed a trail to find one. He desperately needed a drink to ebb the ache in his heart.

The serving girl was a precious thing with black hair, golden eyes, and a blue dress that kept mysteries secret. She looked as if she had been plucked from a whorehouse and delivered to him here, complete with a full mug of ale. The mug of ale interested him more than the girl. He chided himself for the way he used to look at other girls, the countless times he danced with every beauty he could find. *It wasn't right of me to do that to her.* General Clinton intersected him just as he approached the serving girl.

"Ah, Washington," Clinton said, slurring the name after he rescued dark brown liquid from the bottom of a glass. "I've been looking for you, my boy!"

Washington sighed. He'd have to find that ale for himself later.

"I have need to speak with you. Unofficial, of course." Clinton raised an empty glass. "It's a celebration. We don't wish to mix too much business with pleasure."

"Would you like me to get you another drink?" Washington asked with idle fascination. Howe would have never allowed himself to get so inebriated. "I am heading there myself."

"A drink?" Clinton said. "Nonsense. You look a little pink in the cheeks already, my boy. Better lay off for a while."

"If you say so, sir."

Bodies shoved closer together as more men entered the house. Talking and laughing filled the air in all directions. As a result, Washington had to step uncomfortably close to hear the general, who was by no means whispering anyway. Clinton's breath smelled of cooked pork and hops.

"Nothing is finalized, understand."

"Sir?" Washington asked.

"My promotion to Commander has come with a few perks, as it were. Combine that with the French fleet at our doorstop, here and in Honduras, and I have a certain amount of leeway on how best to conclude the war."

"Is the war over? I know Monmouth was a success, but General Gates escaped. The rebels still have an army, displaced as it is."

"Ah, yes, but the poor general fled not just the field but all the way back to Philadelphia," Clinton chuckled. "Once the French hear about this, they will not land troops here. Our Navies may be in a *de facto* war, but I don't think our armies will be. This will give us a position of strength to re-open the peace commission."

Clinton set his empty glass down in an ensign's upturned hat without the young officer knowing. "In light of recent events, I have an opportunity for you." He waved his hand as if he intended to point it somewhere and struck someone nearby. In response, they let loose a string of profanity. When the offended man turned to see who it was, he apologized and sulked away. Clinton paid no heed. "It will look good to have a Yank mop up the last of the rebel resistance and help bring peace back to the Colonies."

Washington stood silent in reflection.

Clinton reached into his jacket and retrieved a sash. "This used to be mine. I am giving it to you. Now, you see, I will not announce this until later, most possibly weeks down the line, but until then, for all intents and purposes, you will hold the rank of Gen—"

"Colonel Washington!"

Washington turned in time to see a big face, a smile, and a large hand come down. The hand hit his back, hard. It emptied his lungs and burned his back even through his thick uniform.

"It is good to see you, Colonel!"

Clinton interrupted, "Ah, Colonel Donop. A pleasure."

Colonel Donop feigned surprise, sloshing his drink with the theatrics. "General Clinton, I did not see you, eh? Forgive this old fool. I was just so happy to see my old friend again." He poked a finger at Washington and wrapped an arm around him, then addressed Clinton. "General, has he not told you of the time we crossed this maddening river, frozen with such chunks of ice that could freeze a man's soul solid?"

Washington sighed.

"Let me get you a drink! It will have to be a weak bitter, as you English know nothing about what makes a stout lager, but it will be something for us to celebrate with."

Washington wanted that drink, but Clinton made a move to hide the sash and epaulette pins he'd been attempting to hand over to Washington from the Hessian officer. The plan backfired, as Donop caught the move.

"General!" Donop roared, officers nearby stopped chatting and turned their heads. "General Washington. Sounds good, from the gut. Congratulations, General!" Whoops and hollers filled the hall.

Washington turned red with embarrassment. Clinton turned red with anger. Donop did not notice either.

"What a great choice for General. Now the English will really run from us. One hundred kilometers, those English will run, just like their General. Everybody runs!"

The Hessian still didn't differentiate the English from one side versus the English on the other. *I suppose from his point of view, we are all English.*

Clinton said, "Now, as I was—"

"Hey everybody, we have a new General here! General Washington." Dunop's voice boomed down the hall, off the walls and floors, as if everyone in the room hadn't heard already. There were a few more half-glances followed by another scattering of hollers. The Hessian continued down the hall, announcing the news.

Donop's not coming back with my drink, is he?

Clinton smiled and handed him the sash. "Well, never mind. News is out. Might as well go have that celebratory swill."

Washington nodded back.

"We still have much work to do. The rebel commander is out there somewhere," Clinton said. "The bulk of their army also still survives, despite Lee."

Charles Lee, the ace up Clinton's sleeve—presumably. That piqued Washington's curiosity. "Hmm. Speaking as one General to another..."

"Don't push it."

Washington shrugged. He'd expected that. Clinton was tight-lipped. "Let me just ask you. Was Lee working for us? Working for you?"

"I have no idea what you are talking about."

Interesting... "But, he was killed? Shot by Simcoe's Rangers?"

"It seems that way."

"Was Lee a turncoat?"

"Of course you know what this means, this promotion, don't you?" The abrupt change of conversation gave Washington the answer. Clinton continued, "You can sell your commission and turn a handsome profit. I've just made you a richer man. You'll have money to rebuild your home once we finish here."

"What of the rebels?"

"They'll be dealt with soon enough. I may perhaps send you to Rhode Island to quell an uprising of the natives there. If we offer the right kind of troops and officers to lead them, it may be enough to draw out what remains of the continentals as well."

You mean, use me as bait.

Clinton eyed the wench with black hair and golden eyes. He turned away from Washington and said, "If you'll excuse me, a matter has arisen that requires my attention. Congratulations, general."

Typical. Well, at least I've made General in word if not on paper. Does that mean I have finally become accepted among the British ranks? Washington may not have succeeded in capturing Gates, but it was clear to anyone who asked that Monmouth was a strong British victory. If the French didn't go any further than sending out a flotilla of ships, then the war could well end soon.

So, what was the point of the promotion? Washington felt a darker motive, something he could not see. He'd been blinded by that darkness before, but now he wasn't as naïve. So long as he fulfilled his duties, he would not protest. He still had personal business to conclude with the Yanks—with General Arnold in particular. His victory at Monmouth had left him far from feeling satisfied.

But once I am finished? That thought left Washington alone and in the same spot he'd been at since the start of the war. *Clinton is right. I have a home to rebuild. Do I rebuild my life back in Virginia without Martha, or do I move to London where I will always be looked at as a Yank?*

Without her, where do I belong, anyway?

Benedict Arnold sat on the sofa, in his home, cup of tea in hand. Coral curtains with gold trim spread wide to let light from the bright, sunny afternoon into the airy room. The sofa matched the curtain trim, its thin pads designed more for style than comfort. Empty chairs with silk embroidery sat opposite the couch. In the middle of it all stood a tall table, set with tea. Hannah swept across the room, straightening things and bringing biscuits to the tea table.

The inactivity was tedious. He said as much to his sister.

"If you are that bored," she replied, "you're welcome to run your apothecary." She hurriedly placed a dusty bottle of Madeira on the table with several wine glasses.

Arnold shuddered at the thought of regular work as he steeped his tea. "No, the public knows you and loves you. Business would shrivel even more if I took over. Besides, it's been so long since I've worked there, I wouldn't recall cloves from catnip." With Hannah gone all day and the boys at boarding school, Arnold spent his days alone.

Besides, it gives me time, too much time, perhaps, to hatch my schemes. Arnold looked at the empty chairs before him. *Those chairs should be hosting British diplomats. Instead, they'll be hosting the President of Congress. Whatever will John Adams have to say? Most importantly,* he thought, *how can I best use this new development to my advantage?*

A little later, his guest arrived, and a servant brought him in. Hannah abruptly stopped working, as if having a guest inconvenienced her tidying. Arnold knew his sister. She could have had one of the servants clean, but then she would have gone right back behind them and redone it to her liking. Hannah sat reluctantly as not one, but two guests arrived.

Arnold nodded at the unexpected arrival of a second man, hiding his shock from his expression as he did so. John Adams, he expected. General Horatio Gates, he did not. *What is the coward doing here?*

"I thought it best for Gates to accompany me," Adams said, as if sensing Arnold's alarm. "I apologize for not sending word ahead. I hope this will meet with your satisfaction?"

Not really.

"Indeed," Arnold said with a pleasant wave. "Please, have a seat." Gates and Adams sat in the chairs. Hannah joined her brother on the sofa. Gates raised an apprehensive brow, when Hannah sat, but said nothing. Adams didn't even seem to notice that a woman joined them.

The Congressional President was a shorter man in his forties and round with pink, puffy cheeks. He dressed in plain yet practical clothing, clean and pressed. He was a staunch supporter of Gates, or had been, and rumors spoke that sometimes, the correspondence between the two broke into discussions of books, rather than talk of the war.

So what were these two compatriots doing here?

Arnold smiled to himself as realization dawned. He hadn't been exactly sure for why Adams would trek out to Connecticut until after Arnold had seen Gates. Now he knew. *Good. This will give me license to have a little fun.*

He wasted no time. Smirking, Arnold asked, "So, Horatio, how was your horse ride from New Jersey? Was it sixty-miles at a gallop, a canter, or did you and your horse casually stroll back to Philadelphia?" *While your men bled in the grass.* Arnold, at least, didn't say that aloud. *See? I can be nice.*

"It was not like that, Arnold. I was about to be captured— or worse," Gates protested. Though he wore his military uniform, there seemed nothing soldierly about him. His eyes were sullen and sad. "I thought it best to report back to Congress the news of General Lee's betrayal and our defeat as soon as possible."

Arnold chuckled. No wonder no one can ever see themselves as the villain. Humans possess such capacity to rationalize any behavior, no matter how abhorrent.

"We didn't come here to discuss that incident, General," Adams said as Arnold cocked his brow. Adams' eyes begged him to stay on topic.

That is exactly *why you two are here. You wouldn't be looking to me if Charles Lee hadn't betrayed you and Gates hadn't fled the field.* "Of course. My apologies, gentleman. And I have also been remiss in my duties as host," Arnold said, referring to the spread laid out on the tea table in front of them. "Would you like some Spanish wine, Mister President?" he asked of Adams.

Adams nodded but said, "Please don't honor me with titles. I am but a servant."

"Understood." A servant poured two glasses of wine and handed one to Adams and one to Arnold. Arnold handed his glass to Gates and poured himself a bit of rum. Hannah did the same.

Gates looked at him. "You're not joining us in your bottle of Madeira?"

"Generals don't drink to wine," Arnold said, prepared for this. "It is not a beverage of war."

Gates slammed his glass down. Thick, red liquid ran out. "I don't have to take this."

"You do, I'm afraid," Arnold responded, turning to his sister. "That's why they've come, Hannah, you realize."

"Yes, I know," she said. "I have real work to get back to, if you boys are just here to jape at one another. I should be going."

Adams interrupted. "If you have business elsewhere, Miss Arnold, we understand. Perhaps it would be best if General Gates left with you, if just for a little while."

Gates jerked toward Adams and said, "I will not be treated—"

"Absolutely not, Mister Adams," Arnold countered. "I enjoy the company of both my sister and the general. His failure cheers me."

"We didn't fail. We held them back and beat them back," Gates said, turning his anger toward his once subordinate.

"General Greene did that after you had already left. After you ran so far away you crossed Colony lines, into—"

"State lines, they are now called," Adams said. "Do think of yourself and things in American terms. We're attempting to create a new nation."

"Well, yes," Arnold said, after being caught off-guard. "But I will always be a man of Connecticut. It will take some getting used to."

Hannah stood, forcing all the men in the room to their feet as well. "Benedict, I've had enough. If you think I'll sit here just to give you another audience member for you to show off your brilliance, you're mistaken. Impress the President. Not me."

She turned around, seeming to notice for the first time that everyone was standing—because she stood. "And furthermore, Mister Adams, what type of nation are you hoping to create? Where do you see women in it? I find it amusing that you boys jump every time a woman enters or leaves a room. I'm not going to bed the man who stands the quickest. It's nonsense."

Adams blushed. "I would not wish for a second for you and my wife to ever meet. The fate of the world would rue the day."

"It would indeed." Hannah huffed. "We just might have a bit of common sense." She shook her head. "Just offer Benedict the position as Commander-in-Chief and stop with all the games."

Adams' pink cheeks brightened with embarrassment, along with the rest of his face. "Yes, of course."

With that, Hannah moved swiftly out of the room.

After they sat again, they sipped their drinks in silence. When a few moments of awkward stares had passed, Gates turned to Adams and whispered, loud enough for Arnold to hear, "Are you sure you want to do this? Arnold is no gentleman."

Adams looked over Arnold for a long moment. Finally, he said with a raised voice, "But he *is* a leader." Adams took another long moment, breathing in and out heavily in thought. "I fear that you've been much maligned, Mister Arnold, many times. But Gates is right—you are a blackguard." Adams held out his hand to stay Arnold's response. "Nevertheless, you are *our* blackguard, and your country calls upon your assistance. In other words, we are in a time of need, and you must help us."

General Gates stewed in silence.

Arnold swilled a glass of rum, eyed Adams, and kept silent.

"General Gates has resigned his position as commander following the... failure at Monmouth."

"My reasons for resigning, Mister President," Gates clarified, shaking his head, "is to spend more time with my son." He turned to Arnold, the sadness in his eyes returning. "My son was gravely wounded in the battle. The physicians say he may not recover."

"I'm sorry for your son, but what of the glory you sought for yourself, for which you impugned me to attain?" Arnold asked.

"What good is glory," Gates choked, "if I have no one to pass it down to?" Tears welled in the general's eyes. "My son is all I have. Without our children to fight for, there is no point, I fear. I wish to spend the remainder of the war by my son's bedside for as long as he has left."

For a long while, no one spoke. "I'm sorry, general." Arnold considered the bottle of rum. *If only my father had believed his fate lived on through his children. Gates has more character than he ever did.* "I truly am sorry for your loss."

Gates looked at Arnold and nodded silently.

Adams spoke, "General Gates has written a retraction of his charges against you, and Congress has dropped the matter. His letter and our apology will be released with tomorrow's gazettes." His expression narrowed. "Will they also run with the headline that says you are to assume command?"

Arnold surprised himself by saying, "No." Adams and Gates sat back in shock.

Now that he had it, he wasn't quite sure he wanted it. The victory felt hollow. "What about Greene?" Arnold asked. "Or Wayne, Lincoln, or even Lord Stirling? Any of them?"

"Remarkable men, all of them capable, to be sure," Adams said. Then he drew silent. "I think you know why."

Arnold nodded. Out of them all, who had seized Ticonderoga and then nearly taken Quebec? Who had beaten Burgoyne? Who had taken Philadelphia away from the British? He had—but this was not how Arnold pictured assuming command. *This may work out better than I thought.* He smiled to himself.

"All we need to do is convince the French we are still in the fight," Adams said. "For that, we need to rally around a hero, someone who has the love of the soldiery and is capable of giving the British one last bloody nose."

Arnold's eyes narrowed. *I will not bed the French. I can and will beat the British bloody.* His mind raced with possibilities. *First, I must speak to the British diplomats. My new station will aid me greatly, but I will still need help.* John Andre's name sprang to mind. He was still a prisoner.

Adams paused. Then, he said slowly, "I will give you aid however I can. I've always argued for strength, and this is true now more than ever. Therefore, you have leave to do what needs to be done." More warily, he said, "I feel the cause of liberty may be lost. Our future lies within a darker realm."

"I will, of course, need full autonomy. Daniel Morgan is to be retroactively promoted to brigadier general. You've overlooked him long enough, and I demand full rights to do whatever I wish with Captain John Andre."

"He is no friend of yours," Adams said. "I trust he will hang."

"Gentlemen, I shall take the role you have entrusted me with. My first duty is to rebuild the army, and for that, I shall beat up for volunteers on the morrow. But first, I will accompany General Gates back home and pay my respects to his son."

They nodded in agreement. Gates swallowed hard, his voice shaking. "Thank you, Benedict. I have perhaps misjudged you."

They all stood and headed out of the house.

"We shall see how my turn as commander fares before you say that," Arnold said, triumphantly. "We should leave today." They stepped through the door.

"Very well. Find us at the inn at the end of Water Street. Good day," Adams said. With that, they boarded an open carriage and rolled away.

Arnold stood on the porch, alone. At that moment, a soft breeze hit him. The wind wrapped around him, transporting him back in time, to the nightfall on the beach in Honduras. He promised himself back then to seek out his fate, though at the time, he did not know what it was. Now, standing in the doorway of home, he was at the cusp of realizing it as the Commander-in-Chief of the Continental Army, though he had something even far greater than that formulating in the back of his mind. He wondered, as the hot July air moved around him, if he were close or if it were just out of reach.

Arnold wanted the world and someone to share it with. His thoughts drifted toward Peggy. *Sibi Totique*, for himself and the whole. He would survive. His name would endure. The Latin inscription was etched into the sign above his apothecary and branded into his heart. Not only would he become great in this New World, he would shape it how he wanted. His sister had been right to question Adams. *What type of nation were they trying to build?* Arnold grinned to himself. He knew the answer to that, too.

And there was no one to stop him.

PART FIVE

"It is next to impossible to unhinge the prejudices that people have for places and things they have long been connected with." --Nathanael Greene

THIRTY

Philadelphia, Pennsylvania
July 4ᵗʰ, 1778.

"WE'VE chased them all the way up to New York, boys!" Commander-in-Chief Benedict Arnold cheered out from on top of his black horse. He shouted the familiar rallying cry: "Remember Corporal Collins!" He reared his horse at just the right time for emphasis.

Columns of soldiers stretched down the street in clean uniforms, brandishing fresh flintlocks with polished barrels and bayonets. They marched to a cheerful cadence of drums as children followed fifers and streamers whipped in the wind.

Along the streets, signs read, "Women want a soldier." Busty ladies from the bordellos surrounded the billboards, bringing attention to them in the way only they could. The parade marched down Chestnut, along ashen scars of the proud city. At the nexus, tables stood near Independence Hall with long lines of would-be soldiers. It was part celebration, part recruitment, and all propaganda.

Arnold knew the dirty truth: some of the people had been paid to stand there. The line moved deliberately slow to keep it looking long. Many of those who waited were already soldiers with active bounties but had fled. No matter. He would take them in again. He would take them all.

A group of grenadiers, tall, large men, worked the taverns. They would go in to return a few moments later, dragging drunks to their feet by their shoulders. Those recruits went into the back of covered wagons. They would realize what happened once they sobered. *I can give these louts a chance to change their fates.* Finally, Arnold had the local jails emptied. Arnold would give the criminals the discipline needed to make the most of themselves. He would take them all—sinners, debauchers, tosspots alike—and give them a chance to redeem themselves under his service.

General Benedict Arnold planned to repeat this process as he crisscrossed all over New England in the coming weeks. As he did, his army would grow. As he traveled the countryside, collecting men, he also vowed to learn the names of county and city authorities loyal to him—and the names of those who weren't. Where he could, he would put his own men in place.

The true numbers of recruits here in the liberated city of Philadelphia, even on this Fourth of July, was pitifully small. But it didn't matter. It was all for show. He didn't need numbers—just loyalty.

Sergeant Martin Stevens grew tired of shoveling dirt. It had already been a long march from Monmouth back to Philadelphia, and the sun baked him like clay. Now, he moved shovelfuls of it. He knew the purpose, and it rankled him. When digging didn't exhaust him, he was angry but could do little about it. *I'm digging a mass grave.*

Stevens should have left when he and Emma had spoken about it, but that was several conversations ago, many weeks past. He hadn't left. Not without her. *At least we're talking again.* She'd even laundered his shirt, though it needed laundering again—caked with sweat and dirt. The field near where Jarosa and his friend had been imprisoned now held a large, empty hole thanks to Stevens and a few other soldiers-turned-diggers.

Not everyone was happy with General Arnold assuming command in the aftermath of Monmouth, or so the wind had whispered. Soldiers from a regiment in Pennsylvania mutinied at the news. During the mutiny, they released the survivors of smallpox still imprisoned. Some of them joined with the mutineers. Others had fled. Some, Stevens heard, stayed in the corral while the gates stood open and the guards were gone.

Is this grave for the mutineers? Or is it for those in Charles Lee's regiment suspected of treason because their general was a turncoat?

General Arnold commanded them to swear oaths, pledging loyalty not to the American nation, but to General Arnold instead. Most had done so; Stevens was among them. Others had not. Now he looked around at the completed grave, glad he had taken that oath. He knew what Arnold could do.

On the grass above Stevens' head, other men busied themselves in construction. They dragged and stacked cheap green pine boards full of resin in rows to create the outline of a frame. Coils of rope remained untouched on the grass. They wouldn't need them until they raised the frame for the gallows.

He stuck his shovel deep into the soft soil and wiped dirt off his face with his sleeve.

"If you and your men are finished, Stevens," Captain Aaron Burr barked, "then fetch yourselves something to quench your thirst and help the men up here finish."

"Your boys stay here, weapons at the ready, while we bring the prisoners out," Burr said to Stevens. "If we have any problems, remember to shoot the *prisoner* this time and not me, eh?" Burr smiled, but it was not a joke. "I'm hanging eight at a time, Stevens, but if I find even a flinch of disloyalty from you, I'll make room up there for a ninth."

Stevens swallowed hard. His skin burned with anger. Of course, it hurt more because it was the truth. *Maybe I belong up there anyway. Not for shooting Burr, but for my other failures.*

The afternoon smelled of sawdust and sweat as men led the first row of prisoners onto the hot field and up to two small, thin platforms just wide enough for a man to walk across. Horror ran down their faces like streaks of sweat. He could see the terror in their eyes. Eight men, some white, others black, stood in front of the ropes. One prisoner retched—it stunk of fear.

From atop a brown mount, Burr said, "For treasons against the lawful authority of the land, including mutiny, the punishment is death, by hanging."

Stevens wondered if Burr understood the irony. *Mutineers hung in the face of a country in the midst of treason. Where did the madness end?* This was all wrong, he knew, but once again, he couldn't to stop it. Stevens' stomach rolled, and acid rose in the back of his mouth.

All the men had hoods placed over their heads by a soldier who edged behind them on the platform. Then he secured ropes around each neck. A minister read passages of scriptures on the grass below, oblivious to the sin on the stage. Stevens continued to hold his rifle at the ready with the rest of his unit, unsure of what to do, particularly if there was trouble.

There was no trouble. The thin platform was kicked from beneath their feet. Bodies lurched downward, then jerked back up. An audible snapping heralded a neck cracking, and a single head flopped to the side. The acid in Stevens' stomach shot upward again, bringing with it bile from deep inside him. He kept it down, even as the life shook out of the men hanging by the ropes.

"At ease."

Several soldiers around Stevens stepped forward. One of them whispered, "This is bullshit." Burr ordered the soldiers to bring down the bodies, which had gone slack by now. They loosened the tight ropes from around each neck. Corpses collapsed with a dull thud onto the ground below.

Finally, men dragged the bodies off through the grass and shoved them into the hole Stevens and others had dug earlier. In a twisted sense, Stevens breathed easier once the gallows hung empty. His relief lasted until a second set of eight mutineers were brought out. Stevens' heart tightened. It grew heavy, grinding into his soul like a millstone. Though it was only in his head, Stevens placed his flintlock upright on the ground to keep himself steady.

He examined the faces of the second crowd. The same as the first, except for one Negro. Stevens wondered if Jarosa or his friend were among the condemned. He breathed relief that, so far, he had seen neither, but this Negro reminded him of Jarosa's friend. He was proud, spine held straight, defiance burning in his eyes.

Stevens lifted his flintlock once more.

Two soldiers held the man from behind, but the Negro stopped and pressed backward against them. His bare heels dug into the dirt. "I'm not goin' to die like this," he said, as the soldiers pushed him over.

As he fell, he grabbed at the nearest one, and they toppled over together. The soldier landed hard, hitting his head on the platform. The Negro hit the same spot but landed roughly on the soldier instead.

Then, he flew upwards and jabbed the other soldier with his hands still tied together. The solid shot to the face took the soldier by surprise. He staggered backward just as the Negro pivoted, jumping with one foot on the bench, then turned around and launched himself over the first prone soldier and into the second, stunned one.

With both soldiers stunned, the Negro had freedom to move, so he darted behind the line of condemned men, moving perpendicular to the line as he ran, making sure to keep human shields between himself and Stevens' flintlock.

Stevens spotted legs speeding away from afar. He wondered if the man would make it and found himself hoping he would. He couldn't fire; he didn't want to fire. Even if he did, he and his boys didn't have a clear shot—which shouldn't have mattered. Who were they going to hit? The men condemned to die? But, Stevens used it as an excuse anyway.

Burr put an end to it. He nudged his horse to the far side of the gallows, pulling his officer's firearm and aiming it. He waited for a long pause... then fired. Stevens saw legs lifting off the ground, then heard a thud. The man screamed but did not die.

"Bring him back," Burr said. "A ball is too honorable a way for this man to die. It must be by the noose."

Stevens felt sick to his stomach once more.

A soldier placed another set of hoods over the rest of the mutineers and fastened the ropes around their necks. The injured man was brought back, screaming and thrashing, until he too was hooded and left standing there on one leg as a noose hung around his throat.

The platforms came out from underneath fifteen feet, and all eight people dropped downwards to their deaths. Stevens winced. Everyone else around him stood still. *Is this normal? Is this how the world is?* Hoods weren't placed over the condemned for their benefit, Stevens realized. Their heads were covered so the audience wouldn't have to face them.

"Sergeant," Burr said, snapping Stevens into focus. "Grab two of your boys and get over here to help."

He knew this was coming, but even so, Stevens felt his blood chill. Burr had been challenging him all morning and all afternoon. It should have been no surprise that he'd call Stevens out now. He walked over with two others. Each step felt like its own lifetime, as if he were the one to hang. He reached it, but made the mistake of looking down and breathing in. He recoiled at a whiff of refuse. Brown, wet splotches stained the grass. Stevens felt sick once more, but he approached Burr.

Burr signaled to bring the next group over. "I have a little test for you. I've got a friend here to see you." He eyed Stevens squarely. "I want you to put the noose on him and hang him yourself."

Stevens stared out at the backs of the condemned men as they walked past him. He shivered despite the sun. Every man stood on the platforms under their respective ropes, hoods placed over each of their heads. Stevens examined them all. Even with the hood, Stevens recognized Jarosa. The Negro clutched his Bible between his hands. Stevens moved to stand beside the one who'd saved his life.

Burr said, "I want you to be the one to do it. Send these mutineers past the ninth circle of Hell, straight into Satan's mouth."

Jarosa reached up, and with the Bible threaded between his fingers, lifted the hood up and over his head. Stevens' heart skipped a beat as the soldiers below jerked back in surprise and began to raise their muskets. Burr shot Stevens a look as if to say, "You better take care of this."

"It's all right. He's no threat," Stevens said, waving his hands up at them. "He can choose not to wear the hood." Jarosa hadn't moved since removing it. The soldiers seemed to settle at Stevens' word.

But in the confusion, Stevens found himself looking Jarosa in the eyes. Jarosa stared back as they locked onto each other. His eyes were filled with peace, his face sat content. It was his usual look. Jarosa was calm. *How did you end up here as a mutineer? Where is your friend?*

"How fortunate to find you here once more," Jarosa smiled. "Did you find my wife?"

Stevens didn't know what to say. He stammered. The rope swung empty in the breeze, rope that he was supposed to place around Jarosa's neck. He tried to speak, to ask questions, but no words came out.

"It's time to prove your loyalty, sergeant," Burr said in a raised voice. "You shot me. I know it was you. Here's a chance to prove I shouldn't hang you, too."

Stevens had a sudden vision of his knife plunging into the girl in the woods. He saw Collins laying there, dead in the street. Then, he recalled Emma's tears. She had been kind to him, saved his life, even after everything he had done. He had done so many things wrong.

"Where is your friend, Jarosa?" Stevens asked.

"Dead," Jarosa said back in a whisper. "Died of pox. In the camps."

Stevens whispered back, "I am sorry." He meant it, but he should have left it at that. He started to place the rope around Jarosa's neck, but he hesitated. "I have to know... how did you end up here?"

"When the soldiers mutinied, when they opened the camps to let the survivors out, I stood there for a long time with this book in my hands. Then, I laid it down on the straw where my friend died, and I joined the soldiers." He looked up at Stevens, staring through him, as if addressing Stevens' soul. "It is all right. Put the rope around my neck while we talk some more."

Stevens did as instructed without knowing why. While he did so, he asked, "Why? Your book does not promote violence."

"I did not do it for God," Jarosa admonished. The rope went snug around his neck. By now, Burr had grown impatient and sent another soldier to secure the ropes around the other men. That left Stevens alone with Jarosa. He finished explaining, "I did it for myself."

"But, why?" Stevens pleaded. His eyes were watering, and he wiped away a tear. "All that did was to get you here. You could've chosen to stay."

"We got a war to win," Burr yelled. "You're wasting time. Hang 'em."

Stevens stepped off the bench. From here, he looked up at Jarosa, standing high above him.

"We all do strange things in the name of friendship," Jarosa said. "Now, I can die knowing I stood for something I believed in. I can be proud of that." Jarosa looked down at him. "And you must do the same."

Stevens looked up at Burr. He remembered his pistol was worthless. *Would his own men fire on him?* A white horse wasn't too far off, tied to a shade tree near the opposite end of the grave. Stevens pictured himself making a dash for it. If he could just keep the gallows between him and his unit, he reasoned he could be safe as he made for the horse. Then, he could ride off, make his way back to Emma, and they could be away before news of his treason reached the camp.

"If you don't kick that platform, I swear by my brass that you will hang next." Burr was right. There was no point in arguing. These men were going to die, by his hand or by someone else's. It was better that he did it himself.

"Did you ever find my wife?" Jarosa asked again.

Stevens hung his head, his face blank. He looked at Jarosa once more. His voice was raspy. "I didn't even know where to look." He tried to hang his head low again, but he could not break eye contact with the man.

Jarosa stood straight. He held his book firmly to his chest. "Then perhaps I will see her soon enough. If not, I shall be able to look down at her." He kept his gaze locked on Stevens. "Thank you, my friend."

Stevens kicked the bench away. It flew out from underneath the men who'd mutinied. They jerked hard as four slack ropes went taut. Jarosa's Bible fell with a thud to the ground.

"Take 'em down and drop 'em in the hole," Burr said.

Stevens stood before Jarosa. He seemed so restful, swaying on the rope in the breeze. Stevens stood the platform upright and hoisted the body onto it. He struggled a bit in getting enough slack in the rope to remove the noose. He had to dig his fingernails into the flesh of the neck. Stevens glanced over at Burr. There was a brief moment where he considered walking over and punching his teeth out.

Like Stevens, the other soldiers had the other corpses down off the rope, but they were rough with the bodies. They rolled one of them across the dirt until the body fell into the grave. Another pair of soldiers picked up and swung a corpse high into the air. It disappeared into the grave with a crunching of bones.

Stevens looked at Jarosa and acted fast. He took Jarosa by the shoulders and gently dragged him toward the edge of the grave. Then he took ahold of Jarosa's chest and tried to carefully lower him in.

It should have been an easy task. But his eyes were still wet, and now there was dirt in them from the ground at the edge of the grave. He held Jarosa in his arms, but he started slipping. Stevens tried to regain control, but the body kept sliding over the edge and into the pit below. A whiff of foul air blew by him.

He coughed as loose dirt blinded his eyes. Stevens couldn't see or breathe. He pushed backward again, but this time, the body slid free. As he fumbled for Jarosa, Stevens fell with him into the grave.

Stevens landed on a mass of corpses which broke his fall. Jarosa lay half underneath him and half on top, pinning Stevens down within a tangle of arms and legs. Death surrounded him. Stevens groaned in pain, the sound vanishing into the dirt walls. His eyes popped open. A face frozen into a broken scream met his gaze. Stevens shot up, but the dead weight on top of him pinned him down. Corpses seemed to contort, twisting in on themselves, to stare at Stevens.

A hand rose from between the bodies.

Stevens stifled a scream, kicked at the body on him, and struggled free. Another hand rose, followed by a face—a girl's. Rebekah. She was near naked. Just below her breasts, a small knife protruded from an oozing wound. Stevens' eyes went wide at the recognition of his knife and the girl he had killed with it. She tried to pull it out, but she screamed in agony each time. Then, her face contorted in confusion. *Why?* She mouthed.

Why?

Martha Washington coalesced in front of him. He remembered her warm smile from a long time ago, when he worked at the estate. Her smile turned downward into a disappointed scowl. Stevens turned away, but when he did, the next thing he saw was—

"Hey friend, it's been a long time. We got to get that backgammon board out—"

Collins looked down. A maroon spot stained his shirt. It grew. "What's happening? What's going on? Why do I hurt?" His smile faded, replaced by a terrible sadness. Collins reached over, arms outstretched as if searching for help. Stevens reached out to grab his hand. Suddenly, Collins stopped and stood up. He screamed, "I see the way you look at her!"

Then, Jarosa rose. He did not stare. He did not even look at Stevens. He opened his Bible and began reading, "and the dead shall rise." Jarosa flipped through the book.

Collins pleaded once more. "I've been shot. I've been killed. Where were you?" A tear rolled down his face. "Take care of my little girl for me."

And the slave girl asked, "You didn't even know me. Why would you do this?"

Then, Martha raised a rifle and pointed it right at Stevens' heart.

Jarosa turned sharply, his voice rising, "Woe be unto those who will not take up my cause, for they will not be seated at the right hand—"

"Take my hand," Burr said. "Open your damned eyes and take my hand!"

Stevens opened his eyes. Tears and dirt no longer stung at them. He could see clearly. There was nothing around. Nothing around except for a pile of corpses. Jarosa's body lay face down, away from him. Stevens looked up and saw Burr on his knees with his left hand outstretched.

Shakily, Stevens made his way toward Burr. He kicked his foot into the dirt, making a foothold, then held on to the wall and sprang upward. Burr grabbed him and pulled him up. A moment later, Stevens was out. He was covered in dirt and the refuse of the corpses. He stank as bad as the pit and wondered if he'd ever be able to get clean again.

Burr patted him on the back, and a cloud of dirt flew off. "Your eyes were closed the whole time, and yet you were screaming. What happened in there?"

Stevens dusted himself off. Chills raced over his skin. He stood still, silent in the sun. He realized the deed was done. There would be no more bodies to fill the grave today. He forced a look back into the pit. It was quiet, and he found himself oddly at peace. Stevens looked back at Burr. "I've got to go. I feel sick." Stevens felt fine. He needed to get away.

"All right, if you must. You look pale. Probably been in the sun too long. Happened to you before in Monmouth, didn't it?"

Stevens stared past the man.

"Well, you've shown your devotion. It's all I've wanted from you. I forgive you for shooting my shoulder. You probably saved my life," Burr said softly. "But do tell, what did you see down there?"

Stevens looked at Burr as he walked over and reached down to retrieve Jarosa's Bible and two small stones. Then, he answered, "I saw what I needed to do."

Manhattan, New York City
One month later

Private Frederick Bakker's mother was dead. She had been dead for many months now, he realized, but the letter had just reached him last week. The news came from his father, still incarcerated with time added to it for running cons in jail as well. Someone had transcribed his father's words and written him. They told him that his mother was killed, butchered by a highway robber over a clutch of eggs. It proved evil could sort its way through war and find itself among people of peace as well. The world, Bakker discovered, was a terrible place.

Bakker was surprised to find he took the news in stride. He thought he should've been sadder, but he found himself detached instead, as if the news hadn't happened. He felt as if, when the war was over and he returned home, his mother would still be there, waiting for him.

Bakker's request to return home was denied. He'd have to wait out the war like everyone else. But he knew, even if he left this instant, life in his old village would've moved on without him. His mother would still be dead, dug deep in the dirt, and there would be nothing for him to do about any of it. So, he threw himself into his duties, surprising even Maximillian in his diligence.

The wilderness and the city in New York wasn't much different than anywhere else he had seen, but it amazed him just how big and fertile the New World was. It both inspired and terrified him. The land was plentiful and diverse, but in a place this big, how could they ever win the war? How could they ever win and return home? Every time the Yankees were defeated, they melted away with the rocks, rivers, and trees.

Bakker thought about that lifestyle himself. It seemed so easy to disappear. The soil was fertile, that much Bakker knew already. And though the winters were frigid and the summers boiled, Bakker wondered what it would be like to live by a roaring fireplace or retreat to a cool cellar on a farm with such rich ground, away from everyone else.

Just then, as if God himself were striking Bakker down for such thoughts, an arrow slammed into the brick wall in front of him. The shaft splintered and pieces rained down into the hot, cracked clay streets. A moment later, another arrow met the same fate as it burst to pieces against the same wall, mortar chipping away.

He dove to the ground, scraping against the wall on his right, and covered his head and neck with his arms. Everyone else in his unit, Maximillian and Anderson included, did the same. The illusion of safety melted away.

"The Yanks?" a newer enlistee asked, panic in his stretched voice.

"Get down!" Bakker said in Prussian. He crawled over to a newer private and found the fool still standing there, because that's what new soldiers did. Bakker had learned better. He lifted himself up just enough to grab a waistcoat and pulled the private down.

"Everybody inside." Maximillian motioned to a shop across the street. He sprinted across and opened the door. "Quick, or you'll lose your dick."

Bakker wanted to know where the attack came from. He knew the Yankees were fond of sending out raiding parties. *But here?* They wouldn't be so dumb as to raid an island with the whole of the British Army on it. *What is going on?* But the answers could be found later. He'd be safe inside... from arrows? These weren't Colonials. The realization struck him as several more arrows shot across the street. He looked up at the rooftops and saw the silhouettes of several men. He yelled to his unit, "Savages!"

Stories about what the Indians here would do to you, stories of hoots and ominous hollers and bird calls filled the air around campfires at night. It was all you heard before they hacked you to pieces with a tomahawk. They scalped you alive, the stories said, then hung your scalp on a tree as a trophy. You could see it hanging there before you died.

It had horrified him on the ship over here. The stories grew more gruesome with each retelling every night that passed on board. However, savages proved to be less of a problem than he had expected them to be. Come to think of it, this was the first time he'd had any experience with them at all.

Well, they are here now. Bakker shook his head to clear it. "Get inside," he yelled at the private. *It couldn't be Indians.* The stories he'd heard after he arrived were closer to the truth. The natives were just like everyone else—most lived peacefully; some did not.

Bakker dove through the door as several more arrows rained down.

The private wasn't so fortunate. An arrow struck him in the gut. He shot back and let out a scream of pain. Bakker covered his ears, then crossed himself—he had no one but himself to blame. He should've made sure the private made it into the store safely. Now... he was sure the boy was dead.

But the private didn't collapse. There was no blood, just the anguish of pain and shock. It was the only noise in the street. The hail of arrows stopped as suddenly as it began. Curious, Bakker stepped out from the doorway, taking a slow step, then crept toward the man. Bakker almost snickered.

"Stop your yelling. It's hurting my ears."

"But it stings!"

"And if it did anything more than sting, you wouldn't be hollerin' right now. Just sit down, and it'll be all right."

The private looked at him with his neck pitched sideways. Confusion rolled over his face. Bakker bent over and picked up the arrow. It was blunted, nearly harmless. Maximillian stepped out a moment later and gave a laugh. "Leaflets."

Now it was Bakker's turn to share in the confusion. He looked at the arrow again. This time, he saw several pieces of brown paper wrapped around the shaft. He looked around. The same papers were wrapped around each arrow lying on the ground. Bakker scanned the rooftops for signs of the savages, but they were already gone. He sighed. He looked at the arrow in his hands. He tore off the paper and read it. The fact that it was in Prussian surprised him. He read the paper again, and his eyes opened wide.

"It's the Yankees' way of keeping you from your duties." Maximillian ripped the paper out of his hand and shredded it. "Ignore it." The sergeant looked around at the men and gathered them up. "Come on, get your things. General Washington is moving us out tomorrow at first light."

That was news to Bakker. His shoulders dropped. He recalled the leaflet. It may have been destroyed, but the words were already in his head. To do as the scrip of paper requested meant leaving his homeland behind. It meant he would never see it again. Ever since stepping onto these shores, he had done nothing but dream of going back. Now that his mother had passed, and the shadow of his father's sins hung over him like a storm cloud, Bakker had to ask himself, *Do I really want to?*

Bakker made sure no one else was looking, then picked up another leaflet.

THIRTY-ONE

Tappan, New York, '76 House
August 1st, 1778.

CAPTAIN John Andre's cell was empty. It had sat empty for the last few weeks, and rumor had it that Andre was now a major. General Benedict Arnold shrugged. The man who killed Corporal Collins and threatened to steal Peggy's heart was free, but it was necessary.

The longer Arnold was commander, the more he found himself fighting the war with paper bullets instead of bayonets. He shrugged at that, too. In a war of attrition, the longer the British stayed holed in New York, the more successful he would be in his diplomatic pursuits. But, that did not satisfy the battlefield commander inside him.

True, there were minor skirmishes where the British veered too far from sanctuary. They fell all too easily to Arnold's army. However, in a major battle, Arnold was sad to say, the British still held the advantage. The siphoning of troops to The Bahamas had already begun. England had to think globally. From their point of view, this whole war was a small skirmish. If the British hadn't thought poorly of her Colonial cousins in the beginning—if they had sent more than what amounted to an enhanced expeditionary force... *I'd be swinging from a rope.*

Of course, if Britain had sent a larger force to America and left her white cliffs unprotected, France might have landed its fleet in England. That would have been an interesting turn of events. There lay the rub: France. They were salt in the wound. No matter how the cards were dealt, France remained the wildcard among kings.

Therefore, Arnold saw his job as twofold: encourage England to continue thinning out her troops and keep France from landing theirs. He would never allow Comte d'Estaing, the French Naval Commander, to land forces in America. Arnold would not transfer power from a British king to a French one. If Congress were so keen, so blind to that idea, then Arnold would indeed give them one.

"General," Eleazer Oswald said, "we have reports of naval vessels leaving the docks at Long Island. We think—"

Another aide entered the tavern. Arnold raised a brow. Oswald stopped and went over to speak with him. He returned, saying, "The diplomats you sent for have arrived."

Arnold's spine stiffened. He stood straight and said nothing at all for a moment. Finally, he said, "Good. Send everybody out, yourself included, and post guards at the front." He paused again at Oswald's head, cocked in confusion. "I want to ensure their safety—set the British gentlemen at ease." It wasn't so much an explanation as it was plausible deniability. Oswald nodded with understanding, then left.

He returned a moment later with two men.

"You will have to excuse us for being late. We had to correct our error in assuming you would be in camp, instead of the tavern." Frederick Howard, Fifth Earl of Carlisle, slid through the partially open door, his thin frame and grey, silk attire making it through easily. He flowed into the room. "You can imagine our unease as we were led here, especially after hearing about the loyal subjects of the Crown you had hung outside Philadelphia." He drew a wooden chair out but remained standing. A moment later, his partner arrived.

"There were some Tories hung, yes, convicted of crimes," Arnold said without missing a beat. "But the men punished were leaders of a mutiny and had to be dealt with, you understand. I assure you, it was a sad but necessary measure. I didn't want to do it." He eyed the earl carefully as the other diplomat reached the table. "You are perfectly safe and welcome here."

"Safe, what?" George Johnstone looked around the tavern as if lost. "Whew, stuffy in here, in'it. What'd I miss?" It was odd to see the man wearing a buff and blue uniform, but those were the colors of the British Navy. The older man, partially bald with long, grey hair worn in the manner of Benjamin Franklin, jumped over to shake Arnold's hands.

"We are perfectly safe," Arnold said, returning the gesture.

"Why wouldn't we be?" he asked.

"If you gentlemen would just take a seat. I realize your time is precious." Arnold motioned to the chairs and raised a brow at the quizzical character.

"Ah," Johnstone returned, finding a chair and pulling it out. It scraped against the floor.

The earl, however, remained standing. "We have been through all of this before with Mister Adams and your Congress. I do not see the point in talking with you. It is highly unusual."

"Don't be daft, Frederick. This man handled Captain Andre's release. We owe him a debt of gratitude." Johnstone turned to Arnold. "You'll have the ears of everyone you wish to speak to, no doubt. Andre is a close friend of Clinton's, as is William Eden, the man we report to. We all thank you for Andre's safe return." He leaned forward in the chair slightly. "But my friend here is right—we are here because of your gesture of goodwill. Congress has already turned down our offers of peace. We must report back to London that our mission has failed."

"Your mission was doomed even before you got on the boat," Arnold said. "Your Parliament didn't inform you of General Clinton's orders to retreat from Philadelphia. How were you ever supposed to broker peace when your army is in—"

"Lord North ordered Clinton to reposition," the earl said in a soft yet stern voice. He sat down, followed by Arnold. "But yes, sadly, it came as a surprise, though it's irrelevant. Our terms are more than fair. Self-rule, elected representation, all of that. British in name only. However, your provisional government will never accept terms of peace when the French are so eager to step in. If that happens, this war explodes globally, America is caught in the middle, and Britain is stretched even further. We wanted to avoid all that, you see."

"You do not want to involve the French," Johnstone said. "It is more than just allying with a former enemy—it is trading your dependence on us with the same dependence on them. You will be right back where you started." Johnstone shrugged. "I hardly see the point."

"And that is why I asked you here. We share the same motivation." Arnold turned, pointing to both. "Have either of you spoken with anyone outside of Congress?"

"We were bidden to speak with a General Joseph Reed, I believe," Johnstone said, "but that was before your predecessor lost so decisively at Monmouth."

"You have no authority to negotiate with us," the earl said. "Your Congress legislates. You enforce." This was true, Arnold thought. Adams had given him much leeway, but it went only so far.

Johnstone nodded in agreement. "Sorry about that."

"We must be going." They rose as if to exit.

"Guards!" Two large grenadiers came into the tavern. They stood there like stone golems. Arnold hadn't come this far to let them walk away without listening to his proposal. "I can be quite persuasive when the mood strikes."

"You said we were safe!" The earl turned to Johnstone. "It was idiotic to come—"

"Indeed, you are perfectly safe," Arnold said, his voice quieting. "I just needed your attention."

"Well, sir, you have it. I hope you know you have spent your goodwill," the earl said.

"I'll earn it back, in spades." Arnold dismissed the grenadiers. He turned his attention back to the diplomats. "Now, which one of you two dislikes the French more?"

"What do you mean?" Johnstone asked. "I have never had a particular interest in the French." That was an understatement, Arnold knew. Johnstone had challenged Lafayette to a duel, but the Frenchman had politely declined.

"You say your goal is to keep Britain out of war with the French." Arnold explained. "Settling our affairs here could either stop the conflict with them in the Caribbean before it escalates—" Arnold paused for effect— "or it will allow England to focus entirely on the French instead of splitting the Crown's attention between them and your cousin countrymen."

"Cousins," Johnstone said, nodding. "We should have said that to Adams, eh?"

"Never mind that now. This fellow is a lunatic," the earl suggested. "Or a scoundrel, perhaps."

Arnold responded in a clear, slow voice, so that there was no mistaking him. "Yes... I am." He ordered drinks and a cheese platter for the table and spent the next hour outlining his plan.

A long silence dominated the tent after the hour of nonstop discussion. Finally, even that silence was broken. "Interesting." The Earl of Carlisle rubbed at his smooth, lavender-scented chin. "You had me going for a bit there, but now I see the method in your madness. Your idea is quite clever, and I foresee few obstacles. Your traitor, Charles Lee, was from Virginia, as is Washington, so you may not have as much resistance to your idea as one might think." He looked around the room, as if gathering his thoughts. His eyes did not focus on anything in particular. "I was wrong about you, General."

"Have you been listening to this?" Johnstone raged. "He strong-armed us, do you not recall? It just happened." Johnston's attitude somehow shifted in tandem with Carlisle's.

"Pish, we were being a bit hasty, yes? Now that we've listened to the man, it makes perfect sense, doesn't it?"

"Impossible," Johnstone said. "This goes beyond our allowances."

"Way beyond," the Earl of Carlisle agreed, "but, do you not see? That is the interesting part. Everyone walks away with something. So long as we can get the French to agree to these terms, everyone else will have no choice but to follow along. That is the end game. There's much work to be done before we get that far."

Johnstone pleaded with Arnold, "But how will you fulfill your end? You are not—"

"By the same way I got your attention." Arnold spread his fingers on the table. "If I must."

"Then what you are talking about is treason."

"I'd say that is redundant, as our whole war is treasonous," Arnold said, drumming his fingers on the table. Then, he stopped and pointed with the same fingers. "No, what I'm trying to do is save what I can of my country. I do this because I am a true patriot. This, my friends, is necessary," Arnold argued, as if trying to convince the Commission and not himself. "The real challenge is to persuade General Clinton and Mister Eden to take my proposal seriously."

"In exchange for Andre's life, you will have their attention. We will give them your words, but I cannot speak to their response," the earl said. He stood. "I think we have everything. With any luck, we can get you and General Clinton to the negotiation table and agree to terms. We can bring your proposal to Parliament by the end of next month."

"Parliament, eh? Not your King?" Now it was Arnold's turn to be skeptical. Arnold knew this was the first step, but they were right; he could bypass Congress by entreating directly with the British commander, but progress might stop once it reached the British bureaucrats. *Why not speak directly to King George?*

"Contrary to your propaganda, the king is not malevolent, nor is he tyrannical. He works with Parliament, unlike what you are planning." Johnstone remained seated as he continued to berate Arnold. "The king does what is best for his people, and—you will excuse me for all this—the fate of the American Colonies is a trivial matter at best. I would worry less about our end and concern yourself with what it is you are about to do. Can you go through with it? Will the people here follow?"

"Are you sure you can hold up your end?" the earl added to Johnstone's concerns. They both eyed him skeptically.

"Generals are gods," Arnold assured them. He stood. Now that the cards were out on the table, his nerves had settled. "From Caesar to Charlemagne, the people in the streets have always followed their Generals."

Johnstone continued, "I am not convinced. It relies too heavily on French involvement. Even if they agree, it still puts Britain in an uncomfortable relationship with her Colonies."

"It will work." The comment came from the Earl of Carlisle, which surprised Arnold.

Arnold smiled pleasantly. "Then we all have work to do. Come, I'll see you both out."

"No surprises?" Johnstone asked, standing.

"No surprises." Arnold had plenty of surprises left, but none for these two.

"Well, then, jolly pleasant to meet with you." Johnstone returned to his chipper self as if nothing had happened. "It is good to see someone with sense enough not to side with the French, even if you are a bit of a wonky cannon."

The earl concluded, "With any luck, we will see you again at year's end."

"I'm certain of it." Arnold took a moment to map it all out in his mind. The timeline came out as most agreeable. Hopefully, this would all come to an end soon.

"You just worry about what you are going to say once you get Clinton to the peace table," the earl said as they walked out the door.

Arnold stood alone in the tavern. It had gone as well as he'd hoped. In his mind, Arnold knew he was doing the right thing. It was the only way to salvage any amount of true independence.

But now, the desire to return to the field burned hot within him. He wasn't made for such backdoor dealings—he was made to fight, and America needed that right now. If he could just bloody the British one last time, it would make up for Monmouth. It would give Arnold the leverage he needed with Clinton at the negotiation table. *I just need one good victory against the British to hammer in the final nail of my plan.*

The problem was, the British boarded themselves up in Long Island, the one place even Arnold knew he couldn't take down without both a massive army and navy behind him. He was stuck waiting for the British to come out.

His mind clicked with something his aide had discussed with him earlier that morning. "Oswald," Arnold called. A moment later, he appeared. "What about the Navy movement reported out of Long Island?"

His aide-de-camp filled him in.

After Oswald finished, Arnold nodded with excitement. The uprising in Rhode Island interested him. If the British wanted to maintain the Colonies, they had to keep them safe, which meant quelling unrest from any source. They had no choice but to come out of hiding and respond. *How amusing.*

"Oh, and that's not the best part, sir."

"Yes?"

"Washington may be aboard."

"How convenient indeed..." Arnold thought for a long moment. "We'll have to travel lightly, forage for ourselves, and take just light infantry, but if we leave now, we can catch them before they conclude their business." Arnold stopped and wrote a few notes. "Make sure we have snipers with us. Morgan's men are a must. Make sure what's his—Stevens is transferred back to his unit. He's a damned good shot. Nicked Burr when Burr mangled the—never mind. Do you have that?"

Oswald had selective hearing. The best aides did. "Yes, sir. Who do you want to lead this? Morgan or Greene?"

"Me, of course."

"Sir?"

"Don't look at me that way."

"We're still building up our forces. Pardon me for overstepping, but is it wise to split them once more? That was one of General Gates' mistakes."

Arnold thought for a moment. Oswald might be right, but it didn't matter. This was his opportunity to hurt the British, and he meant to take it. "I'm not making his mistake. I know what I'm doing. Nevertheless, bring in Burr. I have an idea for reinforcements, should we need them."

All the pieces were moving into their final places. He'd have Burr, he'd have Morgan and his snipers, and he'd have Greene. He'd beat the British and discuss his plans with Clinton and the Carlisle Commission.

The capture or death of General Washington, patriotic puppet of the British Government, however, would make the perfect leverage.

THIRTY-TWO

Newport Docks, Rhode Island
August 28th, 1778.

GENERAL George Washington was once a Virginian. The times he spent prattling around Sally Fairfax as a youth now seemed so distant. He'd long since realized he'd never be accepted as a British soldier, even if he wore the trappings of one. But he was so far down the path he'd started over twenty-five years ago, he had no choice now but to continue. He would do his duty and serve his country to the best of his abilities, as they required of him. That would help him avenge Martha.

The ocean breeze of the Newport Docks kept the heat at bay as Washington walked in solitude, deep in thought. This city was an older one by New World standards. Its streets were made of dirt, muddy at the edges by refuse. Homes and businesses stacked against each other along narrow streets. Everywhere he went, wood warped and cracked from salt and sun.

He could see Goat Island before him through the slips of the sails of the British frigates and transports. The furthest tip of Long Island, and the safety of the British Army, lay a hundred miles away by sea. It was a trivial distance by ship, but by foot, it would take days to reach sanctuary. A gust of wind blew the smell of seaweed across the bay. Washington wrinkled his nose, preferring the smells of his farm and the rushing Potomac to the sea.

His duties finished, Washington headed away from the wharf and back to St. Thames Street, still deep in thought. At the end of his journey, he found little meaning in it. He'd just be a footnote, a general on a long list of forgotten generals, as if nothing he had done had even mattered. *Perhaps I would have been more useful to the Americans, if that would have kept my wife alive, but my duty is to this uniform.* If everything went as planned, then the war would finally end. *What then?*

He would just have to wait and see.

Right now, he looked up and examined the city. General Washington, along with his large detachment of Hessians, were quartered within the homes of the harbor. During the day, they paraded down streets and drilled in the open. Major John Graves Simcoe and his Queen's Rangers had taken to the trees, far from the city. They all awaited the arrival of General Benedict Arnold with bated breath.

Washington hoped he would come. And when he did, Washington would destroy him.

Miantonomi's Hill, Newport

"Do you think he knows we are here?" asked General Morgan, dressed in white.

"They will soon enough." Arnold sat astride his black horse, Henry—named after the fallen corporal—perched high upon a hill along a crest overlooking Newport and its docks to the east. To the north, back the way they came, hills of green rolled for miles past the city of Portsmouth and Turkey Hill. Arnold would've preferred to face the British among the knolls and gullies of the smaller city, but Washington and his forces were here on the docks and city below.

Ocean surrounded them as the peninsula jutted out and kicked around like a boot. Baby-blue skies and salty sea winds made Arnold smile in reminiscence. He missed the ocean and felt more at home near it.

Morgan asked, "When do you wish to engage?"

Arnold took his time answering. His horse bent his head down and grabbed a mouthful of grass. "Hmm... tomorrow sometime."

"Sir?" Morgan jerked his head and stiffened his spine. "Once they discover we're here, they'll slip away on their boats back to Long Island. Unless we do something about their ships, we'll never catch them."

"I'm aware. But tonight, I want to watch the fireworks." Arnold's old sloop, *Fortune*, was due to arrive this evening, dispatched from New Haven. That is, if its captain had sneaked or sped by the British blockade. Arnold would find out soon enough.

A few moments later, Morgan conceded a grin. "I know what you're up to." He swallowed a laugh. "I'll take another gander at the ground, I suppose, but I'll be back in time to join you tonight. Should be a spectacular show, though I'm afraid it's the wrong night for fireworks. It's too late for the Fourth of July and too early for the Fifth of November." He roared again, "As Americans, we're likely to side with Guy Fawkes."

"I don't think we'll remember November anymore."

"Huh," Morgan said in thoughtful repose. "Unless we fail. Then they'll probably set us on fire, right alongside Guy. The British aren't too fond of traitors, you know."

"No one is," Arnold said, "but, if you fail to stand up for what you believe, you betray yourself." He turned to face Morgan. "Still, there are others who betray because they've simply had enough. For them, it's payback. Justice even. Like you, Morgan... and those are the ones who are truly dangerous."

Morgan nodded a response.

It feels good to be working with the old bear again. Towering cumulus clouds blew in from the shoreline to the grassy ravine where Arnold hid his camp, threatening a storm this evening. Arnold turned his eyes skyward, then said, "Tonight is a great night for fireworks, even with the rain."

The black deluge fell heavy and cold. In the darkness, General Washington made out the foggiest outline of a small sloop in the water. If it hadn't been brought to his attention by others with fresher eyes, Washington would not have seen it. The craft moved closer, sneaking out from behind Goat Island.

"Rebels?"

"I can't make out any movement above decks. There are no lights," warned the night watchman who'd roused Washington out of bed.

This cannot be good. He thought for a moment, rubbing the sleep out of his eyes, dreaming of what deception it might be. Suddenly, he knew, and his eyes shot open and the fogginess in his head dissipated. "Get all the injured off our ships and clear the dock. And for God's sake, unload the powder stores." Then he added, "Get word to the captains: Do not engage the approaching vessel."

The young watchman ran off, up the nearest gangplank, asked permission to board, then disappeared. A few moments later, he returned, and Washington thought that odd. The gangplank ripped away from the pier as the watchman reached the dock, followed by a frenzy of movement onboard. Sails unfurled and anchors hoisted from the water on thick chains. Six cast-iron cannons poked out of portholes. Washington's eyebrows squeezed together, his chin thrust out.

"I am sorry, sir," the watchman said with sorrowful green eyes. "The ship's captain said he does not take orders from—"

"You did your duty." Washington saved the young man the embarrassment of finishing the thought. Washington did not take offense, though fury slid through him. British naval officers were stubborn. "An act of Providence itself could not have shaken their steadfast adherence to stupidity. Come, let us remove ourselves and warn the others." It was too late, Washington realized. Instead, they hurried off the wharf as the ship lurched, catching the storm's wind.

A moment later, cannons roared. It sounded like the fury of an angry god thundering his rage at the earth. The night watchman jerked his hands up to cover his ears. Washington stood still on a rise, watching the scene unfold just as he feared it would. Smoke and fire erupted from each cannon as the ship shook in response.

Washington could no longer see the approaching ship, but he heard the crash of eight-pound cannon balls when they met their mark. The dying sounds of the cannonade met the cracking and shattering of wood. Then, as if a match had been lit, the sneaking ship burst into a white-hot sun.

It was a fire-ship, you damned fool.

Washington didn't know if the British captain had ordered the use of incendiary shot or if the fire-ship had been rigged to blow at just that moment, but the effect was the same. Wooden splinters aflame rained down on the docks. They tore through the sails of the ships and set them on fire, but that was not the worst of it. After the initial blast, everything went dark except for the burning hull of the phantom vessel, still sailing more or less on course, headed straight for the pier and the other ships. Once again, cannons roared. Washington clenched his jaw. The ship captain was as stupid as he was stubborn.

The cannon fire, of course, had no effect. Instead, the fiery ship rammed into the stern, crashing into the other ships in port. Washington watched the craft collide with the full realization that he could do nothing but witness the wreck. One by one, the ships lit up as each store of black powder went up in flames. Their means of escape by sea was now an impossibility.

Arnold.

This was his work. The rebel commander was here. General George Washington smiled. Arnold had wounded them, for sure, but the rebel general didn't know that Washington never had any intention of leaving.

Arnold had taken the bait.

Washington threw off his coat and sword, ran down to what remained of the docks, and dove into the black, whipping water. Tomorrow, he would worry about Arnold. Right now, there were wounded sailors in the debris. He surfaced, shivering in the frigid Atlantic waters, and swam toward the closest injured man he found floating among the wreckage.

General Arnold should've been unhappy. His personal fortunes were depleted, and his sloop, *Fortune*, had gone up in flames last night. The likelihood of victory against the superior British forces over the coming years was not likely, particularly without French military intervention or a diplomatic solution. The chance that he would hang was much higher.

Despite that, General Arnold grinned at the morning sky with a feeling of triumph. The familiar ocean breeze of the warm August air filled him with a youthful confidence. His horse shuffled eagerly as Arnold once again surveyed the small town of Newport from his perch. The French fleet, under Comte d'Estaing, floated there in place of the smaller British flotilla Arnold had damaged last night, trapping them in the harbor. *The French could be useful without ever having to step foot on our land.*

The contingent of Hessian and British forces under Washington hadn't budged, staying right where he wanted them, unable to escape and too outmatched to fight. All that remained was to wait until Washington sent out a white flag. Of course, Arnold despised waiting, so he'd already sent Oswald into the city to formally ask for their surrender.

And here, Arnold waited.

Finally, Oswald returned, and Arnold's smile disappeared.

"You weren't gone long enough to have received any formal letters of surrender."

"No, sir."

The wind blew a salty breeze as Arnold's patience dwindled. He found himself taking it out on his friend and aide. "No... what? No, you weren't gone long enough, or no, they didn't surrender? Do they just need more time? What is it? Speak up and be quick about it, Oswald."

General Daniel Morgan moved his white horse between Arnold and his aide in a silent but overt gesture of warding Arnold's anger off the poor aide. He settled in his saddle and took a deep breath. Oswald looked uncomfortably from one general to the other.

"Well?" Arnold asked.

Oswald said, "They've decided not to surrender at this juncture."

"What?" Arnold's anger returned. His knuckles turned white-hot on the reigns. "Does Washington not know how daft a decision that is? Does he not realize he is surrounded? Did I not put on enough of a fireworks show for him?"

Oswald's mouth moved, but no words came out.

Arnold scowled. "What is it? Out with it."

"They said, 'Thank you for the show.'"

Arnold gasped. He was so close to his goal—the new nation almost within his grasp. Terms of surrender, he expected. *Or resistance. Something.* But, to be ignored...

"Perhaps we should invite Washington to meet with us personally," Morgan said.

Always clear-headed, that one. Morgan could be pretty annoying, but he wasn't now. Arnold took another second to gather his wits. Then he said, "Yes. Oswald, go back and set it up. I'll meet with him myself."

Morgan spoke up in that big bear voice of his. "Perhaps that's not the most reasonable course—"

Sound advice. Arnold interrupted him anyway. "Remember our plan. If I must sacrifice my safety for the safety of our coun—"

"Understood, sir." Morgan turned away to address the aide. "Arnold will meet with Washington at a neutral location outside the city. You'll direct him there." He pointed to a ridge about a mile from where they stood, about a mile away from Newport. A grove of trees stood, placed there by divine providence no doubt, for Arnold's purposes. *Morgan knows what I have planned for the British General.*

"What if General Washington doesn't wish to come?" Oswald asked, wiping sweat out of his eyes with a damp, white cloth. He intended the question for Morgan, who had not bitten his head off. Arnold answered anyway.

"Be persuasive," Arnold said. "The fate of our freedom may depend on it." Oswald, did not know the full details of his plan, nor would he have been so quick to help had he known.

"Yes, Generals." Oswald rode back down the ridge and returned to the city.

Arnold addressed Morgan. "Are you ready?"

The bear let out a loud snort. "Now that we're getting down to it, I find I have my reservations. It's not sporting, capturing a general under flag. It's against all conventions. But I'll do it. I'll follow you. Though, where you have us going, we might end up much hotter than an August afternoon, if you get my meaning."

"Just make sure Sergeant Stevens is there on point. If Washington tries to flee, one good shot in the leg will stop him." Arnold looked to Morgan, assuaging the older man's concerns. "When this is all said and done, they'll build a monument to you. You know that, right? You can show it to St Peter."

Morgan smiled. "I'm not interested in shrines." He jerked a thumb at his scarred back. "I seek requite."

Arnold nodded and ran a hand out over his white-and-blue uniform. He patted the usual spot where his firelock pistol rested, the same one he'd carried for a lifetime now. His sword, ready in its scabbard. He knew he looked every bit a leader and it struck him as a perfect painting to commission. *Me astride Henry, heroes of the war.*

He turned to Burr on his way down the path and said, "We'll do more than leave our mark on them. Once I'm down there, you and Greene get everyone into position." Arnold kicked his horse, but it didn't need much prompting. As his steed started off, Arnold turned and said, "It's going to be a messy morning."

Arnold once again found himself waiting along a thin swathe of grass off Broad Street, closer to the city. Though his earlier anger had subsided, in its place grew a restless irritability. Everything depended on today running somewhat smoothly. It didn't have to follow a precise plan. As a strategist, Arnold saw the folly in that. It just had to go *mostly* right. Standing here alone in a ditch a hundred yards from the nearest tree, was not how Arnold saw *mostly* right working out.

He'd heard word from Lt. Arntz of Morgan's rifleman that Sergeant Stevens' name came up missing on the rolls of the last few days. He did not make the crossing with them into Newport. Arnold cursed the news. He was relying on the sharpshooter to aid him. *Where the bloody hell had he gone? Was he sick?* Arnold could do nothing about it now. The treeline held marksmen, true, but none so good as Stevens.

After some time had passed, Oswald returned up the hill along the road, near the grove of trees, followed by a figure Arnold didn't recognize. He wore a military uniform, but it looked Hessian.

"This was who they sent out to parlay, sir," Oswald rushed to get out of the way.

The Hessian introduced himself. "Colonel Von Donop, at your service."

"You are not Washington." Arnold eyed the grove nervously. This was not their target, and he didn't want any itchy trigger finger giving the game away. Now, more than ever, he needed Sergeant Stevens.

"Washington? *Nein, nein, mein freund.*" Donop let out a laugh. In poor English he called out with a boisterous burst, "Call me Colonel Carl Von Donop."

"I don't want to call you anything but a waste of my time," Arnold said angrily. "Where is Washington?"

Donop paused, as if searching for the right word. "Are you, uh, surrendering?"

Arnold hung his head. His blood boiled under the noonday sun. *Damn it all to hell.*

"Oswald, what is the meaning of this? Do they not realize how horrible an insult this is?"

"I do rather think that is the point, sir," Oswald returned.

A moment later, another Hessian ran up on foot, out of breath. Sweat beaded and rolled off his black hair from underneath his trifold hat. This one, Arnold noticed, wasn't even an officer, nor even a grenadier; otherwise he'd be wearing one of those ridiculous looking brass mitre caps.

"My apologies, sir, I couldn't keep up with the count."

"And you are?"

"Frederick Maximillian, First Sergeant. I am your translator, in case any confusion arises."

"Really?"

"At your service, sir."

Oswald lowered his head and covered his eyes.

"This disrespect will not stand." Arnold reared back on the horse. "Forget the British, and damn the Hessians. I'm not even talking to an officer." He turned to them both. "I shall have your souls for this, the lot of you. Damn you." War was a dirty business, but there was supposed to be some honor in it, he thought, ignoring his own hypocrisy.

He'd shown grace to Burgoyne during the British surrender. He dined with the Baroness Von Riedesel at Freeman's Farm. He'd even shown respect for his peers as they were promoted ahead of him. In fact, he'd been respectful all his life. Even during his youth, he'd intended to show respect to Captain Croskie when Arnold ignored tradition at the port in Honduras. That had led to a duel—

A duel. That's it!

Arnold lowered his head and let out a slow, sly grin. "Go back, the both of you. Let it be known that I, General Benedict Arnold, challenge your commander, George Washington, to a duel over a matter of honor." He let it sink in. "I will not be so disrespected. And now, he must answer it." Arnold glowered. "If he tries to deny me, remind him that I burned his home to a cinder and murdered his wife."

Oswald's head shot up as if in horror. Donop stood there, blankly, as if knowing full well what had been said but unable to hide the shock, while his unnecessary translator, Maximillian, looked on expectantly.

Oswald spoke in a calm voice. "I will accompany you both to make sure the words are not minced. I suggest we make haste and do what he says."

Maximillian translated. Donop shook his head in confusion and asked aloud in English, "Surrender?"

No, Arnold thought. He would not be surrendering.

Maximillian and Donop continued to whisper as they rode back into Newport with Oswald.

Arnold headed back to camp. He was done waiting. They could send word to him at his leisure.

Half an hour later, Oswald returned with a letter from Washington. He accepted the challenge, though Washington had changed the location.

It didn't matter. Now, he wouldn't have to set a trap for Washington. He wouldn't capture the general. He'd kill him instead, and he would do it himself.

THIRTY-THREE

Newport, Rhode Island
August 29th, 1778.

"A T last," General Benedict Arnold said, walking down the dirt road where Thames and Farewell Streets met at an angle. At this section of the city, the roads were askew, with residences and taverns stacked in every free square of grass. Benedict approached within earshot of Washington and his British companions, who milled about on the opposite angle of the cross streets. "Here we are."

Arnold, Oswald, Morgan, and Captain Horner, along with several dragoons, took shelter under the shade of King's Tavern as they waited. He snorted in derision. King's Tavern? *As if King George had ever stepped into the place.* Like everything in Newport, moldy planks clung to a rotting frame, whose blue-green paint faded from sun and salt. The sea-worn city reminded him of New Haven, his hometown.

Finally, Washington turned to face Arnold for the first time. General George Washington stood a few paces away dressed in red wool despite the August heat, and his wig showed fresh powder. Though he looked immaculate and imposing on the outside, his eyes looked sullen, and his shoulders slumped as if a heavy weight lay on them. He looked older than when Arnold had seen him dancing with Peggy.

Washington took a slow step toward Arnold and said in a deep, plain voice that sent Arnold's spine crawling, "The Dark Eagle comes to claim the wilderness, I see."

Arnold stopped. For a moment, he was caught off-guard. When he recovered, he said, "You've read up on me. Few people know me by that name, most of whom are natives to this land."

"This land is full of natives. Some, more savage than others," Washington said through gritted teeth. "But not all savages are natives and not all wear it so plainly."

"Me?" The slight grated on him, but he bounced it back. "You are a Virginian. You used to be one of us, long ago."

Washington pointed to his uniform. "I stopped being a Virginian the moment you killed my wife." He walked over to a small table placed outside for the duel. A familiar, decorative box made of dark wood—lacquered and polished—sat on the table. An aide opened it. Inside rested two dueling pistols and the accoutrements to fire them. "This land belongs to the English Crown. You and your people betrayed that."

Washington offered Arnold a pistol.

Arnold held his hands up and said, "Thank you, but no, I have my own." He handed his pistol over to Washington's second for examination. When Arnold retrieved the weapon, he spoke loud so everyone could hear, "This land is no longer the king's. The war is over. You are on American soil now."

Arnold looked back over to Morgan, who shook his head. He ignored him. "The French fleet has you penned in. I have you surrounded. I could have starved you out, but I come with a more reasonable offer. After our duel, and you are dead, I will allow your troops to surrender with honor."

"The war is near over. That much, we can agree on," Washington countered through gritted teeth. "But once the head is cut off the snake, your army will fall." Washington remained confident, his head high and back straight. "Even if you were to kill me and somehow defeat us here, the bulk of the British army remains on Long Island." The general flashed a rare smile. "You won't beat us here. You won't beat us here because I split my forces. While I've drawn you into the city, Major Simcoe and his Rangers have engaged your men to the north. I've kept them hidden until now. You have already failed."

So, the Virginian outsmarted me. The verbal bullet staggered Arnold. He almost took a step back but remained firm, as if trapped and rigid within quicksand. *Washington may have started the game off well, but his army is still surrounded, and I shall put a ball through him.* It was a shame. Washington could've been a formidable opponent.

Still, Arnold needed to respond with some sort of counter. He had only two aces left, so he played one now. "General Greene nearly beat you at Monmouth. I have no doubt that, without you overseeing Simcoe, Greene will beat your Rangers." Arnold shrugged as if it were no bother. "It is no matter. I have already made a deal that will end this war."

"Please, go on," Washington said, anger lacing his words. He loaded his pistol in practiced steps as he spoke. "But please hurry. I recall that we had a duel scheduled."

"I've made a deal that keeps the British and French Empires out of New England. The nine northern states gain their independence. You can keep your Virginia and the three southernmost Colonies. Keep your tobacco, as long as you can hold it. We will come for the south soon enough."

Now, it was Washington's turn to share that same wide-eyed state of shock, as if he'd been struck by lightning. "That's preposterous. Our governments will never—"

"France recognizes our government. They've sent ships here, as you can see for yourself. You're nearly at war with them," Arnold explained. "Your own Parliament recognizes our government. That much is clear with your peacekeeping delegation." Arnold glared down at Washington, watching his face turn white.

Washington's face turned from pale to red, silence burning in his eyes. Arnold went on, "It's all about posturing. King George and Lord North cannot recognize our independence without losing face. So, I leave them with a choice: They either walk away now with some sense of victory, or choose to fight against the French as their treasury depletes and every other country that wants a piece of the British Empire nips at their heels."

Arnold arrived at his mark, pistol in hand. "As if that weren't enough incentive to end the war, France gets a piece, too. It hurt me to do it, but I would rather give them a small piece now than all of it later." The more Arnold spoke, the more he realized he was convincing himself. *It's a concession for the greater good. With France walking away with the Ohio Valley in exchange for a bit of blockading, it all but guarantees they'll agree, which means our government will have no choice but to acquiesce to the treaty. I control the military, if they need any further persuading. It is all but over, and by my—*

"You are a damned Yank and a damned traitor to your cause," Washington barked. He'd apparently heard enough. His breath raced and his arms fell to his sides, stiff as wooden planks. "You could have been somebody to these people, a father. Instead you have betrayed them!"

Arnold cocked his head in confusion. "What do you mean? What I'm doing is for my country. I will lead them."

"You are far worse than I imagined," Washington said, his voice strained, as if the wind had left from him. He shook his head. "You are doing this for yourself. You're nothing short of a tyrant." Washington's eyes grew big, and his soul poured out through them. "I will see you deposed."

The words cut through Arnold, wounding him as if sliced by a sword. *How can I make Washington see that it was for the best? Doesn't Washington see his own sin?* He snarled at the Virginian, letting his anger flow. "Look at you with your righteousness. You are the real traitor, allied with the real tyrant! You don't even have a country. You left us, remember?" Arnold swallowed hard. "You could have led us. Together, we could have set this whole country free. Instead, it will be a piecemeal victory with years of war. Look at what you have done. Look what happened to your family. Look what your actions created!"

"My allegiance is to the King I serve, as yours should have been."

"Ha! You must know that, to King George, you and I are nothing but a pair of damned Yanks—too uncivilized for his own court. Look at you, with your red coat and ceremonial sash. You may have the trappings, but you don't have the soul. You're wild, and they know it. You've only betrayed yourself."

"Enough!" Washington bellowed. The sun bore down on him. His men had their arms up and ready. Arnold's men responded in kind. "You're the monster! You destroyed my home, murdered my wife, and come to me as if I am the villain. So be it. I will come at you with everything I have." He took a deep breath and said with a still calmness, like a lake on a clear day, "Your reign ends."

"And your death here today will seal your king's fate. Are we not here to duel?"

"Quite right."

With that, General George Washington aimed and fired.

A chunk of flesh flew off Arnold's left leg. Both legs flew back as they were picked up and tossed by the sudden force. He slammed to the ground. As he lay there, all he saw through closed eyes were white-hot flashes as pain streaked through his body, like fire through tinder.

"It was somewhat inconvenient for you to destroy our small Navy here and then pen us in," Washington said. All traces of anger were gone. "But, sadly for you, we will survive. You and your men will not. Simcoe and Donop will tear your army apart. I have you here, bleeding on the ground, and your men captive. You knew this might happen, yet your arrogance wouldn't allow you to do anything else. I thank you for your predictability."

"You bloody—" Arnold cried out in pain before he could finish. His leg burned and bled. He felt more than saw Morgan and the others come to his side. He felt a presence near his wound, then a trigger of pain as someone placed pressure on his leg, "You should have put your bullet through my heart."

Washington scoffed. "The reason I did not outright kill you is because I am an English gentleman." His voice sounded muddled to Arnold's ears. "Let it be known, that in your defeat, you are nothing but a damned Yank."

Martin Stevens underestimated the difficulties he, Emma, and Jane would endure once they chose to flee camp. It had been difficult enough to convince Emma to come, but once he explained what he had done... *most* everything he had done, Emma agreed to leave. "My husband would've wanted me to aid the war," she said the morning they slipped away, "but if what you say is true, then it's all too likely that Arnold killed Collins, even if it wasn't his finger on the trigger."

While the rest of the continentals crossed into Aquidneck Island near Newport, the three of them headed back toward Providence. They were nowhere near home with no reliable transportation but their feet. Jane fussed, teething. She had to eat often, which meant that they stopped just as often. Emma's nipples must have been painful—her shirt held blood stains from the jagged edge of Jane's jutting tooth, though Emma made little complaint. They hadn't packed many provisions, and the land was not as plentiful near harvest as they had hoped. Fields in the farms they passed lay fallow or rotted with worms. Stevens snagged a wild watermelon for the girls earlier, but that was about it. *Maybe I was wrong. Maybe we should head back to camp.*

Emma took long strides beside him. He could feel her warmth. He glowed every time their arms or shoulders bumped. Even so, Emma took no notice, and her attention remained on Jane. She carried her, as heavy as she was, and Stevens admired her strength. It wasn't just physical strength, nor stamina, but the resolve she put forth despite everything she'd endured. His own mind, he confessed, had not held up.

Jane was not so small anymore, and she'd recently learned how to wiggle free. Nobody liked to be held against their will, not even the smallest ones. Emma struggled to keep Jane in her arms, but on occasion, she would squirm out of them. Stevens shook his head. *Do all children wish to be free of their parents, if for no other reason than to feel the grass beneath their own feet?*

They made their way down the rutted road as quietly as they could. In upper New England, on the outskirts of Providence, the path ahead was overgrown, little more than trampled dirt with brittle leaves and flattened grasses that sprouted up in patches among the rocks and dirt. But it would take them home.

When they reached Maryland, everything would be—

Stevens looked at Emma.

He knew he could not stay in Maryland, not with her. Not with what he had done. Not with how he felt about her. He would see her safe, find some way of keeping her in her home, perhaps taking the odd job until Emma and Jane were secure. Then, he would leave, but to where, he did not know.

Emma stopped, drawing him from his thoughts, and whispered, an edge of alarm in her voice, "Mister Stevens, I see a couple soldiers coming around the bend. Should you hide?"

He'd done enough hiding. Besides, it would make him appear more suspicious if discovered, especially as he wore no uniform—just his familiar flax shirt and dusty breeches. He looked ahead and saw two men. They wore the buff and blue of Continental uniforms. What they were doing out here, he didn't know, though he'd heard there was a hospital nearby.

Stevens swore silently to himself. *We should've kept off the roads.* It would slow them down, but it would keep them away from unexpected company. He'd kept to the easier paths because he was with Emma, but now worried he'd made mistake. Emma could handle herself. She and Jane would have been fine in the forests. He sighed. The only choice they had now was to keep walking with purpose and their heads down. Perhaps the soldiers wouldn't get too talkative.

"Just keep moving," Stevens said. "Walk fast."

She picked up her pace and almost went past Stevens. As she moved ahead, she surprised him by saying, "If anyone asks, we're married."

He looked at her and nodded as he hid his giddiness at the thought. Then, he chastised himself. He was lousy at this stuff when it came to Emma. Maybe he should just tell her here and now how he felt—how he'd always felt—and be done with it. But of course, he could never do that. *What purpose would that serve? What good would it do?*

The two soldiers drew closer. One of them had stark-white hair and a bandaged hand. The other looked wide and tall. If bricks were blue, a wall built of them would've looked like the second man. His leg sported a bandage, but it did not appear to slow him down. Both were caught up in conversation with each other. As they passed, the pair glanced at him and then moved on. Stevens sighed in relief and turned to tell Emma that the danger had passed.

Then, Jane cooed.

The two soldiers stopped to smile at the baby. Who could resist? Jane smiled back. It was cute and adorable because that's what babies were. *Attention grabbers.*

"What's her name?" asked the soldier with the white hair. Stevens noticed now that he was missing the smaller fingers on his right hand. Red bled through the bandages wrapped around the wound.

"Jane," Emma said. "Her name is Jane." She smiled, too. All parents loved to show off their children.

"How old?" the brick wall asked. Stevens had never even been around kids, yet the rules seemed relatively universal. *What's your name? How old are you?* Children were cute, so long as they weren't yours. Everyone wanted to compare notes. The stratification process started young. *My child is better than your child.* "I got a two-year-old at home in Vermont. Your daughter's tall. Has she started crawling yet?"

The first soldier turned to talk to Stevens. "You must be the lucky father—"

The soldier soured as a hint of recognition hit him.

Stevens' blood chilled in response. He shivered as if a winter wind blew through him. He knew these two. He'd fought with them at Monmouth, before he'd transferred back to Morgan. They knew him, too. *Whitehall?*

"Hey, you didn't have a wife, not least I remember. You move fast, my friend. Congratulations." Sergeant Whitehall smiled. He went to shake hands, then remembered his wound. He withdrew it and continued smiling an increasingly ominous smile.

Jane cooed.

"Ah, how precious," both soldiers said.

Stevens swallowed nervously.

"Well, it was nice meeting with you," Emma said, speaking fast. "We must be leaving—"

"Now just where're you headed off to?" Whitehall asked. "The road isn't safe, not for a family with a small child. With the war making things scarce, there are some unscrupulous people trying to make a living, if you get my meanin'."

"You're in the war, sure enough? But all the action's over at Newport," the big soldier said. "What would you be doing out anyway? Only injured ones like us were left in Providence. I don't see any wounds on you."

"Our business is our own, and he hasn't been at war since the baby," Emma said. "You must be mistaken."

The two soldiers looked at each other. Sergeant Whitehall responded, "But I know this bloke. This is the man who shot General Frasier up north. Changed the whole outcome of the battle in a single second. General Arnold won that day on account of you. He even awarded the prize money to you. Fifty dollars, was it? Surely, you aren't out of the ranks. No one would have it."

Emma looked up in surprise, her eyes big and bright. She hadn't known where Collins had gotten the money. Now she did. Stevens ignored the look for now and said, "Gentlemen, please, I ask leave to go my way with my lovely lady and child—"

"I believe we have here a runner," the other soldier said. He detached his bayonet and held the sharp, triangular blade between his fingers and away from Emma and the baby, as if it were a message meant for Stevens.

As Emma continued to look at Stevens as if searching for answers, her surprise turned to fear. *Not like Collins*, her eyes seemed to scream. *I cannot lose you, too.* Jane started to fuss.

It was one thing for a man to think about betraying his cause and his country. It was quite another feat to act. Stevens had always been the quiet one, the follower, the one who tried to do right by doing what others wanted him to do. He'd followed his friend to war. He'd followed Arnold, and he followed it all to ruin.

Now, he could well make matters worse.

He could either accompany these soldiers, hoping to explain it all away, or he could take up arms against the people he once fought side by side with during battle. The choice was his.

THIRTY-FOUR

Newport, Rhode Island
August 29th, 1778.

GENERAL Arnold, bloody and fallen, pushed himself to fight as he lay on the ground in Newport with a lead ball lodged within his left leg. *I didn't give up when I was shot at Quebec, when they came for me, to take me prisoner. I shot my would-be captor and survived until help came. I can do it again.* He remembered his pistol and realized that he had not yet fired it...

Arnold still had one shot to change everything.

He struggled in search of it. *It must have fallen away when I hit the ground.* Every time he moved, someone, Morgan or Oswald, or maybe both, held him down. He fought against them and every time he did, white flares of pain shot through his leg, as if Neptune pinned his leg with his trident.

Morgan—he saw through tears—placed something cold and hard against Arnold's chest. Arnold mouthed as if to say, "Thanks," but no sound came out—only a low moan. Morgan nodded with understanding as Arnold lifted the pistol with a grunt of pain and aimed it at Washington.

The redcoat general froze. Arnold fired.

The shot did not hit its mark. Arnold was already firing high from his low positon on the ground, so when fired, his right arm jerked upward against the kick, leaving the ball to sail harmlessly over the target's head.

Washington sighed in relief. "You missed."

"That was just a signal, you fool." Arnold coughed out the words with no small amount of pain. At that, the doors to the King's Tavern flew open as plain-clothed soldiers poured out or crawled over the roof. There weren't more than a dozen marksmen, but they were all primed and ready.

A hail of gunfire erupted from the tavern. Washington remained still; not even an eyelid flinched. As a reward, every ball flew by him. He stood just at the edge of accurate fire, and he knew it. Dirt flew out of missed marks, creating divots all around him.

But not all the shots were as harmless. Some found their marks among Washington's companions. Splinters shot off posts nearby and showered down daggers which tore into flesh. British officers collapsed onto the street without even knowing what had happened.

Washington remained unharmed. *Dammit,* Arnold thought. *If Stevens were there, that miserable man would be dead. What the hell happened to my best shooter?* Unfortunately, the time had come to retreat, so he pushed the thought to the back of his mind and tried to stand. All the while, he glared at the general. *Washington's standing right there...*

"Confound it, Oswald, help me get him up!" It was Morgan's voice. It sounded foggy and far away, but he recognized Morgan's booming voice like a rolling thunderstorm.

As his senses and bearings returned to him, Arnold tried to stand. Then, he realized where he'd been hit. His leg. *The same damned leg as before.* This was worse, though. At least, it seemed that way. He looked down, then jerked away. He could see a hole and bits of bone. Blood ran out of the wound like a tap on a cask of thick, red wine. His stomach churned.

He lifted his arms for the two men. Somehow, they wanted Arnold to put weight on the leg, but he didn't know how he'd be able to accomplish that. As a hail of musketfire shot out on all sides, Arnold realized he didn't have much of a choice. The British responded with fire of their own, though it appeared directed on the soldiers near the tavern. He saw his own men fall.

Arnold turned angrily toward Washington, who returned the look as he knelt down to care for a wounded man. Morgan and Oswald tried to drag Arnold away, but he protested as much as he could in spite of the wound and blood loss. *We have unfinished business.*

But Morgan, with his large, hairy arms, wouldn't have it. "Come on, Benedict, it's a trap. We're surrounded. We've got to get you safe."

"No. I want another crack at Washington. Give me your pistol."

"If we stick around here, we'll all end up dead."

Washington made the final decision. As he closed the wounded man's eyes, Washington stood and came forward, then launched himself at Arnold. Washington was a large man, as large as the bear, but younger and with more strength.

Morgan stepped in front of Arnold as the Virginian dove into him. The two giants toppled over. Arnold dropped to the ground. Oswald tried to break the fall, but Arnold collapsed on his aide.

Washington recovered before Morgan. He lurched as Morgan grabbed the general by the legs. It wasn't enough to stop Washington from diving on top of Arnold. Washington threw a punch at Arnold's face. Then he threw another as he yelled, "Murderer!"

Arnold attempted to throw Washington off, but with his leg wounded, he lacked leverage. Instead, he reached for his discharged pistol and cracked Washington over the skull with it. Washington recoiled, his neck snapping back, blood trailing down from the wound, but it didn't stop him. He threw his fist down on Arnold's left leg. Arnold erupted into agony, letting loose a yell that gave Washington pause.

"I should have killed you!" Washington roared.

Several redcoats approached Washington, dodging fire as they did so. As Morgan recovered, they reached their general and attempted to drag him off. Morgan was about to address the two newcomers, but Washington shoved them away.

The standoff continued until Captain Horner dug his pistol into Washington's back. "I'd stop if I were you."

Washington did so.

Horner's dragoons had joined the riflemen at the tavern. Now, with his pistol embedded in Washington's back, he said, "The general will make a fine hostage. Gentlemen, I suggest we take those two redcoats, too, and head for the safety of the tavern. They won't shoot at us with the general inside."

It took a moment for Arnold to fully understand the captain. He hadn't recovered from the blows. His head spun, and one eye started to swell. However, what Horner said made sense. Through the pain in his leg and face, Arnold managed to speak. "Quick, into the tavern. follow the good Captain."

They all used what shots they had at their disposal to cover their retreat into the King's Tavern. The marksmen, now all on the rooftop, let loose another volley. But, so long as they had Washington, the redcoats didn't return fire.

Someone carried Arnold inside. Before the door closed, he glimpsed redcoats marching right down the street, along with Hessian blue. His whole view erupted into blue-red waves, all heading out of the city toward Arnold's boys in the field.

"It doesn't matter what happens now," Washington said. "I have your army cut off. They are trapped, just as you thought you had me trapped. I will wait here until I have word of your army's surrender." With that, Washington sunk into a chair, grabbing a mug of beer left on the table and drinking it down.

Arnold felt more faint by the second. Watching his plan collapse stole the last of his strength. Oswald tied compresses onto his leg, but Arnold knew he'd lost a lot of blood. He saw out the window that the tavern was surrounded by redcoats and Hessians. More Hessians marched up the road toward Arnold's camp.

He turned to Morgan but addressed the room. "Boys, it appears we have a problem."

Stevens also had a problem. In front of him, Sergeant Whitehall fumbled to get his knife out. He wasn't used to using his less-dominant hand. *One wounded man, I could handle.* But on the other side of Emma, a rather large and imposing soldier held the sharp end of a bayonet out as if to skewer Stevens.

If Stevens were by himself, he would've either gone back with the two, or run as fast as he could until he was safe. However, anything he did would affect Emma and Jane. Even surrendering carried risks. The girl Stevens had killed in the woods would agree with that.

"We don't take well to runaways. We got ourselves a proper army now. The only ones who break are those militia folk, and I know you ain't militia," the three-fingered Whitehall said. "So why don't you come clean? You're not a spy now, are you?"

Stevens let out an exasperated sigh. He'd come a long way since playing backgammon with Collins. He made up his mind; he knew what he had to do. "I'm not a spy," he said. He shot his elbow out and connected it with Whitehall's face before the soldier could get a proper hold of his knife. It clattered onto granite rocks on the ground. Whitehall let out a sharp cry and moved his uninjured hand out to cover his face.

The bayonet came toward him. Stevens was glad it was directed at him instead of Emma. His biggest fear was that the man made of bricks would hold Emma hostage. Then, it would be over. He relaxed as the brute's focus remained on him. *This won't be easy, but it could've been worse.*

The large man's size slowed him down, which gave Stevens an extra moment to prepare. He grabbed ahold of his own longrifle by the barrel and smashed the butt of the weapon into the brute's chest. The brick man sucked wind and stumbled backward.

Unfortunately, by now, Whitehall had recovered. He threw a punch. Stevens was in no position to block it, so the left-handed jab landed squarely into Steven's jaw. He groaned as his head jerked with the impact, lucky the sergeant hit him with his off hand.

Stevens righted himself, faced both men, and rubbed his sore jaw. He looked at Emma to make sure she was safe. She had already stepped away and held Jane in one hand, a large stick in the other, lest one of them got too close.

The large man still had his bayonet in his hand, and Whitehall looked ready to throw another punch. Stevens' knees wobbled a little. Maybe they would listen to reason instead. "I don't want to fight either of you. You guys are my brothers, but I am done with General Arnold's war."

"The general's war?" the man with the bayonet asked. "This isn't his war. This war is about our freedom. We'd follow the general anywhere."

"That's exactly the problem. You're not freeing yourselves of anything. You're betraying one master to serve—"

"I think we ought to just kill you and be done with it. Take the lady instead."

Emma stepped back in shock and clung to her daughter. Whitehall turned toward her, as if sensing weaker prey. He was wrong. Emma reacted as a mother bear with her cub endangered. She placed Jane down behind her and held the long, thick branch like a club. Whitehall ignored the threat and laughed as he took several quick steps toward her. She jabbed the man hard in the face, and the end of the stick splintered off. Then she raised it high and brought it down on his bleeding head. Whitehall collapsed.

Emma stood, triumphant.

Stevens took the advantage she had given him and let out a right hook that connected on the side of the brute's face. The punch took him off-guard. Stevens heard a small crack and felt a tooth loosen, though nothing popped out. The large man brought the bayonet down hard as Emma screamed, "Look out!"

Stevens deflected a blow that would've pierced his throat with his rifle. He knocked away the bayonet, turned the flintlock to face the correct way, and pointed it at the large man's face.

"Take off your shoes," Stevens said. The brute didn't need to know the rifle was empty.

Whitehall came to, but remained lying on the dirt, groggy and broken. They looked at Stevens as they rubbed their wounds. Blood poured from Emma's victim's nose. The other man bled from his mouth. Stevens repeated himself. "Take off your shoes."

They did, albeit reluctantly.

Stevens dug into his haversack, moving a Bible to grasp a ball of twine, which he tossed to Emma. She bound Whitehall's wrists and ankles. He looked at her through scornful eyes. There was nothing either of the soldiers could do about it while Stevens kept the longrifle pointed at them. Then, she moved toward the brute and bound him, too.

When she finished, Stevens said, "You'll stay here and await rescue. Say you were robbed, or don't. You'll never find us again." Stevens remained vigilant until Jane was back in Emma's arms, and the two were down the road a ways. Then he said, with a grin, "I hadn't loaded it. Sorry."

The two soldiers sighed and groaned.

Stevens' heart raced. He caught up to the girls, unsure how to feel. He'd just committed treason. He'd beaten two fellow soldiers, soldiers wounded in a war that they believed in.

But Stevens did not share their ideals. General Arnold was no less of a problem than King George, perhaps worse. Stevens had supported it, through it all, until now. Now, all he could hope for was redemption. He could no longer stand on the sideline as a phantom passing through events as they came. He had to take a stand. After Maryland, after he said goodbye to Emma—

He looked at Emma. She looked at him, and he fell deep into her eyes.

"Emma, I love you," he said. The words just tumbled out of his mouth without much thought.

Her pupils contracted, her mouth opening wide. She went to say something, but nothing came out.

Martin Stevens hung his head low. *My God, what did I just say?*

"My leg," Benedict Arnold groaned. He tried rubbing the leg to comfort it, but it only made the pain worse. He looked up at Washington, wondering how that man was still alive. "Why couldn't you have just shot my heart and be done with it?"

"I assure you, that is now my sincerest regret."

Morgan met Oswald on the floor of the tavern with Arnold. He looked at the wound and the makeshift wrappings and then frowned. "We need to get you a surgeon. You're going to lose the leg."

Arnold sobered. For a moment, his head swam in clear water. One thought rang clear as he looked down. "There's no way, by God's bones, I'm losing this leg. I won't end the war a cripple. Better to kill me now and make me a martyr."

"If you are offering." Washington stood but kept another rescued drink in hand. "I shall oblige."

Morgan shot up, placing his bulk between Arnold and the British general.

Arnold interrupted and asked, "Why is he even still alive? Can somebody please kill him?"

Morgan boomed, "With respect, sir, if we kill him, the redcoats outside will be on us in seconds."

"Quite right." Washington stood there, as if sizing his massive frame against that of Morgan. "I do think you and I would have gotten along rather well."

Arnold groaned again. His leg felt heavy and wooden and altogether on fire. If it meant keeping his leg, however, then he would endure the pain. "Morgan, we've got to get you out of here. You need to re-establish our ranks and ensure Captain Burr is on the move."

Washington leaned closer, his eyes asking, *Burr?*

"I can't leave you here," Morgan said. "If I do, I leave you in the hands of the redcoats."

"Just get out there and regroup. Spread the word that I've fallen, but don't be too specific about it. Let them draw their own conclusions. It'll do our cause some good."

"You, sir, are a hypocrite as well as a traitor," Washington added.

Arnold shot the general a look of scorn.

"You would lie to your own men to help you in your cause," Washington said, "yet you would take no help from the French who are willing to give it?"

"Would you have, if you were in my position?" Arnold sat himself up as much as the pain would permit. "Would you have accepted support from the French Army? You're asking me to trust in our enemy, our mutual enemy. That, I cannot abide. We have too much to lose to the French to allow it."

"Much to our advantage. I would have given myself whole to the cause and not thought for an instant what the cause should have given me. Betrayal is born out of selfishness." Washington sipped his drink. "I would have served nobly beside my men and fought with every means available."

Arnold ignored the noble man. His ears couldn't take it. Instead, he pointed to Captain Horner. "Fire a volley out this window, and get them to return fire. Morgan will leave right after."

Morgan nodded in agreement and instructed the men in the room to prepare for his departure. They reinforced the wall where they expected return fire, then moved Arnold and the two British hostages, bound and tied, out of the way. Washington moved himself. No one dared to tie him.

A moment later, the dragoons and rifleman fired, then dove for cover against bar stools and upright tables. The redcoats outside shot back despite their officer's admonishment to cease. At that moment, Morgan burst out a side entrance, near where he'd left his mount, and disappeared from Arnold's view.

"You've sent him to his death."

"Morgan will make it."

"All you had to do was to land the French troops right outside in the harbor. You would have won. Now, your cause is finished. You should have sought help."

Arnold smiled through the pain. "Who said I haven't?"

"I've always loved you." Stevens said. There was nothing for it now. Might as well keep going. His face felt pale and his heart pounded. There was dizziness to his steps. He could hardly even see Emma now.

For her part, she seemed to have passed it off as if she hadn't heard him or he had been joking.

The two Continental soldiers, now bound, barefoot and sitting on the side of the road, faded out of earshot as the two continued onward. Emma walked ahead, holding onto Jane.

"Emma," Stevens ran another few steps to catch up to her. He grabbed her free arm, gently spinning her toward him. A strong breeze blew auburn wisps of hair around her face. She wiped it back across her face with her fingers. Tears came with it.

"No," she said. A gentle smiled appeared on her lips for a second before vanishing.

"Emma, you are no stranger to how I have felt all these years. Please don't pretend otherwise." He rubbed her shoulder. Baby Jane looked up at him and reached out a hand with a smile. "Do you still blame me for your husband's death? I understand if you do." Stevens fell silent.

"He died standing up for what he believed." Emma took a deep breath and somehow kept tears from escaping. "I wish he had believed in his family more."

"He did. I'm sure he did. He loved you so much. I truly believe he wanted a better life for you both." At that moment, Stevens knew he was betraying much more than just his friend; he was betraying everything his friend had fought and died for. But he had to tell her.

Tears welled up in his eyes. This was far more painful than he realized. "I will watch out for you, take care of you, and be there for Jane."

"I know you will, and I will always be thankful for you."

The baby started to fuss. Emma cajoled her as she walked. The three of them continued on the path for some time in silence with Stevens wracking her riddled speech around his head. Finally, she broke the spell.

"We cannot wed, if that's what you desire. I must tell you something, something you'll hate me for... but if you must talk of love, then you need to hear it."

Curious.

"I was the first woman in my family to marry for love. My mother always encouraged it as I grew of age. Father is a nice man, a good man, but like most marriages, he wed my mother for her father's fortune rather than her love.

"But, with my security certain, my mother wanted something different for me. When she passed, I vowed to do what she asked. That was the same summer I fell in love with Henry Collins, a man with no ability whatsoever to provide for me except that he made me happy—and I loved him for it. Of course, Father disapproved, but I didn't care. I was marrying for love. And I don't regret that decision at all," she cried. "Not even now."

Then, she looked at him, as if to warn him that her words would sting. "And if I were to marry again, it would be for love."

But the words did not hurt. Instead, he felt free. It was like Atlas no longer held a massive boulder above Stevens' shoulders. His tears flowed freely, and he didn't care. He had nothing to prove.

Twice now in as many minutes, he had acted on his feelings. In many ways, it felt good. In other ways, he knew he had much to think about in order to discover the person he was meant to be. But now, he could understand how Collins felt, always trying to win over the woman he had already won. Stevens would always love Emma, but in his heart, he knew they could never be together.

Still, she knew. And they were better for it.

He would always take care of her and her daughter. He'd be there for them in Collins' absence. He'd honor his friend's memory and avenge his death.

"I miss him." Emma let tears fall. Stevens did the same.

"Me, too."

Private Frederick Bakker was surprised at just how quick the Yankees fled. From the first shot fired hours ago, to Bakker's latest bayonet charge, the rebels dropped and ran. Some fled into the woods and ravines around Portsmouth. Others fled back to the guns of the Rangers. There was nowhere for them to go. Now, Bakker found himself pushing into the woods, taking out straggling rebel units piecemeal.

There was some resistance, of course. The Colonial unit in front of them was not militia, and they had not broken ranks. Now they both fought, surrounded by thin foliage, just before thick dark trees overwhelmed them. It was strange. As bloody as the war was, all he could think about was how plentiful and beautiful the trees were. *Maybe I could live here...*

"Fire," Maximillian ordered, interrupting his thoughts. Once again, Bakker discharged his flintlock, emptying its contents at the rebels in blue and buff ahead of them. No one fell from their burst of fire, but one Yank looked as if on the brink of collapsing from the heat. Others looked as if they were about to break and run. A Yank lieutenant grabbed the nearest man's arm, and their resolve returned.

These rebels are harder to break than they were before. But Bakker was happy to know he would get the best of them after all. *I'm glad I didn't take them up on their offer of land for my surrender. I'll be going home soon.* But to what? Part of Bakker would miss the vastness and beauty of the New World, the place he'd despised since landing on its shores so long ago. He still kept the piece of paper in his pocket. *I guess I won't be needing it.*

The rebels were almost all on the run...

And that's when he heard it.

At first, it came as a loud whisper, like the forest itself was stirring. The war whoops he heard seemed more like bird calls, so he ignored them. But, they grew louder, and they grew closer. Cold blood flowed through his veins despite the heat. He looked to his sergeant for guidance. Maximillian's face went white as ice.

Savages?

Bakker was no longer a stranger to natives. The Iroquois tribes allied with Britain and fought side by side with them against the Americans, and there were a few natives who'd lived in Rhode Island and walked its streets, but now lay long dead. According to campfire stories, they had been all but murdered by New Englanders over a hundred years ago. Ghosts roamed the grasses and forests and made for stories passed around at night.

But, these weren't ghosts.

The savages fell on them now; there was no mistaking it. Natives looked so different from everyone else—tanned, agile, lithe, and so altogether natural, as if they belonged and everyone else did not. They wore war paint, leathers, and moccasins. Other details, he could not see, as they darted silently past rock and tree. They came from everywhere, yet nowhere, like whispers in the wind.

It would've been magical had it not been so deadly. Maximillian and Bakker held their unit in position. He felt the confidence of a veteran soldier, but the bravado evaporated in an instant as his fears became reality. *There are so many of them...*

As the forest closed in around them, everything changed. The Yankees in front of them no longer backed away. Bakker saw scalps nailed on the trees. *Where did those come from? They weren't there before.* Then everyone was on them, as if the forest came alive and attacked him.

An arrow whipped by, missing Bakker. He sighed with relief until he saw Maximillian. The arrow went through his throat. His sergeant gurgled blood and went down wet. Bakker saw the look Maximillian gave him as he died—eyes bulging, mouth ripped open with shock. He knew it would stay with him forever.

Of course, that depends on how long forever lasts. Bakker looked around, searching for guidance, but the other Hessians in his unit did the same. Except that their looks fell to him.

Oh shit.

The scrip of paper was the first thing Bakker thought of. He didn't want his scalp hanging on a tree, nor an arrow to come hissing at him, harbingering an unseen death. The Americans ahead seemed safer. Bakker jammed his hand into his pocket, searching around for the scrip of salvation. He found it as he knelt, closed Maximillian's eyes, and whispered both a prayer and an apology to his friend.

Bakker threw down his musket and scurried over to the Americans, hands held high. He looked at them and they eyed him, then cast their looks behind him. He turned to see that his whole unit came with him, just as arrows whipped by at Hessians further back. Bodies fell dead, but Bakker and his men, who surrendered to the Americans in front of them, were spared.

"*Ich egerbe mich!*" Bakker said. He looked over the Yankees. Not one of them moved. Bakker shook his head in frustration. *What was the English word for surrender?* He had to make them understand. His whole unit was at the mercy of the Americans. His whole unit was under his care.

He held up the scrip of paper. The lieutenant took it and looked it over. He turned back to the Yanks and said something Bakker did not understand. Then, they all aimed their rifles. Bakker froze. He did not even so much as blink or breathe. Everything went still except for his racing heart.

Major John Graves Simcoe had endured hurricane-like weather over the last three weeks as his Rangers remained hidden from Arnold's forces. Today, the summer sun was sultry as he roused his men to fight against the rebels, outflanking them and catching them unaware. For the last several hours, Simcoe had thought the surprise attack had gone splendidly.

All that had changed without warning. His men were the ones cut off now. Natives had come from nowhere, wrecking their momentum and pushing his men back as the Yanks regrouped. Simcoe knew he would have to call for a retreat into the city soon.

He found it ironic the one person that could aid them the most was the one man he'd reviled, as did all British officers: Washington. More than anyone, Washington had proven he could manage chaos into order. He'd done it twenty years ago with Braddock in the wilderness, and done it time and again since against the rebels. Washington could put an end to their retreat, and Simcoe could regroup, reform, and welcome the Yanks with fresh zeal and bayonet.

Simcoe soured. He'd realized too late that the British really *did* need Washington. If anyone could have salvaged the day, it would have been the hero of Braddock's Road. But Washington was not here.

The task fell to him. *That is all right. I am a British officer. I am more than a match for these wild savages and Yanks. They caught us by surprise, is all. We will still persevere.* He was one of the best officers of the finest fighting forces the world had ever seen. The British were the new Romans, Greeks, and Mongols of the entire globe. *Soon, the sun will never set on the British Empire.*

Major John Graves Simcoe felt something bite into him. It stung as if a giant bee had jabbed him with a white-hot stinger just below his heart. He looked down and saw just a tiny bit of blood. *That's odd*, he thought. Bees didn't normally leave blood.

Simcoe tried to keep going, to ride through battle, rallying his Rangers, but he couldn't. He slumped atop his horse. He felt dizzy and lightheaded, as if tiny grains of sand pelted his brain. He looked down but could not see. He felt the strangest sensation that hands were on him, grabbing him from his horse and laying him down as if he were flying.

He did not quite understand why he felt that way, until he saw the looks of their faces over him. They were distraught—screaming at him, though he couldn't hear or make out the words. Their pleading faces said it all. *I am about to die.* He didn't fight it. Somehow, it all felt right. He looked around at the New World one last time, absorbing it. Now, he knew his mistake—he'd underestimated this land. They all had.

Who would have thought?

EPILOGUE

July, 1779.

PRESIDENT-GENERAL Benedict Arnold hobbled from his unadorned office chair around his desk to his last of many guests of the evening. His left leg hurt worse at night. Every step he took sent a wave of pain from his leg straight up his spine. The doctors told him he would carry that pain to the end of his days.

The wound would never heal. It needed constant re-bandaging and examination, amputation always lingering as a threat. He was also an inch shorter in that leg now, too. It made his gait awkward, like that of a duck, something that took all his control to hide in front of his audiences. After all, he had appearances to maintain.

Earlier, his guest had been the British Ambassador of Arnold's choosing. Major John Andre had been curt in his business with Arnold and walked out stiffly when dismissed. It always made Arnold smile. As ambassador, Andre was always close by. More importantly, it kept Peggy within reach as well. The two still had not wed, and that gave Arnold hope. Peggy, like everything else, would eventually be his.

He met with this particular guest after hours and out of sight and ears of as many workers as possible. General Nathanael Greene was instrumental in the next phase of Arnold's plan. He shook his hand as the general entered the room.

"Congratulations, General Arnold." Greene gave the requisite courtesies. Arnold was never sure if his guests were genuine or not. He hoped Greene was.

"I would have you sit down," Arnold said, "but my business with you is brief, I'm afraid. We will have to get together for pleasantries some other time when the business of the country is put to rest, you understand?" The truth was, if Arnold sat back down again, he doubted he could get back up, at least not easily. He would not show his weakness to one of his top generals.

"I understand, sir. I am at your service and the service of the Free States."

"Excellent, my boy, I'm glad to hear it. I have something only you and a few other people can know about, or will ever hear about, understand?"

Greene nodded.

"Good, good." Arnold took out a bundle of cloth out he had tucked away for the occasion. "I need you to go south."

General Greene licked his lips. "How far south are you talking, General?"

"The Carolinas, if you will. Discreetly, of course." Arnold waved a hand over Greene's blue and buff attire. "You'll have to take all that off. Embed yourself with the locals, and become friends with the natives. Do what you must, if you get my meaning."

Greene gave an unusually long pause, then finally answered, "I understand, sir. If you hadn't told me to do it, I probably would've done it anyway. The war isn't won until we have 'em all."

Arnold nodded. "I knew I could count on you." He gave Greene the bundle, tugging its string as he did so. The nine red-and-white striped flag of the Free States unfurled on display. "Take this and rally our people." Arnold eyed the general. "Give the British hell."

Greene gingerly took ahold of the flag and, with practiced aplomb, folded it back up. "I'll do my best."

"I know you will. Come, let me walk you out. I told you it would be brief. I have much work yet to do." Again, in truth, Arnold needed to stretch his leg. The fresh air would do him good, too. A while later, in the warm night breeze, he dismissed the general and left Greene to his own devices. Soon, Arnold stood alone outside against the darkened sky.

The warm July breeze took Arnold back to the beaches of Honduras where he had once looked up at the sky, pondering his future. He had watched the North Star then, as he often did at night as a sailor. The North Star always guided him. It had once guided him back to America to claim the wilderness. Now, it beckoned him again. He was far from the man he wished he was, but that day would soon come.

Everyone assumed General Benedict Arnold, President and Commander-in-Chief of the Army and Navy, would look south to claim the Colonies from the British. Arnold, however, had other plans. While the British were distracted by civil unrest and outright revolt, Arnold would turn his attention to the north, to the land and city that eluded him—Quebec.

The north would be his.

After the treaty and subsequent parole, General George Washington was now the highest-ranking British officer in what remained of the four British American Colonies—the Carolinas, Georgia, and of course, Virginia. His achievement was predicated more on exile than reward. Many blamed him for the British loss. A more selfish man might have left the British forces altogether. He could rebuild his life at Mt. Vernon, but Vernon held no meaning to him anymore. He was a soldier of the British Crown, and in the humid city of Savannah, Georgia, he still had service to provide for his country.

Washington had his hands full as the Southern Colonies still struggled in a state of civil unrest. He set about his work with the same diligence as before, starting each morning at sunrise. The difference now was, for the most part, he could do things his way. More importantly, he had drive, more so than ever before. Arnold had bested him. With Arnold leading the laughably proclaimed 'Free' States, no one was safe. Arnold remained a wildcard, as selfish and ambitious as they came—a villain.

Washington's heart burned with the desire to see General Arnold defeated. He would save this land. All of it. General George Washington vowed it would become his mission in life to stop the man who had murdered his wife.

But there was something else. Something more which caused his sleepless nights and evenings spent at the liquor bottle— the possibility that Martha might somehow be alive. Her body was never recovered, and the war had displaced many people. He wondered if Martha was out there, one of them, injured or unable to communicate. He owed it to her and to himself to find closure, to either rescue her or uncover her remains. He would plow every inch of the land until he did so.

Frederick Bakker farmed his own land. There had been much to adjust to—the people, the way of life, and the quirks of living in the New World. He settled in a city near Reading, Pennsylvania, somewhere north of the town, away from the crowd. There, he lived the quiet life he'd always wanted.

Looking out at the expanse of his own land, he understood why people called this the New World. Everything appeared fresh and novel. He took his hoe and checked on his squash. He'd already harvested one big batch of watermelons. He would take a cart load and sell them piecemeal at the local farmers market, the only time he ventured into town nowadays. That was where he saw *her*.

Her name was Margaret, and she was a widow. She often had a stall at the farmers' market, selling butter and jams. She'd even agreed to teach him English. Their courtship began there, and she was the reason for his happiness. He hummed with delight as he dug into the earth, all the while thinking of her and her fine, fulsome hair and thin smile.

Frederick Bakker was home.

Martin Stevens paid his usual Sunday visit to the Collins' household. Of course, Henry Collins didn't greet him. Instead, Emma opened the door to him. Jane, now an energetic toddler, had taken to running around the farmhouse, picking daffodils and laughing at the wind.

Today, she played in the yard with her usual playmate, a boy of about ten months, already taking his first tentative steps in the bigger world. The boy was black, but lighter than most Negros. White skin fell like droplets on the boy's left arm. He was the son of one of Emma's servants, a Negro woman by the name of Abigail. He didn't know who the father was, nor was that information ever discussed. Though the boy was a darker shade than Jane, she did not mind. Children, Stevens learned, did not know hate. Their world was too simple for that.

Stevens looked to Emma. She had kept the farmhouse—Stevens made sure of it. Of course, it had been Emma who demanded monthly entitlements from Congress, not just for herself, but for widows and wounded soldiers who had fought for their country. President Adams, at the behest of General Arnold, eventually gave in.

Despite the entitlement, Emma was not without need, which is where Stevens helped. The young country struggled with high inflation and low wages. Cupboards stood empty. There was trouble with natives and Tories. Tensions ran hot at the border between Maryland and Virginia. Eventually, things would stabilize, or the Free States would be swallowed by the British to the north and south, or the French to the West. But that was not Stevens' concern.

He had come on a mission with today's visit. There was something important he had to tell Emma. He said hello to Jane, playing and chasing dreams, and promised to say goodbye before he left. *It will be hard to say goodbye to her.*

Abigail came and went, linens in hand. He passed her on the way in as he announced himself, stepping in to the familiar home. A moment later, he sat at the table with Emma where he had once sat with Collins. Emma spoke first after she handed him an ale.

"I saw you playing in the yard with Jane and the boy." Emma sat down at the table with an ale of her own. Stevens sat across from her in the same chair he sat in to play backgammon with Collins. He pushed the thought back and took a sip.

"She's quite taken with me, lil' Jane. She wants to marry me."

Emma smiled. "It's going to be hard for her to understand why you won't be visiting anymore."

Stevens sat his ale down and opened his mouth in shock. "I—I didn't tell her." He thought for a second. "How did you—"

"You've changed. You've been vocal, displeased with the war, with everything that's happened after the treaty... with Arnold." She cast her eyes down. "I know you can't sit idly by and watch what's happening."

"Then you know I have to go. Take Jane and come with me. You've done it once before."

"You know I can't leave. This is all I have left of Henry. This is my home, for better or worse. I've made something of myself here. Crops are doing well, and I'll be able to repay you the money you lent us soon."

"I don't care about the money. You know that," Stevens protested. "Everything you've achieved will be uprooted in seconds if you stay. I don't trust Arnold. He'll have us at war soon enough. You must see that."

"If there is to be war—" Emma stopped and stared at Stevens. "Wait, you don't mean to just leave. You're going to Savannah with Washington. You mean to fight for the other side? You shouldn't! If there's war, you'll be fighting against us, against your friend." She took a short breath as she realized, "That's why you wish us to come."

"I wish you to come because I care for you and Jane, because I wish to protect you. I can't do that from afar, but I will leave alone if I must."

Emma studied him. "Then you must."

Stevens stammered for a moment and recovered. "I'll still write. I'll visit as often as I can. If you change your mind, I'll send for you in a heart—"

"Don't." Tears rolled down her eyes. She stirred her drink. "Take your time saying goodbye to Jane."

"Of course."

Abigail came in again at that moment. Emma subdued her sadness, wiping away her tears and composing herself into the strong woman Stevens had fallen for so long ago.

"We were just talking about you, Abigail," Emma said.

Stevens looked confused. So did Abigail. "You were, ma'am?" The servant caught a look that Stevens must've missed. "Oh yes, what about?"

Emma wiped away another tear. "I've told you the story about how she came here, of how she stumbled by, big as a whale, alone and pregnant?" She turned from Stevens to Abigail. "You're a mystery to me. There's so much I still don't know about you." She turned back to Stevens. "She lost her husband in the war. I just found out the other day."

"Yes?" Stevens asked. He was being polite.

"Yes, sir. I did. I was owned by a family in Philly. My husband was sold to General Washington. I assumed he was killed in the same fire that destroyed the man's home. I'm not sure if I was blessed or damned for not being there, too. If I was there, I suppose I would've died, too. But I never got to say goodbye to him."

"What?" Stevens asked. He turned to Emma. "When did you learn of this?"

"Like I said, it only came up yesterday. I knew you were coming today to tell us you were leaving. I... Abigail and I got to talking."

"Your husband's name, what was it?" The words had jumped out of his mouth, but Stevens knew the answer.

"Jarosa."

Stevens felt the chair go out from underneath him. In his mind, he flew out of it. Instead, he sat still—still as a fresh snowfall. A moment later, Stevens ruffled through his bag. He pulled out a Bible.

"Abigail, I believe that this is yours. I don't have much use for its contents, but it served its purpose in reminding me of things I needed to learn. I don't know how fate played this out, or how this could've happened, but I ran into your husband long ago, and I made a promise to find you. That promise was broken, until now."

Abigail placed a hand over the worn Bible. Her hands trembled, then her lips. She took it from him and grasped it to her bosom. "Oh, thank you, Lord," she cried. She looked at him. "How did you ever...?"

Stevens told them the whole story, even the parts he was ashamed of. He told it as a sinner would at the pearly gates, but neither of them judged him.

A short while afterward, Stevens found himself alone. He had played a little with Jane, and she urged him on to play some more. There was so much spirit in her. She would grow up and be strong like her mom, too.

Emma stood beside him. She whispered, "I know why you have to go."

He didn't respond, and she didn't say anything more. Emma put her hands around his arm and laid her head on his shoulder. He watched Jane, playing in the setting sun, wishing for one more chance to be chased around.

He smiled.

Benjamin Franklin rose from an overstuffed chair in the pavilion of the *Hotel de Valentinois*, overlooking the swift waters of the Seine. It was the time of day when sunlight streamed directly into the room, blinding any who looked out the window. So, as was routine, he picked up his drink, left the naked Parisian woman adorning the *laisse* chair, and shambled to the window to shuffle the shades.

As was custom, he spent some time peering out the window down into the streets on the outskirts of Paris. This small ritual done at this time gave him purpose, for he felt he failed at all others. To Franklin, his purpose was freedom... and America was not free.

France was a far cry from it as well.

He'd spent much time in the country, enough time to know France had many problems. Filth filled the streets. People were poor. Bellies ran empty. The beacon of hope that was to be America was not lit. Therefore, those most needing a guiding light in Europe did not see it. The people here had no one to rally with, no one to hear their cry. *What will happen in these streets?*

Instead of America transferring her success to Europe, Europe transferred its failures to the New World. America was weak, fractured, surrounded on all sides by bitter rivals and would-be enemies. The pettiness that plagued kings here would play out in the same manner, but on a different stage. The New World was a duplicate of the Old, and it was all because of a single man who would be called king, given the chance.

Franklin took a swig of sherry.

He looked out at the sun, wondering for a moment if it were dusk or dawn. He stared out, longing for an answer, but in that moment, the sun merely stared back.

The story continues in
DARK EAGLE: Fire and Sword
Coming Soon.

Brent A. Harris enjoys history, science fiction, and fantasy and is a Sidewise Award nominated author of alternate history. Previous works of speculative fiction have been published by Inklings Press, Rivenstone Press, and Rhetoric Askew. He has a degree in history with a focus in sociology and is pursuing an MFA in creative writing.

He currently resides in Southern California, where he's lived long enough to think Joshua trees are in fact, real trees. When not writing, he focuses on his family, shuttling children around as a stay-at-home dad, while his wife serves as a Lt. in the USN.

Brent welcomes feedback through his website:
www.BrentAHarris.com

CPSIA information can be obtained
at www.ICGtesting.com
Printed in the USA
BVOW06s0130180917
494782BV00013B/500/P